Quantum Synapse

Russell Blake

Books@RussellBlake.com

ISBN: 978-1720080497

Published by

Reprobatio Limited

What has been will be again,
What has been done will be done again;
there is nothing new under the sun.

-Ecclesiastes 1:9

Chapter 1

AD 2040
Tall Kayf, Iraq

The blades of the latest generation SU-430 stealth helicopter pounded the hot night air. The hum of its turbine was shielded to near silence, the only sound in its wake a rhythmic thwacking like the beating of a prehistoric bird's wings. Moonlight silvered the instrument console through antireflective windows, where a pair of pilots gazed at the landscape rushing by, occasionally monitoring the radar as the autopilot performed its job with robotic precision.

Blast furnace updrafts buffeted the helicopter from the hills below, sending tremors through the cabin. A lone figure, his helmet and NV gear lending him the appearance of a giant insect, sat on one of the steel benches in the cargo bay, staring into the darkness through the open door.

The pilots hadn't spoken since taking off from a provisional air base near Baghdad twenty minutes earlier, a remnant of an occupation that had stretched for decades with no end in sight. Their flight was secret, their destination classified, the passenger a ghost with no name. They'd remarked on the unusualness of the mission before he'd loaded aboard but had kept their thoughts to themselves, other than to raise their eyebrows at his sophisticated weaponry – his assault rifle was a type they'd never seen, and the cables leading from its stock to his backpack were almost as unusual as the man himself.

He'd been bouncing his boots against the titanium floor almost the entire flight, and they'd picked up snatches of unfamiliar words muttered in his gruff baritone with an exotic intonation. Both pilots understood Arabic, but whatever it was the soldier was speaking wasn't any language they recognized.

They'd opened their orders once in the cockpit and had been surprised by the flight plan, not to mention only a single passenger, for what was described as a neutralization mission of a terrorist faction that had been plaguing the region for years. Normally there would have been three or four birds in formation, with at least two dozen commandos and enough ordnance to destroy a fortress. A single fighter with a high-tech rifle, a handgun strapped to his hip, and an assortment of unusual field gear appeared to be woefully inadequate for the job, but they didn't question the orders. Why the geniuses at headquarters had decided to send a lone commando defied logic, but so did many of the decisions that emanated from high.

The target was a compound at the edge of the town of Tall Kayf, an isolated hamlet home to a population of twenty-two thousand. They were flying low over the rugged terrain as they hurtled through space at nearly three hundred miles per hour. For most, even in the new aircraft, the high velocity in rough air and complete darkness would have been frightening, but the pilots had been conducting clandestine runs in this theater for years.

"Four minutes from target," Captain Baxter, the senior pilot, said into his mic. A single click on the close-quarters comm line was the only indication from the passenger that he'd heard. Baxter glanced over at Lieutenant Reynolds, his copilot, and shrugged. Reynolds didn't respond, preferring to keep his eyes on the faint radiance illuminating the horizon, where the town's lights warmed the desert in the distance.

Iraq had technically been self-determining for decades, but coalition forces had been stationed there for the duration to prevent undesirable opposition groups from overthrowing the puppet regime that was dependent on the invaders to remain in power. The area around Tall Kayf was one of numerous strongholds where the coalition forces dared not travel except in substantial numbers, and there wasn't a family there that didn't have a relative who'd been maimed or killed at the hands of foreign fighters.

Death at the hands of coalition soldiers was so common that a term had entered the popular vernacular, which loosely translated meant "martyred angels."

Baxter thumbed a toggle and depressed a button, and the autopilot switched off and control of the helo returned to manual. The bumpy air rising from the baked sand demanded his full concentration, and he pushed aside any doubts about the mission and focused on piloting the helicopter. Reynolds squinted behind his night vision goggles at the threat-detection computer, relieved that no incoming fire greeted their approach – even though the helo was virtually undetectable on a night flight like this, years of harsh experience had conditioned him to never let down his guard.

"On the mark in ten seconds," Baxter announced, and the craft's forward momentum slowed before it shed the last of its altitude and settled onto the ground.

The pilots watched as the commando leapt through the cargo door before the dust cleared, and took off at a run toward a string of buildings a half klick away.

The commando's boots thumped with snare drum cadence on hard-packed dirt, joining the hiss of his breathing and the moan of the arid breeze through husks of ruined structures on the perimeter of the primary compound's security wall. In the near distance, a pair of minarets jutted into the midnight sky like skeletal fingers silhouetted against the city's dim glow.

The commando neared the wall and veered to his right, slowing only long enough to free a miniature drone from his backpack. He tossed it into the sky and watched as the feed from its camera played on his helmet's display screen. The drone scanned the area beyond the wall, its software identifying threats and highlighting their positions. After he was confident about the layout, he summoned the drone back to his hand like a trained pigeon. He replaced it in the pack and removed a grappling hook attached to a length of black rappelling cord, and eyed the top of the wall. Spotting a promising section, he ran toward it and hurled the hook skyward without hesitation.

The hook clanked against the inner wall and bit into the top when he pulled the cord taut. The commando shouldered his Gauss rifle – an experimental design light-years ahead of anything deployed in the field, which used compact micro-fission batteries and smart bolts for heightened accuracy – and was up and over in moments, scaling the sheer twelve-foot face as though leaping over a low hedge.

He landed in a crouch and freed the rifle and, after surveying the collection of buildings in front of him, took off at a jog, weapon in hand.

Twenty-two hundred kilometers away in a bunker near Karachi, six men watched the feed from the commando's helmet cam play across a wall screen in the eerie green luminosity of night vision. Nobody spoke as the image bounced with each running step, and then a pair of gunmen materialized from a darkened doorway and opened fire, the blossoms of their AK-47s like flares in the NV lens. The commando opened up with the Gauss rifle, and both men were cut down by a silent stream of high-velocity bolts that struck them mid-torso.

Another shooter with an AK fired from one of the windows, and the next instant three more joined it. The commando moved with startling speed, picking off the various shooters without slowing, the accuracy of his fire miraculous given the conditions.

"He's performing exactly as predicted," one of the men said in a hushed voice, and offered the others a triumphant smile.

"You aren't troubled by the gibberish he was mumbling on the trip in?" the figure at the head of the table asked.

"Probably nerves, Louis. Everyone deals with them differently. What matters is how he's doing now that he's in the thick of it."

Louis ran long fingers through thick silver hair and nodded. "It was just a question, Edgar. Nothing more."

Their man neutralized a dozen shooters before kicking a door open and pounding through a room with an overturned table, where a dead gunman's form lay sprawled on the floor. They scanned the room with him, their point of view his, and then they were moving deeper into the compound, killing anything that showed itself.

After a brief shoot-out with three guards in a spacious parlor appointed with antiques, the commando approached a Persian carpet on the stone floor. His gloved hand appeared in the field of view and pulled the rug aside, revealing a wooden trapdoor. He jerked it open and dropped a flash bang into the opening even as a flurry of rifle fire lit the gap.

He dropped the door back into place, and the whump of the grenade blew it ajar. An instant after the detonation, he heaved it wide and fired a long burst from the Gauss rifle before lowering himself down a rickety wooden stairway to the chamber below.

Four bodies lay on the floor, their blood black on the bunker's wall screen. One of the downed men struggled to reach a rifle by his hand, and the Gauss rifle clicked twice, dropping the man where he stood.

A quick sweep of the room recorded its contents, and then the fighter was mounting the stairs and retracing his steps to the courtyard.

At the entryway, he retrieved a self-guided drone and a console with a tiny screen from his backpack and watched as the miniature aircraft made a slow orbit of the compound, recording heat signatures with its infrared and scanning the defenders' faces. It paused at the fifth signature, and then a message blinked to life on the control screen: *Target confirmed.*

He studied the target's location, as well as the heat signatures converging on it, and debated shooting his way to the man who was the object of the mission. After a brief pause, he keyed a command and transmitted it.

Neutralize.

The drone's video feed zoomed on the target's face and began its silent attack run at breakneck speed. When it was no more than five meters from the man, it fired a .40-caliber explosive projectile from its integrated barrel that struck the target in the center of the forehead and blew the back of the man's skull apart like a rotten melon.

The commando smiled and recalled the drone even as the other heat signatures raced toward the dead man.

Louis grunted his approval, and Edgar keyed a transmitter to life and spoke into a microphone. "Excellent work, Alpha. Return to the LZ and call it a night."

The fighter growled into his helmet mic. "Still more to mop up."

Edgar and Louis exchanged a glance, and Edgar tried again. "Negative. Mission is over. Return to the landing zone, stat."

A pause. "Not a chance."

Edgar keyed the mic. "Repeat. Mission is over. Return to—"

The line went dead, leaving the room to stare at the broadcast from the helmet cam, unable to do anything but watch and listen.

"What's he doing?" Louis asked in a hushed voice.

"He disabled his comm line," Donald Adair, the technician director, said. "I'm afraid we know what comes next."

"Not necessarily," Edgar said.

"Bullshit. Why else would he have disobeyed a direct order?" Donald snapped.

"He…he might have identified another threat," Edgar tried, but even to his own ears his tone was unconvinced.

"Can we use the quantum link?"

"It won't do any good. We've seen this eight times in the field. Do you really think the ninth will be different? He'll just ignore it like he ignored your direct order to end the mission," Donald said.

The helmet cam image neared the perimeter wall, and then it was up and over again, only this time moving away from where the helo waited. A pair of ancient trucks, their beds packed with armed men, raced toward the wall along a dirt road from town, their headlights blinding as the high beams lit the fighter up.

The Gauss rifle spat death. The lead truck's lights blinked out in a spray of shards, and the vehicle careened to the side, its windshield an opaque curtain of shattered safety glass. The Gauss bolts ripped through the sidewall of the truck bed and cut the gunmen apart before they could get off a shot, and then the second truck was slowing and the shooters in the back were firing at the commando on full auto.

"Turn the goddamn sound down," Louis ordered; the roar of the shooting was deafening in the bunker's confines. Edgar twisted a knob and the noise level halved, but not before they all heard the fighter's voice laughing maniacally as he moved at lightning speed, closing on the truck in a suicide run and lobbing a frag grenade at it as he sped past.

The truck exploded in a fireball, and body parts arced through the sky. The commando was still in motion and had increased his pace to the town as he babbled to himself in his hoarse voice, the words guttural and abrasive.

"Still think this is anything but what it looks like?" Louis asked the room. Nobody said a word.

The camera picked up the first of the buildings on the edge of town, and Edgar shook his head. "We obviously need to abort."

"Do it, before this gets any worse," Louis instructed.

Donald nodded and moved to a small console. "We built an explosive charge into his pack in the event it went wrong."

"Make it happen."

Donald flipped a switch on the console, entered a security code, and then depressed the only button.

Nothing happened.

"Shit," Donald said.

"Malfunction?" Louis snapped.

"Not likely. He must have disabled it on the ride in."

"What about the drone?"

"Already in the air," Edgar said. "Just in case." He turned to Louis, eyes glued to the screen, where the commando was now gunning down anyone in sight. "ETA is four minutes."

"Thank god for that," Donald muttered. "He never should have been sent in."

"We all voted in favor," Louis snapped.

"With serious reservations," Donald corrected. "But what's done is done."

The fighter kicked in a door and sawed a woman and two small children in half with Gauss bolts before their screams could echo off the stone walls. A little girl no more than seven showed herself in a far doorway, panic twisting her young face. The commando laughed again and loosed a burst from his weapon, stippling the wall behind the child with her blood.

Louis looked at Edgar. "How much longer?"

"Two minutes."

A pause as another chilling cackle echoed through the bunker.

"This isn't going to get any better."

"No, it won't," Donald agreed. "He's completely lost his mind."

"Like the rest," Louis spat.

Edgar frowned. "We had to see."

"Sure."

The commando lobbed a grenade at a fuel station, and the resulting explosion sent a bright fireball streaking into the air. A police truck screeched around a corner, and he called to the officers in Arabic, offering to perform impossible sexual acts with their mothers and daughters. The police fired at him, but he dodged the bullets and sprayed a long burst of Gauss rounds. The hardened projectiles shredded the truck like it was made of soft cheese, killing everyone within moments.

Another laugh shattered the night, and then a string of profanities in Arabic that finished with a blood-chilling ululation.

"Drone's overhead in twenty seconds," Edward reported.

"Tell the helo to be ready to clear his body out of there before the military arrives. There can be no trace," Louis said.

"I'll relay the message." Edward tapped a few keys on his keyboard, and the image on the wall went split screen. On the right was the commando's helmet feed and on the left the drone's. "It's programmed to neutralize him without warning," he said.

"Let's hope it does the—"

The drone video went white with static, and then black.

Louis's frown deepened. "He spotted it."

A second later the helmet feed went offline, leaving the men staring at a blank screen.

"Shit," Edward said. He squinted at a smaller monitor with a map of the city on it. The blue icon that represented the commando had also gone dark. "We lost him."

Louis sighed heavily. "Gentlemen, I'm afraid we have no choice. Edward, do we have a tactical nuke we can deploy?"

"A G-12 on standby in Baghdad. But the heat signature will alert the Russians and Chinese. The outcry will be—"

Louis cut him off. "Order the bird into the air. How many minutes will it take to wipe the place off the map?"

"A couple of minutes after deployment, no more. But what about the Russians? And…the press?"

"We'll disseminate a story about a terrorist faction having gotten their hands on a field nuke. The press will say it was only a matter of time and that it was a miracle a remote town in the middle of nowhere went up instead of downtown D.C." He paused. "Hell, we can probably use this to escalate things again."

"Assuming nobody leaks that it was our bird."

"Make the call."

Edgar did and, when he hung up, reached for the transmitter.

"What are you doing?" Louis growled.

"We need to get the helo clear or it'll go up with the rest of the place."

"Stand down, Edward. There can be no witnesses."

Edgar hesitated and then nodded grimly and sat heavily in his swivel chair. He switched the screen to a satellite image and zoomed in on the small city. "This is real time."

"Let's just pray he doesn't anticipate it."

"Unlikely. Nuking an entire city to eliminate one man wouldn't come up in his possible scenarios."

"Better hope so."

A silence as heavy as morning fog hung over the bunker as the digital counter at the side of the screen blinked the local and Greenwich Mean time in green. The phone by Edgar's hand chirped, and he answered it, listened, and then stabbed the call off. "It's in the air," he said, his tone flat.

"Won't be long now."

Seventy-three seconds later, the sat image changed from darkness to a massive blast, yellow and orange and red, bright as a small sun. When the image normalized, they could see the top of a mushroom cloud rising into the heavens and the buildings at the edge of the city flattened like an angry toddler's toys.

After three minutes, Edward confirmed that everything for five miles from the epicenter had been destroyed, and the possibility of anyone surviving was approximately zero.

The bunker cleared and the men disappeared into the night. The operation was over, its failure both spectacular and unambiguous. While the mission target had been eliminated, the repercussions of the use of a tactical nuke would send shockwaves around the world, and even if the cover story held with the public, the clandestine arms of adversarial governments would know the truth.

A dangerous state of affairs, and an unintended consequence that would, like a pebble tossed into a placid lake, cause ripples that would continue long after the stone had disappeared from view.

Chapter 2

Three years later
San Francisco, California

Gray clouds hovered over the Mission District as the light went out
of the western sky. The streets were clogged with rush-hour traffic,
and the air was heavy with approaching rain and filled with a
symphony of impatient horns. An unending stream of pedestrians
hurried along grimy sidewalks past boarded-up shops marred with
graffiti. Tent cities clogged the major arteries, and the gutters
overflowed with trash and feces. The area had long been a zone
where the police didn't venture except in significant strength and
rarely after dark.

Inside a run-down three-story brick building on the corner of
Twelfth and Mission, in a dingy ground-floor room that doubled as a
TV lounge, sixteen people sat in a rough circle on folding chairs. The
air was thick with cigarette smoke. A woman in her thirties was
concluding a familiar story of bottoming out, losing her children, and
an ongoing battle with the pipe and bottle that she barely won each
day.

When she finished speaking, she sat down, and the chairperson, a
man in his fifties with eyes a blue so vivid they seemed painted,
nodded and gazed around the room. His eyes settled on a hulking
young man with caramel skin and close-cropped black hair seated at
the back of the room. "Anyone want to share? Veritas?"

Veritas Grey shifted in his seat and stared at his scuffed combat boots. He hadn't felt the urge to discuss any difficulty he was having with the steps, and he knew nobody would force him to, but even so he felt vaguely dishonest, as though the fact that he felt no cravings for the poisons that had ruined so many of the participants' lives was somehow cheating.

"Not tonight," Veritas answered.

He'd told his story often enough in meetings like these – the years of narcotic debauchery in Thailand, the near misses with the grim reaper that had been as regular as the phases of the moon, his hiatus in a rural monastery as he battled withdrawals before returning home a burned-out husk – but for the last month of meetings he hadn't actively participated, preferring to listen, not exactly despondent, but feeling like he didn't have anything to add.

The chairman nodded again and passed a cylinder to the man on his right, a Rastafarian with ratty dreadlocks and rumpled clothes. The Rasta withdrew a phone, pulled up a pay app and tapped in a nominal amount, and scanned it with the cylinder. The cylinder beeped, and he handed it to the person beside him, a pretty young woman in her twenties whose beauty was marred by frown lines that had taken up permanent residence at the corners of her mouth.

When it reached Veritas, he held the cylinder's retinal scanner to his eye. It blinked twice. He keyed in a few new dollars and passed it to the next attendee. He shifted again and regarded his hands: strong, thick fingers; knuckles as prominent as a street fighter's; the blue and green ink of full-sleeve tattoos ending mid-metacarpal like a hastily donned shirt several sizes too large.

Everyone rose and said the Lord's Prayer, and then the meeting was over. Veritas swallowed the dregs of his coffee, pulled on his leather jacket, and shouldered his messenger bag. The chairman approached with his backpack in hand, the man's expression serious but friendly, as was typical. He had to tilt his head back to look at Veritas, who at six four was almost a foot taller, and offered a wan smile.

"Good to see you here, Ver. You look well." Ben was Veritas's sponsor and rarely asked anything of him. He'd had Veritas over to his apartment a few times in the early days, for conversation and a movie when Veritas had been working through a difficult period, but lately their socialization had been limited to meetings.

"Thanks, Ben. You too."

A whine issued from Ben's backpack and a furry face poked from the top. A ten-week-old yellow Lab eyed Veritas and panted excitedly.

Ben smiled. "This is Moxie. He showed up at my place a couple of weeks ago and never left."

Veritas reached out and scratched the puppy's head and received a lick in return. "He was really good during the meeting. I didn't hear a thing."

"He's well mannered. Hard to believe someone dumped him on the street. People suck sometimes." Ben studied Veritas's face. "Things okay with you?"

"A little down lately, but trying to walk the walk. One day at a time. You?"

"The same." Ben paused, looked furtively around, and lowered his voice. "If you have some time this evening, I'd like to talk to you about something important."

Veritas sighed and checked his cheap mechanical watch – a relic of a bygone era with a scratched crystal and weathered leather strap. "I can't tonight, Ben. I'm on in half an hour, and I really need the money. It's hard enough getting any job these days, much less if you're an ex-junkie covered in tats. I can't afford to lose it."

"Yeah, I understand…but like I said, it's important."

"Ben, my mom's been sick all week, and I haven't gotten in the hours I need… This isn't a great time."

"I'm sorry to hear that. Hope it's not the new flu."

"I don't think so, but she's stubborn. I can't get her to go to the doctor. Between the meds and handling the shopping and looking after her…it's cut into my pay more than I can really afford."

"Veritas, it's important, or I wouldn't be insisting."

"Okay – maybe after work if I get off early enough. Let me get over this hump and I'll call," Veritas said, and gave Moxie a final chin scratch before moving toward the door. Veritas's statuesque physique projected an authority he seldom felt, and the other attendees parted in front of him. He stepped into the lobby, which stank of decay and broken dreams, and eyed the clerk in passing. The thin Asian man looked away quickly, as though fearing Veritas would leap over the counter and throttle him.

Veritas was used to it and didn't take the sidelong glances personally. He looked like what he was – a young man barely hanging on, living in squalor, trying to atone for a past of self-abuse and to live down dangerous choices his prominent ink announced as clearly as a snake's rattle.

His bicycle was chained to a steel rack just inside the door. The hotel's residents were usually indigents without many possessions, and bikes were their preferred transportation, assuming they could still ride one. In a world filled with technological miracles, that so many couldn't manage even the basics always struck Veritas as typical of the way things worked. But the anger he'd once felt at the injustice no longer consumed him as it once had. That rage had been replaced by a dull acceptance and a resignation he'd spent many hours in meetings trying to develop.

He unlocked the padlock, unable to afford one of the new iris- or thumb-scan locking systems, and then slung the chain into his backpack and thumbed on his phone to see what his evening looked like. Thursday was always a big night, and depending on the delivery queue, he might be able to score some decent tips.

The screen flickered as he carried the bike onto the street, and he swore silently. He wasn't superstitious, but it seemed like anything with a microprocessor hated him with the intensity of a jilted bride and invariably malfunctioned when he needed it most. It was one of the reasons he didn't mind having a bicycle rather than a car. Not that he could afford to buy a vehicle, much less to fuel one, with electricity through the roof for the seventh year in a row and gasoline an impossible luxury for most.

He ducked into the market next door and snagged a bottle of

Pow! energy drink. He extracted a five new-dollar coin and handed it to the woman working the counter, and she shook her head and pointed at a sign behind her. "Sorry. Only doing Nexus payments or scans. No more cash."

"Come on, Jan. It's me. You always take cash."

"Big crackdown, sorry. Only Nexus or phone credit from now on. It's not my choice; the owner doesn't want the heat."

Veritas replaced the drink in the cooler and carried his bike back onto the street. He supposed it figured that a government that couldn't protect its population would eliminate all but their trackable payment systems of choice – in the case of the Nexus chip, one that required a huge investment by the user for the implant.

A bearded man draped in black rags stood on the corner with a Bible in one hand and a gnarled finger pointed at the clouds. He spoke in the strident cadence of a tent preacher, his voice a rasp.

Those who submit to being chipped, you take the number of the beast into you and become the servants of Lucifer! Repent or burn in eternal hellfire!

The top pop song in the country played from speakers above a New Dollar Store, acting as an ironic backdrop to the sidewalk preacher.

Oooh, stick it in, stick it, stick it, stick it in

Oooh, stick it in

Uh, stick it, Daddy, stick it.

A poster affixed to a light post caught Veritas's eye. It bore the logo of the Luds, an underground organization branded terrorists by the government after they'd questioned the legitimacy of a federal apparatus that dictated increasingly oppressive terms to the population.

His phone pinged, and he smiled. If he could make it to the restaurant in five minutes, there was a big order to a section of the city that might make the effort to bike through miserable traffic worthwhile. Rush hour was both a curse and a boon for him – the same snarl of steel and glass that barred his way also ensured he would have consistent employment. Evening traffic was almost impossible to navigate in a car, and motorbike licenses in the city were heavily restricted due to their use by criminal gangs that had modeled themselves after those in the Brazilian favelas, leaving bicycles as the only viable delivery mechanism.

An electric truck with speakers on its roof crawled by, blaring an advertisement for discount plastic surgery on credit. An animated woman's voice screeched over the street sounds with orgiastic excitement. "Better Tomorrows will give you the look you always wanted! Start living your dream today! Prices so low they're practically illegal! Because you deserve it!"

The ad changed to a man's voice. "The new Nexus X implant has ten times the power of the previous generation of chips. For the discerning man or woman who wants it all! Quantities limited."

Veritas clamped his bicycle helmet on his head and swung a leg over the seat. A pair of girls, obviously young, strutted past him wearing latex pants and halter tops in spite of the chill, and the taller one threw him an inviting smile. "Looking for something special?" she purred.

Veritas matched her smile and shrugged. "Aren't we all?"

"For you, half price," she said in a husky voice.

"Sorry, gorgeous. I couldn't afford the double condom."

The two girls giggled and continued down the street, swinging their charms with each stab of their stiletto heels. Prostitution was rampant in the city, the financial situation so dire that many teens worked as semi-pros to help their families make ends meet.

A light drizzle moistened Veritas's face, and he wiped it away with the sleeve of his jacket. After checking the traffic, he pushed off into the street and narrowly avoided being crushed by a bus as he accelerated, the exertion a welcome relief after an hour of sitting. Two passenger electric vehicles dodged between older gas cars and delivery trucks with a soft whir, their plastic forms blinking with LEDs.

He frowned as he sped along the block and a familiar feeling of disorientation blurred his vision at the edges. Veritas shook his head to clear it, but the effect intensified. The street seemed to elongate as he rode, stretching as though made of taffy, while his peripheral vision distorted in a hallucinatory haze.

Veritas swallowed hard and willed the spell away. He didn't have time for a flashback from his drug-addled past; there was food to deliver and money to be made.

The street tilted like the deck of a ship in a storm, and his field of vision began to compress until he felt like he was hurtling through a tunnel. His breathing came in rasps and he gripped the handlebars with white knuckles, a searing coil of anxiety churning in his stomach.

A screech of brakes and the blare of a horn sounded from his right, and then he was arcing through the air, his leg radiating pain where a car had struck him. The blurred horizon pinwheeled before he hit the pavement, and everything went black.

Chapter 3

A flock of birds flapped from the jungle canopy with shrieks of alarm as detonations shook the ground. The night was shattered by fighter jets strafing the surroundings, and the darkness exploded in a wall of fire as they dropped payloads of guided bombs loaded with white phosphorous. The air filled with the sickly aroma of burning flesh and screams of agony from an ancient edifice at the base of mountains that thrust into the sky like broken teeth.

Only minutes earlier the valley had been silent, the residents of the monastery asleep within an hour of the sun sinking into the hills. The nearby village was dark, electricity an undreamed of luxury in the rural area. Now the area was an inferno, the jungle ablaze, the centuries-old stone building reduced to ruins, and the river that ran alongside boiling from the scorching heat.

Sweat coursed down Veritas's face as a guide pulled him by the hand through a tunnel deep beneath the mountain. The walls were carved from solid rock, and the passage narrowed in some places so that he had to crawl behind his escort, whose features he couldn't make out in the darkness. The mountain above trembled from continued explosions, and after a particularly violent one, the tunnel twenty yards behind him collapsed in a shower of stone, blowing a cloud of dust and debris down its length and clogging his nose and mouth.

Veritas cracked his eyes open and found himself staring at the frowning face of a paramedic. An ambulance's red and blue roof lights strobed off the building façades and the faces of curious bystanders.

Another man joined the first, who looked around with a somber expression and then back at Veritas.

"Let's get him into the ambulance," he said.

Veritas shivered – someone had removed his jacket – and felt himself bouncing along the pavement, the gurney beneath him squeaking from his weight as the men pushed him toward the vehicle. He tried to speak, to tell them not to give him morphine because of his addiction issues, but he couldn't seem to form the words, and he closed his eyes as his rescuers lifted the gurney and slid it into the back of the ambulance with a scrape of metal on metal.

One of the paramedics climbed into the bay with Veritas's jacket and backpack, and the doors closed. Veritas tried again to speak, but whatever they were pumping into him was numbing him to the point of indifference. After a final try, he gave up on the effort and allowed himself to drift weightlessly in a warm narcotic haze.

When he came to, it was in the corridor of a hospital. The paramedics were wheeling him down a hall, the astringent smell of antiseptic in the air as distinctive as the orderlies in surgical scrubs accompanying his gurney. The ER was packed with people, and the corridors in every direction lined with the sick on cots, hacking and wheezing.

Veritas's tongue felt thick, and he struggled to form words when a physician approached him in a curtained area of the emergency room. The doctor performed a brusque, cursory examination, the discoloration beneath his eyes a testament to long hours of thankless duty, and then snapped orders to the nurse.

"I want a head and neck CT and X-rays of his legs. Clean up the abrasions, watch his vitals, and get the scans done immediately."

"Yes, Doctor."

"I…" Veritas managed.

The doctor leaned into him and shined a penlight in one eye and then the other. "Follow the light," he instructed.

Veritas did, and the doctor nodded and stepped back.

"How do you feel?"

"I'm…I'm okay. But the drug's making me…" Veritas tried, his voice a croak.

"You took a hell of a tumble. It's a miracle you're in one piece," the doctor said.

"Please. No more drugs," Veritas said.

"I'll make a note on your chart," the doctor agreed.

Another nurse in a white lab coat approached with a clipboard, and the doctor and the first nurse moved away, leaving Veritas to the newcomer. She brushed a lock of platinum hair from her forehead and gave him a sympathetic smile that never reached her eyes.

"Mr. Grey?"

"Yeah."

"A few questions. Do you have insurance?"

"No."

The smile faded and her lips compressed into a line. "Next of kin?"

"My mother." He gave the woman his address.

"Are you taking any medications?"

"No."

Her eyes roamed over his tattoos before settling on his face again. "Drugs?"

"No."

She looked like she didn't believe him, but continued with the questions for another couple of minutes. When she was done, Veritas inhaled deeply. "Do you know what happened to my bike?" he asked.

"I'm sorry. No idea."

"How much…how much is all this going to cost?"

She was already moving away. "You'll be billed."

After a half hour in a room adjacent to the ER, Veritas's head began clearing as the painkiller flushed from his system, and by the time another orderly arrived and wheeled him to the basement for his CT scan, he felt marginally coherent, although still punchy. He tested his legs by pressing down against the gurney, and to his surprise, other than muscle aches, they seemed fine. Same for his arms – the leather jacket he'd been wearing had shielded him from road rash, and his helmet had done its job. His head hurt, but no worse than if he'd taken a few punches.

The X-ray machine was older than he was, and after several images of his hurt leg, next up was the CT – a pristine new Mitsubishi XL6 that took only a few seconds to draw a blood sample, record vital stats, and perform a whole-body scan before uploading the results to a national database.

Ten minutes on the table waiting for the scan crawled by, and then the technician emerged from the control room, shaking his head.

"Sorry. We seem to be having some sort of problem with the system," he said. "We'll get you back up to the waiting area, and whenever we figure it out, we'll try again." He picked up the wall phone and called while Veritas waited on the gurney. "Weird. Just scanned another patient five minutes ago and it worked fine. Never seen the fault before," he said. "Error A42992. Just shut down and won't respond. Says to call some customer support number."

Veritas didn't say anything about the tendency of electronic appliances to go on the blink when he was around. Another orderly took him back to the ER and, after a hushed discussion with the woman in the lab coat, wheeled him to an empty room. "You'll be in here for a while," he said. "The ER's swamped. The damned flu is laying everyone low."

"That's fine," Veritas said, not particularly worried about where they stuck him.

Moments later an attractive woman in the starched blues of the SFPD entered, the badge on her right breast pocket glinting in the harsh light. "Mr. Grey?"

She was about his age, a brunette with a serious expression that was only slightly softened by intelligent hazel eyes.

"Yes?" Veritas tried.

"I'm Officer Selena Aames. Do you have a moment?"

Veritas looked around the empty room and then returned his attention to her. He tried a smile. "I'm not going anywhere. Why?"

She returned the smile, and Veritas felt a stirring in spite of his condition. Her eyes seemed to dance with a trace of amusement as she regarded him, but when she spoke, her tone was all business. "I have some questions about the accident. I need to fill in some blanks for my report."

"Sure. But I don't really remember much. One minute I was on my bike, the next I was airborne. That's about it."

"You never saw the car?"

"Not really."

The woman paused. "It's a yes or no question, Mr. Grey."

"I didn't register it until it was too late."

She looked at him oddly, her expression unreadable, and was about to say something when the doctor entered with the orderly. He scowled at her. "I'm afraid we need to get this young man scanned. Any interview will have to come later," he said.

A final smile for Veritas was followed by a shrug. "I can wait," she replied.

The doctor turned to the orderly. "Get him down to the fluoroscopy unit while the CT's out of commission. It'll give us at least some idea of what we're dealing with."

The orderly wheeled Veritas to the basement again, and a different technician positioned an old fluoroscopy unit over his head. He adjusted some parameters and stabbed several buttons, and then retreated behind a leaded partition. After a few moments he emerged and strode to a wall phone. He placed a call and spoke in a hushed voice.

The doctor appeared and conferred with the technician, and after he ducked behind the screen with the tech, they both approached Veritas.

"The CT's working again. Let's get you on it, shall we?" the doctor suggested.

"Is…is everything okay? I mean, I actually don't feel that bad. Just a headache and some scrapes and bruises. This probably isn't necessary…"

"Won't take but a moment," the doctor said, ignoring his question.

The orderly wheeled Veritas down the hall to the CT room, and this time the device appeared willing to cooperate. The gantry whirred and clicked and then beeped once before shutting down, leaving him in frigid silence as the operator and the doctor studied the results in the adjacent room. One minute stretched to five, and then the orderly returned, transferred Veritas from the CT back to the gurney, and pushed him through the door.

The doctor was standing in the hall with a troubled expression. Veritas looked up at him and raised his eyebrows. "Well? Am I going to live?"

"Sorry about the delay. I had to send your scans to a radiologist to read. We should have the results shortly," he explained.

"You must have seen enough of these to be able to give me some idea. Like I said, I don't feel too bad."

"Yes, well, we have a protocol to follow." The doctor looked to the orderly. "Take him back to his room, and–"

The sound of a voice raised in protest from the stairwell at the end of the hall interrupted him, and then heavy footsteps reverberated from the open door. The doctor looked up at the commotion, and then the voice carried from the stairs, louder than before.

"You can't go down there. I'm calling security. If you don't–"

The warning ended in a strangled gasp, and then the jackhammer pounding of hard soles on concrete steps echoed from the stairwell, loud as pistol shots in the still of the basement corridor.

Chapter 4

Jamaica, New York

A lanky young man stood patiently in the immigration line at the Monsanto International Terminal of JFK airport, tired after the long flight in economy class from Frankfurt, after a layover from his starting point in Istanbul.

The line snaked as far as he could see, his fellow travelers silent as they waited for their turn to present their paperwork to a phalanx of bored officers who manned the stations. After an hour shuffling forward like cattle to slaughter, any irritation he'd felt at how slowly the passengers were being processed had faded, replaced by apathy and the hope that, with only two in front of him, his chance would soon arrive.

The couple ahead shambled to where a portly middle-aged man with a crown of gray hair was motioning for to them to approach, and then he was at the head of the line, anxious to get this part of the ordeal over with so he could collect his luggage and get clear of the airport. He sneaked a surreptitious glance at the cameras that monitored the area and concentrated on breathing evenly so he would be composed when it was his turn with one of the immigration officials.

A heavyset woman with a face like a bulldog waved a lazy hand at him, and he walked to her station, his carry-on satchel with his laptop and personal effects hanging from his shoulder. He presented his passport and student visa, and tried a tired smile. The woman adjusted her uniform hat, which was embossed with the distinctive Netflix logo above the immigration agency crest, and pointed at a device to his left.

"Jamal Hereluf?" she asked.

He nodded. "That's right."

"Look at the green light and keep your eyes open," she ordered, in a pronounced New Jersey accent.

He did as instructed, and the retinal scanner worked its magic – a formality he was accustomed to from his last trip abroad. When it chirped, he stepped back and waited for the inevitable questions.

"Purpose of your trip?" the officer asked.

"Visiting my family for the holidays."

"You're enrolled at Goldman Sachs University?" she asked.

"That's right. This is my second year," he confirmed, and bit his tongue, not wanting to appear too chatty.

She frowned and set his passport aside, switched off the audio for her station, and then tapped an earbud and spoke for several moments. When she finished, she switched the audio back on.

"Is there a problem?" Jamal asked.

"My supervisor's on his way."

"My visa is current," he said. "I've only been gone three weeks."

She pursed her lips and looked him up and down. "I can read."

Jamal bit back the retort that came to mind, and waited while a tall man in his forties made his way to the station. He entered the pod and spoke with the officer before regarding Jamal.

"You don't have the Nexus chip?" the officer asked. The Nexus chip hooked into the auditory and ocular vestibular nerves and enabled the host to view and hear internet content without any other hardware, and provided a full-immersion VR and augmented reality experience at will, as well as identity confirmation.

Jamal shook his head. "No."

"I'm afraid you can't enter the U.S. without one now."

"Since when?" Jamal asked.

"The regulation went into effect three days ago. Student and work visas require one now. Sorry."

Jamal's eyes widened. "But my visa…"

The man shrugged. "It's in order, but I don't make the rules." He paused. "There's a station over there that can chip you if you have enough credits on your card."

"I thought I had ninety more days to get one. That's what the woman who processed my visa said."

"Looks like she was wrong."

The skin around Jamal's eyes tightened. "How much?"

"Ten grand, with the subsidy."

The blood drained from Jamal's face. "You're joking."

The supervisor's scowl deepened. "Do I look like a comedian? You don't want the chip, no problem. You can wait in the holding area for the next flight back to Turkey."

"But this is… All my documents are in order. I'm a student. I can't afford ten grand."

"I hear you. But that's the new reg. You want to come here to study, you have to follow the rules. It's a chip or no entry, except for a tourist visa. You're lucky the chip's being subsidized."

Jamal did a quick calculation. The chip would burn three months of living expenses, which his parents had contributed to his education. It was extortionate, but he couldn't risk having to go home and bear the expense of another flight to New York once he'd been chipped in Turkey – the price of having it done at the airport would be higher than in Istanbul, but not after paying for a return flight home and yet another to New York.

"Fine. Where do I sign up?"

"This way," the supervisor said, and exited the booth. He escorted Jamal to an area to the side with a banner over it announcing the Carl's Junior Insta-Chip Station. Most of the official functions had long ago been subsidized by corporations as the government had been increasingly privatized after the national debt had grown so onerous that the state and federal apparatuses were effectively broke. "Have a seat, and someone will run your card and get this taken care of. When you're done, just go back to the station where we're holding your paperwork, and you'll be through in no time."

A young woman approached. Her Carl's name tag said Pamela. Jamal felt in his jacket for his wallet, resigned to being blackmailed out of ten thousand new dollars' worth of credits he didn't have, and handed her his emergency card, figuring that if this didn't qualify as one, he didn't know what did.

Chapter 5

San Francisco, California

Three hard-looking men in dark suits marched down the hall toward Veritas. The tall lead figure, with a pockmarked face and eyes the color of lead, stopped in front of the gurney and flipped out a badge holder.

"Veritas Grey?" he asked, his voice as rough as sandpaper.

"Who wants to know?" the doctor demanded.

"Agent Hersh. DSS." The Domestic Security Service had combined the duties of Homeland Security, Immigration, and the FBI into a single entity. Hersh fixed the doctor with a hard stare. "Now answer the question."

The doctor cleared his throat. "That's right. Veritas Grey. But he's still undergoing evaluation."

"Negative, Doctor. We're authorized to remove him from the hospital and take him into custody."

"Not until he's been pronounced fit for transport, Agent. He suffered substantial trauma–"

"I'll take full responsibility."

Veritas glared at Hersh. "I don't understand. What does DSS have to do with somebody practically running me down?"

"I'd keep my mouth shut if I were you, Grey," Hersh growled.

"It's a fair question," the doctor said. "What's he being charged with?"

28

"He's a potential terrorist. Now get out of the way and let us do our jobs," Hersh said.

Veritas gasped. "What? That's crazy. I deliver pizzas. There must be some mistake."

"Shut it," Hersh said.

The doctor took a step forward. "This is most unusual—"

"These are unusual times, Doctor. But this isn't a negotiation. We're taking him. Now."

"I...I need to call the hospital legal counsel," the doctor stammered.

"Call whoever you want," Hersh said, and nodded to his companions. "Get him out of here."

The doctor's expression darkened. "Now see here—"

"No, Doctor, *you* see here. We're taking a dangerous terror suspect into custody before he has a chance to escape. Nothing you say or do is going to stop us from doing our job."

"I'm not a terrorist," Veritas interrupted. "You've got the wrong guy."

Hersh chuckled, the sound as mean as a fighting dog's snarl. "Another innocent man. We've yet to bust anyone who's done anything wrong."

"It's true," Veritas pressed.

"Sure it is, buddy."

The two agents beside Hersh moved to either side of the gurney, and the one holding Veritas's jacket and backpack withdrew a pair of cuffs while the other retrieved a pistol from his shoulder holster and motioned to Veritas with it. "Hold out your hands. No funny moves, understand?"

The first agent locked one of the bracelets around Veritas's right wrist while the other trained the pistol on Veritas's head. The doctor and orderly backed away at the sight of the gun, and Veritas blinked in confusion as the agent snapped the cuffs into place.

"I was in an accident," Veritas said. "I didn't do anything. You seriously have the wrong guy."

Hersh ignored him. "Move him to the elevator," he instructed the others. The one with the gun slipped it back into its holster and then helped push the gurney toward the gleaming bank of steel doors at the opposite end of the hall.

Veritas struggled fruitlessly against the cuffs. One of the doors slid open with a ping, and the men trundled the gurney into the oversized elevator. Veritas decided to save his strength and cursed inwardly at the drug that had numbed his responses. He closed his eyes, his mind reeling and his trip-hammering pulse thudding in his ears.

The elevator opened at the ground floor, and the agents rolled him toward the ER. Selena Aames's voice from just ahead broke the agents' silence.

"What's going on here? Where do you think you're taking that man?" she demanded, her tone hard.

"Into custody," Hersh answered. He flipped out his badge, flashed it at her, and slid it back into his suit pocket. "Agent Hersh. DSS."

"On what grounds?" Aames parried.

"Terrorism."

"Let's see your badge again. I'm going to scan it."

"The hell you are," Hersh snapped. "Officer, this is a matter of national security. Way over your pay grade."

"He's in my custody until I complete my report and verify your ID, sport. So let's have another look at your badge," she said, one hand on the pistol at her hip.

Hersh sighed, removed the badge, and stepped closer so she could scan it with her phone. Then the air crackled and she stiffened; her eyes bugged out like a puffer fish, and her complexion instantly paled.

Hersh pocketed the stun gun he'd zapped her with and moved to catch her before she hit the floor. He looked in both directions and dragged her to a chair outside of one of the doors while the agents picked up their pace toward the ER. Veritas gaped at the sight of a uniformed police officer incapacitated by a DSS agent, and swallowed a softball-size knot in his throat.

"What the hell's going on here?" he demanded.

Hersh closed the distance between them in an instant. Veritas's back arched and he nearly bit through his tongue when Hersh hit him with the stun gun. The walls closed in on Veritas and a starburst of flares clouded his vision, and then the agony of the shock subsided, and consciousness slipped away.

The agents pushed through the throng clogging the ER, past hospital security, who had their hands full with the crowd, and loaded Veritas into a large electro-drive ambulance flanked by a pair of black diesel SUVs.

Hersh climbed into the back with Veritas and pulled the door closed behind him. He folded a jump seat down and sat with a grunt as the ambulance pulled away. Once the convoy was off the hospital grounds, he withdrew a pistol from beneath his coat and held it casually in his lap, watching Veritas's inert form on the gurney with dead eyes.

Chapter 6

Los Angeles, California

A stiff Santa Ana wind blew hot off the high desert, churning the Pacific into white froth and sandblasting the expensive homes perched near the canyons. Palm fronds clapped like rifle fire in the violent gusts, and semi-rigs on the interstate pulled to the side of the road for fear of overturning.

Servants struggled to secure the patio furniture on the veranda of a sprawling faux-Tuscan estate in an area so exclusive most had no idea it existed. Stars glimmered in the night sky, the ever-present beige blanket of pollution blown out to sea, and a gibbous moon lit the grounds with an amber glow. The nearest home was an eighth of a mile away, hidden from view by a line of senile trees that swayed in the wind like a procession of old women.

Inside, in a dining room large enough to house a private jet, a thin man in his seventies, his long face mottled with liver spots, sat at an enormous dining table whose mahogany surface was polished to a reflective gleam. A stained-glass window of an elaborately rendered three-mast sailing vessel firing its cannon at another warship stretched from head height to the vaulted ceiling high above. The old man fingered an oxblood silk cravat with spindled fingers; a smoking jacket buttoned over a pastel blue shirt shone in the light from a thousand facets of an elaborate chandelier eighteen feet above his head. A paper-thin goblet a quarter full of Bordeaux sat on the table in front of him, and he lifted it slowly to his nose, gave it a perfunctory sniff, and sipped it with closed eyes and intense concentration.

A servant stepped into the dining room and cleared his throat. The old man's eyes snapped open, and he frowned at the interruption and then set down his glass with obvious reluctance.

"Yes, Simon. What is it?" he asked, his voice as dry as parchment.

"Your guest is here, Mr. Abbot."

Abbot consulted his watch, an antique rose-gold Patek Philippe perpetual calendar worth several million dollars.

"Ah. Very good. Kindly show him in, and then leave us."

"Of course, sir."

Abbot took another cautious sip of the wine, swirling it around in his mouth before swallowing, savoring the complexity of the bouquet as he exhaled through his nose. Footsteps rang out on the Italian marble floor, the only other sound besides the low moan of the wind outside and the faint strains of a piano concerto drifting from hidden speakers. A muscular man in his late twenties with skin bronzed a deep copper appeared at the dining room threshold. His black hair was slicked straight back off his forehead, and a faint white scar ran from his hairline to flinty gray eyes, one of which was artificial, the color slightly different than the other. He nodded to Abbot, who motioned for him to approach and indicated a chair.

"Azra, have a seat. I don't suppose you want any wine, do you? It's a '95 Cheval Blanc."

"No, thank you, Mr. Abbot. I don't drink," Azra said gruffly. He moved to the chair and sat.

"You don't know what you're missing. An amazing sensory experience, and one of the few I can still entertain without fear of my doctor having to fly out to give me CPR."

The corners of Azra's lips twitched, but he didn't respond.

Abbot grunted, set his glass down, and fixed Azra with a stare, his gaze unwavering and direct. "We have a problem."

"Yes, sir. I gathered that from your call."

"One of your little group has surfaced. Which should have been impossible. Supposedly everyone but you was…neutralized."

"I wasn't directing that operation, sir, so I can't speak to the veracity of the reports you received."

"Yes, well, I intend to deal with that in my own time."

Azra nodded. "There's good news. After you alerted me, I did as you requested and called in some favors. We have him in custody."

Abbot frowned and shook his head, the movement lending him the appearance of an angry, startled bird. "That's good news. Take the plane and deal with this personally. I need to understand how he escaped – and who, if anyone, betrayed us." Abbot paused. "Use whatever means you like to arrive at the truth. But get it one way or another."

Azra nodded once. "Yes, sir. I'll see to it." He held the old man's stare without blinking. "And once I have it?"

"At that point he is of no further use. Terminate him. I don't want a trace of him left."

"What about the team that brought him in?"

"Up to you. But I'll hold you responsible for any breach of security."

"There's only one way to ensure secrecy, Mr. Abbot."

Abbot waved a hand and eyed his wine. "I'll leave it to you. But I do want his CPU. It may yield some clues that could be vital, moving forward."

"That's all that will be left. I'll deliver it myself."

Abbot squinted at him. "How did your team manage to take him? I would have thought that would have been nearly impossible."

"He was in a car accident and took a blow to the head. Also, it looks like he's been altered in some way. None of his special abilities seem to be active, based on the agents' preliminary report."

Abbot nodded. "That makes sense, then. We received his scans from a hospital, which is how we were alerted. But there were…anomalies that we couldn't explain from a remote read. I want to know how they happened."

"Of course. I'll get to the bottom of it."

"See that you do."

A particularly brutal gust of wind buffeted the house. Azra's eyes narrowed, and he shook his head. "Nothing will be taking off in this weather."

"I've ordered an LS700 drone vehicle to take you over the mountains to the north, and chartered a plane to pick you up at the first airstrip on that side. You'll have any resources you require."

Azra left, and Abbot swirled the crimson treasure in his glass before taking another sip.

"Really remarkable," he whispered to himself, and closed his eyes again, the trill of violins over a sonorous cello barely audible over the Santa Ana's fury, the rare French wine liquid velvet in his puckered mouth.

Chapter 7

The rumble of the ambulance's tires on the uneven pavement died as the big vehicle slowed at an intersection near South San Francisco, heading into an area that made the Mission look like Park Avenue. The right front wheel hit a particularly ugly pothole, and Veritas opened his eyes, jarred back to consciousness by the ambulance bucking like a scared bronco.

Veritas inhaled and flexed his fingers, his gaze unfocused in the artificial light. The skin on his wrists was raw from the steel handcuffs, and his whole body tingled like a limb that had fallen asleep and was coming back to life, which was close to how he felt after taking the full charge of the stun gun in his drugged and disabled state.

Hersh rocked in the jump seat, leaden eyes locked on Veritas and the gun clenched in his hand. Veritas had just cleared his throat to speak when the ambulance screeched to a stop, slamming the gurney against the bulkhead in spite of the wheel locks holding it in place.

"What the—" Veritas blurted, and then an explosion rocked the vehicle.

Hersh tapped his earbud, his gun still trained on Veritas. "Raptor One, what's going on out there?"

The rattle of machine-gun fire sounded from outside, followed by three more detonations in quick succession. Veritas cringed as

36

shrapnel tore through the top of the ambulance only a few feet from his head, shattering the overhead light and shredding the power line that supplied the patient cabin.

Hersh cursed and extracted a miniature flashlight from his pocket. He switched it on and pointed it at Veritas, the gun steady in his hand. His earbud chirped. He listened intently and then cursed.

"I don't care what you have to do. Hold them off and call for backup. You say they used grenade launchers or antitank rockets?"

He listened, and louder booms from nearby answered the machine-gun fire. He frowned and tapped the earbud again.

"Come in, Raptor One. I lost you."

He glared at Veritas as though he were responsible for the attack. More explosions shook the ambulance, and Hersh slowly straightened until his head was against the ceiling, the flashlight beam blinding Veritas.

Hersh's concentration was broken by more shooting near the ambulance doors, and he appeared torn about where to direct his attention, the impulse to shoot Veritas obvious in his eyes. Veritas considered kicking at him but hesitated – given the proximity, it was a nearly hundred percent certainty Hersh would shoot if he tried.

Slugs punched through the metal wall where Hersh had been sitting only moments before, and the agent instinctively backed away from the doors, his focus jarred away from Veritas. Veritas kicked Hersh in the ribs as hard as he could, putting all his strength into it and following the first blow with a pile-driver second. Hersh woofed like a stunned dog as his breath exploded from his mouth, and Veritas managed a third kick. The snap of ribs was as clear in the confined space as the pop of firecrackers, and the pistol skittered across the floor.

Veritas was in motion as Hersh fell against the doors, and he rolled off the gurney and onto the steel floor, landing hard. As he grappled for the gun, a part of his brain rebelled at the idea he was attacking a DSS agent – an act that automatically carried years in prison, even if he was guilty of nothing and the whole episode was a case of mistaken identity.

The intensity of the shooting outside increased, and Veritas's fingers felt the distinctive shape of the gun butt. He tried to get hold of it, but Hersh threw himself toward Veritas and delivered a kick that Veritas was only partially able to block with his hip. His leg went instantly numb and his eyes streamed with tears, but he forced his other leg to piston into Hersh's crotch, dropping him with a crash.

"Grnnnphh–" Hersh exclaimed, but another kick to the head cut him off.

Shotgun blasts from outside the ambulance were followed by a two-second sustained burst of submachine-gun fire, the chattering so rapid the shots seemed like a single uninterrupted bark. The shotguns fell silent, and Veritas's fingers again found the pistol. The feeling in his leg returned as needles of pain. He fumbled with the gun and tried for the flashlight, the interior of the ambulance so dark he could scarcely make out his captor.

His attempt to grip them with cuffed hands proved difficult, though, and the aluminum penlight slipped from his fingers and rolled away. He was reaching for it again when Hersh threw himself at Veritas, fists flailing. Veritas swung the pistol toward him, but Hersh knocked it aside. The weapon fired, and the round went wide and struck one of the steel cabinets that framed the bay.

Veritas's ears rang from the discharge. Two punches to the face instantly cleared his head, and he tried to level the gun at Hersh again. The agent anticipated the move and used both fists to slam the back of Veritas's hand, knocking the pistol away. The gun clattered to the floor, bounced against a cabinet, and banked toward the rear doors. Hersh followed the trajectory in the flashlight's dim glow and reacted a split second faster than Veritas. He launched backward and scooped up the pistol as Veritas was struggling to his feet.

An ugly smirk twisted Hersh's features as he leveled the muzzle at Veritas's forehead. "That was your lucky break, and you blew it," he snarled. "Game over."

Veritas shrank back against the bulkhead, trying to make himself as small as possible, the agent's expression telegraphing his intent. He winced in anticipation, and then the rear doors flew open, and three pistol shots in rapid succession blew through Hersh's back, speckling Veritas with blood when the slugs exited Hersh's chest and slammed into the bulkhead above his head. Veritas gasped as Hersh crumpled. He hit the floor with a gurgle, and Veritas drew back at the lake of blood spreading toward him. Hersh's eyes glared at him uncomprehendingly, and pink froth burbled from his mouth with each ragged gasp.

"Are you hurt?" a familiar face asked from the doors.

Veritas blinked unbelievingly. "Officer…Aames?" he stammered.

"I asked whether you're hurt," Selena snapped.

He shook his head and registered that the shooting outside had stopped. "A little bloody, but I think I'm fine."

"Can you stand?"

Veritas nodded and struggled to his feet, eyes locked on the spreading pool of crimson around Hersh.

Selena looked to her left and lowered her pistol. "Grab his gun and get out here. We don't have much time."

"His gun?"

"Did you touch it?"

"Yes."

"Then you can't leave it." She cocked her head. "See if he's got the keys to your cuffs in his pockets."

Veritas patted the dead man's jacket and heard a telltale clink. He fished out Hersh's keys and tossed them to her. "I don't know what a handcuff key looks like. Is it one of those?"

"Yes. Step over him and avoid the blood."

Veritas did so, and she unlocked the cuffs, wiped them off on the fleece lining of her windbreaker, and tossed them on the ground. He flexed his fingers and rubbed his wrists, the skin chafed an angry red.

"Can I get my clothes?" he asked. "It's freezing outside."

Selena nodded, and Veritas found his backpack beneath the gurney and quickly pulled on his torn jeans, leather jacket, and boots.

"The gun," she repeated.

Veritas leaned over and scooped up the pistol and then made his way to the doors, his head spinning.

"Hand me the weapon, butt first," Selena instructed. Veritas did as she asked, and she took the gun from him, examined it for a moment, and then slipped it into her waistband at the small of her back. "Okay. Hop down and follow me."

"I don't understand."

"I was close by when the 'shots fired' report came over the air. You're lucky I got here before anyone else."

He stepped onto the street and took in the scene. The SUVs looked like they'd been put through a car crusher – their fenders and chassis were mangled, their tires were flat, and flames were licking them both. The DSS agents' bodies were strewn around the area, and two were hanging halfway out of the doors of the first vehicle. Others whom Veritas didn't recognize, clad in dark camo, lay dead nearby, their machine guns and RPGs dropped where they'd fallen.

"Jesus," Veritas whispered. "What happened here? Everyone's dead…"

"You feel strong enough to hoof it?" she asked.

"I think so." He paused. "What's going on? What is all this?"

She ignored his questions. "This way," she said, and took off at a run toward an alley. Veritas followed her, but as he neared the alley mouth, hesitated at the sound of big motors and squealing tires approaching.

Selena called to him from the alley. "Hurry up. I don't hear sirens, so those aren't friendlies."

"Where are we going?" he asked.

"I don't know yet. Someplace where they won't shoot you on sight seems like the safest bet."

He caught up to her. "Why would they–"

She grabbed his arm and studied him for a moment before spinning and sprinting away.

"Shut up and follow me."

Chapter 8

Selena ran full out until she reached the next block, and only slowed when it was obvious Veritas wasn't keeping up. She stopped, replaced her pistol in its holster, and withdrew Hersh's gun, removed the magazine and ejected the round in the chamber, and wiped the weapon down as Veritas approached.

"What are you doing?" he asked.

She strode to an overflowing dumpster, holding the weapon with the bottom of her windbreaker, and tossed the gun into the depths. She pocketed the magazine and bullet and eyed him in the gloom. "You ask a lot of questions."

"We just walked out of a bloodbath. I want to know what happened."

"Looks to me like someone attacked the convoy. Maybe one of the local warlords. This is a rough area. We're not out of the woods yet."

She pirouetted and sprinted away. Veritas had little choice but to tail her. To call the area *rough* was like describing the result of the attack *untidy*. Nobody went into this section of town if they could help it, especially after dark. The Hunter's Point district was infamous even among the denizens of the Mission, which was dangerous in its own right – but child's play compared to where they were now.

Veritas put on a burst of speed and pulled even with Selena in front of an abandoned factory with broken windows. The electrified fence above the six-foot-high wall was adorned with rusting yellow

41

signs every twenty feet warning of high voltage. He grabbed her arm and stopped her.

"I think I deserve some answers," he said.

One of her eyebrows lifted and she held his stare. "Deserve? One of us just saved the other's life. Did I miss where I was tied to the railroad tracks and you rescued me?"

"Okay, poor choice of words. You know what I mean."

Her expression softened slightly. "You're going to have to play along, Veritas."

He frowned. "Trusting the cops isn't high on my list. When you look like I do, you get rousted all the time for nothing."

She nodded. "I hear you. But I also just pulled you out of the fire and killed a DSS agent to do it."

"I know. I was there. Thank you. But I still want to know what's going on. Why did they drag me out of the hospital? And why are you helping me?"

Her face darkened. "Things aren't the way you think they are. Now get a move on, or they're going to catch us, and then all of this will be for nothing."

"I'm not going anywhere until I get answers."

She sighed. "I should have shot you myself."

That earned an ugly look from him. She tried again. "Veritas, you have no idea what you're involved in. I'll tell you more once we're clear, but right now you have to do exactly as I say or you won't live to see morning. Now let's find a car."

"Didn't you drive?"

"A round blew out my front tire."

"So you were there during the fight?"

"I got there at the end."

His eyes narrowed. "Pretty coincidental that you were nearby, huh?"

"You'd be dead now if I hadn't been. The universe works in mysterious ways. Now move your ass or you're going to catch a bullet."

She didn't wait for a response and instead dashed along the

sidewalk, the concrete still slick from the earlier showers. A foghorn lowed in the distance as they ran along the deserted street, and Veritas's stamina improved as his head gradually cleared of the drugs.

Selena stopped in front of another building and pointed at the parking lot. "We'll take one of those," she said, indicating a huddle of rusting cars, not one less than twenty years old.

"We're going to steal a car? Are you really a cop?"

"Desperate times demand desperate measures."

"Do you know how?"

She gave him a disgusted look. "Of course." She hesitated. "They teach us in training."

"They'll have alarms."

"I can bypass anything older than the last two generations. Don't sweat it." She peered down the street. "Wait here."

"You aren't kidding, are you?"

"Enough with the questions."

Selena crept into the lot and moved to the closest vehicle to the street. She withdrew something from her belt and held it beneath the driver's side door, and then tried the handle. It didn't open, so she drew her pistol, and when the foghorn droned again, shattered the window with a sharp blow. Nobody appeared from within the building, and a few moments later she had the door open and was fiddling beneath the dashboard as Veritas kept an eye on the street.

The engine roared to life. She pulled the door closed and put the car into gear. Veritas came at a run, and then they careened out of the lot, blowing through the chain that ran across the driveway, and peeled out on the slick street.

Selena glanced at the rearview mirror and then over at Veritas, who was feeling for the seatbelt with no success.

"This thing's a relic. You're lucky it started," he grumbled.

Her mouth twisted in a smirk. "We're lucky, you mean."

"Couldn't you have picked something newer?"

"That would report itself as stolen the moment I overrode the computer, you mean?" She exhaled hard at his question.

He frowned. "All right. Time for you to come clean. Why did DSS drag me out of the hospital?"

She paused and took a deep breath. "Veritas, you're not who you think you are. I know that's hard to get your mind around, but it's true."

"Bullshit. I'm no terrorist."

"That's where you're wrong. To the machine, you're their worst enemy."

"The machine?"

"The people who run things."

"You've got the wrong guy. This is some kind of mistaken-identity thing, like in the vids."

She shook her head. "No. But now that they know about you, they'll never give up until they get you."

"That's insane." He looked at her. "You were at the hospital, and then during the fight. What's your angle?"

"Veritas, listen to me. You're…you're part of a military experiment that went wrong. An augmented hybrid soldier. What you think are your memories? They aren't real. Everything you think is true is a lie. Everything. Everything you believe, everything you know. It's all fake."

Veritas snorted. "Sure it is. I deliver pizzas, but I'm really the Terminator." He looked away. "I've heard enough. Let me out."

"You need to listen with an open mind. I understand your reaction, but–"

His eyes widened. "You were part of the attack, weren't you?"

"I told you. I showed up at the tail end…" Her gaze flashed to the rearview mirror again as headlights brightened the interior of the car. "Shit."

He twisted to see. "They're gaining on us."

"I know. I'd say buckle up, but…" She gritted her teeth and stomped on the accelerator. "Hang on."

The engine strained to power the car faster, and at the next street she twisted the wheel viciously, and they rounded the corner with all four tires shrieking in protest. The car fishtailed and nearly struck the façade of a building before she got control of it, and she floored the gas, her expression grim.

They were nearly to the end of the block when the headlights bounced onto the road behind them, followed by a second pair. Veritas held onto the door and armrest with a death grip, his stomach churning.

"Now there's two," he yelled.

"I see them." She jagged left at the next street, and the car caught air as it soared over a rise. It slammed down against the pavement and shed a horsetail of sparks, and the undercarriage scraped as the shocks bottomed out. Selena switched off the headlights and wrenched the wheel hard right, and then they were racing down a narrow alleyway, engine redlining as she downshifted. A row of metal trashcans materialized in front of them, and she braked as they slammed into them, sending the containers flying. One smashed the passenger-side windshield, and half the glass frosted over.

"You need to jump out of the car after the next turn," she said.

"Jump? Are you nuts?"

"You're too important to allow them to capture you again. A lot of good people died freeing you. I'm not going to let that be in vain."

His eyes narrowed. "So you *were* involved in the attack!"

"I'll slow down some, and you jump out and hide wherever you can. I'll lead them away."

"I can't throw myself out of a moving car. I'll break every bone in my body."

"No, you won't. Just don't try to land on your feet. Roll when you hit the ground and you'll be fine. Your bones are stronger than you think."

He looked at her incredulously. "You're certifiable."

"They're gaining on us. You're only going to get one shot. Here we go," she said, and yanked the steering wheel right at the alley mouth. The car's tires howled like a wounded animal, and then she was braking. "Now!" she screamed.

Against every instinct, Veritas threw the door open and hurled himself from the car. He landed in a puddle of foul-smelling water and tumbled over and over, protecting his skull with his arms, letting his leather jacket absorb the worst of the fall. When he came to a stop, he gasped and then flexed his legs to confirm they were still attached.

To his surprise, he was still in one piece.

The rumble of SUVs from the alley drove him to his feet, and after a few tentative steps, he darted to a doorway and pressed himself into the shadows. The big vehicles turned the corner and sped past his hiding place, leaving him dripping and stunned as they disappeared down the block. He stood motionless for half a minute and then exhaled loudly, only then realizing he'd been holding his breath.

The foghorn bayed, urging him to action. Veritas stepped from the doorway and glanced up the empty street and, after orienting himself, headed toward the black expanse of water at the bottom of the hill, the wail of sirens from the scene of the ambush trailing him like a curse.

Chapter 9

Chula Vista, California

A van with the logo of a cleaning company emblazoned on its side rolled to a stop in front of a building in an industrial park a stone's throw from the Mexican border. A crew of four emptied out of it and made for the glowing entrance, one of them rolling a cart in front of her, another carrying a large shop vacuum, and the rest toting mops and brooms.

Inside, a trio of security guards looked up at the new arrivals. The oldest of the three guards, obviously the supervisor, checked the time. "Late, aren't you?"

The woman with the cart shrugged. "The van with the regular crew broke down. We had to divert from another job," she explained.

The guard studied her, taking in her gaunt features and gray complexion before looking over the rest. "Everyone got their IDs?"

The woman nodded and handed over four driver's licenses. The supervisor scanned the cards and handed them back with a smirk. "Any of them speak English?"

"That isn't as important as whether they're hard workers, is it?" she asked.

He checked the time. "Pretty sure nobody's going to raid us at this hour." He turned to one of the younger guards. "Check out the cart and the vac."

The guard did so, and after rummaging around and inspecting the cleaning supplies and the vacuum cleaner, he nodded. "You're good to go."

The head guard cleared his throat. "Tell your people that under no circumstances should they go near the restricted areas. They're all clearly marked. No exceptions."

"I remember the place from a few years ago. Before your time. Where do you want us to start?" the woman asked, thumbing a blueprint of the building on her phone to life and showing it to the supervisor.

"Where it says administrative offices. After that just do the hallways, and you're done."

She smiled. "Sounds easy. Maybe we'll get off early tonight."

"If you get to work and they don't dawdle," he said, eyeing the others. "No *tacos* or *cerveza, comprende?*" he asked in a grating gringo accent.

The cleaners grinned sheepishly and nodded. The woman said something in rapid-fire Spanish, and the group made for a steel security door with a palm scanner beside it. She raised her hand and the screen blinked twice and then turned green when the bolt clicked open.

Once in the administrative area, the workers followed her down a long hall to a large open area filled with gray cubicles. Her eyes roved over the ceiling, taking in the security cameras in each corner. She stopped the cart at the first cubicle, and the workers gathered around while she doled out coveralls. When everyone was suited up, she handed each a tackle box filled with cleaning fluid, scuff pads, and brushes. She and a young man rolled the cart and vacuum to one corner of the room, and the others moved to the opposite corner and began to clean.

The young man leaned toward the woman, his gaze skittish, flitting to the cameras and then back to her. "We're in," he whispered.

"Told you this would work, Greg."

"We're still a long way from the labs."

"Give them some time to get bored with us, and then we'll make our move."

"Hope the gizmos work as advertised."

Her lips hardened into a line. "They will."

Greg plugged in the shop vac and began cleaning around a pair of doors, and she extracted a bottle of cleanser and a yellow rag from the cart and walked to the break room. An hour passed, and as midnight approached, Greg and the others joined her in a small conference area that had no camera.

She opened a hidden panel in the base of the cart, removed a white lab coat, and quickly stripped off her coveralls and slipped on the jacket. Next, she unscrewed the vacuum motor housing and withdrew four compact 9mm pistols and passed them around before sliding one into her jacket. She extracted a black nylon backpack, and Greg shouldered it. After feeling inside, he removed four tiny boxes with toggle switches and pocketed them, his expression serious.

The woman nodded to the workers, and they dispersed, leaving her with Greg.

"Ready?" she murmured.

He nodded, his eyes bright with excitement and a hint of fear.

She took a deep breath. "Let's do this."

They exited the cubicle and walked at a deliberate pace toward the hallway at the far end of the office. Greg jumped and slapped one of the boxes onto the side of the camera, and then stepped back a pace to consider his handiwork. The woman exhaled slowly.

"We'll find out whether they work soon enough."

She pushed open the door, and they ran down the corridor until they arrived at a T intersection. The woman studied the blueprint and pointed to the left, and whispered to Greg, "Camera right around the corner. You need to nail it before we're in its field of view."

He leapt and stuck another box on the intersection camera housing and activated it, and then the woman strode to a door with a biohazard warning sign several yards away. She peeled a latex coating with the handprint of the woman who'd worked at the plant years ago from her hand, beneath which was another, similar layer. She held her palm to the scanner beside the door and it winked green. After a moment's hesitation, her face hardened, and she twisted the handle and half-turned to Greg.

"I should be back in a few minutes. I'll take the backpack. Station yourself at the junction by the stairwell up ahead. If anyone comes, you know what to do."

He nodded, handed her the bag, and removed the gun from the pocket of his overalls. "Good luck."

"Thanks."

When he was gone, she shouldered through the doorway and found herself staring through a long glass window, beyond which were rows of hospital beds. Men and women lay atop them, vital signs monitors recording their pulses and temperatures. Nobody was moving in the dim light. Her breath caught in her throat at the sight, even though she'd known what to expect from an informant.

Her eyes drifted to the door of a changing room that was connected to the biocontainment room – a clandestine facility not on any official list. The building belonged to a biotech firm whose largest client was the U.S. military, but even the highest echelons in the Pentagon had no idea that the lab existed.

The woman moved to open the outer door, and when she stepped inside, she repeated her hand scanning in order to unlock the second airtight door that led to the shower and changing area. She ignored the showers and crossed to another airlock. That one opened with a hiss, and then she was in a sanitization cell.

She made short work of donning a hazmat suit and deposited her lab coat and backpack on the bench before entering yet another chamber outfitted with nozzles and UV lamps, beyond which was the final door that led into the main room.

Once in the lab, she went straight to a thermal unit and opened it. Inside were rows of vials of blood samples. To her right were those dated earlier that day. She removed three of these and read the identity codes, and then moved to the beds, where the codes were repeated on plastic plaques. She matched the first sample with a bed and regarded the Hispanic man in it. His breathing was obviously labored, and his heartrate was 128 with his blood pressure through the roof. His eyes were closed, a sheen of sweat glistened on his forehead, and his pasty appendages twitched slightly with palsy.

The woman knew from their informant those in the beds were illegal aliens who didn't officially exist in the U.S. system and whose presence wouldn't be missed if they disappeared – which they would, after they'd served their purpose. She forced herself to concentrate on identifying the beds that corresponded with the other two vials, and confronted the same scene – migrant workers in the final stages of a horrific death.

Her verification took less than a minute, but she was conscious of the passage of time. She hurried back to the airlock and entered it just as an alarm shattered the quiet. She cursed and rushed to the other airtight door to push it open, now racing the clock. She fitted the vials into the backpack and unfastened the hazmat suit, and once free of the bulk, pulled on the lab coat and ran through the remaining doors, backpack in hand.

A gunshot rang out from the administrative office area as she was retracing her steps to the hall, answered by a volley of shots. More gunshots echoed through the building as the pair of workers she'd left in the cubicles battled it out with security. She ran to the junction where Greg was waiting, his skin white as chalk.

"You get it?" he asked.

"Yes."

"I'll stay here and hold them off."

She frowned. "Do the best you can."

"It was an honor, Leslie."

"For me too, Greg."

Her eyes were moist as she brushed past him and made for the stairs. She was opening the door when Greg's pistol barked four times, and then she was through, the sounds of a gunfight reverberating in her ears as she climbed the stairs, cursing her lack of stamina with every step. Her legs burned like fire from the strain, and when she reached the roof door, her breathing was a wet burble.

The shooting downstairs stopped, and she checked her watch as she crept to the edge of the roof.

A minute later she was cinching rappelling cord to a pipe when the roof door burst open and two guards with bullpup machine guns appeared. She dropped the cord, whipped her pistol free, and fired at them, squeezing the trigger as fast as she could.

A burst from the guards caught her in the chest, and she tumbled back. The pain was excruciating. Her weapon clattered harmlessly beside her as she hit the roof. A bright flash of agony flared from the back of her skull, and then there was nothing but a million stars above her as her awareness drifted to a place far away.

Chapter 10

Ghostly tendrils of fog floated above the frontage road, and the bay was a carpet of white that stretched as far as Veritas could see in the darkness. He jogged at a comfortable pace as his mind raced over the night's events. One minute he'd been on his bike, and the next he was in the middle of a war zone, with a man shot right in front of him a split second before he could put a bullet in Veritas.

None of it made any sense, including Selena. Why had a cop executed a fellow officer of the law in cold blood and shown zero remorse? And what about her oblique assurances – what the hell did any of her babble about him being a hybrid and everything being a lie mean? And his memories weren't real? Nuts. He remembered his drug-addled years and his painful detox ordeal in the Thai monastery like it was yesterday. Maybe this was all some kind of wish-fulfillment hallucination, that he was special and none of the damage he'd done to himself or others because of his addictions had actually happened.

He would have liked to believe it was some really bad drug flashback or a residual effect of the painkillers he'd received, or that he'd wake up any minute to discover his skull had been traumatized and he was dreaming everything. Even now, as he made his way back toward the city, a lone figure running through the fog, the whole thing had the otherworldly feel of a nightmare.

It was enticing to think he was inventing it all, but the lances of pain from his leg told him otherwise. Dreams weren't that realistic, or at least not so fully developed. He might have thought he was running along the water, but if he'd been dreaming, he wouldn't have been simultaneously aware of the sting of frigid air in his lungs, his feet beginning to blister in his boots, or the headache throbbing just behind his eyes that had been his constant companion since regaining consciousness.

No, like it or not, this was real – which meant he really was wanted by DSS, or at least someone they'd mistaken him for was. Which also didn't make any sense. He'd been living at his mother's since returning from Thailand. His whereabouts weren't a secret. His employer had done a background check before hiring him, so he was in the system. None of it added up, and the more he thought about it, the more jumbled it got.

What he couldn't deny was that some group had waylaid the ambulance and come at it as heavy as a combat platoon. Selena's admission in the car had confirmed her involvement – which meant she'd been stalking him, or at least that there was far more to the situation that he could fathom based on her ambiguous declarations.

Veritas shivered. The chill was creeping into his bones in spite of the exertion and his heavy jacket; at least, he told himself that was the reason.

So now both the police and DSS were looking for him. Given that the security agency controlled everything, he had no doubt that resources would be mobilized to find him, especially after their agents had been cut apart in an ambush. They would want to interrogate him and find out what he knew, and when. The irony being that if Selena was to be believed, what he thought he knew wasn't true, so it would do them even less good than it was doing him.

"What now?" he whispered.

He had to get help. He was broke and hurt, a fugitive, and couldn't trust his instincts – a losing combo no matter how he sliced it.

A face popped into his mind: Ben, his sponsor.

Ben had always been able to offer sound counsel and was never disapproving or judgmental; plus nobody outside of the program knew they had a relationship of any kind.

Headlights approached through the fog, and he ducked behind a dumpster. A police cruiser glided by, its electric drive silent, the Pfizer logo above the SFPD emblem glowing blue on the door.

It was just a matter of time until he ran out of luck, alone on the mean streets of the city.

When the car disappeared, Veritas altered course and moved away from the water's edge, toward the Mission district. Ben had a flat over a music store, and at the rate Veritas was going, he could probably make it in under an hour.

Veritas increased his pace and reached Ben's building after another narrow miss with the police. Once in the Mission he wasn't worried – he knew the streets cold, and the cops avoided the area unless extenuating circumstances were involved. Routine patrols were a thing of the past; the ongoing budget crisis had left the city shorthanded thanks to the legions of homeless and criminals who'd overwhelmed the government's ability to fund itself, in part aided by the will of the bureaucrats who'd mismanaged the chaos for a decade.

Veritas scoped out the street before ascending the three steps to a narrow entryway with four buzzers. Ben's was the flat that overlooked the street, and Veritas pressed the button with trepidation, hesitant to put him in a bind by being there but with nowhere else to turn.

Thirty seconds later, Ben's voice croaked from the speaker. "Yes?"

"Ben? It's Ver. Sorry to bug you so late…"

"No problem," Ben said, and the lock buzzed to let Veritas in.

Ben was waiting with his door open, his face lined from the years but his eyes clear in spite of the hour. He took in Veritas's scuffed and stained jacket, torn jeans, and disheveled appearance, and stepped aside without speaking. Veritas brushed by him, and he bolted the door before following Veritas into the living room. The rich aroma of coffee wafted from the kitchen, and as though reading Veritas's mind, Ben turned to him.

"Have a seat. Coffee?" Ben asked.

"Please."

Veritas sank onto the old couch and sighed in relief. The room was unchanged from the last time he'd been there, and the familiarity was reassuring after the surreal events of the evening. A yellow blur streaked across the room, and Moxie leapt into Veritas's lap, startling him but making him smile. The dog's bottom wiggled with frantic energy, and it groaned contentedly when Veritas stroked its belly.

Ben reappeared with two oversized mugs and set one on the table in front of Veritas before sitting in an overstuffed easy chair.

"Sorry about Moxie," he said. "Moxie. Get down. Now!"

"No problem, Ben. He's fine here."

Ben took a sip and cocked an eyebrow at Veritas, obviously waiting for him to speak.

Veritas swallowed half his mug in two gulps. The scalding brew warmed him, and after another sip, he placed it back on the table.

"Again, I'm really sorry about this, Ben," Veritas began.

Ben nodded, his expression concerned but caring. "Care to tell me what happened?"

Veritas knew the invitation was an encouragement to confess if he'd fallen off the wagon. He shook his head. "I'm not sure where to start."

"Hasn't been but a few hours since we spoke at the meeting. How about there?"

Veritas nodded. "I had an accident."

Ben didn't blink. "What kind of accident? Are you hurt?"

"A bit beaten up, but nothing broken. But that's the least of my problems."

Ben sipped his coffee before responding. "What brings you here, Veritas?"

Veritas cleared his throat. "Like I said, I had an accident. I was on my bike, riding to work, and I had one of my…one of my spells."

Ben nodded for him to continue.

"A car hit me. Thrashed my bike. But then, while they were scanning me at the hospital, DSS showed up and arrested me." Veritas told him about Selena, about Hersh stun gunning her, and about the attack on the DSS convoy and his ultimate escape.

Ben's face could have been cast in bronze. When Veritas finished, Ben sat back and sighed heavily. "Quite a story, Ver. You're obviously in trouble. I...I should have leveled with you earlier, but it wasn't the right time. But...now it sounds like it might be too late."

Veritas's expression radiated confusion. "What are you talking about?"

"It's...it's complicated. But the important thing is you're here. I wanted to talk to you this evening, remember? It's because circumstances have been moving fast, and the decision was made to bring you into the circle."

"You're losing me, Ben. What circle?"

Ben's face hardened. "We need to get out of town."

"How? I don't have any money, and my mom's sick as a dog."

"I'm sorry about that, but after I explain a few things, you'll understand why we need to leave."

"What things? And where can we go?"

"McCleary, Washington. West of Olympia."

"Washington? What's there? Family or something?"

Ben sighed again. "Ver, there's so much to tell you. There's someone you need to meet who can explain everything. His name's Cassius, and he has a big retreat a couple of miles east of town. I only know small pieces of the story, but he knows all of it."

Veritas stared at Ben. "What story is that?"

Ben didn't say anything for a long beat. "Cassius can tell you what you need to know. I wish I could, but I don't know enough to be dangerous."

Moxie snuggled in Veritas's lap as he downed the last of the coffee. "You're kind of freaking me out, Ben."

"Sorry. Refill? You might need it. It's going to be a long one."

"Please."

Ben padded to the kitchen, and Veritas's gaze settled on Ben's phone. He felt in his jacket and was relieved to find the familiar lump of his cell zipped in the inside pocket. He took it out and powered it on, and it beeped at him. He thumbed to the inbox and saw he had a message time-stamped about when he'd been in the ambulance with Hersh.

His mother's voice, faint and obviously strained, emanated from the speaker. "Sweetheart? It's me. I know you're busy, but I…I'm getting worse. I think I should go to the hospital. I'm having problems breathing. Call me as soon as you can."

Veritas called her back, but the number just rang. He stabbed his phone off in frustration and pushed to his feet. "Ben? I need to go home. Now. My mom's getting sicker. And that was hours ago."

Ben's face fell. "It's too dangerous, Ver. It's a safe bet the police are looking for you, so we need to get out of town immediately. You're only one unlucky break from going down for the count."

"I'm not going to leave my mother when she's this sick. That's not an option."

The older man studied him in silence. "It's a foolish risk. We'll be lucky to get clear of the city, much less show up at your mother's." He paused. "At least turn your phone off. Or don't you think the police can track it?"

"Shit," Veritas muttered under his breath, and removed the battery and pocketed it. "I must still be out of it from the accident. I'm not thinking straight."

"Another reason you shouldn't go home."

Veritas's jaw clenched. "I have to do this, Ben. I hear you, but she's my mom, for God's sake. She said she needs to go to the hospital."

Ben shook his head. "Stubborn as a mule, as usual. I don't know why I ever expected it to be otherwise." He hesitated and nodded once. "Okay, I'll drive you. But you have to promise that once we get her to the hospital, we leave immediately. You can't hang around or you're a dead man."

Chapter 11

Ben's vehicle was a cheap Chinese four-door that rolled along the empty streets like it was on glass, the only sound the muffled hum of its hydrogen fuel cell and Moxie's panting from Ben's backpack. The self-driving economy vehicle moved painfully slowly for Veritas's taste, but the logical part of his brain knew that any faster might get them pulled over. Normally it wouldn't have been an issue, but given the attacks, there would likely be an enhanced police presence on the streets. Even in the present impoverished climate, when cops were killed, the government pulled out all the stops.

They passed a huddle of street people in the shadows of a gutted building, and Ben shook his head.

"It always saddens me how such a high percentage of the population's destitute in the richest country in the world," he said.

"Why do you think that is?" Veritas asked.

"Oh, it's all engineered. If you know your history, you can see how the country was asset-stripped by powerful interests over generations. The only thing left is unpayable debt that was run up to enslave them. Worked like a charm."

"It can't continue." Veritas looked out the window for another few blocks and then spoke quietly. "Ben…that cop told me I was a…a hybrid. Any idea what she was referring to?"

For the first time since Veritas had known him, Ben sounded

uncertain. "I don't want to speculate. Cassius will know."

"Can you be any more nonspecific?"

"I'm sorry. All I can tell you with any certainty is that the reason you feel different from everyone else is that you are."

Veritas frowned. "That's incredibly helpful. We're all snowflakes. Got it." He paused. "The cop told me I'm some sort of military experiment. You know anything about that?"

"She sounds intriguing."

"So she's not one of your 'circle'?"

His eyes flitted to Veritas and then back to the road. "I'm not in the top tier, so I have no idea how many of us there are."

"What – are you some kind of secret society? Blood brothers or something?"

Ben laughed. "If you're asking whether we dress up in black robes and dance around a bonfire, the answer's no."

"No orgies or human sacrifices?"

Ben chuckled. "Haven't been to a good orgy in forever, so afraid not."

They fell silent and watched the blocks pass. Eventually Veritas ran a hand over his face and looked at Ben. "I'm really worried about my mom. The hospital was jammed with flu patients. This year's seems way worse than the media is letting on."

Ben frowned. "Let's hope for the best."

The car turned down a smaller street and drove past Veritas's home, a shabby shotgun house little wider than a garage and with bars on every window, crowded between a pair of two-story Victorian townhomes on similar lots. Veritas scanned the surroundings carefully, but saw nothing unusual – no police cruisers, no windows with lights on, no parked cars with windows fogged.

After circling the block, Ben directed the car to park down the street from the house and powered down the engine.

Veritas resisted the urge to run to the front door and instead waited as Ben climbed from the car and locked it. Veritas stepped from the vehicle and accompanied Ben at a moderate pace that wouldn't attract attention – although anyone foolhardy enough to be on the streets at that hour was suspicious enough.

They reached the house, and Veritas felt for the key in his pocket.

The door swung open into a tiny darkened living room.

"Mom?" he called as he stepped inside.

No answer.

Ben followed him in, and Veritas flipped on a light.

They both gasped at the sight of a frail woman lying on the couch, a crocheted blanket over her legs, her olive complexion unnaturally white and her open eyes staring at the stained ceiling as though surprised by some final thought as she'd died.

Ben grabbed Veritas's arm and leaned into him. "I'm so sorry, Ver..."

Veritas shrugged him off and moved to the sofa. He stared at his mother for a long moment and then reached out to close her eyes. Her skin was cold, and the fingers that clutched the comforter had curled into rigid claws. Tears welled in his eyes and rolled down his cheeks. He bowed his head, and his shoulders shook as he sobbed silently, his breath coming in agonized gasps.

After half a minute, Ben approached him. "Ver?" he said in a soft voice. "There's nothing we can do for her now. We have to go."

"We can't just leave her here, Ben. Not like thi–"

The door crashed open and a pair of uniformed police burst in, guns pointed at them.

"Freeze. You're under arrest!" the nearest of the two shouted.

Veritas raised his hands, but Ben reached toward his jacket. The shorter of the cops fired at him twice. Ben stumbled backward with his mouth agape and then sank to his knees as though in slow motion before he pitched forward and lay still.

"You shot him!" Veritas cried. "He was unarmed, and you...you killed him."

"Shut up. Stay where you are or you're next," the bigger cop ordered.

The smaller officer stepped past Ben's body to the dining area and kitchen, leading with his gun. The bigger one kept his pistol on Veritas, murder in his eyes. After verifying that the house was empty, the smaller one returned.

"Okay," he instructed. "Real slow. Keep your hands up. Walk to that wall, face it, and lean your hands against it over your head, legs spread. One false move and you join your buddy there."

Veritas obeyed. The smaller man approached, and Veritas heard the tinkle of cuffs.

"Left hand. Lower it behind you," the cop ordered.

Once he was cuffed and searched, the other cop toed Ben's corpse and then leaned down and felt with his free hand to see what he'd been reaching for. He found Ben's phone in his pocket and swore.

"The guy was reaching for his cell. Idiot. Why do people do that shit?" he said.

The smaller cop shrugged and holstered his weapon. "Let's get this one to the car. We can call in the shooting."

"I make it as good," the other cop said. "Shouldn't be any problem."

"The hell it was good," Veritas spat. "You shot him in cold blood. You're murderers."

The big cop's eyes were slits. "You going to cause problems? I'll be happy to club you a few times if you don't keep your mouth shut."

"He was just an old man," Veritas repeated.

"Who was given a direct order by the police and ignored it."

They read Veritas his rights, escorted him to an electric cruiser at the curb, and stuffed him into the backseat. Lights now glowed in the windows of the nearby houses, the gunshots having drawn spectators. After five uncomfortable minutes, another squad car pulled up, followed by a coroner's van. More patrol cars arrived, and soon the street was full of police, several in full assault gear, who scanned the surroundings with automatic rifles and night vision goggles, wary of being attacked. After offering a terse report to a detective, the two who had gunned Ben down drove to the police station, leaving Veritas to fume in the rear.

The officers led him past the booking area, passed his belongings through a bulletproof glass window to a female cop, and after a short booking procedure, handed Veritas off to another pair of cops, who eyed him like he was going to try to kill them with his bare hands.

"I want my phone call," Veritas said.

The men ignored him.

"How about a policewoman named Selena Aames? Can you please contact her?" he tried.

"Better button it, tough guy," warned the one with a face that looked like it had been smashed with a baseball bat.

"She's a cop. She was interrogating me when all this started."

They each took one of his arms and half dragged him into the back of the building. Hoots and swearing and catcalls filled the air, and the pungent stench of vomit and urine hit him like a brick to the head. He glanced to the side as he passed one of the cells. The wing was packed with junkies and drunks, none of whom had bathed in weeks. Bile rose in his throat, and he choked it down as they continued past until they arrived at a small empty cell at the end of the row.

The guard on Veritas's right held a card to the reader. The door opened, and the other pushed him in. The door clanged shut behind him, and the smashed-face cop motioned to him. "Put your hands through the food slot and I'll unlock the cuffs."

"When do I get my call?" Veritas asked, slipping his hands through.

The cuffs opened with a snap. "You don't get a call, hot lips. DSS is on its way to pick you up. They want you bad."

"I still get a call. You can't arrest me without letting me contact someone."

The guards smiled at each other, and the one with the scarred face grunted. "We should brush up on the rule book. Cop killer here's schooling us. My feelings are hurt."

"What about a statement? About the shooting."

The big guard snorted and elbowed the other one with a roll of his eyes.

Their boots thudded back down the hallway as they headed back to the station, leaving Veritas alone. He sat on the steel bench attached to the wall, nearly retching from the disgusting fumes that wafted from a metal toilet in the corner. After a quarter hour of alternating between breathing through his mouth and holding his breath, he lay down and closed his eyes, visions of his dead mother filling his thoughts, her hands clutching her blanket as though trying not to slip from life, her surprised expression an accusation in Veritas's mind – she'd held on as long as she could, certain he would come for her and take her to the hospital.

Chapter 12

The moment of Ben's death replayed in Veritas's mind in an endless loop, blood blossoming on his mentor's shirt in technicolor before he collapsed. Sweat beaded Veritas's forehead in spite of the cold in the cell, and he stirred, the bench unyielding beneath him. He tried to roll over, but it was too narrow, and he fell to the floor. He cursed as he came awake, and then whooping and shouts filled the corridor.

He shook his head to clear it. Selena stepped into view, and he scrambled to his feet.

"They called you!" he exclaimed.

She glanced back down the hall and then up at a security camera near the ceiling. "Step close and listen to me. We don't have much time."

Veritas followed her gaze to the CCTV lens. "The guards said DSS is coming for me."

"That's right. Now don't talk – listen," she whispered. The noise from the prisoners nearly drowned her out. "I told you that you're a hybrid. But I didn't get a chance to give you the rest of the story. You were part of a secret program. You were chemically modded and your bones were strengthened with polymers, but you were also equipped with an implanted processor that contains a memory module. That got wiped along with your old memories when you escaped, which is why you don't have any of your hybrid strength or skills. But all the plumbing's still there." She slipped a vial through the feeding slot, and he palmed the plastic tube without looking at it. "The nanotechnology in this fluid will begin to repair your systems and bring them back online. It won't return everything to normal right away, but it will improve your strength and reaction time. Drink it. Takes about five minutes." She paused. "Oh, and you can call me Selena."

Veritas's face darkened. "Are you for real?"

"When DSS gets here, it'll give you the edge so you can catch them by surprise. They think you're normal, so they won't be expecting you to try anything. But don't wait until you're outside the building. Do it just as they're about to haul you out – that's your best bet. I'll meet you when you've dealt with them."

"I'm supposed to overcome God knows how many trained agents with some magic potion and waltz out of here?"

"Shut up and drink it. Enough will come back to you so you'll know what to do."

Selena stepped away and looked him up and down. "You're DSS's problem now," she said in an officious voice. "Sorry, buddy. Them's the breaks. I'm washing my hands of you."

She retraced her steps along the cellblock without a backward look. Veritas stepped away from the door and walked slowly to the steel sink. He snuck a glance at the vial, holding his breath to avoid the worst of the toilet. The tube, sealed with a purple rubber stopper, was filled with coffee-colored fluid. He twisted to look back at the corridor and then unstopped the vial and tossed back the contents in a single gulp.

It was almost tasteless, like watery syrup with a metallic flavor. He dropped the container in the toilet and returned to the bench, his mind racing. He had no idea what was going on, but Selena was his only lifeline with DSS on the way, so he had little choice but to trust her.

He hoped he hadn't made the mistake of his life.

The jabbering from the other cells quieted, and Veritas closed his eyes again. The headache he'd been battling since the accident pulsed with each beat of his heart. He wasn't sure what he was expecting to feel from the juice, but so far it was a zero. He rolled his head to get a kink out of his neck, and the base of his skull tingled, but otherwise, nothing.

The tingling increased and spread down his spine and along his appendages. He flexed his fingers and felt his face. His eyes opened and he looked around.

Is it my imagination, or is it slightly brighter?

He could now make out countless names etched into the paint on the wall across from him, and his vision seemed crisper than only moments before. Even the smallest lettering was legible, whereas earlier everything had looked like dark smudges.

The dull ache in his head receded and his thoughts seemed clearer, his ideas more wholly formed, as though his synapses were firing more efficiently. The sensation wasn't entirely pleasant, and he fought to keep his breathing slow, the urge to hyperventilate or panic at the unfamiliar feeling strong.

He closed his eyes again and calmed himself the best he could. The tingling slowly abated, and a sense of clarity and well-being wholly out of place given his circumstances flooded through him. Each breath seemed to rejuvenate him, and his fatigue slipped away, replaced by strength and confidence.

"I'll be damned," he muttered, flexing his fingers and staring at them as though for the first time.

The cellblock came alive ten minutes later, providing Veritas with an early warning. He closed his eyes and slumped against the wall in feigned sleep. Footsteps approached with authority – at least four that he could make out.

"Grey!" a rough male voice called out. Veritas opened his eyes as though groggy and looked through the glass at where a pair of DSS agents in their customary suits waited behind two burly guards; different ones from earlier, he noted.

"What?" Veritas demanded as he struggled to his feet.

"Approach the door and slide your hands through the slot."

Veritas complied, and one of the guards cuffed him again while the other stared him down with a malevolent gleam in his eye. Veritas knew the look and focused on something a thousand miles away just over the other guard's shoulder, offering the first no excuse to club him.

"Step away from the door."

Veritas backed away and the door swung open.

"These here gentlemen are here to take you into custody, Grey," the first guard said. "Give them any trouble and they'll return the favor double, believe you me."

"I never got my phone call," Veritas said.

"I wanted to win the lottery for my birthday and didn't get that, either. Life's a bitch. Now step out and behave yourself, or we'll beat the crap out of you – understand?"

Veritas nodded. He slowly moved from the cell, limping a little even though his leg no longer hurt, his eyes downcast.

Once in the administrative section of the station, the guards handed Veritas over to the agents. "Prisoner transport exit's down there and to the left," the first guard told them. "You've been cleared to use it. Just sign out at the desk."

"Thanks," said the agent gripping Veritas's right arm. "Come on, sunshine," he growled, and squeezed Veritas's bicep hard enough to make him wince.

"You're making a mistake," Veritas said.

The agents ignored him and guided him to the transport area, which was deserted at the late hour except for a paunchy, bald officer with skin the color of coal, who was seated behind a metal desk, watching a handheld vid player. He looked up from his program and pointed to a digital screen.

"Scan your badge and sign there," he said in a bored voice.

"They never gave me my call," Veritas complained to the man.

"I just watch the door," the officer said, without looking him in the eye.

The nearest DSS agent placed the stylus on the screen and scrawled a signature.

"What about my stuff? It's still in the station," Veritas said.

"Where I'm sure it will be safe," the agent fired back. "Are you done, or do you need some convincing to shut your trap and follow instructions?"

Veritas studied his boots. "Just don't hurt me. I'm cooperating. Officer, make a note that I've cooperated with everything they've asked me to do, will you?"

The cop nodded without interest. "Sure."

Veritas allowed the DSS agents to manhandle him to the door. When he reached the threshold, he pretended to stumble, forcing the men to steady him and throwing them off balance. His right foot snaked out and knocked the feet out from under the agent on his right. Time seemed to slow as the man staggered forward, trying to keep his balance, and Veritas tore his left arm free from the other agent and leveled a brutal two-handed uppercut at him. The blow caught him on the chin with the cuffs and snapped his head back like a crash dummy. He grunted and tumbled backward, and Veritas slammed the cuffs into the back of the first agent's neck, dropping him onto the concrete floor with a smack.

Blood seeped in a pool around the agent's head from where he'd struck the floor nose first, and Veritas spun and kicked the other agent in the crotch, recalling that it had worked like magic with Hersh.

He didn't wait to see the result and instead leapt toward the desk officer, who was fumbling with his holstered pistol. Veritas stopped in front of the desk and glared at him.

"I've got no beef with you. Sorry," Veritas said, and then his hands were a blur as he struck the man in the neck. The cop's eyes rolled up into his head and he moaned and slid from his chair onto the floor, the strike to the pressure point surgically effective. Veritas grappled with his pistol, pulled it loose, and darted to the door, gun in his cuffed hands.

Selena stepped from the shadows. "You're not going to need the gun," she said. "But it can't hurt to have an extra. Follow me," she said, and took off back down the hall toward the station. Veritas was on her heels when she stopped at a metal door halfway down the corridor and pushed it open. She entered the stairwell and waited for

Veritas to join her, and then descended the steps two at a time.

At the basement, she cracked the door and peered through the gap, and then turned to Veritas. "Stay with me."

"How are we going to get out of here?"

"We can't go out the transport door, unless you want to walk into the arms of half the Bay Area DSS contingent. So we need to create some confusion and slip through the main entrance in the chaos."

"And you're going to do that how?"

"Fire alarm, and then cut the power," she said, and slipped through the doorway. Veritas followed her to a room with Maintenance stenciled across its door and tried the lever handle. It was locked. She knelt and removed a leather pouch with lock picks, and in under a minute they were in the darkened room.

"The main breakers are over here," she said. "These two levers. Stay here, and when you hear the fire alarm trigger, cut the power after about ten seconds."

"Won't that shut off the alarm?"

"Nope. Battery backup."

"And then what?"

"I'll come back for you."

"What about the cuffs?"

"We're going to need you cuffed until we make it out." She held his stare. "Put the gun away unless you plan to shoot me." She studied him for a moment and then smiled. "Nice work with the DSS thugs. I told you it would come back. Like riding a bicycle."

"Yeah. Which is how all this started tonight."

Another faint smile and then she was gone, leaving Veritas staring at the door in the dim illumination from the green and red power lights on the various panels, the only sound a faint whirring of equipment and the fading reverberation of Selena's departing boots in the hall.

Chapter 13

The fire alarm's howl was as loud as an approaching train, and Veritas's newly enhanced hearing amplified it to a painful level. He counted backward from ten, forcing himself not to rush, and then flipped the breakers. The equipment lights died as the room plunged into complete darkness, but even so Veritas found that he could make out the panels. The siren continued to klaxon in the hallway, and the only thing that kept him from holding his hands over his ears was the cuffs.

Selena appeared a few moments later with her service flashlight in hand. "Okay," she yelled over the alarm. "All hell should be breaking loose upstairs. Let's make tracks before anyone figures this out. Whatever I do, follow my lead."

When they entered the hall, the alarm was deafening, and it was all Veritas could do to focus on following Selena's bouncing flashlight beam. They reached the stairs, and Selena turned to him. "When we get to the main floor, I'm going to pretend that you're my prisoner. Hopefully in the pandemonium, nobody's going to question it."

"Sounds good to me."

They climbed the steps, and when they were out of the stairwell, Selena adjusted Veritas's jacket and shirt so it hid the pistol in his waistband. Yells and loud voices reached them from the station area. The fire alarm continued to bay as they hurried to the administrative area, where cops with flashlights barked orders at suspects they'd been in the process of booking, and frightened witnesses demanded to know what they were supposed to do.

Selena took Veritas's arm and marched him to the front entrance. A desk sergeant was directing everyone to the exits while advising them in a loud voice to remain calm, and Selena squeezed Veritas's arm to let him know their ruse was working.

Until they reached the lobby and a tall officer in his forties with a graying crew cut and a mean look stopped them and shined his light in Veritas's face.

"What's this?" he demanded.

"He's cuffed. I was taking him for booking and the damned alarm went off. Is the fire department on its way? I don't have all night," she said.

The cop looked Selena up and down. "I don't think I've seen you around."

"Normally I'm day shift over at Presidio. But things are all messed this week. They transferred me to night duty and sent me down here because you're shorthanded."

He looked to Veritas. "What did he do?"

"B and E. Over in the Mission."

The cop's expression relaxed a trifle. "Lucky he didn't get his ass shot, breaking and entering in that neighborhood."

"True," Selena agreed. "A neighbor had him at gunpoint until I got the call. Not the area you want to be trying that."

"Where are you taking him?"

"My car's outside. I'll lock him in the back until the lights come on. Don't want him making a break for it."

"You can cuff him to a chair."

She snorted. "Right. And get sued by some a-hole ambulance chaser for risking the poor victim's life while a fire was under way. No thanks."

He took a final look at Veritas and shrugged. "You're probably right. Damned vultures. I'd love to see any of 'em spend a shift here. That would be good for a hell of an attitude adjustment."

Selena squeezed Veritas's arm again. "Come on. Don't want you to get your perp ass all singed."

They were at the entrance when the cop called out, "Stop."

Selena stiffened, her hand resting on her pistol butt, and the cop marched over, pushing through the frightened civilians. He stopped in front of them, hands on his hips, and looked down at her. "Name's O'Reilly. Where's your car? I'll come get you when we have this under control."

Selena smiled. "End of the block in the red. Can't miss it."

"You got it."

Selena exhaled heavily and then they were on the sidewalk, where several dozen officers and civilians were thronged, talking excitedly.

"I can't believe that dude was hitting on you in the middle of all this," Veritas said.

"Takes all kinds."

She escorted him down the block and stopped at a black-and-white cruiser that was at least ten years old. The Pillsbury Doughboy beamed from above the SFPD crest on the dented door. She checked around and unlocked the door, and leaned into Veritas.

"Get in the back. Once we're out of here, I'll work on your cuffs."

"Nice ride."

"With the budget cuts I'm lucky I'm not on a moped-glide. We'll ditch this thing as soon as we can. They'll have every traffic cam in the city looking for you once the DSS agents come to. We can't take the chance of them connecting my name to yours. It's bad enough I'm on the roster as visiting you."

"How are you going to explain that?"

"I'll think of something."

Selena closed the door and slipped behind the wheel. The engine sputtered and hiccupped, but didn't start. She gave it a rest and depressed the starter button again, frowning at the dashboard.

"The damn thing has at least half a million miles on it, and they don't maintain them for squat," she explained as the starter ground. "It does this sometimes."

"Great."

The car radio squawked, and a frantic voice called in Veritas's escape.

"Shit," she said. "That was too fast."

"What now?"

"If the car doesn't start, we go on foot."

"What about the traffic cams?"

"A lot of them don't work. Same deal as the car – no money for maintenance."

The starter whined as the engine coughed but refused to start. After another ten seconds, she sat back with an exasperated sigh. "All right. We do this the hard way."

She climbed from the car and opened the back door for Veritas. One of the black SUVs was now parked in front of the precinct entrance, a dome light on its roof strobing red across the façades. Selena took his arm again and pointed him away from the station. "Let's hope backup doesn't arrive for a few minutes or we're screwed."

Selena picked up the pace after they rounded the corner. They hurried another block and then stopped in an alley.

"Hold out the cuffs," she instructed. He did, and she removed a lock-pick kit from her tactical vest pocket and went to work, frowning in concentration as she coaxed the locking mechanism open. Veritas watched her without comment, grateful that she was helping, although unsure why she was risking her neck to do so.

The first lock clicked, and she pulled it open while maintaining pressure on the pick until Veritas's hand was free. The next one went faster, and after unlocking it, she slipped the picks back in her vest and checked the time.

"We need a car," she announced.

He thought for a minute. "I know where there's one that won't be missed."

"Gas or electric?"

"Fuel cell, but a really early one."

Her eyes sparkled in the darkness. "That'll work. The new models are almost impossible to hotwire. Where is it?"

"About ten blocks away. At my…at my mom's house, where they shot my sponsor. It's his. It won't be reported as stolen."

"Lead the way," she said.

He nodded. "That stuff you gave me worked. What was it?"

"A partial software upgrade. They've been using liquid upgrades on military implants for a while. As far as I know, yours is light-years more advanced than what they let on. Same with many of their weapons."

"Why haven't I heard of any of this?"

She shrugged. "Money. If they let on that they knew how to make dependable Gauss miniguns, or rail guns, or any of the rest, a lot of companies with fat contracts would lose out. Same reason gas cars still get terrible fuel economy and electric's so expensive."

His eyebrows rose. "There's such a thing as a Gauss minigun? As in one that actually works?"

"We can talk later. Right now we need to get your sponsor's car and avoid the entire SFPD. Not to mention the DSS. You're going to be public enemy number one by morning."

Chapter 14

They stuck to the shadows as they made their way deeper into the Mission, avoiding streets that were drug-distribution points or small tent cities filled with vagrants. Veritas knew the entire district cold, and he and Selena navigated the empty arteries wordlessly until they reached his street.

Ben's car was right where he'd parked it, and the police were long gone; nobody wanted to stay any longer than absolutely necessary where they could be picked off by an aspiring gang member trying to make his bones. They crept to the vehicle, and Selena smirked when she reached it.

"Piece of cake. These things have a primitive contact on the doors, and the same system for the ignition lock. But there's a code that the manufacturer uses for towing companies and police to access it and disable the auto-drive, and I have them all in my phone."

Selena got the door open in seconds, and a relieved whine greeted Veritas when he swung his wide.

"What's that?" she asked.

"Damn. I forgot. It's Ben's dog. Moxie," Veritas said as he slipped into the partially destroyed passenger seat. Moxie flopped down in his lap, tail wagging furiously, and then bolted up and bathed his face with kisses as he took in the interior, which the little dog had shredded to pieces while locked in the car. Veritas twisted to look at the backseat, which was covered with synthetic stuffing, and couldn't help but smile.

"You've been busy, haven't you?" he asked the dog, who looked at him with the innocence of a newborn lamb.

"He's a wrecking ball," Selena said.

"He was in here for hours, bored out of his mind. It isn't his fault."

Moxie licked him again, and Selena's mouth crinkled in a smile. "He's awfully cute, I'll give you that. And he seems to love you."

"No accounting for taste." He exhaled and bounced Moxie on his lap. "That stuff you gave me is amazing. It feels…I don't know. Like I can fly or something. Crazy strong."

"I'm glad. What's important is that it worked."

"I guess. But…what's in it? Drugs? This euphoria thing…I've never felt anything like it."

"No drugs. Just the upgrade."

Two minutes later they were driving along Mission Street, Selena at the wheel. They were the only vehicle on the street, and she entered coordinates into the nav system as she motored along, sticking to the speed limit using the auto-limiter.

"Where to?" he asked.

"We need to get you out of the city – somewhere there's no internet, cell service, or traffic cams."

"That would be…Tibet? The middle of the Pacific?"

"Close. I have a safe apartment in Redwood City. Down the peninsula."

"And then what?"

"I don't know. I'll contact my superiors and find out what they want to do next."

Veritas shook his head. "No."

"What do you mean, no? It isn't safe to stay here."

"I want answers. You keep double-talking. Everybody claims they don't know enough to be dangerous. I've had it with that. I want to talk to someone who can answer my questions without giving me the runaround. So no. We're not going to Redwood City. We're going wherever we need to for me to meet your people."

"It's not that easy, Veritas. And right now–"

"Stop the car."

Selena didn't slow. "I can't let you do this."

"Then you'd better take me to someone who can explain what's going on."

"I…I can't just snap my fingers and do that." She frowned. "Although… No, the first thing we need to do is get somewhere where there are no cell phones or cameras. From there we might have a chance."

"I told you I'm not going to Redwood City."

"I heard you the first time. So we'll do this the hard way." She made a U-turn at the next intersection and sighed in obvious annoyance.

"Where are we going?"

"Oakland. No cell or internet."

Oakland had become a criminal wasteland six years earlier, when the biggest food riot in California history had destroyed a third of the downtown area and it had become a no-go zone for the East Bay police. After numerous failed takeover attempts by law enforcement, the district had been officially abandoned and declared off-limits. Now it was a quasi-war zone, run by gangs that functioned like fourth-world warlords. The county had shut off all internet in the early days of the rioting and it had never come back on, there being no way for the providers to get paid for its use. Looters had destroyed the traffic cameras and the city had walked away, just as it had refused to waste resources on the cell towers that had been ultimately stripped of their wiring and anything of value.

"Why would internet or cell be a problem for us, anyway?" Veritas asked.

"This isn't widely known, but the government has the ability to activate anyone who's chipped and use them as remote cams. Like the old cell phones, where they could turn on the mic even if the device was off, or switch on a computer's cam or mic. So even if you're not spotted by a traffic cam in an area with coverage, anyone walking by could be a surveillance device."

"How would they know if someone saw me?"

"They have the power to filter all the data from a limited area, like San Francisco, and enter your mug shot or ID photo to automatically flag it. Last I checked, they can run it on as many as a million simultaneous users."

"But that completely violates the right to privacy and about a dozen other constitutional prohibitions."

That drew a smile. "It's not common knowledge, if that's what you're asking. It's a secret aspect of the surveillance system the state uses to control the population. If you're asking whether it's legal, well, anything they can get a judge to okay is, whether you like it or not." She paused. "As you learned tonight, DSS doesn't have to obey any laws. They can lock you up, torture you, disappear you like the bad old days in Russia or Argentina, and there's not a thing anyone can do about it."

"Aren't there toll booths on the bridge? Cameras?"

"Only going in the other direction. This way there's nothing."

"I've never been across the bridge in a car. The only times I ever did it was on the subway, back when it still ran to Oakland."

By the time Selena motored onto the Bank of America Bay Bridge, the fog had thickened to the point where visibility was near zero, and she slowed to a crawl so as not to rear-end anyone. Brightly lit panels on either side of the lanes flashed images of nearly naked women in matching blue wigs drinking Crankoid Energy Boost, the sporadic glare making the thick haze even more hazardous. Hidden speakers moaned orgiastic oohs and aahhs as the women savored their drinks, and Selena rolled her eyes. When they crossed through the toll gates, with Veritas lying flat on the backseat, the road was a ghostly strip enshrouded by a brume with the density of cotton candy.

Veritas got his first confirmation of how dangerous the area they were heading into was when the first three freeway off-ramps were barricaded. The one for the port was guarded by a heavily militarized security contingent of assault police and robotic antipersonnel drones, and signs warning that only official traffic would be allowed through. If Selena was worried, she didn't show it, and Veritas frowned at her with trepidation.

"You okay going into Oakland wearing a cop uniform?"

Selena looked down at her windbreaker and tactical vest. "Crap. I didn't even think about that." She pulled off the windbreaker and vest, and then unbuttoned her uniform shirt while steering with her knee. She removed the shirt, beneath which she was wearing an olive tank top with a sports bra. "This better?"

Veritas did his best not to stare. "I don't know. You still look like a cop to me."

"The guy I'm going to be looking for will fix things for us. He'll get me some clothes."

"I thought we were heading to Oakland to drop off the radar."

"We are. But there are all kinds of interesting characters there. One of them owes a friend of mine a favor or ten. I plan to call in some markers. But we can't hide out there indefinitely. This is just a stop."

Veritas frowned. "Maybe you should stop talking in circles and level with me, Selena. Right now I'm flying blind. I have no choice but to trust you, but I have no money, no hope of ever going back to a normal life, and the most powerful entity in the country pulling out all the stops to find me. What's this all about? And no more generalities about me being some military hybrid."

"That upgrade I gave you to drink worked, didn't it? You just got finished telling me how awesome you feel, and you were able to tackle those agents without breaking a sweat. Let me concentrate on what I'm doing, and we can play twenty questions later, okay? Once we're somewhere safe, I'll tell you everything I know. But the short version is we need to get to Burning Man, and the guy we need to find in Oakland will help us do it."

He stared at her, clearly befuddled. "Burning Man?"

"You want answers; that's where you'll get them."

She took an exit at the southern end of Oakland, and her face hardened as she slowed and peered ahead into the gloom.

"You might want to pull your gun, Veritas. Looks like you're going to need it."

Chapter 15

A fire was burning bright in a fifty-five-gallon drum in front of a crumbling building, blocking their way. A group huddled around it, assault rifles, shotguns, and pistols clearly visible as Selena and Veritas approached. The rusting hulks of stripped cars lined the street, and most of the tenements appeared to be abandoned.

"Maybe you should back up and turn down a different street," Veritas said.

"They're all going to be like this. Many of them worse."

"I'm not sure how. Those guys look like stone killers."

"Oh, they are."

"Isn't the idea to live out the night?"

A smirk lit her face before it grew serious. "And to find someone to help us. I'm sure these nice young men will be able to point us in the right direction. Have a little faith. I got you out of custody, didn't I?"

"Is that what you call me having to take on three armed men single-handed?"

"Come on. Two and a half. Don't exaggerate."

Veritas fell silent, and Selena slowed the car. Angry faces caught in the headlights glared at them, and five of the youths separated from the rest and sauntered to where Selena had coasted to a stop, pistols in hand. She lowered her window part of the way, and Veritas could see that she had her gun resting in her lap, pointed at the door.

A leering face leaned close with a flash of gold-capped teeth. "You in the wrong neighborhood," the thug said, brandishing a chrome Desert Eagle with nonchalant ease. "What you want? Synth? Race? Loco?"

"Not really."

The punk's smile faded to something tense and mean. "Bitch, I hope you brought backup, 'cause you gonna need it."

"I'm looking for Zeke."

The thug's hostile stare faltered at the mention of the name. "What you want with him? You got no business here."

"We're friends of his. He told me anyone on the street knows where to find him."

"Maybe. But I'm not getting my ass shot bringing no five-oh to his crib."

"Too bad. There's a payday in it if you do."

"Can't spend nothin' if you dead."

"Maybe one of your homeboys wants to make some easy scrip. Doesn't have to be you," she countered.

"How 'bout instead I just take your money, and me and the crew has us a little party with you?"

Veritas bristled, but a half-raised hand from Selena silenced whatever he was about to say.

"You really think you'll be in the mood after you're gut shot?" Selena asked, her tone friendly. "How about we cut to the chase and you tell me where to find Zeke so we can get on with our business? It's too late for this shit."

"I don't know no Zeke. Got no idea what you talkin' about."

"He runs this section of O-Town. You must be new."

His hand tightened on his gun. "You got a mouth on you, huh?"

"I've shot three people tonight, youngblood," Selena said. "You want to be number four, keep it up. We want to see Zeke, not waste our time."

The gunman's stare hardened. "You come on my block and talk shit? Who you think you are? You got no clout here. You nothin', hear? Talking smack like some angry ho. I oughta pop a cap in you for fun."

Selena nodded as though in agreement. "Are we done? Zeke's going to be pissed we got held up on his turf. You don't believe me, you will when we find him. Or you can give us a hand and earn up. Your choice."

"Like you going to walk away unless I say so." The youth's bluster had lost the earlier conviction, though, and he stepped away from the car to where his companions stood. Veritas tensed, but Selena didn't flinch. The gunman had a terse discussion with the others and then returned.

"Five hundred if I take you to him," he said.

"Is he in Vegas? Try a hundred," Selena countered. "That's all I have on me."

He looked over the car and then Selena and grudgingly nodded. "I believe it, driving this piece of shit. What the hell happened to the seats?"

"Don't get me started."

He waved the Desert Eagle. "Unlock it. I'll ride in the back."

Veritas shook his head. "I'll hop in back. You ride shotgun."

The youth looked ready to argue, but Veritas was already opening his door. When he stood, he was five inches taller than the younger man, and his expression didn't invite an argument. The thug grunted and rounded the hood, and Veritas climbed into the backseat, his pistol in his right hand, Moxie in his left.

When everyone was in the car, the youth directed them down the main street and then along a smaller tributary framed by darkened walk-ups. Every block had armed gangs gathered on porches and corners, and the almost complete absence of lights made the area even more ominous.

They rolled up to a bar where a pair of tough-looking guards was standing outside with shotguns.

"What's this?" Veritas asked.

"Zeke moves around a lot. But his guys hang here. Ask around. They'll hook you up."

Selena shook her head. "I didn't agree to pay a Benjamin to get pointed at a bar. You were supposed to take us to him."

"Nobody but his crew can do that. This is close as I can get you."

She exhaled in frustration and pulled a fifty-dollar token from her pocket. "Then this is what that's worth."

"Deal was a hundred."

"We're going to need money to buy drinks and ask around. You didn't take us *to* him."

The thug took the coin and grumbled, "Bitch," before swinging the door open and stepping out. Veritas and Selena did the same, and without another word the youth slipped into the darkness like a ghost, one moment there, the next, gone.

The guards watched them approach, and the one on the left demanded they leave any weapons at the door. They complied, and the guard dropped their guns into a milk crate along with at least twenty others. He seemed uncertain about Moxie in the backpack, but eventually nodded. Veritas and Selena exchanged a glance and then pushed past the men and into the bar.

The interior was painted flat brown, with the lighting provided by strategically placed camp lanterns. A coal-black bartender who could have easily worked as a pro wrestler stood behind a long bar, watching the patrons with a wary eye. His expression clouded as they approached.

"You in the right place?" he growled.

Selena nodded and offered a smile. "I think so. We need to find Zeke."

The bartender's brow creased and he looked away. "I sell drinks. You want one?"

"What do you have?" she fired back.

"We got ice earlier, so the beer's cold. Got everything you can think of, but cash only."

"Couple of Steamboats," Selena said, naming a popular beer.

"Make that one, and a Coke," Veritas corrected.

One of the bartender's eyebrows twitched. "Pepsi work?"

"Sure."

The man went to get their drinks, and Veritas smiled. "I don't drink."

Selena nodded. "That's right. Sorry. I forgot. Although you actually don't have an alcohol or drug problem. That was an implanted memory. All your memories are. They never happened."

He blinked, and then his brow wrinkled. "You're telling me I'm imagining my time in Thailand? My childhood?"

Another nod. "That's right."

"So I'm imagining my mother as well? That seems pretty real to me."

Selena swallowed hard. "She wasn't your mother. She was one of us."

Her words hit him like blows. His mouth was hanging open when the bartender returned with a can of PepsiUltra and a Steamboat so cold ice had formed on the top half of the bottle.

"But Ben...my sponsor...he took me there himself, and—"

"He didn't know."

The bartender set the drinks on the bar. "Twelve bucks."

Selena pulled a couple of tokens from her pocket and placed them beside the bottles. "Keep it."

The bartender scooped them up and walked to the far end of the bar.

Veritas was still staring at her. "I don't believe you."

"Even after drinking the upgrade? Come on." She paused. "I know it's hard to accept, but the woman you thought was your mother was our operative. You were placed with her so she could keep an eye on you."

His frown deepened. "Prove it."

She looked around the room. "Can we do this later? This probably isn't the place, Veritas."

"You can call me Ver. But I still don't believe you."

"Okay, Ver. We can talk about it when we're alone."

The patrons were largely gangbangers and hoods, with a few hookers salted through the crowd. Veritas and Selena could feel their eyes boring into them with undisguised hostility. Selena gave no indication that she noticed the aggressive attention, though, and Ver followed her lead.

"Now what?" he asked.

"We ask around and see who knows Zeke."

A thin man shuffled from the end of the bar where the bartender was cleaning a bottle with a rag. The man sniffed and wiped his nose with the back of his hand. "You looking for someone?" he asked in a nasal whine.

"Could be," Selena said.

"I'm Willie. I know everybody. Man over there say you wanna talk to Zeke?"

"That's right."

"What about?"

"That's between me and Zeke," she said.

"Yeah, yeah, no problem. Well, I can find him."

Selena regarded him, skepticism clear in her stare. "For a price, no doubt."

"Man's gotta eat," Willie agreed.

"Take us to him and it's worth a hundred bucks."

Willie rubbed his hand over the stubble on his face. "I'm awful thirsty," he said, eyeing her beer.

"Just think how many of these you can buy when you find him," she countered. His face fell and his jaundiced eyes darted to Veritas.

"You want anything else besides that? I can get anything. I mean, anything you can think of," he said with a smirk.

"Zeke's all we want," Veritas said, straightening to his full height and staring the smaller man down.

"Yeah, um, sure. No problem. Don't go anywhere," he said, backing away.

Willie scuttled off and made for the door. Veritas rolled his eyes as he popped the top of his soda can. "I thought you said you only had a hundred."

She flashed a smile. "I lied."

"This bunch doesn't seem like the kind that's going to be too helpful," he observed.

"We have to try. Maybe Willie will come through."

"That junkie? Not a chance."

"You never know."

"If I had any money, I'd bet it all on no."

Half an hour later Selena had asked the two waitresses and been rewarded with blank stares, as well as several of the stragglers who'd walked to the bar for drinks, but had gotten nowhere. Veritas had done the same with the three working girls who'd propositioned him, but they'd quickly backed off at the mention of Zeke, and their enthusiasm for Veritas's charms had died an early death.

Their drinks empty, Selena checked the time. "This sucks."

"What's plan B?" he asked.

"That was plan B."

The youth who'd shown them to the bar entered with three others and sat at a table in the back, glowering at them sullenly. Veritas edged closer to Selena. "That looks like trouble."

"We should give Willie some more time."

"Willie's passed out in a doorway somewhere. He isn't coming back."

"He looked like he really wanted the hundred."

"I might want to be able to fly, but it doesn't mean I can."

One of the group stood and swaggered to the bar. He was tall, almost as big as Veritas, with an old knife scar running from his ear to his chin, the skin puckered tight. He looked Selena up and down and shook his head.

"Mmm, mmm, mmm. Sweet little rig you got there, sugar," he said.

Selena ignored him. He moved closer to her until he was looming over her. "What's wrong? Can't take a compliment?"

She reached for her empty bottle, but the bartender had swept it away moments before. "I've got no beef with you."

"Home boy here ain't floatin' your boat? Is that it? I can take care of that for you real good," he said, one hand on his crotch.

Veritas bristled, but Selena remained cool. "We were just leaving," she said.

"Maybe he is, but you can stay," the tough snarled, and reached for her. She twisted away and put a hand on Veritas's chest.

"Don't," she warned him.

"I don't want to hurt you," Veritas said, his voice quiet. "But I will if you don't get out of here."

The punk laughed and groped Selena's breast. Her eyes remained locked on Veritas's, and then she spun and stomped on the arch of the tough's foot with all her weight. He howled in pain when the metatarsals splintered, and he fell against the bar; and then Selena had Veritas's hand and they were rushing to the exit as the crowd parted to let them through.

They exploded through the door and sprinted toward the car. Footsteps pounded behind them. Selena spotted a figure leaning against their vehicle and pulled Veritas's arm, directing him into an alley to her right. They turned the corner and Selena skidded to a stop on the wet pavement – the way was blocked by a mountain of trash and rubble. They spun to try to get clear before their pursuers caught up with them, but it was too late. The trio rounded the corner and approached, fists balled by their sides and faces twisted with rage.

Chapter 16

"That's far enough," Selena said evenly. "We didn't come to fight. You came at us, not the other way around."

"Too late," the lead punk said. "You crippled my boy back there. You gonna pay for that."

Veritas stepped forward. "You won't walk away from this. Let it go."

"See, you come to my hood and talk shit – nobody does that," the thug said. He looked to his companions, and their postures tensed as they prepared to rush Veritas.

Veritas waited for them to make their move. "Stay back," he whispered to Selena, and handed her the backpack with Moxie's head sticking from the flap. "I'll deal with this."

The leader drew a ceramic-blade stiletto and flicked it open. One of the others leaned over and picked up a length of rusting pipe. "You going down, punkass," the leader snarled, the knife clutched in front of him, the gleaming blade tracing a hypnotic pattern in the air.

They moved as one, and Veritas stood his ground as they closed on him. At the last possible second, the one with the pipe swung it at Veritas's head. He blocked the blow with his forearm so the pipe glanced off his jacket, and Veritas kicked him, dislocating his kneecap. The thug howled and dropped the pipe, and the one with the knife stabbed at Veritas, moving in low like a practiced street fighter. Veritas countered with a butterfly kick that sent the punk slamming into the wall with enough force to break most of his ribs.

The knife hit the pavement and Veritas addressed the third thug. "You want to spend the next year walking on sticks, or you had enough?"

The punk's eyes told Veritas that the pack bravery they'd displayed when they'd thought Veritas would be easy prey had been replaced by fear. He shook his head. "You making a big mistake."

"Yeah, I do that," Veritas said. "Now either step aside or I'll go through you. Your choice."

Indecision radiated from the tough's face, and then he moved to his downed companions, both of whom were moaning in pain. Selena gave Veritas the backpack with Moxie. Veritas patted the dog's head and then took Selena's hand and guided her to the intersection, looking back periodically to ensure that the remaining attacker hadn't gotten any bright ideas.

"They'll be down for a while, but out for blood once they rally," Veritas said. "What do we do now? Get our weapons and car?"

She nodded. "We probably should. No chance we'll be able to once they put word out about us."

"And then?"

"If we haven't found Zeke, we'll have to scratch that and try to make our way to Burning Man on our own."

They hurried back to the bar. The two bouncers seemed surprised to see them, but returned their pistols without comment. Veritas moved to the car and stopped beside it.

"Shit," he said, staring at the flat front tires. "Should have figured they'd vandalize it. Probably before they went inside."

"Well, we can't stay here."

"So now what?"

Selena sighed and checked her watch. "We should find someplace to rest and see if we can't locate Zeke in the morning."

"How about we get out of Dodge instead?"

"The problem is trying to make it to Burning Man on our own. DSS will have checkpoints in place – you can bet on that – and your image will be all over the news. We'd never make it without some serious help, which is why we need Zeke."

"Wherever he is." Veritas eyed the surroundings. "You have any idea where we can lie low? This all looks the same to me."

"Let's put some distance between us and our friends back there." She unlocked the car and snagged her backpack and tactical vest, and then tossed Veritas the backpack and relocked it. "This way."

Selena set the pace and stopped at each new street to peer around the corner before continuing. Many of the bonfires had died down, and when they found a deserted street lined with bombed-out buildings, she paused at a door hanging half off the jamb on broken hinges, and looked at Veritas.

"This is probably as good as any. Let's see if there's anybody home."

Veritas peered beyond her into the darkness, and his nose wrinkled at the sour stink of urine. "Are you serious?"

"We don't want company."

He nodded. "Nobody in their right mind would go in there."

"Exactly."

Once past the barrier, she switched on her flashlight and played it over the walls, which were covered with graffiti. The floor was scarcely any better, littered with a carpet of used syringes and condoms.

"Charming," she muttered. At the stairway to the second level, she shined the beam on a gap where the wooden steps had collapsed. "Looks like we're staying on the ground floor."

They continued to the back of the row house, and when they reached what had once been the kitchen, she froze. Veritas looked over her shoulder at a skeleton sprawled on the floor, ratty jeans and work boots flattened against bone, a dark T-shirt rotted away.

"Probably a junkie who got a hot shot," Selena whispered, and then jumped back as a dark form shot from beneath the corpse and tore into the gloom.

"Rat," Veritas observed.

She nodded and swept the area with her lamp. A stained sofa with half its stuffing hanging from long rents in the cushions sat by one of the broken windows, a pool of water near it. Anything made from wood that could be burned had long since been carted away. She looked the sofa over and grimaced.

"Not exactly the Ritz, but it'll have to do," she said, and lowered herself onto the couch. The frigid air in the room was heavy with must and the dank odor of mold. She surveyed the room impassively and then shrugged. "This is the only game in town. You can sit next to me. I won't bite."

He managed a wan smile and moved to the sofa. "Looks like nobody's been here for a while. Corpses tend to lower rental values, even here."

"Apparently so," she said, and switched off the light. They sat wordlessly while their eyes adjusted, and after several minutes lost in their thoughts, Veritas turned to her. He could make out her face in the glow from the window, the cloud layer having yielded to the stars and a tangerine half-moon.

"You promised to tell me what's going on once we were in a quiet place. Can't get much quieter than this," he said.

She sank back into the sofa and set her vest on the arm. "I did," she agreed.

"Let's start with who are you, and why are you helping me?"

"It's…complicated. And it'll sound kind of crazy," she warned.

Veritas removed Moxie from the backpack, and he trotted to the corner, relieved himself, and came running back to Veritas, tongue lolling from his mouth. Veritas scooped him up and stroked him while eyeing Selena.

"We're in a shooting gallery with a corpse for company. Try me."

She nodded. "I'm not really sure where to start. It goes back to the dawn of time."

"How about keeping it simple? Who are you? Who is it we're going to see in Burning Man?" he asked, referring to the city that had grown into a legendary outpost of lawlessness in the Black Rock Desert, named after the annual festival that had been the precursor to the permanent encampment.

"He's one of the leaders of what, for lack of any better term, I'll call the Tribe."

"The Tribe? What the hell is that?"

"That's where it gets convoluted, Veritas."

"Ver," he corrected.

"Right. Well, the Tribe's been around in one incarnation or another for…for practically ever."

"You're losing me, Selena. Please. All the ambiguous stuff isn't helping me understand any of this."

Her brow creased and she nodded again. "Okay, I'll start with my history with the group. Or rather, my family's. It was a long time ago. In Venice, Italy. The year was 1631, and the plague was decimating the city, with a third of the population dead or dying."

~ ~ ~

A cart heaped high with corpses rolled along one of the narrow cobblestone passageways that served as streets in Venice, pulled by a donkey with sad eyes. Its master was a short man with a barrel chest, his companion tall and thin with a hollowed-out face.

"Bring out your dead," the short man called, ringing a bell, a black scarf doused with rosewater to mask the stench of death wrapped around his nose and mouth. The air around the cart was thick with flies, and the men's clothes were seeped in grime and bodily fluids, their lowly station in life dooming them to toil at a job nobody wanted before they too succumbed to the scourge that was ravaging Europe.

A cleaning woman wiped dust from the legs of a statue in front of a palatial residence near Piazza San Marco, the basilica's famous lead-clad wooden domes and the clock tower jutting into a morning drizzle. A kit of pigeons took flight and soared into the gray sky before disappearing, startled by the ringing of the plague cart's bell as it worked its way to the square.

A pair of noblemen in richly embroidered finery materialized from the direction of the Grand Canal and approached the residence. The guards greeted them with reverence, their typically abrasive demeanor transformed into the fawning of sycophants, and waved them through. When the visitors had disappeared into the building, Lorenzo, the captain of the guards, motioned to the cleaning woman.

"Yes?" she asked, her tone hesitant. One word from Lorenzo and she could lose her job, which he reminded her of whenever he had the chance.

"Get inside and make yourself useful. Help the staff with the china. They're shorthanded because of the damned plague."

"Of course," she said, and brushed past him. He reached for her, and she ignored the groping that was a routine part of their interactions and hurried into the depths of the massive edifice.

Guillermo, the head of the domestic servants, raised an eyebrow when she appeared. "What do you want, Claudia? I thought I assigned you to clean the exterior this week."

"I know. But because of the rain Lorenzo suggested I help in here."

"Lorenzo, eh? Well, I suppose I have no issue with you helping Maria upstairs. Go on, then. Second floor." He indicated the scrap of cloth in her hand. "And get yourself a proper rag, not that filthy thing. You'll be the death of us all yet."

"Yes, sir. I will, sir. Right away," she said, and made for the service stairway.

At the second floor she padded on silent feet down the long hall, peering into each room she passed, looking for Maria, her sister. She neared a corner but stopped when men's voices raised in anger reached her from one of the salons.

"I made clear that you weren't to mention this to a soul – and now you say you told your daughter? Fool. When we give you an order, you're to follow it, not do as you please."

Claudia didn't recognize the speaker, but the next voice was familiar – it was the owner of the home, one of the most powerful men in Venice.

"I was simply trying to reassure her. She was panicked over the plague. The only way I could calm her was to tell her that we had a cure."

"I give not a care for your familial issues. She's an outsider, and now she knows our secret."

"She won't talk. I made clear that she mustn't."

"Idiot. You doomed her. We cannot take the risk. Her death will be on your head. We don't allow women in our ranks for good reason."

"No! You can't."

"You're lucky you don't join her. Now roll up your sleeve and I'll inoculate you, although I'm of a mind to let you suffer the fate of the rest of these sheep."

Claudia almost choked on the knot in her throat. The words of the men were impossible to believe. A cure for the plague? Impossible! Everyone knew there was no cure – it had spread across Italy like wildfire, killing indiscriminately.

"Claudia!" Maria whispered from an alcove to Claudia's right. "Come. Now."

Claudia followed her to one of the rooms, where Maria, two years older than Claudia, held her at arm's length, steel in her stare. "How much did you hear?" she demanded.

"I...I didn't hear anything," Claudia stammered.

"Liar. I see it in your eyes."

Claudia gave her sister a frightened nod. "They're going to kill his daughter. And...they claim they have a cure for the plague. It's crazy talk."

Maria's face tightened. "I suppose it's time you knew the truth about why we're here. To spy, and to report on everything that goes on. I've kept you out of it so far, but it's too late now – you heard too much."

"Spy?" Claudia blurted. "What are you talking about?"

"For Father. He arranged for us to get these jobs."

"Why would Father want you to spy on the master?"

"He's an evil man, Claudia. In league with powerful forces working against us."

"Us?"

"Humanity. He's part of a secret society, old as time itself. You've heard of the Knights Templar?"

A flicker of recognition greeted the name. "But they're…they're just a legend, aren't they?" Claudia asked. "There are no more of them. Not for hundreds of years."

"They're alive and well, Claudia. You just heard two of their leadership scolding the master like a schoolboy. He is their creature. Throughout history they have visited misery on the population – that was why they were hunted down and killed. But some survived, and they're stronger than ever. They always survive. This plague is likely their doing, so of course they have a cure for it – but only for their anointed. That's typical of the way they operate."

"I don't understand, Maria. You're scaring me. This is nonsense. There's no cure."

"I'll allow Father to explain. But for now, you're to go back downstairs and claim to be feeling sick. Guillermo will excuse you; nobody wants to risk the plague. Go straight home and tell Father what you heard. Don't speak to anyone else. Now, go, before they find you up here and you're implicated. If they think you were eavesdropping, you won't live to see supper."

"What about you?"

Maria's gaze hardened further. "I have a job to do."

"You can't let them kill her, Maria."

"I have no choice in the matter. If they've condemned her, she's dead. One of their assassins will have already been dispatched. For all I know, she's already cold. It's not our problem. Now do as I say, and run all the way home. Father will know what to do."

~ ~ ~

"The Templars? Is this a joke?" Veritas asked, staring skeptically at Selena in the gloom.

"Claudia and Maria were my ancestors, Ver. Our calling runs in our blood. Claudia was spirited away by her father and trained in the dark arts, as her sister had been. But that was just one of many similar episodes through the ages. They…the ones who're after you have been a part of humanity since forever. And so have we, countering their influence whenever we can."

"So you're...you expect me to believe your...tribe...is hundreds of years old?"

"Thousands. But when we get to Burning Man, my superior will tell you the full story. Our adversary has had many names: Knights Templar, Hashashin, Brotherhood of Babylon, Illuminati, and now the Brethren...but it doesn't matter which cloak they wear. They're always the same, and always have the same goal—"

Voices from the street silenced Selena, and they both drew their pistols, ears straining for any hint of who was approaching. The click of animal claws scrabbling on the sidewalk outside reached them, and they froze.

"It's them," she whispered. "They found us."

"They've got a dog."

"Damn. There's no back way out of this dump."

Veritas looked around the room for anything they could use for cover, but there was nothing but the walls – the sofa wouldn't stop a bullet, much less a hail of them. He stuffed Moxie into the backpack and shouldered it.

"You take one side of the doorway and I'll take the other," Selena said. "When they come inside, I'll shine the light in their eyes – it'll blind them long enough for us to take them down."

She crept to the doorway. Veritas did the same, and they waited to see whether their pursuers would continue down the street or enter the building.

The plywood that served as a front door scraped as it opened, and then the sound of a dog panting carried down the hall, followed by the crunching of debris underfoot as a group made its way toward them.

Chapter 17

Veritas's awareness narrowed to the exclusion of anything but the approaching threat. His breath caught in his throat, and he fingered his pistol's trigger guard, hoping that the thugs wouldn't start shooting through the sheetrock walls without waiting to find a target. Selena stood across from him, her eyes narrowed in concentration, the flashlight in one hand and her gun in the other. Veritas slowly crouched so she wouldn't be in danger of shooting him accidentally, and his index finger crept to the trigger, hovering over it as the footsteps in the hall drew near.

A whiney voice called out from the hallway. "You in here?"

Confusion flitted across Selena's face, and then her eyes widened. "Willie? Is that you?"

"Damn right it is. Now don't you go and shoot me."

"We won't," she said, but didn't lower the pistol.

Willie stepped into the room, and then a young man entered with a Belgian shepherd on a short leash. Selena switched on her flashlight, and Willie and the man winced in its glare and turned their heads away.

"Shit. Turn that thing off, would you?" Willie said. "Can't see a thing."

She lowered the beam to his chest, but kept her gun trained on Willie. "Who's this?"

"My nephew. Kyle. Dog's name is Bear."

"You carrying, Kyle?" Selena asked.

"No."

"How about you, Willie? Got an insurance policy in your belt?"

"No, ma'am. Got nothing worth stealing, and everybody knows me around here. Don't have no business with no gun."

"Search them," Selena said. Veritas thumbed the safety back on and slid his pistol into the waist of his jeans, and did a quick frisk of both men, ignoring Bear's growl.

"They're clean," he said.

Selena lowered her weapon and the flashlight. "Why are you tracking us?"

"I found Zeke. Told him someone was looking for him. He wants me to bring you to his place. And I really need that hundred bucks."

"Any chance you were followed?" Veritas asked.

"Hell no. You think I want to lose my paycheck?" Willie hesitated. "Although I heard you beat up some of the local bangers pretty good. Best watch your backs – they hold a grudge."

"Doesn't Zeke run these streets? We didn't pick the fight," Veritas said.

"He does, but that don't mean he's God. Punk decides he's gonna pop a cap in your asses, he's gonna do it, and nobody's gonna be able to stop him."

"I'll take my chances," Selena said.

Bear whined and strained at the leash, and Willie glanced over at the skeleton without comment. "Zeke ain't that far from here. Best move before your new friends get it into their heads to pull out all the stops to pop you."

Selena nodded. "Fine."

"And turn that light off. Don't want anyone seeing it from outside and deciding to shoot up the place for fun."

She complied and pocketed the flashlight. Willie and Kyle led them out to the street, and Willie grinned in the moonlight. "Kyle needs fifty bucks for getting dragged outta bed."

Selena felt in her pants for her money and turned away from Willie to sort through the bills. She peeled off a fifty note and handed it to Kyle. "Glad you found us."

Kyle and Bear disappeared down the street, and Veritas eyed their surroundings. "You think they're going to be searching for us?"

Willie shook his head. "Probably not that much of a chance this late. Them boys is bone lazy. But they'll put the word out, and there's a lot of eyes on the street." He looked around. "Not here, though. You picked a spot even the worst of them steer clear of."

"I can't imagine why," she said.

Willie led them through a maze of alleys and deserted streets until they arrived at a four-story brick building with a half dozen heavily armed men standing sentry outside. Willie threw them a salute, and the nearest one shifted his shotgun so it was pointed in Veritas and Selena's direction.

"They're here to see Zeke," Willie announced.

The guard nodded once. "Only them. You stay out here," he ordered Willie.

"How about that hundred?" he asked Selena, his eyes feverish in the dim light.

"When we come out," Selena said.

"But I brought you here!"

She looked around. "I don't see any Zeke, do you?"

"He's here," Willie insisted.

"Then you have nothing to worry about."

"Guns," the guard demanded, with an outstretched hand.

Selena drew hers, holding the butt with two fingers, and Veritas did the same. The big man nodded to one of the others, and the second guard moved forward and took the pistols.

"This way," the first guard said, and made his way up the steps to the oversized doorway.

The interior of the building was black as pitch, but the guard had no trouble finding the stairs. Selena and Veritas followed quietly, and at the second-floor landing, two more gunmen sat on wooden chairs outside a doorway. The guard rapped on the door three times, and a muffled voice answered from inside.

"Come."

The big man twisted the knob and pushed the door open. Selena and Veritas entered a large room lit by battery-powered LED lamps. A man with a coffee complexion and a lupine face studied them from behind an expansive desk, a submachine gun on the tabletop beside a bottle of beer. He motioned to the guard, who nodded and pulled the door closed, leaving them alone.

"You know who I am," he said. "Now who're you, and what do you want?"

"I'm a friend of a friend. You parted on…difficult terms. But I was hoping you could help us," Selena said, her voice quiet.

"Who's your friend?"

"Jordan. He said if I ever needed a serious favor, you owe him one."

Veritas thought he detected a slight tremor in Zeke's hand as he reached for the beer. He took a long swallow and gestured to a pair of chairs in front of the desk. "Sit."

They did, and he studied them like they were from another planet. "Haven't heard that name in a while," he said.

"He told me you could help."

"He's still an optimist, I see."

"I'm part of his group."

"Yeah? Well, it's been a long time since I was, lady." He took another pull on his beer. "I don't want any part of his game. I got it pretty good here, and I see no reason to fight an unwinnable battle." He regarded Veritas. "He one of you?"

She sidestepped the question. "We need to get to Burning Man. But half the state's looking for him."

"Yeah? What did you do?"

"Got into it with DSS," he answered. "They got the worse end of the deal. They're not happy."

Zeke sat back and fixed them with a cold stare. "I want nothing to do with DSS."

"We're not asking you to get involved with them," Selena said. "Just to get us to Black Rock. We'll deal with it from there. It'll be like you never heard of us. I promise."

Zeke shook his head and eyed Veritas again. "You have any idea what you're up against? Did she tell you? The people she's fighting control everything. You name it, they've got it under their thumbs. Cops, military, banks, newspapers. You don't stand a chance."

"Maybe," Veritas said. "But so far they haven't done too well."

"Don't underestimate them. They never lose. Never."

Selena frowned. "That's not true, and you know it."

"You want to take on the people who run the world, leave me out of it," Zeke said.

"We will. Just get us to Burning Man," Selena said. "You owe Jordan. This is for him. It's important, or I wouldn't be here to call in the marker."

Zeke stared at her for several beats. His scowl deepened. "You're lucky. I have a shipment going to Reno tomorrow morning. If you don't mind riding in the back of a truck, that will get you close enough. I can have him run you up to the desert – it's about a hundred miles, but not like he's got a pressing schedule."

"A shipment?" Veritas asked, and immediately regretted it.

Zeke nodded. "That's right. I supply most of the west coast with whatever they need. You got a problem with that?"

Veritas shook his head. "No. I was just trying to figure out the risk."

"No risk at all. Truck's shielded, and I pay off the checkpoints on the way. He'll get you there. Then you're on your own." Zeke paused. "And you can tell Jordan we're even."

"We've got another problem," Selena said, and told him about the gang that they'd tangled with.

Zeke laughed. "Kicked their asses, huh? They deserve it. Don't worry about them – they won't mess with you now that you're under my protection. You'll just disappear and they'll never know what happened."

"What time does the truck leave?" Selena asked.

Zeke looked at his watch. "Two hours – gotta be on the road before dawn. The cops don't work the highways at night because of snipers, so we're clear of the Bay Area before sunup." He cocked his head and studied Selena. "You know you're on a suicide run if they've got DSS looking for you. It's just a matter of time."

She held his stare. "I don't see it that way. But I won't try to convince you. You made your choice."

"Fighting the Brethren is futile. They can't be beaten. Jordan's delusional if he thinks he, or anyone, can win against them. Once I figured it out, I bailed – do you blame me? I've got a nice thing going now: plenty of juice, anything I want with the snap of my fingers. Beats the hell out of a lungful of dust in a freezing desert. But I won't try to talk you out of it. I spent enough time in Jordan's circle of true believers to understand I'd be wasting my time."

Selena sighed. "You know the stakes. You have all the facts. Yet you still turned away."

"I chose living well while I can, instead of tilting at windmills. Look around. I command an army now. I'm rich beyond imagination and getting richer by the day. I don't have to worry about the world – the world keeps on turning without me."

"I can't pretend to understand, and I won't judge. But your path isn't mine," she said. "This is far bigger than my wants and needs."

"Maybe. But it isn't a battle that can be won." He stood. "I'll tell the driver you're going with him. We'll prepare an area with the cargo in the back of the truck. Probably unnecessary, but better safe than sorry." He regarded Veritas. "Don't get sucked into something you don't understand, buddy, that's my advice. They're good at that. But it's your life, and there's no refunds."

They rose, and Zeke escorted them to the door. He opened it and called to the guards. "Put them in one of the rooms upstairs, and get Louie in here."

Two hours later, Veritas and Selena were nestled in the cargo bay of a fifteen-year-old hybrid-drive bobtail truck with a miniature two-way radio the size of a butane lighter. They were near the bulkhead, hidden behind pallets of crates, and the load shifted ominously when the driver struck a particularly bad pothole on the way to the freeway. Selena fell against Veritas as the bed swayed, and he held her for a moment before she inched away. The ride settled out once the truck hit cruising speed, but the roar of the muffler prevented any discussion as the old vehicle labored to make it up the grade on the road east.

Selena tried to find a position where the hard riveted steel of the walls didn't slam into her back.

Veritas yelled to her, "You can lean against me. My jacket's taking most of the pounding."

She didn't answer, and he tried again. "Let's try to get some sleep while we can."

He could barely make her out in the darkness, even with the heightened acuity he'd developed since ingesting the liquid she'd given him. When she didn't say anything, he got as comfortable as he could with Moxie beside him, and closed his eyes. He was nearly asleep when she moved to him and lay with her back against his chest.

"Am I hurting you?" she asked.

"No. Not at all."

Veritas smiled at the smell of her hair and the warmth of her body against his. By the time the truck leveled and was chugging along a flat section, he'd drifted off with Selena snug in his arms, headed into a future as uncertain as any he'd faced.

Chapter 18

California/Nevada border

The two-way radio crackled to life, and Veritas started awake. The truck was slowing, and when the driver's voice squawked from the tiny speaker, it sounded tense.

"Checkpoint. Not one of the usual. Right at the border. Stay quiet no matter what happens and you'll be fine."

Selena took the radio from Veritas and turned the volume down. Veritas grunted and noted that she didn't pull away from him as the truck rolled to a stop.

They heard muffled voices from the road, and then the driver's door slammed shut. Seconds later, the rear cargo doors opened. Shafts of sunlight pierced the darkness, and they winced at the sudden glare that shot through the gaps between the stacked pallets.

"Where are you coming from?" a male voice asked.

"East Bay, with a shipment of medical gear. Varies based on the client. The boxes say that this one's artificial kidneys," the driver said.

"That's a lot of kidneys."

"Hundred and forty-four of 'em, according to the manifest. Taking them to the medical center in Reno."

The truck bounced as a search robot climbed onto the back. Veritas's hand tightened on his pistol as he thumbed the safety off.

A handheld computer beeped as the robot scanned one of the boxes.

"It's all there on the manifest," the driver said, his voice relaxed.

Several minutes dragged by while the robot inventoried random crates and compared them to the manifest, and then the cargo bay doors closed and the truck got under way again. Veritas flipped on the pistol's safety and exhaled in relief.

"If we're at the border, we should be at Black Rock in, what, a few hours?" Veritas asked.

"Figure an hour to Reno, tops, then at least a couple to the desert. You feel the elevation? We're probably at seven thousand feet right now."

Zeke had explained that the driver would drop his shipment before continuing on to Black Rock, and that the people involved wouldn't ask questions about Veritas and Selena. The setup made them both nervous, but there was no way around it, and they'd reluctantly agreed. Veritas scratched his arm and removed his jacket. The interior of the bay was quite warm now that the sun was hitting it, and there was little ventilation to cool the air.

"Switch your flashlight on," Veritas said.

Selena complied, and he examined the full-sleeve tattoos that adorned his arms. "You said that they augmented my bones?"

"That's right. You can see faint scarring. The tattoos were to cover anything still visible, although their micro-surgeon did a good job. You can hardly make out the lines."

"Then…they did this? Or your group?"

"They did the augmentation. Once you escaped, our group handled the tattoos. But you chose the art."

He shook his head. "I don't remember any of it."

"It was the memory wipe."

"Why was that necessary?"

"I wasn't involved," she said, and switched off the lamp. "We may need this again."

"So…the government was in charge of all this? Or the…Brethren?"

"Both. The program was conceived by them and implemented by the government. The Brethren prefers to have the taxpayer cover the bill for their projects, and this was perfect. Supersecret, requiring tech that nobody knew existed, and tightly controlled. Best of all, the agency that carried it out ensured that everyone involved was expendable and didn't officially exist. It was decades in the making."

"What happened?"

"I don't know all the details, but they decided to shut down the program."

"It was a failure?"

"Again, I only know what Jordan shares with me. They wanted to create super commandos that could single-handedly wipe out anything they came up against. But something went wrong, and they canceled it. As far as we know, you're the only surviving member."

"Who can't remember anything about it." He paused. "Every memory I have is fake?"

"I wouldn't say fake. Just…different than your actual past."

"Memories of my mom, of my birthdays, of girlfriends…"

"All invented so you had a coherent backstory."

"Why the substance-abuse angle?"

"We were afraid some of your original memories would leak through – think of them as artifacts you can never completely scrub clean. If they did, and you remembered a monastery, you'd think that was from your time in Thailand, not from your training. And it gave us a chance to keep tabs on you."

"Ben, my sponsor, didn't seem to know you, or about my mom."

"Makes sense. The cells operate that way so if one's compromised, they can't give up the others."

"But my mom?"

"She was part of my cell."

"You knew her?"

"I knew of her. I never met her. She had no need to know about me."

"Ben mentioned someone in Washington. Is that also you?"

"First I heard of it."

Veritas thought for a long moment. "This is a lot to swallow. It's all so…surreal. I mean, who am I? Really? And how can I trust my instincts if they're based on false memories? Seems like that would make them unreliable."

"I don't have an answer for you, Ver. I wish I did. That's why we're headed to Burning Man. Jordan will have the answers, I'm sure."

"Like why your group is helping me in the first place?"

He could sense her stiffen. "For everything," she said.

"Let's say I buy all this. Is it possible to get my real memories back?"

When she answered, her voice was quiet. "I don't know."

He shook his head. "This is so weird. I'm not really me, my past is something complete strangers cooked up for reasons I don't understand, and the most powerful people in the world are after me. You heard Zeke. He didn't sound like he was making it up."

"Zeke served his purpose. But, Ver, he has an obvious character flaw, and he chose a dark path rather than to fight the battle he signed up for. Jordan was nothing but good to him, but when he saw an opportunity to walk away, he took it. A part of him has to regret that decision every day, so of course he's going to come up with fifty reasons why he made the right call. That doesn't mean he did."

"He said they're unbeatable."

"Yet here we are."

"For now."

She sighed. "I'll settle for that."

The truck stopped and the radio squealed.

"We're at the warehouse," the driver announced. "Just stay put and we'll be out of here in a few minutes."

The doors opened, and four workers removed a couple of dozen boxes from the middle of the bay. If any of them noticed Veritas and Selena at the far end, nobody said anything, and fifteen minutes later they were back on the road.

"Once we're at Black Rock, I'll clear a path to the door for you," the driver said over the radio. "Until then, hang loose. We should be there by lunchtime. Shouldn't be any more checkpoints, but no point risking it."

Veritas chuckled grimly. "Hang loose, the man says, after transporting dope and felons across state lines."

They rode in silence for about half an hour, Moxie sleeping in Veritas's lap. "What about you? What are you planning to do?" Veritas asked.

"What do you mean?"

"You've been seen with me. The cameras at the jail; the punks in Oakland. Just a matter of time until DSS picks you up."

She shrugged. "I was ready for a change anyway. Being a cop isn't all that rewarding in a city like San Francisco these days. Terrible hours, pay's late half the time, equipment's junk, and everybody hates you until they need help. So I'll do whatever Jordan wants me to do, I guess."

"Just like that? How many years have you been on the force?"

"Six. But yeah, just like that. See, our view of things like jobs is that they're expendable. That's not my primary purpose, if that makes any sense. The Tribe is my life. Everything else is sort of cover – like Maria being a cleaning woman. She did it for a reason, not because that was all she could be."

"You never finished that story."

"Somehow the Templars got hold of her, and she was found dead. It wasn't a happy ending. But she did her part, even if it meant sacrificing her life."

Veritas considered that kind of commitment and couldn't imagine it. "Her father put her in danger like that, and no regrets?"

"I'm sure he had regrets at losing his daughter, but we all play our roles. We're part of something way bigger than any individual's life. Once you understand that, the rest falls into place. It's about duty and who you are. My family's been at this for centuries. It's what we do."

"I'm still trying to get my mind around that. I mean, I've been struggling to stay sober, and now you tell me I was never an addict. I never thought about sacrificing my life for others – I thought I was barely hanging on to my own by a thread."

"I learned early that the only way to really find meaning is by having a bigger purpose than just eating, sleeping, and whatever. I was indoctrinated in that since childhood. Which I don't regret. It's completely true. If you're only concerned with yourself, you're missing out on most of what makes life worth living. Responsibility makes it meaningful." She sighed. "You were like me, once. Before the wipe."

"So you say. Right now I'm not sure what I believe."

The truck eventually stopped, and the driver shifted some of the cargo out of the way until they could squeeze through the gap. He gave them each a bottle of water and pointed at train tracks that stretched into a beige valley with a collection of structures in the middle of it. "You can follow the tracks until you get close enough to find your way. Good luck. You should be able to make it before it gets dark."

They watched him drive away, and when the truck had disappeared on the highway back to Reno, they were left with the whistle of the wind through the scrub, and nothing else. Veritas squinted at the tracks. "No way of guessing how far down the line it is. I always heard distances were deceptive in the desert."

"I hope he was right about making it before nightfall. It can get freezing after dark."

"You've been here before, right?"

"It's been a long time. But I remember the train tracks."

"Why did Jordan pick someplace this remote? Why not a city?"

"Surveillance. Most places have cameras and tracking devices everywhere. This is an outlaw encampment. They don't allow cell or sat phones, so it's a step back in time. There's a lot of appeal to that."

"What does everyone do for money?"

"In Burning Man? Barter, mostly, and some of the craftspeople sell stuff in the nearby town. They use new dollars, too."

Veritas gave Moxie half his water and set him in the backpack again. The little dog was obviously hungry and tired of being contained, but limited his complaint to whining. They began their hike with a dust devil for company as it traced its way along the tracks before veering toward the hills. Veritas tied his soiled red bandana over his nose and mouth like an Old West outlaw, and they trudged toward the makeshift city. As time wore on, the wind picked up and the clarity of the high desert was replaced by a dusty haze.

Dusk had arrived by the time they were near enough to make out the buildings through an otherworldly distortion of heat waves rising from the sand, streaking the heavens with magenta and apricot as the sun sank into the mountains behind them. They paused to rest as the light faded, and sat to drink the last of their water.

Selena smiled grimly. "Hope we get there soon or we're going to be awfully thirsty."

"And hungry. I know how Moxie feels." Veritas considered the structures in the distance. "I don't suppose they have power or water, do they?"

"Water's trucked in. The only power's solar. A lot of the places have arrays to run things like refrigerators, but it's pretty primitive."

"I can see some fires."

Another smile. "Well, it is called Burning Man."

Veritas was getting to his feet when a gruff voice yelled from the shadows, and the distinctive sound of a pump shotgun chambering a round emanated from the darkness behind them.

"Neither of you move or it'll be the last thing you ever do."

Chapter 19

Four men stepped into view, and Veritas's eyes widened at the sight of them, their shotguns and rifles at the ready, two of them with wild beards and long hair, a third with a gravity-defying Mohawk, and the fourth with a shaved head and reptilian slits for eyes.

The bald man motioned to them with the barrel of a battered AK-47 he held with practiced ease. "Place is invitation only. You'll have to keep moving."

"Who're you?" Selena demanded.

"Security."

"We're here to see Jordan," she said. "He's expecting us."

The group's demeanor changed from aggressive to more relaxed. "You look familiar," one of the bearded men said to Selena.

"This isn't my first time here," she said, not elaborating further. "But I don't remember any patrols. When did that start?"

"As it got bigger. Eventually we had to limit the size. We had all kinds of problems with sewage, water, food, you name it. And some of the newcomers didn't like the rules and caused trouble. So now we have patrols at night and whenever anyone's spotted on approach during the day." He gave a half shrug. "Everyone's free to do what they want, as usual, as long as it doesn't hurt anyone else. You know about the phones?"

She nodded. "I remember."

He held out his hand. "Let's have 'em."

Selena produced hers and the man took it. "What about you?" the man asked Veritas.

"I don't have one."

The guard stepped closer. "Gonna have to pat you down."

Veritas shrugged. The man did a perfunctory search, pausing at Veritas's pistol.

"You shoot anyone, we got our own laws here. Nobody hurts anybody else here. Other than that, use your head. You hurt or kill someone, you get the same treatment as you dealt," he said. "Let's see your face, buddy."

Veritas pulled the bandana down, and the guard stared at him for a long beat before looking at the others and then back to Veritas and Selena. "I'll take you in while they finish patrolling," he said. "Ready?"

"Lead the way."

They covered the remaining stretch of desert and approached the strange collection of buildings, and Selena frowned when she saw how many there were. "I see what you mean by it's grown."

"Yeah. As things got worse out in the world, word spread about us, and for a while we were seeing dozens of newbies showing up every day. We had to put a stop to it – a lot of them had no plan when they got here, and there were robberies and a couple of stabbings. So now we have the patrols, and things have quieted down, kind of like old times."

"You been here a while?" Veritas asked.

"Little over a year. But I'm still not used to the sandstorms. They come out of nowhere and peel your skin off if you aren't protected."

A pair of men armed with assault rifles stopped them at the outer perimeter of the sprawl, but relaxed when they saw the bald man.

"Hey, Sloane. Who do we have here?" one of them asked, gesturing to Veritas and Selena.

"Visitors to see the hermit," Sloane said.

The man grunted. "That's a first, isn't it?"

"First time for everything."

They continued walking until they reached the structures. Sloane paused and indicated one of the buildings – an elaborate pyramid shape with ornate carvings adorning its wood walls. "That's Jordan's place. Same as always."

"I remember," she said. "How do I get my phone back when we leave?"

"Security's that old Airstream trailer over there. Just tell whoever's working that you want it back. I'll mark it with today's date and my name so there's no confusion. I'm Sloane, by the way."

Sloane departed, and they walked to the pyramid.

"I let Jordan know we'd be coming after they took you from the hospital," Selena said.

"Then why didn't he let his goons know?"

"They aren't his. Nobody knows who he is except a few of our group who live here with him."

Once they were outside the wide entrance, Veritas could see that the structure was larger than he'd thought. Selena knocked on the ten-foot-high teakwood door, the carved panels weathered by the elements, and an instant later it swung open to reveal a tall man with long, straw-colored hair pulled into a ponytail. His face changed from serious to relieved when he saw Selena and Veritas, and he stepped back.

"You made it! Please come in."

They entered, and Selena turned to Veritas. "Ver, this is Jordan. Jordan, you've met Veritas, even though he doesn't remember."

Jordan shook Veritas's hand and smiled. "Good to see you again. I'm glad you arrived safely."

Veritas nodded but didn't say anything, processing the exchange and Selena's revelation that he was no stranger to Jordan.

The interior of the pyramid was bathed in a warm glow from a pair of amber LED lamps, and Jordan showed them to a sitting area adjacent to a small, tidy kitchen. "What can I offer you? Food? Drink? I'm well stocked."

"We haven't eaten since yesterday, so anything," Selena said. "And if you have a top that will fit me, I'll marry you."

He laughed. "Nothing grows out here, so we have to truck everything in except the bread, which is delicious. I'll whip something up, and you can tell me what happened." He sized her up. "And I think I can find a shirt and jacket that'll fit you." He looked to Veritas. "How about you?"

"I could use one too," Veritas said. He slid the backpack off and freed Moxie, who scampered around the room before returning to Veritas. "This is Moxie. He could probably use some food and water, too."

"Let's see what we can do about that," Jordan said. He disappeared and returned with clothes for them both before moving to the kitchen and pulling pans from a cupboard. Veritas and Selena took turns cleaning up in the bathroom while Moxie wolfed down food, and by the time they were done and changed, Jordan had made them a hearty meal.

Veritas studied Jordan as he plowed through a heaping preparation of eggs, sausage, and fresh baked bread. Jordan appeared to be in his late thirties, fit and trim, with a boyish twinkle to his hazel eyes, tanned skin, and a strong jawline.

"Are you absolutely certain you weren't followed?" Jordan asked, halfway through their meal.

"It would be almost impossible. Although Zeke and the truck driver know."

Jordan scowled. "If anything goes sideways, the same protocol's in place as the last time you were here."

Veritas looked to Selena in confusion. "Protocol?"

Jordan nodded. "We have a safe house on the other side of Burning Man. Hopefully we won't need it."

Selena provided a running commentary while they devoured their food, and Jordan sat back and listened, nodding occasionally as she spoke. When she finished, he smiled again.

"Quite a story. I imagine you have a lot of questions," he said, eyeing Veritas.

"That's the understatement of the year."

"I'll give you a short rundown, and then you can hit me with them. Roughly twenty years ago, the group known as the Brethren conceived of a program to create a team of super soldiers. To do it, they worked with the CIA and the DOD, as well as their counterparts in China and Europe, and set up a test case using orphans with specific characteristics. They worked together to train them in a variety of disciplines to refine their skills. In your case, you were of mixed blood – an American smuggler who'd spent his final years in Vietnam with a French-Vietnamese girlfriend, who was forced to give you up when the American disappeared. The program initially had five hundred children raised in a monastery in Myanmar, but by the time they were eighteen, the number had dropped to fewer than a hundred, with the rest washing out for one reason or another."

"What happened to the washouts?" Veritas asked.

"They disappeared." Jordan paused. "You were one of the success stories. They chemically altered your central nervous system, which heightened the techniques you'd become adept at through meditation and by mastering a slew of martial arts. When you didn't reject the chemical augmentation, they chipped you, only with a far more advanced version than they're currently foisting off on the public. Those are supposed to be replacements for smartphones – a next-generation advance that eliminates identity theft and makes life easier – which is an irrelevant tangent to your chip's story. Yours is exponentially more powerful and interacts with your brain and your synapses. In other words, it's active, not passive like the civilian version."

He paused for a moment for his words to sink in. "The combination of the spiritual, chemical, and hardware augmentation was supposed to create the ultimate fighter – an unstoppable killing machine unlike anything the world's ever seen. But something went wrong in the trials, and they decided to shut down the program and eliminate everyone involved. With our help, you survived. We had a source who alerted us before it happened, and we were able to sneak you out of your base on the roof of a laundry truck only hours before the extermination program was implemented. You made it. The rest didn't."

"Why did you help me?"

Jordan gave a flat smile. "If you suspect it wasn't altruism, you're correct. We wanted to save you so that when the time was right, we could enlist you in our battle against those who created you and robbed you of your real life."

"The Brethren," Veritas stated flatly.

"That's but one of their names. The oldest references to them were as the messengers of the Anunnaki, in Mesopotamia, who were revered as Gods. They're always depicted in carvings in elaborate robes with horned caps. That was the basis of both our groups. At one time there was just one group, known as the Brotherhood of Babylon, but at some point thousands of years ago, there was a difference of ideology between some of the leadership. Our faction went our separate way, committed to stopping the other one from achieving their ultimate goal."

"Which is?"

"The complete enslavement of humanity." He sat back. "We date back to the dawn of civilization – which is far older than is commonly believed, largely due to their efforts. They've worked hard to mask the true history of human development, because if the truth were known, it would undermine their power."

"And for them, power is everything," Selena said.

Jordan nodded. "After we split off, they became known as Melki-Tsedeq – the basis of the King of the World legend. Later that morphed into the Hashashin – the Assassins – and after that, the Knights Templar, and still later, the alchemists. All of those were notorious for having occult power and secret knowledge that made them virtually invincible."

"King of the World?" Veritas asked.

"It's the basis of the idea of the divine rights of kings – the belief that a special group was in direct communication with God, or the Gods, and ruled by divine decree. They went from being the right hand of the Gods – the Anunnaki – to a lower profile group, but still one of ultimate power, which developed into the hidden power behind the throne. They learned that wielding power anonymously kept them from being recognized for the manipulators they are."

"And they've been doing it ever since," Selena interjected.

Jordan nodded. "After the Templars were nearly eradicated, they went underground and never returned to the limelight. Our group also tried to remain clandestine, although we were stigmatized in every era. Whenever we were discovered, the Brethren used their power to attempt to wipe us out and color us as evil. We've been known as the Igigi, the Roshaniya, the Cathars, the Gnostics, the Druids, the Cabala, and as the Brotherhood of the Snake. That's why the verses in the Bible selected by the Romans as Catholicism's narrative paint the snake as evil and deceptive, and its role in bringing humanity knowledge was colored as damnable rather than enlightened."

Selena pursed her lips. "The Brotherhood of the Snake is where the serpent and staff that's the most recognized medical symbol in the world came from. It was only later that the Brethren worked to make our symbol of healing enlightenment into something the masses would consider evil, by some judicious editing of what the Romans decided would be the official version of the Bible after Emperor Constantine convened the First Council of Nicaea in AD 325."

Jordan shrugged and took a sip of water. "There are hundreds of thousands of clay tablets, which were recently discovered in Iraq just before the turn of the twenty-first century, that describe every aspect of Sumerian civilization. Most haven't been translated – for a reason. One of the things that's puzzled historians is how such an advanced society sprang into being almost overnight, yet the accounts on the tablets remain hidden from view, and that's because of the Brethren. It's no accident that the area of the world where Mesopotamia flourished has been a war zone for as long as I've been alive – the invasion took place after those archeological finds, where the tablets that chronicled the world's true history were uncovered, as well as relics of alien design. Our adversaries don't want the truth of humanity's origins, and theirs, to come out. They'll use any means necessary to ensure it doesn't."

Selena nodded. "We're talking thousands of years of human history, all of it the same – the Brethren working to keep humanity in mental and physical chains of ignorance, and our group seeking to defeat them for the good of the species. Darkness and light, evil and good, ignorance and knowledge, if you view it metaphorically."

Jordan smiled sadly. "She's correct. Although it's been more than a few thousand years. Going back further than the Anunnaki, one of the great mysteries of anthropology was why the Neanderthals, with bigger brains and hardier physiques, went extinct, while *Homo sapiens* prospered. The short answer is that *Homo sapiens* had help."

Veritas frowned. "What does that mean?"

"*Homo sapiens* and Neanderthals coexisted for thousands of years and mated and bred. The Neanderthals' bigger brains allowed them to perceive the nature of the universe differently than Sapiens, and those that bred created the hybrids that are modern humans, which had a significant advantage over those who didn't, due to the mixing of DNA that's in much of the current planet's blood – they got the best of both species, so to speak."

"Wait. Modern humans have Neanderthal DNA?"

Jordan nodded. "It was only recently discovered that most of us have somewhere around two percent."

"Why not all humans?" Veritas asked.

"Neanderthals prospered in cold climates. There weren't any in the tropics. But the important point is that our group's ancestors, as well as those of the Brethren, have more of that Neanderthal DNA than average – around five percent. That's been advantageous because it enables us to perceive reality differently than most, but that advantage also makes our faction dangerous to the Brethren's designs."

"You kind of lost me," Veritas said.

Selena cleared her throat. "They want to be the only ones with that bloodline, which is the basis of the fabled bloodlines of those who searched for the Holy Grail, which are in turn based on the bloodlines of the twelve apostles, which are based on the bloodlines of the twelve tribes of Israel – which date back to the bloodlines of the twelve Anunnaki."

Jordan took a sip of water and nodded. "Which is also the basis of the twelve signs of the zodiac. As time passes, we see the same patterns in mythology because they're all based on the same stories, modified as cultures grow and change."

"The higher Neanderthal DNA gives them, and us, enhanced perceptual abilities that are dormant in normal humans. That works well for them because they want humanity to be mostly slaves, with them as the masters."

"So, you're telling me that a bunch of alien Mesopotamian gods were trying to create super soldiers in…Myanmar?" Veritas said, skepticism plain in his tone. "Why? Sounds like they already control the world, if they can get the CIA and the Chinese to collaborate to do it."

"One of the things you discover as you're more familiar with the story is that the perceived differences between countries and races is engineered to keep populations subjugated. To the Brethren, there is no China or Europe or America. There are just themselves, who control all the world's governments through a number of mechanisms, and the rest of the world."

"What mechanisms?"

"Now? Present day? Well, the global financial system via the central banks, all of whom answer to the Bank for International Settlements in Basel, Switzerland, as well as the IMF and World Bank and a host of others. The basis of their power is the creation of money based on nothing but the population's willingness to slave away for it, and they've been able to use that to control for generations – for a long time, banking was one of their ultimate secrets, as it was during the time of the Templars. The global financial system is just their latest control mechanism."

Veritas eyed Jordan skeptically. "You're telling me it's a bunch of bankers?"

Jordan shook his head. "No. As I said, that's their current control mechanism, nothing more. True wealth isn't material. That's an illusion to keep humans enslaved."

"Try buying a hamburger without that illusion. You'll have a hard time," Veritas said.

"I won't bore you with the evolution of money, but consider that never before in history has there been a time where a small group creates it from thin air, and the rest of the world has to trade its resources for it. In the past, it was always something of scarcity that had innate value, or at least perceived value – like precious metals that were scarce and had to be mined to get them out of the ground, which limited the amount that could be created at any given time. Now? It's just a bunch of digits tapped into a computer. But again, that's immaterial. None of it's real."

"It's real enough for you to continue fighting them," Veritas observed.

"Because their ultimate plan is beyond evil." He looked away, his face suddenly older, and when he looked back at Veritas, his expression was bleak. "One of the ways they manipulated the world before the monetary system was through religion and disease – plagues, flu, that sort of thing. Religion to keep scientific inquiry from prospering, disease to keep societies terrified and malleable."

Selena sat forward. "If they had their way, antibiotics would never have been invented, and we'd all still be drinking water from rivers where we dumped our sewage. And they also used these viruses as ways to alter human brains in steps, so they'd be easier to harvest."

"Harvest," Veritas repeated.

Jordan nodded. "They use our brains as computers. The first operating system upgrade I know of was in 2200 BC. The accounts of Moses are partially based on that plague. The next major upgrade was the Plague of Justinian in the sixth century, which wiped out almost fifteen percent of humanity. But as medicine became more science based and cures for those plagues were discovered, they had to pivot to something else. They only focused on money after their tried-and-true approach failed and religion became less effective. But now…they're using a new strain of flu to thin the population and prepare the survivors for what's to come. That Levant flu's the one that's beginning to spread. It killed the woman you knew as your mother, and it's in the process of killing far more."

"Why?"

"It's the first stage in a two-step process. This first will eliminate those with unsuitable genetic material – those without the DNA – and leave the rest prepared for the second phase. After the flu's run its course and decimated the global population, a second virus will be introduced that achieves their end game in conjunction with the chips. It's their final solution."

"What final solution?"

"The second virus will exterminate anyone without a chip and do a final wetware upgrade on those who have one – they'll make the chip mandatory for the survivors of this first round, but the catch is that they'll screen the DNA of everyone who's to receive it and deny those who don't fit their criteria. Of course they won't say so – they'll say that some people aren't candidates for invented medical reasons. It's the ultimate filtering of thousands of years of evolution."

Selena interrupted. "Why do you think the world's governments have been subsidizing the chip? Paying for people to get implanted? When the Levant flu becomes a crisis, they'll require everyone to have one if they want medical care or student loans or to travel. They'll claim the health care system is overwhelmed and the chip's required for it to work efficiently."

Jordan sighed. "That's why the man you knew as your sponsor needed to speak with you confidentially. The plan's accelerating, so it was time to tell you the truth about your past, as well as your destiny. But your being hit by the car changed everything because it put you on the Brethren's radar, and now that they know you exist, they'll stop at nothing to capture, interrogate, and eliminate you."

"Because you threaten their plan," Selena added.

"I deliver pizzas," Veritas said. "This is crazy. I'm broke, and now I'm running from the law. I can't change a ten, much less some Sumerian super plan."

Jordan didn't blink. "Selena gave you a partial update to drink in jail. What happened after that?"

"We...we escaped."

"But it's more than that, isn't it? You gained strength and mental acuity. You react faster now; process thoughts faster. Your synapses are more efficient, and that translates into speedier responses. That was only a partial update – the rest of your capabilities are still dormant."

"Like what?" Veritas asked.

"Superior speed – nearly blinding. Greater duration and stamina in anything you attempt. The ability to jump higher, run faster, you name it – anything physical. But perhaps the most important requires something more, and we haven't developed it yet. But we're working on it. The problem is that we're running out of time. The first virus has been released, and it's spreading fast. There isn't much we can do about this first phase, but the second phase must not be allowed to enter the population, or it will be the end of humanity as we know it."

Veritas's eyes narrowed. "Why didn't Ben know about my mom? That makes no sense, not that any of the rest of this does."

"Within our resistance group, there are two camps. One wants to be proactive and stop our adversaries at any cost. The other...the other has a different philosophy, one that's more pacifistic, you could say. They don't believe in using violence or matching the tactics our adversaries use. Ben was a member of that group. We don't really communicate with each other, even though we both have a stake in you."

"What do they believe in, then? Letting them win?"

"They're of the opinion that the fate of humanity doesn't matter. Obviously, we see things differently."

"If humanity doesn't matter, what do they think does?"

Jordan shrugged. "Nothing. That's their ideology. We have our own."

"They're nihilists?"

"Well, it's more that their perception of reality is different from ours. But we both agree that the Brethren are working against the interests of the human race. The other faction thinks those interests are meaningless, whereas we believe that every person has meaning and should be allowed to be self-determining and self-actualized. Regardless of who's right, we're now at a point where humans will be doomed to an eternity of slavery unless we stop the Brethren's plan. And that doesn't even count everyone who'll die because of the first virus."

"Is there some way to stop it?"

"We're working on a vaccine for both. But unfortunately that takes time, time we don't have. Even once we deploy a vaccine, presuming we can…"

"Millions, or billions, will still die," Selena said, her voice quiet.

"And if we fail, those who're left will be automatons," Jordan finished.

"Back up. You said that *Homo sapiens* had help. What did you mean by that?"

"Everything is linked. The Anunnaki were viewed as gods on earth by the Sumerians, but specifically, gods with the ability to fly through the sky, and who descended from the heavens. In other words, extraterrestrial visitors. Those visitors determined that *Homo sapiens* were more malleable than Neanderthals and gave *Homo sapiens* the knowledge to prosper as the climate changed, whereas the Neanderthals died out. The human offspring with Neanderthal DNA became the dominant species, and those with the most DNA were a select group that were literally the messengers of the gods – the keepers of higher knowledge only they could access. The Brethren and our group's ancestors."

"Now we're all descended from Martians?" Veritas scoffed. "Come on."

"You asked me to explain why you have such amazing strength and what was done to you. I have. If you decide you want to ignore everything I've told you in favor of your preconceived ideas, that'll require that you also ignore the proof I've told you the truth."

"What proof?"

"You. Everything about you. The network of scars that cover your body, where the incisions were made to modify your bones and muscles." He hesitated. "The reason DSS was notified when you got your CT scan is because it picked up something that should be impossible: a hybrid body with an embedded CPU chip. That triggered an alarm, which is why the whole world came crumbling down shortly thereafter. You are the proof, Veritas."

"Is that even my real name?"

Selena looked at him quizzically. "Does it matter?"

"To me it does. I want to know."

"We don't know your real name. We gave you your current one – it means the truth. Because your very existence represents proof of the truth. And because you're important in the coming struggle for the fate of the planet."

"Stopping the virus. Because I have the power of fifty bike delivery grunts," Veritas muttered.

"Mock me all you like, Veritas. But in your heart you know I'm telling the truth," Jordan said.

When Veritas looked up at Jordan, his expression was pained. "How can I know or be sure of anything? My memories are lies, so any of my instincts are based on inventions. If I don't know my past or who I really am, I can't trust anything, including my gut."

"We may have modified your memories, but not your essence, Veritas," Selena said.

"Bullshit. If my instincts are based on lies, then I have no true essence – just whatever you inserted," Veritas snapped.

"That's not true," Jordan countered. "Your memories were scrubbed, but you can never get to the very deepest ones. They're the foundation of your personality, of who you are. What psychologists call the unconscious. Your conscious memories were wiped, but nobody's able to reach your unconscious."

Veritas's eyes widened. "I've always had weird dreams…"

Jordan nodded slowly. "Those are your unconscious mind leaking through." He looked around the room. "We're at a crisis point, Veritas, and we need your help. There's a prophecy that's as ancient as those in Abrahamic religions – all of which center around the return of the messenger of God. It's that of a final battle between the forces of darkness and those of light, where an angel of God wars against the angels of darkness. The Christian depiction of angels are winged beings, but originally *angel* was nothing more than the word for messenger. In our prophecy, one of us – a messenger – battles evil during the final confrontation." He fixed Veritas with an intense stare. "We believe you're that messenger."

Veritas snorted in exasperation. "You can believe whatever you want. I've heard enough."

"You are, Veritas," Selena said. "You're the one."

"I'm an ex-junkie who delivers food to fat asses who're too lazy to get off the couch and get it themselves. You've got the wrong guy."

Jordan shook his head. "You deliver food. That makes you a kind of messenger, doesn't it?"

"If you're smoking synth-meth, maybe." Veritas addressed his next remarks to Selena. "Look, I appreciate everything you've done, but I'm not your angel of death or whatever you think I am."

"Veritas," Selena said, "we saved you."

"So you keep saying." He rose and scooped up Moxie's sleeping form, put him in the backpack, and walked to the door. "I need some time to think about all this. You can't just announce that the world's about to end, and I'm not who I believe I am, and that the woman who raised me isn't really my mother, and I'm part of some super plot going back to cavemen and aliens, and expect me to nod along. That's crazier than your story."

"Where are you going?" Selena asked, alarmed.

"To clear my head." He opened the door and stormed out, not waiting for them to say anything more.

Jordan and Selena exchanged a dark look.

"That went well," she said.

"He'll come to terms with it. He's just overwhelmed. It's a lot to digest, and I hit him with all of it at once. Perhaps I should have gone slower."

"If he refuses…"

Jordan frowned. "That's not who he is."

"You don't know that. Not for sure."

He stood. "Follow him and make sure he doesn't get into any

trouble. Answer any questions, but don't press him. He needs time to process."

Selena moved to the door. "Time being the one thing we don't have."

Chapter 20

Music thumped from mini speakers in the corner of the Burning Bar, a techno grind that was little more than a series of rhythmic noises over a relentless beat. A pall of marijuana smoke hovered near the ceiling, and raucous laughter and shouted conversation filled the air. Finally finished with his guard duty, Sloane made his way to the entrance, pushed through the crowd, and approached the bar, where an impassive man with bronze skin and jet-black hair stared at him without blinking.

"Beer," Sloane said.

The man nodded wordlessly, opened an ice chest, and set a bottle on the pine plank that served as the bar. He popped the cap off and resumed staring at Sloane, the lines on his stony face etched deep by a hard life.

Sloane lifted the beer to his lips and took a long pull before setting the bottle back on the bar. "How's it goin', chuckles?"

"Same shit, different day," the bartender said.

"Devin around?"

The man's eyes flitted to a corner of the room. Sloane twisted to see where he was looking, and spotted a figure seated at a table in the shadows, away from the patrons, a mug and an ashtray on the table and nothing else.

Sloane tossed a few coins on the bar, snagged his beer, and walked to the table. A man in his early thirties, his hatchet face unshaven and his unruly hair greasy, looked up at him with eyes the color of lead.

"What?"

Sloane hesitated before pulling a chair free and sitting across from the man. "I've been keeping an eye peeled, like you asked."

The man nodded. "And?"

"Man and a woman showed up tonight. On foot. Looked like they been dragged behind a truck. Said they're here to see the hermit."

The man's face twitched and he sat forward. "Yeah? What did they look like?"

"I've seen the woman before, a while ago. She's maybe five four, brown hair, white, kind of an 'I'm better than everyone' look."

"What about the guy?"

"Six three or four. Muscular. Some kind of mix. Light brown skin. Short hair." Sloane paused. "Looks like he can handle himself, you know?"

The man nodded. "Anything else? Tats? Piercings?"

Sloane shook his head. "He was wearing a jacket, so maybe, maybe not." He tapped his pocket. "I got images."

The man's thin lips curled into a smirk. "You did, did you?"

Sloane tossed him a tiny data fob. "Yup. Micro-cam. Figured you'd want some."

"Where are they now?"

"In the pyramid. Looked like they're spending the night."

The man's hand snaked out, and the fob disappeared into his pocket. Sloane took another sip of his beer and waited. The man stood and beckoned to Sloane. "Step into my office."

Sloane followed him to a door at the back of the bar, and they entered a small room filled with crates of alcohol. The man fished in his jacket and held out a plastic vial filled with pink-white crystals. "That's a week's worth of synth. If your info bears out, there's more where that came from. On the house."

Sloane's eyes were locked on the vial as he took it with a trembling hand. "Cool."

"Remember. Not a word to anyone."

"Of course."

They returned to the barroom, and Sloane chugged the rest of his drink. "I could use another one," he said. "They're nice and cold tonight."

The man nodded. "Tell Tom it's on me."

When Sloane left, the man waited a few minutes and then strode to the bar. "I'll be gone the rest of the night," he said, and the bartender nodded once, the gesture almost imperceptible.

The man pulled his jacket tight around him, pushed into the cool night air, and strode to a camper van with a dirt bike parked beside it. He removed a key from his pants pocket and started the bike, slung his leg over the saddle, and toed the motorcycle into gear.

The headlight cut through the darkness, bouncing along the hard surface, and when he was clear of the town, he accelerated, working through the gears until he was flying toward the tiny hamlet of Gerlach eleven miles away, leaving a cloud of dust and a faint track in the desert in his wake.

Chapter 21

Selena trailed Veritas as he wended his way along one of the curved strips of unpaved road that served as the arteries of Black Rock City. The encampment's original spontaneous expression of artistic purpose had, as the area had become a permanent fixture, given way to a more pragmatic approach to design, and many of the final festival's structures had been toppled in favor of utilitarian dwellings and small businesses that catered to the enclave's residents.

Still, there were elaborate fixtures crafted from steel, wood, and glass that lent the area the feeling of a post-apocalyptic Neverland, and after dark some of the most elaborate landmarks were lit with colored, solar-powered LEDs.

Veritas stalked past a trio of giant Munch-inspired screaming faces with hands clamped over ears, eyes, and mouth, sculpted from iron beams and rebar, painted iridescent hues that glowed in the starlight. A young woman wearing a leather bikini top adorned with silver diamond studs, a pair of boxer shorts, and goggles over her eyes drifted by him atop a bicycle with bulbous tires before dematerializing in the darkness.

He paused in front of a temple, its elaborate Asian façade and vaulted roof breathtaking against the backdrop of glimmering stars. He looked to his right, where a bonfire was burning twenty yards away and at least thirty young men and women were drinking and dancing and hooting in tribal celebration around the flames. A pang of sudden emptiness shot through him at the sight of their carefree abandon and their enjoyment of a moment from which he was excluded.

He hadn't asked to be the object of some freakish cult's obsession, but now that he knew the truth – or at least their version of it – he had decisions to make. Much as he wanted to dismiss the outlandish story as a flight of deluded fancy, Jordan's sincerity, and the undeniable result of the upgrade Selena had given him, demanded that he take at least the base claims as legitimate.

DSS was scouring the state for him. There was no way he could hide forever or wait them out. If Jordan was telling the truth, they'd never give up, and he was facing an adversary who would stop at nothing to find and silence him.

Which left him with few appealing choices.

A voice from behind him interrupted his rumination. "Ver? Wait up."

He turned as Selena approached from out of the gloom.

"I'm sorry Jordan freaked you out," she said. "It's a lot to process, I know."

A pair of young scantily clad young women with goggles and pigtails rolled by on skateboards with oversized wheels. Music emanated from one of the larger structures ahead, where a man in a black unitard to match his ebony skin blew fire into the night sky at the tower's entrance.

"I'd always heard this place was a zoo," he said.

"It's one of the reasons Jordan likes it. Burning Man is its own insulated world, mainly populated by creatives who wanted out of the system. Every day's like a tour of the bizarre, but you definitely meet a lot of interesting people. And the security's good, as you saw."

"They take your phone, but you can keep your guns? Not sure that makes a lot of sense."

"When you live here, you agree to a mutual self-defense pact. Nobody wants to get booted, so there's virtually no violence; but if a gang of bikers shows up to loot or something, they're going to be facing a thousand guns. It's a good disincentive that's worked wonders."

Veritas nodded. "I don't appreciate being blindsided by Jordan. You obviously knew most of what he told me. You could have at least eased me into it some."

"It wasn't my call, Ver. If I could have, I would. But I'm just a cog in a much bigger machine."

"How many of you are there here in Burning Man?"

She shrugged. "Maybe a dozen. This is just one cell. Jordan's got sort of a council that he meets with. But we have people in a lot of the major cities. And there are other cells in Europe, Russia, the Middle East, and Asia."

"What's he going to try to get me to do? Assuming I decide to play along?"

Selena looked away. "I can't…"

"After telling me everything I believe is a lie and I'm not who I thought, the cat's out of the bag, Selena. If you want me to consider helping you – and note I'm not saying I will – I need to understand what I'm being asked to do."

"I'd prefer if he told you."

"I'd prefer not to have DSS hunting me. Come on. Give."

"I don't know the whole plan, Ver. But I know part of it involves a suitcase nuke and Washington, D.C."

Veritas's jaw dropped. "You're kidding."

"Jordan can explain it better than I can."

"I'll bet." He looked away. "You people are out of your gourds."

"The stakes are too high, Veritas. They have to be stopped."

"You're talking about nuking the most heavily defended area in the country – not to mention a populated urban area."

"That's not the whole plan. It's just part of it. The Brethren is a hydra with many heads. We'll have to launch simultaneous strikes and sever all of them at once, or they'll be back with the same agenda. Remember this has been going on for many, many thousands of years." She took his hand, and in spite of his misgivings, he didn't pull away. "Looks like they're having a ball over there. Come on. I'll buy you a beer."

"I told you I don't drink."

"Right. Because of an addictive past that isn't real. Loosen up, Ver. You're not an addict. You never were. That was just to keep you on the straight and narrow."

"I don't get the logic."

"They weren't sure how you'd react to the memory wipe, and they didn't want you becoming a liability if you decided to use drugs or alcohol to numb yourself. You were more manageable straight, so it was an easy call to make."

"More manageable. How nice," he echoed, his tone bitter.

"Poor choice of words. With the mods to your physiology, they didn't want any surprises. For all they knew, alcohol might have brought your subconscious memories closer to the surface, which would have been a problem." She smiled. "That obviously isn't an issue now that you know the truth. Come on, Mr. Grumpy. You can watch me drink if you don't want any. After the last twenty-four hours, I could sure use one."

She pulled him toward the fire-eater, and he reluctantly accompanied her, the feel of her skin on his pleasant in spite of his anger at the situation. If she was telling the truth, she was a foot soldier, not a general, so he couldn't hold her accountable for the decisions of her superiors.

And she had saved his life. That counted for something.

He glanced at her out of the corner of his eye and remembered how she'd felt in his arms. As if reading his mind, her grip tightened on his fingers and she picked up her pace.

"This a bar?" he asked as they neared the structure. A glowing sign announced that they'd arrived at "The Temple of Doom."

"One of five in town. More like a club than a bar. There's dancing, drinks, whatever you want. Burning Man's the Wild West when it comes to most everything."

"Sodom and Gomorrah in the desert?"

"Something like that," she said, her smile widening.

"I really need to think," he said.

"Nobody's stopping you. Hope you're not easily distracted, though. It's a good-looking crowd."

She handed a few coins to a heavily muscled bouncer, and they entered the building, which was ten times bigger than Jordan's pyramid and designed with a Hindu-temple theme. The walls were painted with depictions of Indian deities in what looked suspiciously like scenes from the *Kama Sutra*, and the dance floor was three-quarters full with a rogues' gallery of misfits worthy of a circus sideshow.

A woman in a sequined G-string and a halter top, every inch of her body inked with elaborate tattoos and an oversized ring through her nose like a prize bull, stopped in front of them and yelled over the music, "What do you want?"

"Beer. Quadra Stout," Selena said, and looked up at Veritas, who shrugged.

"Might as well make it two," he said, and the woman nodded and strutted away, her biker bootstraps glinting in the colored lights. Veritas leaned into Selena. "She seems like a nice girl."

Selena smirked but didn't say anything. The waitress reappeared and handed them two sweating bottles. Selena clinked her beer against Ver's. "Cheers."

Veritas took a cautious sip and made a face. "Blech. It tastes like sweat socks. How can you drink this?"

She shrugged. "It's an acquired taste."

A thin man with a shaved head and tattoos inked across his entire body to the top of his head stepped onto the bar with a burlap sack, his naked torso gleaming with oil. He reached a raised section in the middle and the patrons around it stepped back, apparently knowing what came next. He performed an elaborate bow to the crowd, and then unceremoniously dumped a five-foot-long rattlesnake out of the bag and onto the bar.

The snake coiled and raised its head to strike the man, who began weaving his hands in a mesmerizing fashion, waving them slowly in front of the snake. The reptile's head followed the movements, back and forth, for a good minute before the man stepped closer, and in a single deft motion, grabbed the snake just below its head and dropped it back into the bag to thunderous applause.

"Tell me that thing's been defanged," Veritas said.

"I doubt it. Wouldn't be the same performance without the danger, would it?"

"He's got to be insane."

"He's part of the entertainment. Probably does it three or four times a night. The snake's used to it."

"What if the snake's having a bad day and decides it doesn't want to play?"

Selena shrugged and then nudged Veritas in the ribs as the snake charmer was replaced by a pair of young women in near perfect physical shape, wearing little but a few pieces of string.

"That more your speed?" she asked.

Veritas considered his response. "Might be more dangerous than the snake."

The women linked arms and stood hip to hip, and then each raised their right legs until their feet were touching their ears. They then swiveled to face each other and arched their backs while reaching with their raised foot. The one on the left tapped the top of the one on the right with her foot, and then her counterpart did the same.

The contortionists performed for ten minutes, each act more impossible than the last, and when they finished and curtsied, the ovation was thunderous.

"Impressive," Veritas admitted, as they strutted to the far end of the bar to collect tips from a hat that had been circulating.

"Guess we know what you'll be dreaming about tonight."

They stood together watching the scene for over an hour, taking in the counterculture buzz of the crowd and the electric energy in the air. After they finished their second beers, Veritas took Selena's hand again and led her outside. Branches of dry lightning pulsed in a line of clouds that brooded over the distant mountains to the east, and the breeze smelled of rain and ozone and wet earth. Veritas tilted his head back and inhaled deeply, and regarded Selena's profile as she ran her fingers through her hair.

"We can't hide out here forever," he said.

"No, but we should be fine for a night or two. Jordan will think of something. That's what he does."

"What happens to me if I don't play along?"

She looked him in the eyes. "I don't think it's so much what happens to you, Ver. It's what happens to the human race."

"I get that, and forgive me for selfishly being interested in my own well-being, but if I say no thanks…what happens?"

"I don't know the answer to that," she answered truthfully. "But I hope you don't."

He studied her face and the defiance in her posture, a faint glow from the Temple's external lights warming her skin, and was leaning into her, light-headed from fatigue and alcohol, when she pulled away, her eyes glued on the western horizon.

"You hear that?" she asked, her voice tight.

Veritas cocked his head and listened with his eyes closed. After a moment, they snapped open and he nodded, his expression tense.

"What is it?" he asked.

She looked around and was about to answer when the relative quiet was shattered by a half dozen black helicopters streaking toward them from out of the darkness.

Chapter 22

"What the hell–" Veritas blurted.

The lead chopper banked and fired a pair of missiles. Selena gasped as they seared through the air and struck Jordan's pyramid. A fireball exploded into the air like an orange fist, and chunks of burning wood arced through the air and bounced against the ground near the temple.

"Jesus!" she said, and whipped her pistol from beneath her shirt.

She tried to run to the pyramid, but Veritas grabbed her arm to hold her back.

"There's nothing you can do," he said.

The helos slowed and hovered near the perimeter of town. Ropes dropped down, and commandos slid from the open cargo doors.

"They found us," Veritas said.

"We have to try to save Jordan," she answered, trying to pull free of him.

"Looks like at least thirty guys dropping from the choppers, and they're loaded for bear. What do you think we can do with these peashooters against assault rifles?"

A shotgun boomed in the night, and answering fire from the commandos chattered from sound-suppressed rifles. More gunfire cracked and popped from some of the dwellings, and Selena turned to Veritas and nodded, her expression determined.

"You're right," she acceded. "But remember what I said about the locals. This isn't going to be a cakewalk for the bad guys."

"Who do you think it is?"

"Who else? Doesn't really matter what agency they sent. The target was obviously the pyramid."

Veritas swallowed, but didn't speak for a moment. "No. It was me. They thought we were still in there. This was directed at me, nobody else. Jordan was collateral damage."

"He could still be alive." More shots echoed through the camp as the rhythmic whump of the helicopter blades blew flurries of sand into the air.

"Anything's possible. But the men in black seem like they're on a mission. What do you want to do?"

She thought for an instant, and then her face settled into a frown. "Keeping you safe is the priority. Jordan would want me to get you clear of this."

A submachine gun rattled from nearby, and another shotgun boom joined it.

"Easier said than done. Didn't he say something about a safe house?"

She nodded. "We're not going to have much chance to get out of here. They'll be using infrared. If we make it out of the perimeter, we'll be sitting ducks on foot. We need wheels."

"Bikes?"

"Anything's better than being gunned down."

The helicopters settled onto the hard-packed ground. Helmeted figures in black exchanged fire with camp residents, and more of them joined the fight every second.

"There are a lot of antigovernment preppers who've vowed to fight to the last man if anyone messes with them here. But against a coordinated force like that, it's only a matter of time. They're outgunned." She exhaled hard.

"Then let's go."

Selena sprinted away from the commandos and zigzagged between structures, the sound of the gunfight behind them urging her forward. Veritas followed on her heels and was surprised at how easily he overtook her without breaking a sweat. The staccato bark of more automatic weapons fire from the Burning Man residents confirmed Selena's assertion that the encampment was ready to defend itself.

"A couple of Jordan's men live at the safe house," Selena said. "He told us that if anything ever happened to him, we should rally there."

"Sounds like he was expecting something like this."

"The history of our group has been persecution and periodic purges by whatever government is in power. Our adversaries are always behind them and use them to further their aims."

"Then why didn't they go after Jordan earlier?"

"Probably because they didn't think he mattered, what with the virus already out there and their plan coming to fruition. Besides, you might be right. This isn't about him so much as it is about you. They're obviously desperate to stop you." She paused. "They know of the prophecy too, Veritas. You may think it's all BS, but obviously the powerful interests that are looking for you don't. Which should tell you something." More gunfire exploded from where they'd been, and Selena pointed down a small artery that stretched toward the outer section of the camp. "This way."

They darted from cover to cover, staying low as they ran by denizens of Burning Man who were running toward the battle with assault rifles. They reached a modular building, where a pair of men were standing with shotguns.

"The pyramid took a direct hit from a pair of missiles," Selena announced by way of greeting.

"Shit," one of the gunmen said.

"Jordan said you'd made contingencies?" Veritas said.

The men nodded. "Come inside."

The shorter of the pair held the door open, and Selena and Veritas brushed past him. The interior of the building was utilitarian and the furniture cheap. He walked directly to the kitchen and heaved on the refrigerator, which rolled forward. He stepped around it and lifted a section of linoleum flooring, revealing an opening the size of a manhole.

The guard handed Veritas a flashlight. "Goes down a story and a half, and lets out near the foothills. We created it when we were building the town's sewage system. Jordan figured it might come in handy." He regarded Selena and then studied Veritas for a moment. "You'll be fine, but it'll be a tight fit for him in places."

"What's at the other end?"

"Four all-terrain, amphibious, GPS self-guided ATVs. Each one can haul two people. They have full tanks, and they're each packed with a couple of days' supply of energy bars and water, as well as a first aid kit and some basic survival supplies."

"Keys?"

"Take one from the box at the bottom of the shaft. They're all keyed alike." The sound of shooting drew nearer. "Better get going. Good luck. If it looks like they're onto us, we'll blow the opening on this end." He paused. "Any chance that Jordan made it?"

"Hope so," Selena said. "But I wouldn't count on it."

Veritas lowered himself into the hole and felt the iron rungs of a ladder drop into the darkness. Selena followed him in, and they were at the bottom within seconds. The light from above disappeared when the linoleum flooring was replaced, and Veritas switched on the lamp the man had given him and swept the area.

A plastic box was affixed to the base of the ladder from which he extracted two keys, leaving the rest. He played the beam down the passage that stretched into the darkness, where the vertical chute gave way to a horizontal shaft lined in concrete.

"You want to lead the way, or shall I?" Selena asked.

"Ladies first."

They dog-crawled along the passageway, and after a few yards, the hard concrete was replaced by a culvert pipe that Veritas could barely fit his shoulders through. After nearly a half hour of inching along, an explosion from behind them rocked the tunnel, and their ears popped from the sudden change of air pressure. Veritas pulled his bandana over his nose and mouth as dust blew past them, and closed his eyes until it had settled and the air had become breathable again.

"They blew the entrance," Selena whispered. "That'll buy us some time, but it means that they had no choice. That was their escape route as well."

"None of this is good news," he said.

"No, it isn't."

An hour later, they reached a small chamber with four black ATVs. Selena moved to a ramp that led upward and reached for a trapdoor. She pushed at it with her shoulder, but it barely budged.

"Can you give me a hand?" she called to him. Veritas joined her, and together they raised the hatch and slid it to the side. Sand poured through the opening, which was just big enough to accommodate one of the ATVs. She poked her head out and looked around, and Veritas did the same. Burning Man's outline was silhouetted against the night sky with fires raging through it. An occasional gunshot echoed over the desert, but the furious firefight from earlier had died down.

"I should never have brought you here," she said, her voice quiet.

"You did what you had to do."

"Because of that, Jordan and a whole lot of good people are dead."

"It isn't your fault. You had no way of knowing."

"I should have."

Veritas glanced at the encampment. "Sounds like it's mostly over."

Selena's expression hardened. "Which means we're on borrowed time. If they get one of those birds in the air before we've cleared the area, we're screwed."

"Then we'd better get going."

"Damn. I left my phone back there. It has my nav app on it."

"So we're flying blind?"

"We're on the south side of the town. I say we follow a gorge up into the hills and see what we find. We'll have to cross the railroad tracks and the road, but once we're past those, it should be pretty wild country."

"This was hidden well. We could always stay here until they take off."

She shook her head. "We can't risk it. If anyone talks, we'd be sitting ducks. Too many people know about the work that was done on the sewage system. When they don't find your body in the camp, eventually someone's going to figure out you escaped, and it won't take a rocket scientist to conclude it couldn't have been above ground. Remember, they have access to the smartest minds in the world."

"They aren't all that bright if they have to do a frontal attack on a squatter camp to get one man."

"That should tell you something about how ruthless they are." She looked around. "You can kind of make out an area over there by that rise that looks good. We'll push it until we're out of sight of the town, start it up, and boogie."

"Why not take two?"

"Twice the noise and double the tracks to cover up. Plus, we have to push one until we're far enough so the engine won't draw attention, and I won't be able to push one that far. We can both ride on one – no point in making it easy for them."

"I hope you know what you're doing."

She turned from him before he could see the doubt etched into her face. "Me too."

The ATV must have weighed six hundred pounds, but Veritas had little trouble pushing it up the ramp. The elixir he'd drunk had definitely increased his strength, for which he was grateful as he plodded with the vehicle a hundred yards, past the stench of the crude sewage treatment plant the Burning Man engineers had contrived and across the railroad tracks to an area of rocky terrain that marked the beginning of the foothills.

"Can you drive this?" Selena asked.

"Only one way to find out." He swung onto the saddle, held out the backpack with Moxie, and patted the area of the seat behind him. "Take Moxie and climb on."

She slung the backpack strap over her shoulder and settled onto the nub of cushion while he twisted the key and depressed the starter button. The little motor roared to life and he toed the gear shifter into first and gently worked the thumb throttle until they were bouncing along a ravine. He left the ATV's headlights off and used only the intermittent moonlight to guide them, Selena's arms around his waist as he negotiated the rutted terrain.

The column of storm clouds had drawn nearer since the attack, and lightning flashes lit the desert before thunder exploded several seconds afterward. A few minutes later, they arrived at a rise, beyond which stretched a black ribbon of road. He stopped the ATV and waited in the shadows with the engine idling.

"What do you think?" he asked.

"No time like the…wait. Hear that?"

He shook his head.

"We need to get off the road."

He executed a sharp turn and rolled twenty feet down the bank. Selena leapt off before he'd completely stopped, and freed her pistol. She dropped in a crouch and whispered to him, "Kill the engine and get down."

Veritas shut off the motor and did as instructed.

Headlights rounded a bend to the west, and the sound of a motor reached them from the road. They watched as a Highway Patrol electro-cruiser growled along the highway, its spotlight sweeping over the shoulder of the road as it made its way east. The car and a pair of aerial drones passed their position, which was hidden from the road by brush and a rock outcropping, and when the vehicle's taillights had receded into the darkness, Veritas called to Selena, "Let's get across before more of them show up."

They straddled the ATV and Veritas started the engine again. They practically flew across the asphalt with a rev, and then they were careening over a berm on the other side, moving fast over the shoulder before slowing again. More lightning brightened the night sky, and the heavens let loose. Sheets of cold rain blew over them, dropping visibility to near zero and turning the gravel beneath the vehicle's wheels into a treacherous slurry that slowed their progress to a crawl.

Chapter 23

Azra stood by the lead attack helicopter, glowering at the incinerated remains of Burning Man. He'd been standing by when the message had come in that the target had been traced to the camp, and he hadn't hesitated to take to the air and rain destruction down on the squatters before the target had a chance to escape.

They'd known of the Tribe cell headed by Jordan for months, of course, but had seen no reason to roll it up with the virus plan moving smoothly forward. Azra would have killed them all when he'd first discovered them, but it hadn't been his call to make, and his superiors, in their wisdom, had deemed the cell too trivial to worry about. Now it appeared that they might have underestimated the group's importance; he'd lost half his fighting force to surprisingly stiff resistance, and there was no sign of his prey.

The helo pilot called to him from the cockpit. "The entire perimeter is secure."

"Perfect," Azra said. He tapped his earbud and transmitted on the group comm. "What have we got, people?"

"We're questioning some of the survivors," answered Lars, the head of the mercs. "Most took off when the fighting started – they're scattered in the desert now."

"What about the pyramid?"

"Stand by. We're putting out the last of the fires."

Azra paced in front of the aircraft as its blades orbited lazily overhead, its turbine still running but the rotor in neutral. The comm crackled in his ear.

"Nothing from the latest bunch. How should we proceed?"

"Somebody has to have seen something. We're not pulling out until we've found his body. This shouldn't be that difficult."

"Roger that."

A figure approached with a handheld receiver. Donald Adair, the former technical director for the super-soldier team, looked up at Azra and shook his head. "The scanner's not showing anything."

"How is that possible? I thought that once he was within a half klick, it would pick up his chip."

"Either he isn't here, or his passive stealth tech has been reactivated. Could be the Tribe was able to restore some of his capabilities."

"DSS didn't report anything consistent with that."

"He escaped from jail and took down two agents and a cop. That doesn't sound like a bike messenger to me. They must have figured out some way to bring him back online – at least partially," Donald said.

"Get the helicopters in the air, stat. He's gone."

Azra bit back the anger that surged through him at the possibility that the target had managed to escape him. It was impossible. There was nowhere to go, and the first place they'd struck had been his last confirmed location – the Tribe headquarters, or whatever had passed for that laughable idea in the middle of this shithole.

Azra was well aware of the troubled origins of both the Tribe and his masters, but he didn't particularly care about any of it. He was a purpose-built machine who didn't trouble himself with ideological implications or the vagaries of one faction or another. All he knew was that his masters rewarded him with riches and spoils beyond imagination, and that his loyalty was his ticket to continuing to enjoy a life that would have been the envy of most heads of state. Anything he wished for, be it boys or girls, wealth, power, was his for the asking. If that required that he wipe out a community of parasites in some godforsaken desert, so be it.

Chapter 24

The rainstorm turned the gullies Veritas had been using to ascend into the foothills into raging washes of floodwater, and after three hours of riding through the chilly rain, they'd made it no more than seven or eight miles from the highway, to the top of the nearest mountains. They were freezing from the soaking and wind chill, and when the dark outline of an old pump station materialized out of the gloom, they eased to a stop, and Veritas climbed from the ATV.

He tried the door, but it was locked. Selena joined him and removed the small wallet with her lock picks and went to work on the bolt. After a few minutes, the lock surrendered to her efforts, and she pushed the steel door open and shined her flashlight into the interior.

Dirt and debris covered the floor, along with a few empty plastic beverage bottles and some half-rotted cardboard boxes filled with trash. A corner of the cinderblock roof had collapsed, and rain had collected on a third of the floor before draining out of the open doorway. She cocked her head and listened, and then turned to Veritas.

"It's abandoned. Doesn't seem like anyone's been here for years, judging by the silt on the dry area."

"Think the door's wide enough to get the ATV inside?"

"We can sure as hell try."

They pushed the ATV into the small building, and Veritas closed the door behind them. "We need to start a fire and dry our clothes, or we're going to catch pneumonia."

"Maybe we can soak a little of this garbage with gas."

"I can go forage for some wood. Even if it's wet, it'll dry out quickly over a fire, and then we can use it to keep it going." He eyed the hole in the roof. "Between that and the door, we won't asphyxiate. And with the storm, we don't have to worry about helicopters. They won't be able to see twenty yards in this soup." He frowned. "Don't suppose you have a lighter, do you?"

She walked to the ATV, opened the equipment pack, rummaged around, and removed a tiny butane lighter. "There are some bars if you're hungry."

"How about a knife or a hatchet or something?"

Selena withdrew a silver rectangle and tossed it to him. "Super tool. Should have a saw blade, or at least a serrated one."

"Let me see what I can find out there."

Veritas left in search of promising scrub, and Selena removed Moxie from the backpack and let him nose around. She fed him part of a bar and then did her best to clear the floor and sort the refuse into flammable and useless piles. When she finished, she walked into the rain and returned with rocks with which to make a fire pit near the wet section of floor.

Veritas entered with an armload of branches, and Moxie ran to him like he hadn't seen him in weeks.

Veritas smiled at the dog and then Selena. "They're green, but it's better than nothing."

He arranged a handful of them atop Selena's pile, and then moved to the ATV and soaked several strips of cardboard with gasoline. After placing them near the bottom of the heap, he used the lighter to ignite them with a flash. The scraps of paper caught, and soon the branches were crackling as they flamed to life.

Veritas shrugged out of his leather jacket and stripped off his shirt. His muscular tattooed torso glowed in the firelight as he looked around. He pushed the ATV as close as he dared to the fire, and draped his jacket and Jordan's borrowed shirt from one of the handles. He next removed his boots and set them by the fire pit and pulled off his jeans. "At least with all the rain we won't have any laundry worries for a few days," he said.

Selena removed her shirt and trousers and hung them from the other handle. If she was self-conscious of her near nudity, she didn't show it. She turned from the fire and looked at Veritas. "I'm freezing."

"Me too. It'll get better once our clothes are dry. Stick close to the fire. Once the rain stops, I'll get some more wood."

She glanced at her watch. "Five hours till dawn."

He lowered himself by the fire pit. "Which will bring a whole new set of problems. Biggest being, what do we do then?"

"Don't think I haven't thought about it," she said, and joined him. She leaned into him, and he could smell her wet skin and hair. "Don't get the wrong idea. This is just to stay warm."

He wrapped his arms around her shivering form and nodded. "Strictly business."

"Matter of survival."

"No question."

They both laughed nervously, the tension broken, and she relaxed in his arms. "We need to find another cell," she said. "There's one in Southern California. Jordan mentioned them several times."

"How do you find them if you don't even know where they are? Do you guys have meeting halls or something? Like Shriners or Masons?"

"We have a method of communicating," she said cryptically.

"How? I'd say the time for secrecy's over, Selena. We're on our own in the middle of nowhere with an army of black helicopters after us, not to mention the most powerful law enforcement agency in the country."

"If I can get to a computer, I can leave a message on SexUp," she said. "I post a new profile with several key words. They search it regularly."

He sighed. "Tell me you're joking. A teen hook-up site?"

She shrugged, and he held her tighter. "It's effective," she said. "We used to have to use newspaper classifieds, but since nobody reads anymore and paper's dead, we switched to the internet. The benefit of SexUp is that it's everywhere, so it doesn't attract suspicion."

SexUp had been created by a pair of high school students for easy and anonymous sexual encounters, and had gone viral five years earlier until it was now the fourth most popular site on the internet. Charges that it was a glorified prostitution conduit hadn't stuck, and the founders had become two of the richest celebrities in the world.

He thought for several minutes, watching the mesmerizing dance of the flames, keenly aware of Selena's skin against his and using all his self-control not to show it. His body betrayed him, and he shifted so she wasn't pressed against his abdomen.

"Sorry. Got a crick in my back," he said, hoping she hadn't felt his arousal.

"At least our shirts should be dry pretty soon," she said.

Veritas drew a deep breath and concentrated on anything but Selena's proximity. "Ben, my sponsor, mentioned someone in Washington who could explain everything to me. He told me the name of the town. The guy has a compound just outside it. That's going to be way easier to find, and nobody will be looking for us in the wilds of the Pacific Northwest. I say we head for Washington rather than hoping we can make contact with some anonymous cell in LA or wherever."

He felt her stiffen. "I don't know, Ver. The clock's ticking on the virus. Now that you know what's at stake…"

"No offense, but all I know is what Jordan and you told me. I'd kind of like to hear another perspective before I make the biggest decision of my life." He paused. "Besides, they obviously knew which building was Jordan's, and it follows they knew who he was, so I'm not as sure as you are that your cells aren't compromised. If we try to make it to a big city like Los Angeles or San Diego, they're going to have a lot more firepower than some rural area of Washington."

Selena's chest rose and fell as the minutes ticked by, and eventually she stirred from her half-slumber and pushed herself to her feet. "Fire's almost out," she announced. "And the rain's stopped."

She pulled on her top and felt her pants with a frown. Veritas stood and donned his shirt and his still-damp jeans. "At least my boots are dry. I'll scrounge up some more wood. Then we should try to get some sleep. I have a feeling tomorrow's going to be even longer than today."

Fifteen minutes later, the newly fueled fire was warming them again, and Selena was back in his arms, Moxie slumbering beside him.

"How do you propose we get to Washington?" she asked. "They're going to have an APB out for both of us, so it's not like we can just take a bus."

"You think they'll have roadblocks?"

"Maybe on the major freeways. Maybe not. Hard to say."

"They might stick to traffic cams rather than paralyzing the entire West Coast. Assuming that they don't think we're dead in one of the explosions."

"Don't underestimate them, Ver. You've seen what they're capable of. They'll mobilize all their resources to catch us."

"Maybe we can find a small plane. I don't suppose you know how to fly one, do you?"

She smiled. "My dad was a pilot. But it's been years since I went up with him."

He frowned. "You mentioned money isn't an issue. How much do you have access to?"

"I have a decent amount with me, and an anonymous digital wallet with a high balance. And cards. They aren't in my name. Shell corporations. Jordan issued us a bunch of them along with the wallets. Everybody's are different, and they're untraceable."

"Then we could theoretically charter a plane? Or buy a car?"

She yawned and placed a hand on his thigh, which didn't help his focus. "Theoretically. But you're public enemy number one, Veritas. Even a charter company will want to know who it's flying. Especially

with all the DSS regs in place. And that rules out buses or trains —
they all require ID, and they're packed with cameras."

"We'll figure it out tomorrow. Let's try to rest while we can, okay?
It'll be light out before we know it."

Selena exhaled and snuggled against Veritas's chest, and soon her
breathing slowed to a rhythmic pulsing that told him she was asleep.
He gently laid her on the floor with her knees to her chest and curled
himself around her. She didn't wake, but merely adjusted her legs so
she was melded to him, using his forearm as her pillow.

His last thought as he drifted off was that it figured he'd finally
met someone he was attracted to in more than a cursory way, and the
chances of them surviving to the next sunset without being captured
or killed were slim to none.

Chapter 25

Selena jolted awake at the sound of a helicopter. The fire had died and a chill had settled over the bunker. Veritas was already sitting up, his eyes alert, his gun in hand as the roar of the aircraft rattled the door and filled the air with dust.

Veritas held a finger to his lips as a light played over the exterior of the pump house, the white glare seeping around the edges of the door and through the hole in the roof. Selena nodded, her eyes wide, and chambered a round in her pistol.

"The rain must have eradicated our tracks," Veritas whispered.

"This is probably just a fishing expedition – routine check," she agreed.

"Hope so," Veritas said, wincing at the roar from the turbine.

The door handle turned a half inch as someone tried it. Veritas had locked the handle and the deadbolt, so there was little chance it would open without a key. Something slammed into the door hard enough to shake it on its hinges, and then a voice called out, "Place is abandoned. The door's jammed."

Selena and Veritas sat frozen until the helicopter moved away. Selena checked the time, her expression drawn. "Well, that was a refreshing two hours of sleep."

"Think they'll be back?"

"Probably not. But if they're searching this soon after the storm, it's not good news for us. It'll make it hard to move after it's light out."

"We can always spend the day here and travel at night."

"That's not a terrible idea, except that the next patrol may decide to look through the roof, in which case we're dead meat. We can't chance it."

"But if they're flying patrols…"

"We'll hear them from a ways off. Besides, they're likely working a grid pattern so they don't go over the same ground. Once they're finished with one area, they'll move to the next. If I'm right, that means this one's probably safe for a while."

"Probably. Not sure I like that word." He frowned. "If we stay here, we're sitting ducks. It's probably smart to put as much distance as we can between us and Burning Man."

"Which sounds fine except we have no idea where we're going."

He shrugged. "We'll play it by ear."

They were on the trail again five minutes later, bouncing along a gulch with only a few inches of water coursing along the base. The predawn sky was clear, the clouds having blown west, and the air was crisp and clean, with the snap of altitude in every breath they took. The ravine drifted in an easterly direction, and the horizon brightened with a salmon glow as they came over a ridge.

Veritas braked to a stop and pointed at a scattering of buildings near the dark basin of a pit mine.

"See that?" he asked.

"What?"

"Looks to me like an airstrip. And that building at the end? It's big enough to be a hangar. You said you could fly, right?"

"Not exactly. I told you my dad used to take me up all the time. I mean, if it's a prop plane, I can probably figure it out."

"Then that's what we'll do. Assuming the FAA or whatever won't notice a stolen plane flying across Oregon and Washington."

"Not if we stay low. Drug smugglers use clandestine airstrips all the time. They evade radar by hugging the trees."

"And you know this…"

She smirked. "I'm a cop, Veritas. We know stuff like that. It's my job." She hesitated. "Or at least it was."

Veritas goosed the throttle and they skirted the barbed-wire fence until they were near the hangar. Signs posted just inside the perimeter warned that the compound was private property and that trespassers would be shot. The buildings were dark, any residents asleep, and when Veritas stopped ten yards from the hangar and shut off the engine, the only sound was the low moan of the wind through rock formations near the mine.

They dismounted, and Selena nudged Veritas in the ribs. "Still have that super tool? It's got a mean wire cutter at the base of the pliers. That should make short work of the fence."

He looked around the grounds. "What is that? Some kind of gun range and…obstacle course?"

She nodded. "There are a lot of antigovernment types out here. Prepper camps, survivalist communities, crypto miners, you name it. Ever since the government outlawed crypto mining, rogue outfits have sprung up wherever they can install large enough solar arrays without attracting attention."

He nodded. "Looks like everyone's still asleep. Let's do this before they wake up."

Veritas removed the super tool from his pocket and approached the fence. The wire was thick, but the snipper sliced through it like butter, and in less than a minute there was a gap big enough for them to get through.

"Grab the equipment pack from the ATV. We may need it later," Selena said, and Veritas obliged, slipping one of the pouch's straps over his shoulder. They trotted toward the possible hangar, crossing the ground quickly. Veritas noticed that even though he was running on empty and had sustained a concussion, his body seemed oddly energized; the fatigue he should have felt was a minor irritation rather than debilitating.

When they reached the building, Veritas pointed to the roll-up door. "It's a hangar, all right."

"Let's hope there's a plane inside. And that it has a full tank."

They crept around to the side of the building, where an access door with a frosted window faced the breaking dawn. Veritas tried the knob and shook his head.

"Locked."

She felt for her lock picks and slid her pistol into her waistband. The lock posed no obstacle and popped open in under thirty seconds. Selena pushed the door open and peered into the gloom before turning back to Veritas with a triumphant look.

"It's a plane, all right."

He scowled. "From what, World War One? It looks ancient."

Selena smiled in the darkness. "Hardly. Looks more like late eighties."

"So it's over twice as old as I am? That's reassuring."

They entered the hangar and walked to the plane's single big prop. "Seems like it's in good shape," Selena whispered. "Someone's kept it maintained. Looks like it did duty for cargo – you can see the rear door's been widened and most of the windows sealed."

Selena opened the cockpit door and looked inside. She twisted to Veritas, who was right behind her. "And the keys are in it. Let me check the fuel, and if it's got some, we're off to the races."

She climbed into the cockpit and powered on the instruments. After a quick glance at the gauges, she depressed the pedals and looked to Veritas. "I hope this is like riding a bike. My dad used to let me fly, but I never actually took off or landed. Just once we were in the air."

"Taking off is probably the most important part besides landing, and you haven't done either."

"What are you worried about? You've got hundreds of hours behind the console, right?"

"This thing's prehistoric. The planes in the game are jets."

She pointed at the gloom. "See that cart? It's a battery assist for starting the engine. Wheel it over here and I'll see if I can figure out how to plug it in."

Veritas did as asked, and Selena hopped from the cockpit and studied the underside of the nose before nodding to herself and connecting the heavy cable. She pointed to the roll-up door.

"Let's open it up and get out of here."

156

Veritas heaved on the chain to one side of the door, and the panel rolled upward with a clatter. A low whine sounded from the plane, and then the motor coughed to life with a deafening growl. Selena jumped to the ground and disconnected the starter cable, and then motioned for Veritas to climb in beside her. They were in their seats within moments, and Selena frowned at the controls before adjusting her chair and giving the engine some throttle.

"We have gas?" Veritas yelled over the engine.

"Three-quarters full. Should get us to Washington. What is it, maybe five or six hundred miles?"

"I have no idea."

She tapped the GPS mounted in the console. "Once we're airborne, I'll program that thing and see exactly how far. Buckle up."

Veritas nodded and strapped in. "You really think you can get us off the ground?"

"My dad explained the process a million times. A prop plane like this probably lifts off at around eighty or ninety miles per hour, and cruises at one sixty or thereabouts. We'll burn more fuel flying low, but that can't be helped."

"Can I do anything?"

"Pray."

Lights blinked on inside the low-slung buildings, and Selena frowned in concentration as she worked the pedals and throttle. They taxied to the dirt strip, and she did a final inspection of the instruments.

Veritas tapped his window. "That doesn't look good."

Men were pouring from the buildings, rifles and shotguns in hand. Selena nodded once and pushed the throttle forward, and the plane leapt like a fighting dog freed from the leash. The men were running in their direction, but were too far away to do much damage – at least that was Veritas's hope.

"How long to get in the air?" he yelled over the roaring engine.

She eyed the speedo. "Maybe ten more seconds."

A voice screamed from behind them, "Shut it down or I'll blow your heads off."

Veritas twisted in his seat to see an unshaven man with red eyes pointing a large revolver at the back of Selena's chair from the rear of the plane.

"Selena, he's got a gun," Veritas warned.

"Shit," she exclaimed, and backed off on the fuel.

The plane slowed and she braked to a stop, and as the men with rifles came running, the one with the revolver cocked the hammer with an ugly grin. "You picked the wrong outfit to rob," he growled. Veritas could smell stale alcohol and halitosis reeking from the man, and considered trying for the pistol in his waistband before the gunman kicked the base of his seat. "Make any moves and you'll get a bullet through your spine. Don't even think about it." He stared holes through the back of Selena's seat. "You too, missy. I got no problem spraying the windshield with what little brains you got. Reach for your peashooter and it'll be the last thing you do."

Chapter 26

Robots that resembled large steel wolves roamed the dirt streets, rooting out the rest of the camp survivors the mercenaries had failed to find. The residents were being held in a pen, watched over by armed guards who had instructions to shoot anyone who tried to escape. All appeared frightened, and many of them had lost friends or family in the shoot-out that had spanned over an hour and left hundreds dead and many of the camp's dwellings destroyed.

So far the effort had yielded nothing. No body had been found, and nobody had admitted to seeing the target or the woman he was with. The robots were programmed to identify the chip that had been implanted in the target's cranium, so there could be no mistake. A proximity scan had turned up no trace, and Azra's patience was wearing thin. His instinct was to butcher everyone still alive in the most brutal manner possible, one by one, in the hopes that it prodded the others into remembering something that would be of help, and it was only the knowledge that his masters would be displeased if he gave in to that desire that held him in check.

Lars approached, his features concealed by a black balaclava beneath his helmet. "We pulled a survivor from the pyramid, but he's in bad shape."

"A survivor? Is it…him?"

"Negative. This is a Caucasian male who's ten years too old to be the target."

Azra's eyes narrowed. "Is he the only survivor?"

"Yes. The missiles destroyed most of the structure, but he survived because he was in the bathroom. The shower wall collapsed on detonation, but whatever they built that area out of didn't catch fire. He's got pretty substantial internal injuries, though. Our medic gave him a once-over, and he's not long for this world."

"Where is he?"

"It isn't safe to move him. He's over in the triage area."

"Take me to him."

At least two dozen wounded lay on blankets or pieces of tent spread around the Burning Man central gathering area, groaning or crying out. Two black-clad gunmen watched them without reaction while a third paused periodically and checked a victim's vitals.

The third man stiffened when he saw Lars nearing with Azra.

"Where's the one from the pyramid?" Azra demanded.

"Over there."

Azra followed the medic to where Jordan was lying on a horse blanket, blinking away pain. Azra stared at him for a long moment and then crouched beside him and inspected his wounds. Half of his face was blistered and burned, and his left arm and leg were obviously broken. Bone protruded from his shirt, and Azra studied the compound rib fractures with the detached expression of a lab tech eyeing a test tube.

"Where are they?" Azra whispered.

Jordan tried to focus on Azra's face, but the pain was too great. He moaned and his eyes flickered shut.

Azra grabbed Jordan's broken arm and gave it a vicious wrench. Jordan's scream trailed off into a groan, and he passed out. Azra stood and kicked him out of frustration, and then turned to the medic. "Pump him full of whatever you need to, but I want him talking, and soon."

The medic nodded wordlessly, and Azra was about to snap at him again when his earbud crackled and a voice came over the comm.

"We found something."

"Where are you?"

"At one of the wrecked buildings. I'll be back at the helos shortly."

"Make it fast. It'll be light out in a few minutes."

"Roger that."

Azra stalked back to the helicopters and waited for his man to arrive. When he did, he cut to the chase without delay.

"We talked to a survivor who said that the sewage system runs to a treatment area several hundred yards to the north. He helped build it. And he said that there's more than just black water that runs there – apparently there's an access tunnel. He took us to where it ends in the camp, and the building's been destroyed. Looks like an explosion."

"Damn," Azra blurted, realization dawning on him. "Where's this treatment pond? Get a squad of six men and show me. Now."

"We're thin on the ground."

"Then you, Lars, and I will go. Double time."

They found the vault with the ATVs in minutes. Azra was livid – the slot of the missing one was obvious – and he tapped his earbud as he glared at the desert sand at his feet, ignoring the reek of the holding pond.

"I want satellite of the area and an estimate of the likeliest route someone on an ATV would have taken from a point I'm sending momentarily." He thumbed the satellite phone to its map function and recorded the coordinates before transmitting it to his base, where AI would tell him where to look next. He was marching back to the camp when his phone vibrated. The imagery had three routes outlined in red, yellow, and green, with green the likeliest.

When Azra reached the helos, he barked orders at the pilots. "I'm sending everyone a map. I want all resources on tracing the routes. They're on an ATV. They can't have gotten far with the weather and the police patrols. Assume they stayed off the roads and went overland."

He turned to Lars. "Round everyone up. We need to get out of here. The media and the locals will be all over this once it's light out."

Lars hurried off to relay Azra's orders, and Azra surveyed the destruction. He tapped his earbud. "Medic, I want our prisoner loaded up. There may be something we can get out of him yet."

"What about the rest of them?" the medic asked.

"I don't care. Let them die."

"Roger that. I'll have him there within a few minutes. But it's a bad idea to move him."

"We can't do anything about that. Just do it. If he doesn't make it, we'll toss his carcass out of the helo on the way home."

Chapter 27

December 1917
Étaples, France

The troop hospital at the base camp in Étaples, a notorious seaside staging depot for British and Allied troops headed to the front, was overcrowded with wounded soldiers and those suffering from respiratory failure from gas attacks in the trenches. The war had been long and brutal, with the cost in human suffering astounding to combatants of both sides, and the physicians and nurses who tended to the mass of damaged men gathered in the packed wards were subjected to a stream of misery that was seemingly without end.

Chemical burns and amputations were commonplace among the wounded; the medical techniques available were crude and only marginally effective, man's efficiency at inflicting damage having far outstripped his ability to treat its result. Twelve-hour shifts for the medical staff were commonplace in rooms steeped in death, and hardly an hour went by where a cart bearing corpses headed for the cemetery didn't depart with a full load.

A whippet-thin man in a long white physician's coat strode along one of the aisles, his leather satchel in hand, pausing occasionally at a bedside to inspect a chart. He looked around each time and, when he was sure nobody was paying any attention, felt in his bag and retrieved an old-fashioned perfume atomizer and sprayed some of the men with it.

"What's that, Doc?" asked one of the patients, a young man with bandages over his eyes.

"It's to help you breathe, my lad," he answered. "After what the Hun threw at you, you can use all the help you can get."

"Too right. Feels like my lungs are on fire. Damn mustard gas."

"You're lucky you made it out."

"Reckon there's no chance I'll ever see again, though, eh?"

"You never know. For now, rest and recover. Nobody can say what Providence has in store for any of us."

He continued down the aisle, repeating his ministrations, and then exited from the burn ward and continued through the next one until he'd passed through them all.

When he was finished, he marched with squared shoulders to the empty mess hall and sprayed the remainder of his atomizer on the dining tables before slipping it back in his bag and making for the double doors. Once outside, he breathed deeply, ignoring the faint tang of rotting seaweed and dead fish, and continued to the camp gates, his expression telling anyone who cared to look that he was deep in thought. The guards saluted as he left and strode to a waiting automobile. The driver stepped from behind the wheel and opened the cabin door for him, and he sat down heavily on the rear seat.

A small, plump man with a waxed mustache and impeccably combed hair smiled at him from the other seat.

"Mission accomplished?"

"Exactly as you outlined. I hit the mess hall for some extra coverage."

"Excellent. This flu should spread like wildfire in these conditions. With over a hundred thousand troops passing through here every week, it will propagate to the four corners." The plump man sat back. "We're also disseminating it in America, at the main troop training camp in the Midwest, and in China…Australia…"

"Taking no chances," the doctor said. "Thank God you've got an antidote. From what you describe of the symptoms…"

"A regrettable side effect, but a necessary evil. We estimate that it will eliminate ten to twenty percent of the population by the time it's done. But there's no way around it, and we're on a schedule."

"As long as I've been inoculated, as well as my loved ones, I have no issue." The doctor hesitated. "In fact, when am I to receive the vaccine?"

"Shortly," the plump man said, and indicated something through the darkened car window. "You haven't told anyone about this, correct?"

The doctor frowned and leaned forward to try to make out what his companion had pointed at. When he turned back, the little man was holding a nickel-plated revolver with a steady hand.

"Sorry, old boy, but we know you told your wife about a coming big payday," the man said. "That wasn't part of the agreement. You were told what the penalty for disobedience would be."

The doctor's eyes saucered and he held up his hands. "I said nothing about the virus. Nothing."

The driver put the car in gear and the big engine revved as he negotiated the muddy road. The two gunshots from the cabin were almost inaudible from outside the vehicle, and the car proceeded on its way, toward the sea, where the driver would hose out the interior while his master attended to more pressing matters.

Within three months the Spanish flu, so named because Spain, unlike the combatants, was neutral in the conflict and had reported accurately on the spread, would earn the dubious honor of being the worst outbreak of viral influenza in modern history.

Chapter 28

"Whatcha got there, Chris?" one of the men with rifles called out.

"Couple of plane thieves," Chris shouted back.

"We can explain," Veritas protested.

Chris jabbed the back of his seat with his pistol. "I'm sure you can. Meantime, I want you to toss your guns on the floor back here, or my buddies and I will use you for target practice."

Veritas looked over at Selena and sighed. "You want to go first, Selena?"

Selena slowly withdrew her gun from her belt with her index finger and thumb, and slid it back along the aisle between the seats.

"Now you, big boy," Chris ordered.

Veritas did the same, and Chris kicked both weapons into the depths of the hold. "That it? Nothing strapped to a leg or anything?"

"That's all we have."

"All right. I'm going to back up, and you're going to open the cockpit door and get out with your hands up. Nice and easy. My boys don't appreciate being woken up so early, so they probably got itchy trigger fingers."

"This isn't what it looks like," Selena said.

166

"Yeah, I can totally see that. It's nothing at all like you two stealing a plane worth a small fortune. I've got it all wrong," Chris said, sarcasm dripping from every word.

"We have a good reason," Veritas protested.

"Oh, I'm sure you do. You needed a plane and didn't want to disturb anyone. Got it. Now get out of the plane before I decide to drill you myself."

Selena climbed from the pilot's seat and Veritas followed. The men trained their rifles on them, anger clouding their features. "You picked the wrong bunch, lady," snarled a burly man with a pump shotgun.

"We had no choice," Veritas said.

The burly man clubbed Veritas with the butt of his gun, and Veritas staggered backward but didn't fall. The man appraised him, and his lips curled in a sneer. "Shut up. We'll deal with you once we've had coffee. For now, keep your trap zipped or I'll beat you to a bloody pulp. You got it?"

Veritas nodded wordlessly. Chris hopped from the plane with their pistols in hand and spoke to one of his men. "Buzz, take them to the container and search them before you stick them inside. I need some food. It's too early for this shit."

"You got it," Buzz, the burly man, said. "Let's go. Chop-chop."

After a thorough frisking by one of the gunmen as the rest stood by with weapons aimed at their heads, the big man pushed Selena and Veritas into a shipping container near one of the buildings. The door slammed shut behind them, and the bolt clattered as it was locked in place. Veritas probed his skull with his fingers before sliding down with his back against the steel wall.

"Our luck that some drunk was sleeping it off in the plane," Selena said, and sat beside him with a sigh. "That's one for the record books. How's your head?"

"Not so bad, which surprises me."

"It's the stuff I gave you. It's restored some of your power. Too bad not all of it. You could have taken them all with one hand, from what I've heard."

"So now what?"

"We need to get a feel for what these guys are all about. They're heavily armed and have a compound in the middle of nowhere. For all we know, they could be Luds."

Veritas frowned. "We're pretty much screwed, then. Just a matter of time until DSS or whoever catches up to us."

"We'll figure something out."

"Sure we will," Veritas said.

He closed his eyes and listened intently, hoping to hear anything that would give him an idea of what the gunmen had planned for them. After a few minutes of silence, he gave up and closed his eyes. Selena scooted down and laid her head in his lap, but he decided not to protest given the circumstances.

"You have a girlfriend?" she asked, just as he was drifting off.

"Nobody steady. Which you'd know since you were watching me."

"I was brought into this a half hour before I showed up at the hospital, Ver. I didn't know anything about you until I got the call from Jordan explaining about you having had an accident."

"Need to know, right?"

"Mock it all you want, but it's a smart way to run a cell."

"I'm sorry you got dragged into this. Now there's two of us who're completely screwed."

"I signed up for this, Ver. It's my life. I know you didn't, so I don't blame you for being bitter. I would be too."

"Yeah. My dead mom's an imposter, everything I thought I knew about myself is a lie, and oh, by the way, the most powerful miscreants in the world want to skin me alive if DSS doesn't put a bullet between my shoulders first. That could make a guy bitter." He paused. "What about you?"

"What about me, what?"

"You have a boyfriend? Husband?"

She laughed. "No. When you're active like I am with the Tribe, you don't pair up. Especially now. Who'd want to bring a child into the world, knowing what's coming?"

"I didn't ask if you had a family, just a boyfriend."

"Nobody steady. Wasn't that what you said?"

They fell silent, and Veritas slipped into a restive sleep, his head throbbing like a painful metronome with each beat of his pulse.

When the locking mechanism rattled, they both started awake and scrambled to their feet. The steel door opened, and Veritas shielded his eyes from the sun.

"All right. Come on out of there. Time to spout your lies before we deal with you," Chris said.

"A fair trial before we hang you, huh?" Veritas asked.

"Wasn't me trying to rip off the plane," Chris parried. "You got nobody but yourself to blame for this." He indicated a doorway on one of the nearby buildings with a wave of his pistol. "Thataway."

Selena and Veritas approached the door and waited for one of the gunmen to open it.

"Inside," one of the men ordered.

They filed in and found themselves in a large room lined with stainless steel service tables on one side and two metal folding chairs in the center, with a hodgepodge of seats and sofas clogging the other side of the room.

"Sit," Chris ordered, and they did. Veritas's eyes flitted to an American flag suspended from a pole near the doorway, and then to Selena, whose expression was unreadable. The gunmen arranged themselves on the sofas, and Chris seated himself in an overstuffed recliner, gun in his lap.

"Okay. Explain yourselves. And no bullshit," Chris ordered.

Selena nodded. "Do you get the news up here? Internet or TV? Radio?"

"What's that got to do with anything?" Buzz asked.

"I'm wondering if word's gotten out about the attack on Burning Man," she said, her tone reasonable.

"What the hell are you talking about?" another man demanded. "Who'd wanna attack that bunch of street trash?"

"Last night, six attack helicopters flew into Burning Man and launched missiles before dropping an attack force that massacred

169

most of the camp. We fought back, of course, but these were trained professionals with silenced automatic weapons. We had no chance. I'm wondering what spin the media's putting on it, if they're even reporting on it yet."

Chris's gaze darted to one of the men, who nodded and stood. He crossed the room and left, and Chris resumed glaring at them. "Al there's gonna check on that. What are you saying happened?"

"We escaped," Veritas said. "Rode that ATV all the way from Black Rock Desert in last night's rainstorm. We saw your setup and figured there might be a plane in the hangar. We were trying to get out of here. We didn't mean you any harm. We're being hunted by the group that murdered so many at Burning Man."

"What group? This sounds like some kind of shaggy-dog story to me," Chris said.

Veritas indicated Selena beside him. "I'm Veritas. Her name's Selena. She's a San Francisco cop. We had to duck out of the city two nights ago. We thought we'd lost them, but apparently not for long."

Buzz's eyes widened and he stared at Selena. "You're a cop?"

"A long way from home," Chris said.

Selena nodded. "We're being hunted by several groups. Veritas is wanted by DSS on some trumped-up charges. They tried to kidnap him from my custody, and I fought back. They lost that round. But they're holding a grudge, and now we're both marked."

Chris frowned. "You said several groups. DSS is one."

"You won't believe it," Veritas said.

"Try me," Chris fired back.

"They're called the Brethren," Selena said. "Used to be called the Illuminati. Which supposedly doesn't exist. But it does. It's alive and well, and it wants Veritas more than you can imagine. It's behind the attack on Burning Man. They're willing to kill whoever they have to in order to find him."

Al returned and took his seat. "Internet says terrorists attacked Burning Man. The Luds."

"That's complete crap," Selena said. "Figures. The media's controlled by the Brethren. So's DSS. They'll pin it on the Luds, or whoever they can. Typical."

Chris didn't react. "Why were you stealing the plane?"

"We need to get to Washington State. There's someone there who can help us," Veritas said.

"Washington? Where in Washington?"

"McCleary. Near Olympia."

Chris nodded. "You figured you'd fly there yourself with DSS looking for you?"

"We didn't have much choice. If they catch us, we're dead," Veritas stated flatly.

"So you say," Buzz growled.

"Why else do you think we'd be riding an ATV through a rainstorm into the most uninhabited area around?" Veritas countered. "And why do you think we'd risk breaking into an armed compound to steal a plane? Simple. Because the alternative's worse."

"Why do DSS and the Brethren want you so damn bad?" Chris asked.

Veritas sighed and looked to Selena. She inclined her head toward Veritas. "He's some kind of specialized soldier they created. But he got away."

Chris's expression darkened. "A deserter?"

Veritas shook his head. "No. Part of a secret program they decided to cancel. When they shut it down, they eliminated all the evidence – or so they thought. I was the last of the evidence, but I managed to escape."

Buzz snorted. "Tale keeps getting taller and taller, don't it?"

"It's true," Selena said. "He could have taken you all down without breaking a sweat if he'd wanted to."

"Hogwash," Buzz said and got to his feet. He handed Al his shotgun and pistol and walked to the center of the room to glower at Veritas. "I'm an ex-Ranger, douchebag. Your story's complete bullshit."

Veritas looked to Selena, who pursed her lips and nodded.

Veritas handed her the backpack with Moxie and then shot from the chair at blinding speed. Before Buzz could react, he'd knocked him to the floor and gripped his throat. Buzz's eyes bugged out as Veritas squeezed, and then he released the big man and stepped back. "Sorry. I tried not to hurt you," he said, and offered his hand.

Buzz reached for it and then sweep-kicked Veritas's legs. Veritas barely seemed to move, and Buzz's boot caught nothing but air.

"We done?" Veritas asked, a blank smile on his face.

The room was silent as Buzz struggled to his feet and limped back to his seat. Al handed him back his weapons, and he grunted a thanks.

Buzz and Chris exchanged a glance. Buzz nodded and stood again. "It's your call, Chris. Your plane, your sandbox, your rules." He tromped to the door and swung it open, and the rest of the gunmen followed him out.

"You stay put," Chris said. He rose and made for the door, pistol now in his hip holster.

Selena cradled Moxie while she and Veritas sat wordlessly. After several minutes, she reached over and took his hand. "However this turns out, that was kind of awesome."

"I felt bad. He was so slow. It was like he was moving through Jell-O or something." He exhaled. "I hope I didn't hurt him."

She smiled. "That's what makes you different, Ver. Nobody else would care at this point."

Chris returned alone and sat back in his chair.

"Got a son DSS took away about a year ago. He was living in Vegas. They said he was involved in some terrorist crap because he didn't buy into the government's lies. Said he was a domestic terrorist even though he didn't do anything. Same logic that lets 'em drone a family wherever they want without a trial, I guess. Somebody died and made 'em God, and if you fight it, they drag you off." He stopped for a moment, lost in thought. "The reason I'm telling you is because I got no love for them. Matter of fact, none of us up here do. We got out of the system a while ago because we saw this coming. The country's being run by fascists. Worse than the Soviets were. You buck the system, they disappear you." He spat on the hardwood floor. "That sure as hell isn't what I fought and almost died for. And now they got my boy, and they told my attorney they don't have to tell us anything, that they can hold him without trial long as they want, that he's got no rights 'cause he's a terrorist. Which they haven't proved. They don't have to."

Selena nodded slowly. "I'm sorry. That's horrible."

"It's a common story. The bastards do whatever they want, and there's no way to fight 'em. They got the guns, the money, the judges in their pockets. I always figured there was somebody pulling the strings. Brethren or Illuminati's as good as any, I guess, by way of explanation. Doesn't really matter who they are. They sure been at it a long time, haven't they?"

Selena nodded again. "That they have. Under many different names."

"I thought the Illuminati were a bunch of Germans playing secret society a few centuries ago," Chris said.

Selena cleared her throat. "The original Illuminati were. But they got absorbed into the Freemasons, and at the very top of that group were the ancestors of the ones we're up against today. The names change, but the agenda doesn't. I'd guess 99 percent of Masons have no idea what the top secret tier are actually up to or stand for. That's by design. Their power's always been in their ability to mislead and pretend to be other than they are. It's their defining trait. That misdirection is key in their ability to convince most that there's no conspiracy, ever, and that anyone who thinks so is nuts. As long as they can achieve that – and they have – nobody questions things skeptically for fear of being ostracized. They own the media and control the government, so their power to make life miserable for anyone who starts nosing around is very real."

"As my son discovered." Chris took a deep breath. "I've been waiting for this whole shit show to come apart for a while now. It feels like it's going to any minute, you know?"

Selena nodded. "I know. I'm sorry we tried to take your plane. We really had no choice."

"Apology accepted. If you're telling the truth, you didn't. And I believe you. Not just because superman over here was able to put down Buzz faster than black ice. I just got a feeling about you two. You're not thieves."

Veritas shifted in his seat. "What's your deal with this compound? Seems like you got a pretty good setup. Lot of guns and guys who know how to use them."

"I bought this land when nobody in their right mind wanted it. The mine had been exhausted, and the ground was toxic from the chemicals. But I figured if things ever went critical, it would be better to be in a defendable area a long way from anywhere. So I bought it for a song, and then got some like-minded people together who saw which way things were headed. Everyone's ex-military. I'm Air Force. Buzz there was a three-tour Ranger. The rest are Navy, infantry, SEALs, you name it. But man, I have to say I've never seen anyone get over on Buzz. He's tougher than snot, and you pimp-slapped him good."

"So you're…what? Preppers?" Veritas asked.

"You could say that. We're the government's worst nightmare is what we are. They trained us, but we figured out what they're up to, and we ain't having any. And we got ordnance for days."

"You think that might have something to do with why they took your son?" Veritas asked.

"I don't think so, other than I raised him right. Let's just say it's hard to put one over on him. My hunch is he mouthed off to the wrong person about something – he was part of a group that was against this whole chip thing as a surveillance state rights grab, and he also was vocal about the constant wars. Could have been anything. That boy never learned to keep his trap shut."

"He's not a member of the Luds or some subversive group they might be targeting?" Selena asked.

"Shit, lady, the Luds got nothing on us. Not to brag, but we're some genuine badasses. We could take down half of Vegas anytime we want. Only reason we haven't is we don't want a bunch of innocent people to get hurt, which they would if we pulled the plug. But at some point it's got to happen. Things can't continue like this."

Veritas stood. "So…what? Are we free to go? Because they're not going to give up, and I don't want to be a sitting duck when they come."

"You have any idea how to fly that thing? Didn't sound like it from what I heard. And your friend here was about as rough behind the wheel as a first-day student."

"It's a little older than what I've flown in," Selena admitted.

He nodded. "All analog except for the GPS and the autopilot. Not a lot to go wrong with it. I maintain it myself. I'd fly it to Hawaii and back if it had the range. A real nuts-and-bolts plane." He grinned, displaying yellow teeth, his eyes still bloodshot. "I guess I'm saying I could give you a lift. It'd be an adventure."

"You would?" Selena exclaimed.

"Not much action going on here. Wouldn't mind a chance to jab one in DSS's eye. Any friend of theirs is no friend of mine."

"That would be...awesome. One of your guys took my money, digital wallet, and cards, but if you'll return them, we could pay whatever you want," Selena offered.

He waved a hand. "Money's no problem, although if you want to throw some cash at gas, that wouldn't hurt. My time's my own. Part of being a free man."

"Name a price and it's yours."

"We'd probably burn...seventy-five gallons each way, maybe less since we're going light. Twenty bucks a gallon for aviation fuel..."

"Three grand sounds like it will cover it, right? Done deal."

"Well, you two look like you could eat, and maybe choke down some coffee. Grab some grub and we'll give your stuff back and then we can git. No reason to tempt fate if you're right about them looking for you."

Veritas's forehead creased. "Oh, we're right. And we might want to get that ATV out of sight. Or better yet, lose it somewhere it'll never be found."

Chris smiled again. "The mine's got quite a bit of water in it after all the rain."

Veritas held his gaze and returned the smile. "Accidents happen."

Chapter 29

Selena and Veritas were finishing up a breakfast of fresh eggs and biscuits with Chris when Al barged through the door with a wild look in his eyes.

"There's a group of armed men making their way up the hill. We spotted them when we were ditching the ATV," he said.

Chris dropped his fork with a clatter and stood. "Time to boogie."

"They must have followed the ATV tracks from the pump station," Selena said. "But how did they trace us to there? The rain should have washed everything away."

"Doesn't matter," Veritas said. "What does is that they found us."

Chris looked to Al. "Tell the men we've got company. You know what to do."

"This is it, isn't it?" Al asked.

"Maybe. Maybe not. Depends on what they do. Don't fire unless fired upon, or if they trespass. Then we're within our legal rights unless they produce a warrant."

"They can claim special circumstance if it's DSS," Selena said.

"Not in Nevada, they can't. Courts here don't hold to the feds running roughshod over state's rights," Chris countered. "Come on. We need to get the plane in the air before they show themselves."

Chris scooped up a two-way radio and led them to the exit. Buzz handed Veritas a backpack with their guns and Selena's stuff in it while she gathered up Moxie, and they ran across the open ground to the hangar and were in the plane's cockpit in a flash. The hangar's roll-up door was open, and Veritas climbed through the cargo hatch and into the rear of the fuselage. Chris lowered himself into the pilot's seat and slid on a pair of headphones, and motioned to Selena to sit beside him. "No charge for the lesson," he said, and then started the engine.

"They have helicopters," Veritas warned. "Armed ones. We saw them fire missiles in Burning Man."

Chris nodded as though the information was expected. "Then I've got a hell of a surprise for them."

"What?"

"You'll see. I've been working on it for a few years. Putting my engineering skills to use." He turned to Veritas. "Strap in. This might get ugly before long."

"What does that mean?" Veritas asked.

"It means I'm going to do everything possible to keep from getting shot down, and if you aren't secure, you're liable to break your neck."

"Don't suppose there's a parachute back here?" Veritas said.

"Buckle up."

Chris taxied out of the hangar, his face as calm as a churchgoer's, while Selena scanned the brush line. "There," she said, pointing to an area of fence. "Looks like a half dozen. Their black stands out against the terrain."

Chris's radio screeched, and Buzz's voice came over the air. "We're in position. Maybe they'll back off. They don't have any right to come onto the property."

"Don't count on it. But remember what I said – no shooting unless they shoot first or trespass."

"Shit. They spotted us," Buzz said.

"Send Al out and see what they want," Chris instructed. "Ask to see ID and a warrant."

"Roger that."

The plane bounced along the dirt strip toward the far end. The wind had picked up and now was blowing steadily at fifteen or so knots from the direction of the hangar. They were approaching the turning basin when the radio crackled again, and Buzz's voice rang from the speaker.

"The bastards shot Al. Didn't even hesitate. And you got choppers incoming."

"Take them out. Time to put my surprise to the test."

Gunfire echoed off the foothills as Buzz and his men opened up on the black-clad gunmen with automatic rifles on full auto. Chris continued past the turning basin, and Selena grabbed his arm. "What are you doing?"

"Got a stop to make. Hold your horses. Won't be but a minute."

He stopped the plane by a small cinderblock structure with heavy power lines running to it from one of the nearby towers. He leapt from the cockpit and ran to it as dirt fountained around him – one of the shooters had spotted them and was firing on his position, but at the long range against a moving target, he wasn't having any success. Chris ducked into the structure and returned a few seconds later. Veritas cringed and ducked when three rounds punched through the fuselage of the plane and light streamed through the holes, and was calling out to Selena in warning when she eased the throttle forward and the plane began to move. Chris ran alongside before hooking his hand around the doorframe and pulling himself into the pilot's seat. He slammed the door closed and increased the speed, and then executed a bumpy turn on the grassy field, foregoing the turning basin in favor of expediency.

"They're shooting at us," Veritas warned.

"I saw that. Lucky for us we're too far away for any accuracy."

"What were you doing?"

"You'll see. We got sixty seconds."

"Until what?" Veritas yelled.

Chris grinned. "All hell breaks loose."

Selena pointed through the windshield at the sky. "Crap. Three choppers. See them?"

Chris nodded, and his expression didn't change. "Sure do. They look pretty new, don't they?"

"How would I know?"

He slammed the throttle forward and the plane surged ahead. "You'll find out right around the time we're in the air."

"They'll shoot us down."

"Hang on," he said as the plane picked up speed, bucking and bouncing like a bronco over the washboard strip.

The handheld squawked something indecipherable, and Chris reached out and switched it off before returning both hands to the controls. His eyes roamed over the instruments every few seconds, and when the airspeed indicator had passed his desired mark, he pointed the nose at the sky.

The helicopters were closing on them as the plane lifted over the brush at the end of the runway, and Selena swore softly. "We're not going to make it."

"Bullshit," Chris said with a cackle.

Back on the ground, the concrete structure blew apart in a thousand pieces, and the helicopters lurched like drunks on the deck of a ship in rough seas before plummeting straight down and crashing into the rocky ground near the mine. Two of the three caught fire when they crashed, and the third bounced twice before teetering over, crushed like a soda can by the drop.

Veritas screamed in pain and gripped his head. "What the—" he exclaimed, and then blacked out.

Selena twisted to look at him and then at Chris.

"What did you do?"

"Flux compression generator bomb. Tested a few of them, but this was the finished product. The trick was finding the right combo of capacitors."

"What the hell's a flux...whatever?" Selena demanded.

"It produces a powerful single electromagnetic pulse. EMP. This old bird's fine since everything's analog 'cept the autopilot and GPS, but anything with a microprocessor within half a mile just got fried." He let out a rebel yell and smacked the instrument panel. "I knew it would come in handy. Told the boys a hundred times. Half of 'em thought I was off my gourd. Not anymore. The bad guys' radios won't work, either – all the new ones have GPS chips and processors."

He banked and steadied out at just below a thousand feet above the ground and then dropped until they were flying only five hundred feet above the mountainous terrain.

"The bastards had it coming to up and shoot Al like that. No way they're cops," he said.

"Veritas!" she yelled. When he didn't answer, she swiveled to Chris. "Why would an EMP cause him to pass out?"

"Hell if I know. But not a lot we can do about it now, is there?"

She unbuckled her harness and climbed between the seats to where Veritas lay. She tried to revive him, but with no luck.

"We have to do something," she said.

"Like what? Land and hand him to DSS? All we can do is keep flying unless you want to get caught...or worse."

The engine sputtered, and he leaned forward to look at the gauges. "Well, don't that beat all..." he muttered.

"What is it?"

"Pressure's dropping."

"And?"

"It's nothing to sweat for now, but if it keeps dropping, we're in trouble."

"Why would it be dropping? The EMP?"

"You never know with one of those. I mean, theoretically there's nothing that could have fried. But like I said, nothing's ever guaranteed."

"What do we do if it keeps dropping?"

"If it doesn't steady out, eventually we'll run out of oil and the engine will seize up."

"So?"

"We'll keep our eye on the oil pressure gauge and worry about it if it gets worse. Like I said, for now, it's just a little glitch. We move below that line," he said, tapping the gauge with a dirty fingernail, "and we need to start thinking about putting down."

An updraft buffeted the plane, and it shuddered briefly before steadying. Chris checked his watch and tried the GPS and autopilot. He waited for the screen to flicker on. When it didn't, he shrugged. "I kinda figured it wouldn't work, but you never know."

"So we're flying blind?"

He tapped the analog compass. "Not completely. I mean, we know it's up the coast. Worst case, we fly west until we hit the ocean and then make a sharp right and follow it to Oregon and then on to Washington."

"How far is the coast?"

Another glance at the gauges. "Little over an hour and a half at this rate. I'm heading due west."

"When will we know whether we've got a real problem?"

He managed a smile. "When I ask for the Gatorade bottle." He paused. "How's your friend?"

"He's out cold, but his breathing's regular."

"Weirdest thing I've ever seen. The EMP shouldn't have caused any problem though unless he had something like a pacemaker with a microprocessor in it."

"What about like a Nexus chip?"

He nodded. "Could be. But worst case, I'd think it just wouldn't work anymore."

Selena's face clouded with concern. She sat by Veritas and put his head in her lap. "Holler if we're going to crash into the mountains or something, okay?"

"Stay optimistic. We made it out, didn't we?"

She regarded Veritas and then checked her watch. "Barely," she muttered under her breath, and held a trembling hand to his neck to check his pulse. His heartbeat was strong and regular, and she wondered whether the blow to his head had caused more damage than he'd thought.

She hoped not.

With the plane limping along in questionable shape, piloted by a hungover recluse who didn't seem particularly sure of anything, Veritas being out of commission could be a game changer. It wasn't like they could touch down near a major metro area and take him to a hospital.

She stroked his brow and closed her eyes. "Come on, Ver. Hang in there."

Chapter 30

Bern Thue, the head of the North American faction of the Tribe, parked outside a run-down warehouse in an industrial area of Detroit bordered on all sides by slums that rivaled the worst shanty towns in Mumbai or Rio, where private armies operated by warlords ran the neighborhoods and meted out their versions of justice, or death, with impunity. He strode hurriedly to the barred gate that enclosed the drive, the grounds on either side overgrown with weeds and littered with garbage, and nodded to a lone security guard, who sat behind bulletproof glass in a bunker that could have withstood a direct artillery strike.

The gate creaked open and Bern made his way to the main building, noting the darkened cavities where the window glass had been long ago broken by vandals. At the front door, he unlocked a rusting box mounted by the heavy steel slab and peered into a retinal scanner that affirmed his identity.

Bern surveyed the empty street, his battered economy sedan the only vehicle there now that night was falling, and then turned, pushed the door open, and stepped into a filthy hall that reeked of stale urine and rot. He continued past the discarded syringes and empty port wine bottles to the warehouse floor, where piles of decaying pallets in disorderly piles littered the gloomy interior.

On the far side of the building, he stopped in front of a broken-down forklift and reached beneath the seat and pulled a lever. The vehicle slid to the side on silent tracks, and a stairway appeared beneath it, illuminated in a greenish glow from lights that rimmed the steps. He descended a story and pressed a button on the wall, and the forklift returned to its original position. Another retinal scanner identified him, and a panel rolled to the side, bathing the landing in bright white light.

Bern stepped through the opening into a fully outfitted lab with a half dozen techs in head-to-toe white at workstations. A gaunt woman barely five feet tall approached him, and they embraced. He held her at arm's length and smiled.

"Susan, tell me you have good news."

She frowned and shook her head. "I'm afraid not, Bern. We thought we had something, but when we tried to confirm the results, the virus had already mutated. It must have some sort of properties we haven't seen before that serve as a kind of anti-vaccine."

"I don't understand. We took the samples from their facility, and I personally removed it from the drone the extraction team used, so it hasn't been tampered with. What's the problem?"

"We'd normally reverse engineer the virus, and that would be that. But it isn't cooperating. Every time we think we've successfully sequenced it, it changes. We're also seeing that on the first version that's currently in release. They must have tech that enabled them to create a rapidly mutating variant so that no vaccine could be produced. We've seen early research that hinted at this capability, but it's still ten years from being well understood."

Bern's eyes narrowed. "Then how do we develop a vaccine?"

"Whoever designed this had to have been using the equivalent of a biological encryption key. Without the key, it's impossible to create a working antidote."

"But with it?"

"It's like anything encrypted, I would guess. Once you can unlock it and see the correct sequence, you can build a vaccine. They obviously have one or they wouldn't have released the first one.

What I'm telling you is that without it, they've built the perfect weaponized virus. It's virulent, contagious for several days before any symptoms appear, and attacks specific genetic markers, or rather, the lack of them."

"What are you saying?"

"If you can get your hands on the key, we're game on. Otherwise it doesn't look good."

Bern looked away. "Damn."

"Sorry. I wish I had better news."

He nodded and lowered his voice. "We lost the Burning Man cell."

Her face fell. "Oh, Bern…" She took his hand. "Are you okay?"

"Yes. I'll mourn Jordan in my own way. Once we have a vaccine."

Susan studied Bern's face. "God. Losing your brother…let me know if there's anything I can do."

"I will. Jordan knew the risks. Doesn't make it any easier, but it's just the way that it played." Bern inhaled deeply and frowned. "Please keep working on this. We need a miracle, Susan. For the sake of the human race."

"I won't lie to you. See if you can find the key, Bern. Otherwise we're just stabbing in the dark."

Chapter 31

Chris had grown increasingly worried as the plane droned west, with the engine temperature gradually climbing as the pressure steadily dropped. Selena had eventually taken the copilot seat again after making Veritas as comfortable as she could, strapping him into the jump seat by the cargo door at Chris's urging.

A wall of thunderheads ahead of them towered over the far side of the Sierras as they flew toward the coast, and the engine occasionally labored as a headwind picked up. Occasional gusts from canyons in the mountains below batted them around like a cat toy swatted by a playful tabby, and the ride grew bumpier as they neared the clouds.

"That's the remnants of last night's storm. It's falling apart as it moves to the coast, but looks like there's still a lot of rain and some high winds. It's going to be rough," Chris warned. "Normally I'd try to fly around this kind of front, but with things going against us, we'll never make it to the coast if we have to detour. I'll take us up to buy some altitude, but that's about all I can do."

"Won't we appear on radar if you do that?"

"All this area of Northern California is now Indian Nation. The government handed it to them when the budget crisis cut its ability to provide services or protection north of Redding. So there's no radar monitoring – the airports from here to Eugene closed after they did that. But that's the least of our problems. We're steadily losing oil pressure. At the rate it's going, we're going to have to put down within half an hour, tops. I've backed our airspeed off so the engine's barely ticking over, but once we're in the red, it's game over."

"Why would the EMP have had that effect?"

"I been thinking about that. It might not have been the blast. Could be a round nicked a line or something."

"If that's the case, couldn't we put down and repair it?"

"Maybe. Depends. But the farther into Indian country we are, the better we'll be if we do have to land. Less snoops to report a plane with no flight plan and a bunch of bullet holes in it."

The ride got bumpier as they neared a silver curtain of rain. Chris raised the nose until they were at two thousand feet, and then they were in the storm, buffeted by confused winds in every direction. Chris's knuckles were white on the yoke as he fought to keep the plane under control, and the sky around them darkened from a light gray to anthracite. Flashes of lightning lit the maelstrom as they bounced through squalls of heavy rain, and Selena's heart was in her throat when the little Cessna dropped with freefall speed before shuddering hard and continuing forward.

The air speed indicated they'd slowed to 125 knots, and Chris backed further off the throttle until they were doing 110.

"It stalls out at about seventy," he said. "But I don't want to test that."

"This is terrible," Selena said, her complexion white.

"Told you it wouldn't be much fun," Chris agreed, his eyes on the instruments as he fought to keep the plane level.

"You weren't kidding."

"Grin and bear it. It ain't over yet."

The plane yawed hard right and he adjusted, and then a crosswind knocked them sideways like the plane had been smacked by a giant hand. The engine groaned, and Chris's already tense expression hardened further.

"We're going to have to start thinking about putting down somewhere. Look at the temp," he said.

Selena did and saw that the needle was now in the red near the top of the range. "How are we going to do that in this soup?"

"Good question."

He reduced speed again, and ten minutes later the nose emerged from the rainstorm and visibility increased from a few yards to several hundred. The altimeter said they were a thousand feet above the ground, and Chris raised the nose to buy them more altitude.

"In case it conks out, the higher we are, the more time we have to glide."

"I hope you're joking," she said.

"It's all physics. But we won't have a lot of options if we're five hundred feet above the trees. Start looking for someplace we can land."

"Like what?" she asked.

"Anything. There are a lot of small airstrips cut out of the forest. Drug smugglers use them. Or if you see a stretch of straight road…even an open field, if it comes to that." He tapped the oil gauge. "We're about done, though, so don't be shy. Holler if you see anything."

They both scanned the horizon and the area to both sides of the plane, but all Selena saw was thick forest. The engine sputtered once, continued its drone, and then sputtered again.

Chris pointed to his left. "That could work."

"Really?" she asked, trying to make out what he was indicating. All she could see were treetops.

"Yeah. Looks like maybe a logging road or something. Your boy back there strapped in tight? This could be a rough one."

"Yes." She paused. "How rough?"

"Long as the wings stay on, maybe not too bad. She'll stop with a pretty short length of runway."

"What do you mean about the wings?"

"No telling how wide that is until we're right on top of it."

He banked left and slowed further, and then cursed. "Nope. No go. Looks like only one car width."

He raised the nose again and the engine moaned in protest at the additional load, but the prop pulled the plane higher even as the temperature gauge pegged. Selena clutched Chris's arm and gestured over the nose at a long scar in the treetops. "Is that an airstrip?"

Chris squinted and turned the nose where she was pointing. "I'll be damned. Not much of one, but sure looks like it."

"Think we can make it?"

"I don't think we've got a choice. Hang on."

The plane shed altitude, and beads of water streamed from the wings as Chris coaxed the laboring aircraft toward the gap in the forest. As they drew near, Selena could make out a red clay strip between the trees, and then they were skimming the tops of the conifers as Chris dropped the final feet to the ground.

The wheels struck the wet muck and he struggled to keep the plane on course. It slowed, but then began to turn sideways even as momentum kept it skidding along the dirt strip. Chris cursed and fought for control, and then yelled when the engine froze with a deafening clank.

The right wing clipped a pine tree, and the plane began spinning like a top even as it continued to slide forward along the slick mud. The tail hit a trunk, and part of it broke off with a wrenching screech of metal, and then the opposite wing struck another tree, and half the wing sheared away with a crash. Selena bucked in the seat from the impact, with Moxie in her arms, but the straps across her chest held. The fuselage pounded against the trees, throwing her sideways before she lurched forward against the harness as the plane ground to an abrupt halt.

Chris sat frozen, the only sound the ticking of the engine cooling, and then felt for his buckles. "We need to get clear in case there's a fuel leak. This thing's about half full. One spark and it'll blow sky high."

"Help me get Ver out of the back."

"We don't have a lot of time."

"Then hurry."

They moved into the cargo area and freed Veritas from the harness. His head was hanging forward with his chin on his chest, and Selena felt the side of his throat for a pulse before looking at

Chris. "He's alive. But we're going to need some way of carrying him."

Chris moved farther to the rear of the fuselage and returned with a blanket and a hatchet. "We should be able to make a litter out of branches. But right now we need to get out of here. I smell fuel."

The side cargo door refused to open when Chris tried the handle. He swore and handed Selena the blanket, and then hacked at the metal with the hatchet like a man possessed.

The area around the latch buckled and then gave, and he forced the door halfway open. Selena slipped one of the backpack straps over her shoulder and dragged Veritas by his arms, and the two of them hoisted him out of the plane and carried him down the runway, the toes of his boots carving grooves in the sopping clay.

They paused when they were thirty yards away and lowered him to the ground. The rain had stopped, but water was dripping from the trees, making the footing treacherous.

Chris looked back at his plane and shook his head. "There goes a half mil down the drain."

"I'm sorry, Chris," she said.

He coughed and looked around. "Easy come, isn't that the saying? No point in crying over it. We need to find some saplings, and I'll see if we can't rig something up so we can drag him along without killing ourselves."

"The question is, drag him where? Any idea where we are?"

"Someplace in Humboldt County, I'd guess, or maybe north of it. I'd plotted a course for north of Eureka, but we got tossed around pretty good back there." He looked around. "Not a lot out here."

"How far are we from the coast?"

He shrugged and motioned to a break in the trees farther ahead. "Beats me. But the orientation of the strip was east to west, so if we follow the access road, it should take us north."

"What's north?"

"Hopefully some kind of civilization. If we find a paved road, it should lead somewhere. Your buddy there doesn't look like he's in great shape."

"No, he doesn't," Selena agreed.

Chris took another look at the wreckage and squared his shoulders. He hefted the hatchet and adjusted his gun belt, and then set off into the woods to find suitable fodder for his blade.

He'd chopped down three small trees and fashioned an elongated triangle from them, and was tying the blanket corners to the poles when the Cessna exploded in a fireball. They both ducked as the plane blew apart, and then Chris spit into the woods and put the finishing touches on his project.

"That'll work. A travois. Indians used them to haul stuff, only usually with horses. But the ends of the trees won't have nearly the resistance his legs do, so it should be a lot easier to drag it between us." He handed her the hatchet. "Put that in your backpack, and we'll see how well this thing does."

Selena dropped the hatchet into the bag and retrieved her pistol, which she slid into her waistband, and they lifted Veritas and set him on the soggy blanket. Each of them took one of the longer poles and raised it to hip height, and they began trudging toward the access way that led into the forest, Veritas's unconscious form trailing behind them on the makeshift sled.

They were nearly to the road when Chris abruptly stopped, one finger to his lips. Selena followed his gaze to the woods, and Chris leaned toward her and whispered to her as he drew his gun with his free hand.

"We got to get out of—"

He was interrupted by the roar of a shotgun. The branches to their immediate right shook as buckshot shredded through them and tore divots from the tree trunks, narrowly missing taking off the tops of their heads.

Chapter 32

Selena and Chris ducked as an assault rifle joined the shotgun firing at them, and dragged Veritas into the trees, staying low as they hauled him into the brush. The gunfire stopped, but they kept moving, the only sound the occasional snap of a branch underfoot as they hurried away from the airstrip.

Voices called out behind them, and the sound of pursuit drove them forward, the ends of the travois poles gliding along the carpet of wet pine needles. They reached a felled tree, and Chris paused to whisper to Selena.

"We can't keep running. He's too heavy. They'll catch up in no time." He indicated the log in front of them. "Let's set him behind this and use it for cover. If we stay quiet, they might get close enough that we can use our pistols."

Selena nodded and they dragged Veritas behind the log, and then they split up. Chris crouched behind a tree a few yards away, while Selena lay on the ground on the far side of the log. They waited in silence, pistols at the ready, watching the woods for movement.

Four bearded men in tattered camouflage appeared from the direction of the strip, with rifles and shotguns. Selena forced herself to remain motionless and held her breath as they made their way

192

toward her, leading with their guns. She was sighting on the closest gunman when Chris's revolver barked twice and the man fell backward, his rifle spraying the trees with a burst of lead as he collapsed.

She fired three times, and another of the gunmen tumbled forward with a strangled cry. The remaining two ducked behind trees and blasted at them, one with a pump shotgun and the other with an assault rifle. Selena darted to a nearby tree as she fired, and slugs pounded into it. Pieces of bark blew through the air where her head had been a nanosecond before. The shotgun boomed over and over, and Chris's pistol answered with four shots in quick succession.

The rifle continued to stutter death at her position, and she didn't dare peek around the trunk for fear of the shooter drilling her with one of his three-round bursts. She was under no illusions of her odds of winning a contest between an automatic rifle and a pistol, and knew that it would be near suicide to do anything but bide her time and pray the attackers made a mistake.

There was a lull from the shotgun, and she figured the shooter was reloading, but the rifle continued firing on her position. When it finally stopped peppering the tree, she reached around and fired three shots and then threw herself behind the log again. The shotgun boomed and a fist-sized chunk of wood blew past her head. Chris fired two more times, having reloaded during her last volley, but there was little chance of either of them walking away from the battle with the pair of shooters still alive.

A voice called out, "Drop your guns and we won't kill you."

Selena prayed that Chris had enough smarts not to respond, and she cringed when she heard him answer.

"Got no fight with whoever you are."

Both the shotgun and rifle targeted him at the same time and loosed a withering attack at his position. He returned their fire, but Selena's heart sank when she heard a pained cry from him.

She was about to call out when more gunfire exploded from farther away, this time the steady chatter of assault rifles on full auto, and the men who'd been shooting at them screamed in agony.

Silence descended upon the forest, and then a baritone voice called out, "We got them. Don't shoot. We're the good guys. Hold your guns where we can see them and there won't be any trouble."

"Who are you, and why would we believe you?" Chris shouted. Selena could hear the pain in his voice.

"Because we just saved your ass, for starters." The speaker paused. "We're the law around here. From the town a few klicks north."

Selena bit her lip and considered their options. Chris was hurt, but she didn't know how badly. She had maybe a half dozen more rounds in her pistol, and Veritas's gun was still in the backpack. If the speaker was telling the truth, she'd be insane to continue trying to fight their way out.

She called to Chris, "On my three, okay?"

"It's your funeral," he answered.

Selena held up her gun and glanced over to where Chris was doing the same. When nobody shot them, she placed her pistol on the log and called out again. "Now what?"

"You can come out. The name's Angel. My partners here are Mike and Greg. We heard your plane blow. You're lucky we were in the area, or these thugs would have killed you."

Selena rose slowly and found herself facing three bronzed Native Americans in rain slickers, with rifles pointed at the ground. Chris stepped from behind his tree, holding his arm, his jacket sleeve slick with blood.

"There's one more of us behind the log," Chris said. "He's hurt. We were headed up the road to see if we could get help when they bushwhacked us."

"Are you okay?" Selena asked, her hands still raised.

"The bastard winged me, but I'll live."

"Stay where you are. I'm going to collect your weapons. No sudden moves, all right?" Angel warned, and made his way toward them after checking the dead gunmen. He scooped up her pistol first and, after a glance at Veritas, strode to where Chris was leaning against his tree, and picked up his revolver. "Mike? Greg? Get their guns and ammo and then give me a hand over here." He eyed Chris and frowned. "Probably want to get a tourniquet on that so you don't lose any more blood. What happened to him?" he asked, indicating Veritas.

"Hurt in the crash," Selena said.

Angel nodded at Chris. "Take off your belt and I'll wrap it around your arm."

Chris released his hold on his wound and did as ordered, and Angel pocketed their pistols, set his rifle against a tree, and approached Chris. He wound the buckle end around Chris's bicep and threaded the other end through the clasp, and then cinched it tight and handed Chris the loose end. "Keep pressure on that," he instructed.

Angel turned to Selena. "You hurt?"

"No. Just shaken up. Who were they?" she asked, indicating the dead men.

"Opium growers. Like pot in the old days before it got legalized. They probably have a field of genetically engineered dope nearby and figured you'd be easy pickings when they heard the plane explode. Shit grows in almost all climates – you can tell it by the green blossoms instead of the usual pink. Biggest cash crop in the world now. Most of the growers are fairly peaceful, but some...some obviously aren't. We normally leave them alone, long as they don't try to sell their crap in our towns, but when we heard the shooting..."

Greg and Mike approached with the dead men's weapons. Angel indicated the travois. "Let's get him to the truck."

Selena and Chris followed the men to a beat-up turn-of-the-millennium Dodge crew cab emblazoned with a green shield on a front door that appeared to be more rust than metal. They set Veritas in the bed, and Greg climbed in back with him while Mike took the passenger seat. Angel drove, with Selena and Chris in the rear of the cab.

"How far to your town? My friend back there needs a doctor," Selena said.

"Maybe twenty minutes. The roads kind of suck after a big rain," Angel answered. "What went wrong with the plane?"

"Engine problems," Chris said. "We saw the airstrip and barely made it."

"Yeah, all around a lucky day so far, then," Mike said – the first words he'd uttered since they'd met.

"Do you have a doctor there?" Selena asked.

"We have a shaman – a medicine woman. Good as any doctor I've ever gone to," Angel said. "Although if anyone needs surgery or something major, we take them to Eureka."

"Does she have any training?" Selena asked.

Angel laughed. "She's been caring for us for longer than I've been alive, so I'd say so. She was a physician's assistant in San Francisco a long time ago, but she's also versed in the old ways. A good combination."

"I hope so," Selena said.

Angel caught Chris's eye in the rearview mirror. "She's treated more gunshot wounds than I've had birthdays, so you'll be fine."

"I'm not worried. One of my friends lives up this way, and he swears by the traditional medicine."

"Yeah? What's his name? I may know him."

"Eddie Deerborn. Quite a character. Hell of a fighter, too. We were in the service together."

Angel laughed. "That's funny. He's kind of the mayor of our town."

"Really? Small world."

"He came back to stay when the government bowed out of the area and left it to the tribes. He's not the government's biggest fan. Nobody around here is."

"That makes two of us," Chris said. "Bunch of lying snakes."

Angel chuckled. "Sounds like you'll be right at home with us, then. Happiest day of our lives was when they packed up and left. Good riddance."

"I'm a little surprised you haven't had any more trouble with them."

"The way I see it, we don't have anything left to steal. But they're still making noises about forcing us to get chipped, even though technically we're a sovereign nation. They claim until the courts and Congress give us final approval, we still have to comply with their rules. We say bullshit."

"Not sure how having internet in your head's going to help out here in the wilds."

Angel nodded. "Exactly."

Chapter 33

The town turned out to be an old Indian casino on the Trinity River, surrounded by prefab buildings. Farther along the water, hundreds of single- and double-wide trailers lined the shores near where a highway bridge spanned the river.

The road was deserted except for Angel's truck.

"We have roadblocks to limit access to our lands, and we charge a toll to trucks on the highway for passage. Part of our deal with the government. One of the few it hasn't broken, at least so far," Angel explained.

"How many in your tribe?" Selena asked.

"About three thousand here. With those of us who've settled in cities, maybe four thousand total. But we're just one of many. We're responsible for about a three-hundred-and-fifty-square-mile area, and then another tribe is responsible for each of the adjacent sections. We administer everything for ourselves, though. The government left us with a few abandoned buildings and not much else, but we make do. Even now, some come to gamble at the casino, and between that and the road tax, we're better off than we ever were when the government was supposedly helping us." Angel looked back at Chris. "How's the arm?"

"Hurts like a bitch, but it's only a flesh wound. Hopefully your medicine lady has some antibiotics and can stitch decently. I don't think it did any major damage."

"Like I said, she's the best," Angel said. "And she won't mislead you. If she can't help you, she'll tell you straight up, and then we'll have to take you to Eureka."

"Is that far?" Selena asked.

"Maybe an hour or so, depending on the road. Some of it's iffy since the state gave up on maintaining it."

A pair of men carrying lever-action rifles waved to them as the truck passed, and Angel gave the horn a toot. He turned off the two-lane highway and drove past a line of trailers in various states of disrepair. The dwellings thinned, and he pulled into the lot of a small building with a weathered sign atop a steel pole that announced a medical clinic inside.

Angel killed the engine, and everyone emptied out of the truck. The three men carried the travois to the front entrance and placed Veritas on the ground, and then hoisted him like a sack of potatoes and carried him inside. Chris and Selena followed, where they were met by an old woman with a mahogany complexion, long unruly gray and black hair, and intelligent deep brown eyes.

"We were in a plane crash," Selena explained.

The woman nodded and pointed at an exam table. "Put him there." She looked at Chris. "Looks like more than a crash, judging by the bullet hole."

"Some druggies tried to ambush them," Angel explained. "They shot it out. You might want to have a look at his arm before the other guy, just in case I need to run him down to Eureka."

The woman nodded. "I'm Mabel. You are…?"

"Oh, sorry. Selena, and this is Chris," Selena said. "And that's Veritas."

"Veritas? Interesting name," Mabel said. "All right, Chris, let's see what we've got here."

She walked to a steel cabinet, opened it, and slipped on a white lab coat, and indicated another exam room. "Come in and I'll clean it up and assess the damage. Can you move your fingers?"

Chris waggled them. "Yes. Hurts a bit, but I don't think there's any nerve damage."

Mabel nodded and guided him into the other room. After ten

minutes, she returned and removed a pair of bloody latex gloves and dropped them into a wastebasket. "That was easy. Cleaned, dressed it, and stitched him up. Passed clean through without hitting an artery or bone. A shot of antibiotics and some follow-up and he'll be playing tennis in no time." She regarded Angel and then Selena. "Now let's take a look at your man here."

Mabel probed and prodded Veritas while Selena blotted his brow with a cloth. Chris emerged from the other room with a bandage around his arm and nodded to Angel. "You mentioned that Eddie lives here? Don't suppose you could show me where while they're dealing with him, do you?"

"Sure. Or I can tell him you're here. Might be a better idea with your wound," Angel said.

"You can hang out in the waiting room," Mabel said. "I wouldn't be moving around too much until your body recovers some, Chris. Angel? Maybe have Eddie bring him some orange juice and food? He lost a lot of blood and could use some of both. And get the puppy something to eat and drink."

"Thanks. I'll do that," Chris said.

"There's bottled water in the dispenser. We boil it so it's sterile," Mabel advised.

"Perfect. Let me know if you need anything," Chris said.

"Other than payment, probably not a lot," Mabel said.

"I'll be covering the cost for both of them," Selena said. "Do you take digital wallets?"

Mabel shook her head. "No, but you can go to the casino and convert some into hard money."

"Let me know how much and I will," Selena said, and looked down at Veritas with obvious concern. "What about him? What's wrong with him?"

"He's got a couple of bumps on his head," she said. "How hard did he get hit?"

Chris left the room with the men, and Selena sat down on a stool in the corner. "He passed out after that happened. But it wasn't the blows to the head. We were near an EMP explosion, and something about it affected him. He just…shut down when it exploded."

Mabel's eyes narrowed. "Wait a minute. Back up. You were near an EMP?"

Selena gave her an abridged version of the morning's events. When she was done, the older woman considered her for a long moment before turning back to Veritas. "I'm in uncharted territory. You say he's got a chip in his head? One of those new Nexus jobs, or something older?"

"It's a prototype," she said. "Like the Nexus, only more advanced."

"Don't suppose you know how it interfaces with his brain, do you?"

"I'm afraid not."

"Who installed it?"

"The military."

Mabel grunted. "Then it could be just about anything. Well, hell. I'll brew up something and we'll monitor him. Not a lot more I can think of doing. He should probably go to Eureka."

Selena shook her head. "No. We can't. He's…that's not an option."

Mabel exhaled noisily. "Don't suppose it has anything to do with your crashed plane, does it?" She held up a hand. "I'm not sure I want to know. If you can't take him to a hospital, the best I can do is try to bring him round, hook him up and monitor his vitals, and wait to see what happens. His eyes don't show any signs of intracranial bleeding, so there are no obvious indications of brain damage, but he could have a concussion. You're sure he didn't show any symptoms before the EMP?"

"No. He seemed fine. Lucid. Fit."

Mabel prepared a concoction from herbs and roots and, after steeping them in hot water, used a syringe without the needle to funnel some into Veritas's mouth. When the cup was empty, she placed a cool moist towel on his head, stripped off his jacket, wheeled a medical monitor to his side, and clamped a cable to his index finger. The monitor began to beep in time with his heart, and she took his blood pressure, which was on the high side of normal.

Selena watched from the doorway, holding Moxie like a baby. Mabel eventually looked up at her. "Now it's a waiting game. I'll hook up an IV so he doesn't get dehydrated. In the meantime, you might want to head over to the casino." Mabel named a price. "That's for the gunshot wound and Veritas through tonight. We'll play it by ear from tomorrow." She frowned at Selena. "You may not have any choice about taking him to Eureka. If he's been out for six hours, there could be something–"

Veritas groaned, and Mabel rushed to his side. Selena followed and stood at the foot of the exam table with Moxie squirming in her grasp while Mabel examined him. Veritas moaned again, and then his eyes fluttered open before closing again.

"Where – where...am..." he croaked.

"You're at a doctor's," Selena said. "You passed out."

"I..."

Mabel shushed him. "Don't try to talk. Just rest. There's no hurry."

"I...my...vision..."

"Shhh. Stay still and let your body heal," Mabel said. "You're in a safe place."

His eyes opened, and he looked around the room before his gaze settled on Selena. "Things look...weird..."

"Does your head hurt?" Mabel asked.

"A little."

"Close your eyes and rest. I'll be right here if you need anything," Selena said.

"She's right – that's probably best. I gave you something that might make you feel a little fuzzy," Mabel said. "But it'll wear off. Don't talk anymore."

"I'm...tired."

"Yes, I imagine so," Mabel said. "Go to sleep. I'll check in on you in a little while."

Veritas nodded once, grimacing when he did. Mabel moved to Selena and whispered to her, "Let's leave him alone for a bit. The body has an amazing ability to heal if you let it."

Selena fished her things out of the backpack and left it on the floor by the base of the exam table. Mabel led her into the clinic lobby, where Chris was sitting with a Native American man about his age. Chris looked up when they entered, and Mabel smiled at the newcomer.

"Hello, Eddie. Always nice to see you," she said.

"Likewise, Mabel," Eddie said. He rose, and Chris motioned to Selena.

"This is Selena…sorry, don't remember your last name.

"It's not important," Selena said. "Pleased to meet you."

Eddie shook her hand, appraising her, and then sat again. "Chris tells me you've had quite a morning."

"That's one way of putting it," she said.

"I was telling him about the engine trouble and the shoot-out," Chris said. "If it wasn't for bad luck, sometimes I don't know if I'd have any at all."

"Hell, I could have told you never to get in a plane this man's maintaining," Eddie said with a laugh. "They threw a party when the Air Force finally managed to get rid of him."

"Eddie's always thought of himself as a comedian," Chris said. "Problem is he's the only one who thinks so."

"Well, I'll let you play catch-up. I need to run over to the casino," Selena said.

"I'm not going anywhere," Chris said, holding up his bandaged arm. "How's…our friend?"

"We'll see," Mabel said. "Everyone's been through a lot."

"You might want to get something to eat while you're out," Chris said, indicating the bottle of orange juice and a half sandwich on the coffee table in front of him.

Eddie nodded. "The casino's got the best food in town by far. Has to, or the truckers won't stop in to blow their paychecks."

Selena's stomach growled, and she realized she was starving. "Thanks. I'll do that."

"You can't miss it," Eddie said. "On the main road just after the bridge. Ask anyone if you get lost."

"Will do." She looked at the older woman. "Is there any way you can watch Moxie while I'm gone?"

Mabel smiled and took the puppy from Selena. "He's a little angel, isn't he?"

"I wouldn't let him near anything you don't want chewed to pieces."

"Oh, look at those eyes! How can she say that about you, Moxie? You're adorable. I'm sure you'll be on your best behavior."

Moxie gave Mabel a tentative slurp, and it was settled. "You go on, then. I'll watch this young man for you. Been a long time since I had a puppy in the place, but I think I remember what to do."

"Thanks, Mabel."

Selena pushed through the clinic doors and looked up at the gray sky. It didn't feel like it was going to rain, but she was still chilled by the cool air and pulled her jacket close around her. She set off at a brisk walk, conscious of the eyes of the residents on her as she made her way along the river, many of them sitting on the cement patios of their trailers with apparently nothing else to do. She passed the pair of men with the lever-action rifles, and they smiled and waved, and she felt better about her errand. Mabel had asked for three thousand dollars, which would pose no problem for her digital wallet and seemed reasonable compared to the bills she'd had to sign off on from hospitals for gunshot wounds, which could easily run six figures if they'd done serious damage.

She thought about the attack on Chris's camp and their narrow escape from the Brethren's mercenaries, and replayed the missile attack on Jordan's home over and over as she neared the casino.

Her fear was that Veritas's insistence on making his way north to meet Ben's friend in Washington had been a tactical mistake, and now that their means of getting there had gone up in a burst of flames, they were effectively stuck, with the Brethren combing the state and DSS pulling out all the stops to find them. None of which would be much of a problem if Veritas was seriously injured, which seemed likely given his reactions and the apparent disorientation the

EMP had caused. If he was, she knew it was game over.

She wished she could call someone and ask for guidance, but for the first time since childhood, she was completely on her own – which left her with little choice but to hope the old medicine woman knew what she was doing, and that the EMP hadn't fried something vital in Veritas's makeup.

So now she was stuck with a wanted man who was crippled by an unknown degree of trauma, with no way of making it to Washington barring divine intervention, and the entire power of the government being used by the Brethren to track them down.

If it could get any worse, she didn't see how.

And that was the optimistic spin.

Chapter 34

Sweat streamed down Veritas's face as he slept fitfully. His dreams were filled with vivid images of running through a jungle, climbing a rope ladder up the side of a sheer cliff, and then diving into raging rapids and battling the current as it threatened to pull him under. One moment he was seated in a helicopter manning a .50-caliber machine gun and scanning the landscape below, and the next he was running hard along a mountain ridge with a hundred-pound pack on his back, his muscles bulging from exertion and high-altitude air burning in his straining lungs.

The scene changed, and he was a boy, perhaps seven or eight, bathing in a lagoon beneath a waterfall, surrounded by towering peaks and a turquoise sky dotted with birds of prey so high they were little more than specks. Other boys laughed and splashed each other as they played in the water, but Veritas couldn't hear them, as though he were watching a vid with the sound off.

It changed again, and he was standing on a surface of timber planks, shirtless, barefoot, and wearing only a pair of loose-fitting pants, in a group of twenty other boys the same age, all following the movements of a man with ridges of wiry muscle beneath bronze skin – some sort of martial arts class, judging by the repetition of strikes and blocking moves. Again there was no sound, but some part of him knew that even had there been, the area would have been silent except for the rush of the nearby falls.

Suddenly he was older, perhaps twelve or thirteen, holding a traditional Chinese bow crafted of ox horn and bamboo, its length hand painted with traditional symbols, and drawing an arrow to his ear in a fluid motion after pointing the bow and arrow at the sky. He then released it to drill into the center of a target at the far end of a courtyard. Leaves blew along the smooth rocks that lined the area, and he drew another arrow in the same manner and performed the identical shot. The arrow flew straight and true, and lodged so tightly beside the first that they were indistinguishable from his vantage point.

Veritas's eyes snapped open, and he blinked in confusion. On the periphery of his blurred vision was a stream of data moving so fast he couldn't make any sense out of the seemingly random strings of letters and numbers. He closed his eyes again, but the stream didn't disappear, and he groaned in frustration at his inability to clear his thoughts of the invasive ciphers.

He rubbed away the perspiration from his forehead and tried to calm his mind, but the visions and data continued no matter what he did. He attempted to slow his breathing, inhaling through his nose and exhaling through his mouth, and willed the disturbing images to fade into nothingness. After several fruitless minutes, he gave up and opened his eyes again, the fatigue he'd felt earlier replaced by a feeling of power and alertness. The throb in his temples that had been his constant companion since the bike accident had receded and been replaced by a sense of clarity and strength.

Veritas remembered the old woman squirting some vile-tasting concoction in his mouth before he'd dozed off and wondered if she'd drugged him. He'd meant to tell her not to give him anything addictive, but even as he had the thought, he remembered the young woman's assertion that he wasn't an addict – that those had been false memories implanted for his own good.

What was her name? It danced at the edge of his awareness, teasing him without allowing him to latch onto the prize.

Then he remembered.

Her name was Selena.

"Selena?" he called weakly. He sat up and took in the vital signs monitor and then the IV pole's bag of saline beside him, and he touched the cannula in his left arm. He called out again. "Selena? Hello! Anyone there?"

He was working at the tape on his arm so he could pull the needle from his vein when the door on the far side of the room opened and the old crone stepped in, her eyes as wild as her hair.

"You're up! How do you feel?" she asked.

"I…fine, mostly. But something weird's going on with my vision."

She moved to his side and checked his vitals, and then leaned down, her expression concerned. "I'm going to pull the IV. You have to get out of here."

"What? Why?"

She removed the cannula and pressed a piece of gauze in place. "Maintain pressure for a minute," she ordered, and disconnected the pulse oximeter before pushing the cart with the monitor out of the way.

"What's going on?" Veritas tried again.

"You've been sold out," she whispered, eyeing the door. "Your supposed friend Chris. I overheard him talking to his buddy. You don't have much time."

"I don't understand."

"He told his friend that you're running from DSS, and if they ever found out you'd been here, they'd crush the town. God knows they can do whatever they want."

Veritas's expression hardened. "Shit." He paused. "Where's Selena?"

"She went to the casino almost an hour ago."

"What?" he blurted. He couldn't imagine Selena choosing to gamble when everything was falling apart.

"To change money and eat," Mabel said, seeming to read his thoughts.

"I need to get her."

"They're on their way. There's no time."

"I'm not leaving her," he said stubbornly.

"Can you stand up? Try. Let's see how you do."

He pushed himself off the table and took a deep breath. "I'm fine. Only these damned numbers in my head are driving me nuts."

She handed him his jacket and the backpack. "If you think you can make it, follow me."

Mabel hurried to the door and peered out. Seeing the lobby was empty, she crept to the rear of the building and slid the bolt on the back exit free. She eased the door open and looked out and, when she was sure there was nobody around, stepped aside.

"The forest is impenetrable from the air. If they don't come with dogs, you have a good chance of escaping them. My ancestors roamed the woods for years. Good luck, Veritas."

"Where's the casino?"

She sighed. "That way," she said, pointing up the river. "But you can't go there. They'll be here any second."

"What about you? They'll interrogate you."

"I'll disappear until they're gone. They have no power here. No jurisdiction. My people will never allow them to do anything to me."

"They gut-shot a man for no reason. They aren't who you think."

"Even more reason for me to leave, then." She smiled sadly. "I'd go with you, but I'd slow you down. Don't worry about Moxie – I'll take care of him for you."

Veritas blinked in recognition at the dog's name. "No. I'll take him…"

"You're out of time. Get moving."

"Thank you for–"

The unmistakable sound of helicopters cut him off, and a shadow passed overhead. He looked up and spotted a drone hovering over the front of the clinic and steeled himself to sprint to the tree line.

"Come on. I'm not leaving you here to be tortured by them," he said.

"No. Count to sixty. That'll give me time to go out the front of the clinic. It might distract them long enough for you to make a break for the forest."

"But they'll–"

"They'll lose interest in me when they see it's an old woman with her dog. By the time they figure it out, I'll be long gone, and hopefully so will you."

Mabel didn't wait for him to reply, and pressed a small wad of cash into his hand before turning and rushing back down the hall toward the lobby. Veritas slipped the money into his pocket and continued to watch the sky, counting as she'd instructed. When he reached sixty, he bolted for the trees, running as fast as he could.

Which proved to be far faster than he'd thought possible. He was at the tree line in an instant and beneath the cover of the pines before he'd drawn two full breaths. He remembered the elixir that Selena had given him and nodded once to himself — whatever it was had certainly worked.

A glance at the heavens told him that the drone hadn't spotted him and was no doubt following the old woman until the operator called it off. He hefted the backpack and looked inside, but there was little of use besides a hatchet and the super tool.

The sound of the helicopters grew louder, and Veritas didn't wait to see them appear in the afternoon sky. He took off at a jog, following a track through the trees in a northerly direction, his thoughts on Selena — he had to get to her before they did.

He was halfway to the casino when the first helo landed in the building's largely empty parking lot and a half dozen black-clad commandos sealed the two exits. Another chopper touched down and more men disgorged, assault rifles pointed at the few stunned spectators watching from nearby.

A drone zipped past him, and he drew farther into the trees. When he was sure it was clear, he continued toward the casino and was nearly there when a third aircraft landed in the lot, and two figures emerged and walked to the main entrance.

Veritas cursed when a pair of gunmen exited the building with Selena between them. He had to fight the urge to blindly charge them, and forced his pulse slower by focusing on his breathing. They bundled her, struggling, into one of the helicopters, and then a drone dropped to within twenty yards of Veritas's position and hovered.

He didn't wait for the cries from the fighting force to know he'd been spotted, but tore deeper into the woods, where the branches and brush would make it impossible for the drone to follow. As he ran, the numbers in the periphery of his vision began organizing into something less random, and some part of him intuited how to interpret the strings of characters.

Men came running to where the drone had thwacked into a low-hanging branch and damaged one of its rotors, and Veritas realized that he could "see" their GPS chips on a mental overlay of the terrain. He watched as they spread out in a wide pattern, but he couldn't find his position relative to them, so the display was of limited value. Dozens of icons blinking in his mind's eye were more of a distraction than anything, and he shook his head to clear it before crashing through the vegetation, the gunmen on his tail.

Veritas followed a game trail that traced the river, and powered up a steep rise, hoping his augmented strength would be sufficient edge to leave his pursuers in the dust. He slowed as the trail veered from the tree line and onto a rocky ridge, and spotted the dark water of the river rushing below in a froth where it surged over a rapid. He paused and dared a look back, and his blood chilled when he saw the muzzle of a rifle leveled at him from no more than seventy yards away. Another helmeted soldier joined the first and called out to him.

"Freeze. Not a twitch or you're history!"

Veritas glanced to the side. The river was at least eight stories below, the canyon wall sheer granite, the surface of the water swirling where it deepened as the course narrowed. He slowly raised his hands in surrender and hung his head in defeat, and then threw himself into space before the gunmen could react, his body twisting and tumbling as he dropped.

Gunfire exploded behind him, but he'd been too fast, and the shots missed.

He slammed into the water with a massive splash, unable to adjust in time so his feet would hit first, and the force knocked the wind out of him. He struggled to stay afloat, but the icy current pulled him under. The gunmen on the ridge fired into the water, and the bullets sizzled around him as the undertow dragged him deeper into the darkness, lungs burning, his entire body in shock from the sudden immersion and the impact of his fall.

"Damn," the lead commando blurted, and tapped his comm to life to report on what had happened.

"Follow the river," Azra ordered. "If he's alive, he has to come out somewhere. If he's dead, I want a body, or nobody goes home."

"Roger," the commando acknowledged, and walked to the edge of the sheer drop. He turned to the others and scowled. "You think we hit him?"

"Hard to tell. He moved like lightning. But I'd say there's a good possibility."

"You heard the boss," the commando said. "Make your way along the ridge until we can get to the water."

One of the men eyed the display screen in his goggles. "Doesn't look like it's gonna be easy. This shows canyon for at least a mile."

"They don't pay us for easy. Move out."

Chapter 35

Veritas rolled in the current and hit the rocky bottom of the river. A sharp stab of pain shot through his bruised ribs, and he nearly gave in to the impulse to breathe even though he knew to do so would flood his lungs. He struck again, and this time used his arms to pull himself along the bottom until he felt the level rising and a glimmer of light pierced the inky gloom. He worked with the current, using it to propel him farther up the bank, and then his head broke the surface and he gasped, shielded from view by the low branches of a bush spreading over the water from the shore.

He dug in his boots to keep from being dragged farther downriver, and shivered as he caught his breath. The river was near freezing and swollen from the rain. The dizziness and panic he'd felt faded as his lungs filled with air, and he blinked at the display that seemed determined to dominate his thoughts.

The icons were now superimposed over a map, as though he were watching it on a computer screen or a projection inside his eyes, and he concentrated on organizing it so it made sense. His pursuers were blinking yellow along one side of the river graphic, moving along the bank, and then he saw a stationary blue icon – a representation of his position.

He waited, ignoring the numbness that was creeping into his body from the cold, and when the search party was well past his location, dragged himself from the water and onto the steep gravel bank. He studied the length of the cliff, spied a fissure upriver a dozen yards, and crawled along the water's edge, moving slowly as the icons continued downstream.

The gap in the stone turned out to be a nearly vertical cut in the granite carved by eons of runoff slicing through the rock to meet the river, and he scanned the steep channel. The display in his mind's eye changed, and handholds glowed along the cut, and for the first time since regaining consciousness, he felt a tremor of hope. Somehow, the EMP that had dropped him like a left hook must have rebooted his chip, enabling the tracking and scanning capabilities he was now discovering. Whatever the cause, the result was unmistakable, and he intended to use it to the best of his abilities to evade his trackers.

He reached up, and his fingers gripped an irregularity in the rock. He hauled himself into the crevice, pushing with his legs as he felt for the next hold. He inched higher and his body warmed as he pulled himself toward the crest far above, his muscles straining but performing in spite of the battering he'd endured.

Making sense out of the data stream was still confusing, but the ability to track the search party and mentally call up maps of the terrain seemed to be growing easier with time. Ten minutes later he was again in the woods and running away from the river. The icons that represented his pursuers were on the other side, and the distance between his blue and their yellow grew with each passing moment.

He recalled Jordan's description of the super-soldier program and frowned. A part of Veritas had wanted to believe the entire story was some sort of shared delusion, or that Jordan and Selena had been exaggerating. But now, with some of his additional capabilities restored, he couldn't deny they'd been telling the truth – in which case everything was true, including that his memories were implanted and his mother had been an actress pretending to be the woman who'd brought him into the world.

The realization hit him hard, as did the thought that Selena had been captured by the Brethren and there was nothing he could do about it. Even though he'd only known her for a couple of days, he couldn't deny the attraction he felt, and he believed it to be mutual. He was willing to believe she could have been faking it, but he didn't think so. Much as he distrusted his instincts now, based on the revelations about his memories, the deepest part of him insisted that she was as attracted to him as he was to her.

Which made his abandonment of her that much harder.

Veritas paused beneath a tall pine and considered his limited options. A part of him wanted to go back to the town and try to rescue Selena, even though his rational mind told him it would be suicide. He was up against air and ground forces that were well trained and equipped, completely focused, and utterly ruthless. Even with his speed and newfound abilities, any hope of freeing her was hopeless.

He blinked and the icons refreshed. They'd stopped, probably because he hadn't surfaced, and several were reversing course, which meant he couldn't afford the luxury of entertaining fantasies of circling back and flanking them.

Now his survival was the priority, and he had no choice but to keep moving if he wanted to live until nightfall.

He inhaled deeply and resumed running deeper into the forest, away from the hunters, who for all their technology and numerical superiority, when pitted against Veritas were clumsy pawns on a chessboard they couldn't see.

An hour and a half later, Veritas was nearing the highway that bisected the Indian Nation from south to north. He'd developed no plan other than to find the road and follow it until he dropped or made it to Washington. He still felt strong, which he attributed to the partial upgrade Selena had slipped him in jail. But if that upgrade had been a three, his new capabilities were on the order of an eight. Without them he knew he would have been dead meat – between the helos that had been circling overhead, the drones, and the boots on the ground, he was woefully outmatched.

Not to mention that he didn't even have a weapon. Pathetic as the pistols were, they at least would have provided some defensive capability at close range. But a hatchet? What the hell was he supposed to do with that?

He pushed the thoughts from his mind and called up the map that had become second nature to activate. He was a quarter mile from the road, and the enemy drones and helos were miles west of it.

The question being what to do once he reached it.

Veritas picked up his pace and silenced the voice that kept nagging him with questions about the viability of action with no strategy, and concentrated on crossing the remaining terrain without twisting his ankle or spearing himself on a low branch.

He slowed as he reached the road and remained in the trees for several minutes, his head cocked, listening. Something to the north caught his attention – the faintest hint of a diesel motor his hyper-attenuated hearing picked up. Veritas took off at another of his blistering runs and made it half a mile in under ninety seconds without breaking a sweat.

A semi-rig was parked by the side of the road, its engine idling as its driver relieved himself on the shoulder. The truck was pointed north and presumably would keep going until it reached a population center like Eugene, or if he was lucky, Portland or Seattle. He waited until the driver finished, and when the man had climbed back into the cab, darted from the trees and threw himself under the long trailer. The truck's gears ground and the driver gave it some throttle, and the heavy load lumbered forward, slowly at first and then faster.

Veritas clung to the undercarriage of the trailer and allowed his heels to drag on the pavement as he pulled himself toward the cab. A third of the way an idea occurred to him, and he wrapped his legs around a crossbeam and fumbled the hatchet from the backpack.

Gripping the beam for dear life, he swung the blade at the flat underside of the trailer and was rewarded with a thunk of thin metal over plastic slabs – this was one of the newer trailers that had been built almost entirely out of synthetics to cut weight and improve fuel consumption. He tried again and again until he'd hacked a crude hole through the sheet metal and plastic floor. He slid the hatchet back into the backpack and tried to ignore the road whizzing by at belt-sander speed only a foot from his back, and pulled himself forward until he was directly beneath the gap.

Veritas clasped the rough-hewn edge of the opening with one

hand and, after testing his weight, clamped his other to the opposite edge and heaved himself upward.

And hit his head on the bottom of a pallet in the trailer above.

After another ten minutes of clinging to the beam and chopping like a madman, he'd destroyed enough of the pallet and the crates of oranges that were resting on it to be able to lie on the remains of the pallet in a fetal position, his jacket and jeans slathered in juice and chunks of fruit.

He blinked and called up another map, and then zoomed out and ordered his processor to plot the distance to McCleary. The display immediately blinked three numbers based on a choice of routes. The shortest was the main highway, but even so it was over five hundred miles, which at truck speed and with a meal break wouldn't get him in the vicinity until just before dawn, assuming the truck was headed all the way to Seattle.

Veritas slept as the truck rocked its way north, his body nestled far enough from the hole to keep from falling to his death while slumbering. The driver eventually stopped for a meal at a truck stop, but Veritas stayed hidden and contented himself with oranges for dinner – he remembered too well what Selena had said about the chipped being used as unwitting surveillance cameras, and after his recent experience with the technology, wasn't about to chance it.

He busied himself with counting the money the old woman had given him: ninety-seven dollars of wrinkled and velvet-soft bills. If he ever got out of this mess, he'd find a way to pay her back for her unrequested generosity – without her warning, he would have been taken without a fight, and given what Jordan had said, that would have cost him his life.

When the truck got under way again, he closed his eyes and resigned himself to another uncomfortable stint, his olfactory senses overwhelmed by the sickly-sweet aroma of oranges and his thoughts on Selena and the vision of her being manhandled to the helicopter, prisoner of an enemy more ruthless than any he could have imagined.

Chapter 36

Azra stood by his helicopter, eyeing the woman in the cabin with an impassive stare. It had been three hours since they'd landed and taken her prisoner, and ever since the target had made his suicidal leap off the cliff, they'd had no contact with him. With four helicopters in the search and a score of drones now deployed over the river, it was nearly impossible that he could escape or his body go unfound, but with each passing minute Azra's pessimism was growing.

Donald paced by the casino entrance and then stopped with his hand to his ear. He gave a small wave to Azra and then made his way over to him at a rapid clip.

"Just got word from the medical team. The Burning Man prisoner didn't make it," he reported.

Azra glared at him like Donald had insulted him, and then looked away. "Not surprised. His injuries were bad."

"No, that wasn't it. He had a toxin in one of his molars. He cracked it just before they were putting him under, and was dead in seconds."

"Damn. These cockroaches are nearly impossible to corner." He scowled at Selena. "I'm frankly surprised we captured her. Have the medic do a thorough exam of her before we take off. I don't want a repeat performance."

"If the target's dead..."

"We're still taking her in. For the record, I don't believe for a second that he's dead. If he was, we'd have found the body by now."

"It could have snagged on something at the bottom of the river…"

"We have aquatic robots on the way. I'll bet you a week's pay they find nothing."

Donald frowned. "No deal. But the question is, how did he escape? The men are all over the area."

"We're just assuming that his chip isn't functioning, based on our intel. But if that's wrong, evading us would be child's play for him. I can't believe we can't trace it. Why didn't they build that in? You'd think…"

"I'm not responsible for the final design," Donald said. "Bigger brains than mine made the decision. Supposedly so that they couldn't be tracked by enemy forces."

"How would they have done that, given the secrecy level?"

"It only takes one mole with a gambling or drug problem. Or some whistle-blowing do-gooder. Anyway, it's a moot point. I suspect our intel was wrong."

Azra eyed Donald with obvious frustration. "We'll get all we can out of the woman."

"Assuming she knows anything."

"She was with him, and he was on his way to the casino when the drone spotted him. That tells me that she's important to him. The logical thing to do would have been to run the second he heard the helos. But he didn't. I'm betting there's a reason." He paused. "She's not hard to look at, is she?"

"I hadn't noticed."

"Sure. Well, keep at it. I need to deal with our informant."

Donald returned to his spot by the casino, and Azra walked to the opposite end of the parking lot, where Chris was waiting for him, his bandaged arm in a sling. When Azra reached him, the older man wet his lips.

"I did my part and told you about them. Now you need to do yours," he said.

Azra nodded. "I've already spoken with DSS. Your son will be released within twenty-four hours and his record expunged. I'd try to keep him out of trouble if I were you – they didn't want to let him go. Apparently he's been naughty."

"How do I know you're telling the truth?"

"DSS will be here in about an hour. You can speak to them directly. They won't renege on the deal. They've got no reason to."

"I don't trust them."

"That may be, but you'll have your son back by tomorrow at the latest. And no charges will be pressed for the destruction at your ranch. It'll be cleaned up like it never happened."

"Your people were trespassing. And they shot my foreman for no reason."

"And now they're dead. So I'd say we're even. Besides, I told you they violated orders in doing so. Somebody got panicky. It can happen."

Chris glanced over at the helicopters. "You haven't found him yet?"

Azra's expression hardened. "None of your business. We're done here. If you have any questions, talk to DSS."

"What about McCleary? You going to do roadblocks or something?"

"Maybe I wasn't clear. We're done."

Azra stalked away, biting back the annoyance he felt at having to deal with the snitch. While it was true that his tip had been invaluable in alerting them to the target's location, Azra hated his type – a result of his years in the military as part of the program.

Another helo streaked from the south and settled onto the parking lot, and a trio of figures in civilian clothing got out and hoisted a pair of Anvil cases from the aircraft's hold. Azra approached them, and one of the men, a bearded geek in his thirties, greeted him.

"I'm Carter Levin. We brought the robots. Can someone here take us to the area you need scanned?"

Azra tapped his earbud and called Donald over. "Take them to the river," he said, and then turned to Carter. "How long until we have a definitive?"

"Depending on viz and how large an area, maybe an hour or two.

Have to go by visual since there won't be any thermal to ping by now."

"Get to work, then. We're wasting time."

Azra already knew they wouldn't find anything, but they had to go through the motions anyway. As to whether he wanted to set up roadblocks, the thought of involving the locals or DSS in the hunt at this point was anathema to him. This was his mess to clean up, and given the level of incompetence he'd come to expect from government authorities, alerting the quarry of their knowledge of his ultimate destination would be the worst move he could make. If he was correct about the target's abilities having been reactivated, it would not only prove ineffective, it would cause him to go so far underground they'd never find him.

Which raised the question of why they cared so much about the lone surviving original member of the dream team, as they'd called themselves.

Given what Azra knew about the progress in bringing his masters' ultimate plan to fruition, one man seemed inconsequential. Then again, Azra didn't believe in prophecies, so he wasn't driven by the same fears they were.

No, he had a different idea about how to use the information he'd gleaned from the pilot, which he would corroborate with some vigorous interrogation of the woman once they were in a secure location. With the combination of drugs and persuasion he could bring to bear, there was nobody on the planet who could hold out for long, and he fully expected that she'd beg to tell him everything before he was done.

Or perhaps she could be put to another use.

It remained to be seen. For now, he would entertain the charade that the target's body was snagged on a rock or submerged tree, and once the robots had proven that false, would put his contingency plan into effect.

Chapter 37

Veritas slumbered to the monotone lullaby of the thrum of the tires beneath him as the truck rolled north. His eyes flitted behind closed lids, his dreams as vivid and clear as if he were awake.

He was no more than ten, clad in a saffron robe, seated at the feet of an ancient Asian man with a wizened face and bald pate. They were in a grotto surrounded by jungle plants; the floor he was seated on had been hewn from stone, and the man's throne was a petrified log with Chinese logograms carved into its surface.

"Master, I do not understand," Veritas said, and realized even as he dreamed that his words weren't English.

The man nodded patiently and looked up at where a raven was perched near the top of a tree, grooming its plumes in the morning sun. "You don't understand because your mind refuses to acknowledge the truth. In this way it protects the illusion it has convinced itself is reality. In so doing, it keeps you ignorant of the truth but comfortable in your ignorance. If you are to progress, it is necessary for you to view things differently and not draw conclusions as to their nature, but to simply observe and accept them without conscious judgment, understanding that what you think of as separate from you is actually a part of you, just as you are a part of everything."

Veritas the child studied his hands, embarrassed by his lack of understanding of the message the master was attempting to impart.

The master seemed to sense his discomfiture and smiled kindly, his skin crinkling like old parchment. "We walked by a river on the way here. When we looked out over the water, you saw eddies and swirls that appeared to be separate and distinct, is that not so? If you perceived the effect as you do all things, you might remark that this swirl is where I caught a carp, or that eddy is where the water is warmer when I swim. You would view the areas as separate, yet they are all of the same river. Their semblance of separateness is an incomplete description of their nature. Because each swirl is not a separate thing when you consider it – it is a never-ending stream of water that creates the swirl over and over again, every fraction of every second, only in the exact same pattern, thereby creating the illusion you perceive."

The master looked away for a moment. "By viewing it as other than an aspect of the greater river, you mistake it for a thing that is separate from that from which it is made. In this way you also mistake yourself as separate from all things, rather than simply an expression of something larger than yourself." He paused and his kindly eyes warmed as he gazed at Veritas. "You too are nothing more than patterns of energy. You're composed of atoms in constant movement. Every cell in your body regenerates in two or three days and is a different one than the days before, yet your body appears to be solid and enduring. It is a magician's trick, but one that is masterfully presented and easy to mistake as distinct from all other atoms that create everything you see and touch."

Veritas's serious expression brightened with childlike wonder. "So everything is a part of me, and I am a part of everything," he said, nodding slowly. "But if I stub my toe by the river, is it not my toe that hurts, and not your toe and everyone else's toe?"

"Of course. But that does not mean the pain you feel is unique to your experience, nor that the act of stubbing your toe, or feeling that pain, doesn't affect anything else. If everything is intertwined, the flutter of a butterfly's wings on the other side of the world affects you at some subtle level, even if you don't acknowledge or feel it. If there is no you, no butterfly, no me, but simply varied expressions of the same matter confused as though they are swirls that exist apart from the river, then you might say there is no impact on you. But that is only because you're viewing reality through a limited framework – one that you have learned and that is limited by your awareness and your senses. Your job in becoming enlightened is to move beyond that construct and simply see things as they are, rather than organizing what is so that it makes sense to you."

"I still don't completely understand, Master. I'm sorry. You have been very patient with me. I am unworthy of your time."

"Your mind and your senses are filters, young master. They automatically filter thousands of possible impressions each moment and focus only on those your mind believes are useful. But does that mean those other events, those stimuli, don't exist? That they have disappeared the moment you dismiss them as unworthy of your awareness? No. Of course not. They are still there, taking place every instant, forming the backdrop of reality. But from your perspective, you might say 'I am thirsty' or 'It is hot' or 'The ground is hard' because those are the aspects of reality your mind is focused on. It eliminates from your reality nine hundred and ninety-nine things that are still occurring simultaneously, and leaves you with the impression that all that exists in that moment is your thirst or temperature or feeling."

The master smiled again. "You have blocked out those other things, but they are still there, only without your active involvement – you are not actively observing them, but they are still having an effect on you, whether you know it or not. What I mean by *you must learn to experience reality in the whole, rather than in pieces* is that you must change your learned inclination to filter and instead allow yourself to swim in the stream of what is."

A particularly nasty pothole jostled Veritas awake, and he blinked in the darkness, confused about the dream. Was this a genuine memory finally making itself known, or yet another implanted narrative that had been invented by people he'd never met for some purpose they'd never seen fit to explain?

The data stream in the corner of his eye had gone back to appearing random once he had fallen asleep, and now was just a continuum of seeming gibberish rather than information.

Veritas adjusted his position and leaned farther from the gash in the trailer floor, wishing he still had his watch. Almost instantly the stream solidified into an image like that of a digital clock, and he couldn't help but smile at the power of the chip that was implanted in his cerebral cortex. He willed a map into being and studied the icon that represented him, and saw that he was only a few hours from where the highway would fork to go to Seattle, answering any questions he'd had about its final destination.

Veritas closed his eyes and breathed deeply as he drifted off again, this time without any memory of what he dreamed or whether he did at all.

Chapter 38

Olympia, Washington

The truck driver pulled over for a bathroom break at a truck stop, and Veritas dropped from the trailer and crept away without anyone seeing him. It was four a.m., and the only souls awake were the long-haul truckers who were on schedule to arrive in Seattle first thing in the morning to unload their goods, and if they were lucky, sleep before turning around and heading in the opposite direction with another full load.

Veritas stayed in the shadows and made his way toward the truck stop restaurant, where he could see signs for the restrooms. He tried a thought command, and his inner display highlighted the locations of the CCTV cameras. None were near the restrooms, so he felt safe ducking into the men's lavatory and relieving himself before washing his face and hands, and then he used a damp paper towel to remove the worst of the orange pulp and residue from his jeans. He finished by rinsing his jacket in one of the sinks and blotting it dry before slipping it back on, the air frigid now that he was near the Canadian border.

His stomach growled, but he ignored it. His display indicated a CCTV camera at the cashier and another in the restaurant, so there was no way he could buy anything without being recorded. While electronics seemed to malfunction around him much of the time, he couldn't rely on that happening when he most needed it. He had to assume that with Selena in custody, they would have learned of his ultimate destination, so from this point on he was alone in enemy territory, and wary of being ambushed if they'd figured out he hadn't died in the river.

Veritas had considered the possibility on the long ride north and expected that there would be roadblocks had the authorities been on alert. But the truck had made its way without being stopped after leaving the Indian Nation, which had given him hope that his gambit had worked, at least for the time being.

He called up the distance and saw that he was roughly fifteen miles from McCleary, which appeared to be a small hamlet in the middle of the Washington hills with nothing much to distinguish it from countless others. He did a quick calculation and figured that at a measured trot, he could make it by sunrise. Rested from the ride and with his muscles sore from lying motionless on the hard trailer floor, the prospect of trekking through the countryside actually sounded inviting.

Veritas adjusted the backpack and walked along the highway until he hit the smaller tributary that led to McCleary. He turned onto the road and picked up his pace, sticking to the shoulder, where he could dart into the brush if any cars came along. He doubted it would be a problem, given how rural the route was, but he was taking no chances, and he forced himself to endure plodding through loose gravel versus skimming along the more stable pavement.

Clouds drifted overhead like inky islands in a sea of stars as he pushed west, and each gust of wind felt like a thousand icy needles stabbing into his exposed skin. The landscape was black as the grave once the lights of Olympia faded behind him, and the air was redolent of wet grass and blooming trees and the crisp snap of salt spray blown inland from the Northern Pacific. His legs pumped with methodical precision, and once he'd settled into a comfortable pace, he scarcely noticed the effort, concentrating instead on his mental map and pushing visions of Selena being tortured by faceless black-clad figures from his thoughts.

He rounded a bend, and his mental screen changed from an

unobtrusive background display to a blinking red alert. Icons appeared on the road ahead, and he counted eight of them just off the road, presumably lying in wait. His expectation that he'd moved quickly enough to beat them to his destination had clearly been unrealistic, and now he was faced with a worst-case scenario: alone, with no resources, his one chance of getting answers lost. He cursed under his breath as he slowed and calculated the distance until he reached them – three-quarters of a mile, so even if they had night vision gear, he was still invisible to them, the hills obstructing their view at that distance.

Veritas veered right to a towering pine tree and stopped beneath it. There was no point in continuing to Cassius's retreat – he had no doubt that they would have the place under their control and he'd be walking into a trap. He wiped his face with his hand and muttered to himself, and then his display alerted him of another blue icon like his own, moving extremely fast across rough terrain.

He gauged the distance between them, which was closing quickly, and looked around for a good place to hide. He spotted a tall pine with a trunk nearly two feet thick and made his decision. Veritas ran toward it at full speed and threw himself upward. He caught the lowest branch, easily twelve feet off the ground, and pulled himself up to the next branch. When he was sure it would support his weight without moving, he froze and watched the forest as the icon continued to close on his position.

If the Brethren had some sort of ability to track his chip, then all of Veritas's assumptions were wrong, and they'd have him in minutes. He wished he understood what the different color icons meant, but there was no manual, and he had to make do with guesses. He watched the other icon bearing down on him without slowing, and reached into his backpack for the hatchet – a feeble gesture, he knew, but he'd be damned if he went down without a fight. With his speed and an element of surprise, he might be able to take a single commando if he could drop on top of him.

Veritas listened intently and thought he heard the pounding of footsteps from deeper in the forest, which aligned with the blue icon's trajectory. He craned his neck to see, grateful for his enhanced vision that enabled him to make out objects he wouldn't have normally been able to, and tensed in preparation to spring, hatchet in hand.

The icon stopped just before it merged with his, and he waited, not daring to breathe.

A voice called out in a whisper, "I know you're up in the tree. Smart, but no cigar. You can come down – just don't shoot."

Veritas frowned and tried to make out the speaker, but couldn't. A few seconds went by. The speaker whispered again. "We don't have all day. One of their thermal drones will pick up your heat signature if we're still here when they send one up."

Veritas resumed breathing and lowered himself to the bottom branch, and then dropped to the ground. A tall man about his age, with dark hair clipped close to his skull and high cheekbones that hinted at Slavic genes, faced him from five yards away with his hands on his hips. He chuckled when he saw the hatchet.

"You won't need that." He paused and studied Veritas. "You don't recognize me, do you?"

Veritas still clutched the hatchet and shook his head. "No."

"Not surprising. Figures with the memory wipe you wouldn't. Doesn't matter."

"Who are you?"

"Milo. We grew up together. I was one of the team."

"Milo," Veritas said, repeating the name. "I thought I was the only survivor–"

"We can talk later. Are you hurt?"

"No."

"Then stow the hatchet and get ready to run. I've got a camp a few miles from here, deep in the woods. No roads, good tree coverage, and outside the area they've been patrolling with drones."

"I don't understand," Veritas said, replacing the hatchet in his backpack.

"I'll tell you everything when we get to the camp. Follow me."

Milo took off at a sprint, and it was all Veritas could do to keep up. If his new abilities had been surprising, Milo's were astounding as he cut through the forest without hesitation, moving at motocross speed. The two men ran like the devil was on their heels, twin blurs in the darkness, Veritas trying to make sense of the sudden appearance of another super soldier, who clearly hadn't suffered the same memory wipe Veritas had.

Fifteen minutes later, Milo slowed and spun to face Veritas. "Almost there. Hear the water?"

Veritas hadn't, but the moment Milo mentioned it, he could make out the burble of a stream ahead. Milo regarded him, his face unreadable in the darkness, and then set off again at a walk. "We should be fine. Nobody comes this way. It's too far from even the fire roads. The only beings I've seen so far are some squirrels and a frightened deer. Poor thing couldn't have been very old, and I was right on top of it before I noticed."

"I don't understand any of this. How did you find me?" Veritas asked.

"Easy. You showed up on my head screen. That's what I call it, anyway. Another blue. We were all wired so we could detect each other when in relative proximity."

"Why?"

"So that in battle we wouldn't accidentally kill each other or leave one of our own behind. Of course, we never really got the chance to test that, did we?" Milo said, his final words laced with sarcasm.

"No, I get that. I mean, what are you doing here?"

"Same reason you're here, I bet. I was staying with Cassius. About six hours ago, all hell broke loose – helicopters, drones, combat troops. I sensed their approach and woke up. I tried to get Cassius to come with me, but he's so goddamn stubborn… He wouldn't leave. I took off – the head screen makes it easy to avoid detection – and he stayed behind."

Milo stopped and motioned to an area near the brook. As dawn broke across the hills, Veritas could just make out a dark green four-man tent pitched beneath a pair of towering pines. Besides that sole sign of human life, the rest of the area looked undisturbed.

Milo shook his head. "I heard them land. Cassius wouldn't put up a fight, so it went down quietly. I got away with what I could carry, which fortunately looks like it's enough for a while. A bow and a quiver of arrows, the tent, some TP and food, water purification tablets, a lighter and butane stove, a stack of cash and some gold…"

"No guns?"

Milo nodded. "An old Glock 9mm I'd traded some work for a while back. But Cassius disapproved of even that."

"He just let them take him?"

"He wasn't a fighter. I don't blame him. Nothing in all human history has been solved with violence."

"You say I know you. We grew up together?"

Milo walked to the brook and rinsed his face and hands in the bracing water. "That's right. We've known each other since we were toddlers."

"What's my name? My real name?"

"Anton. From your mother, who was French-Vietnamese."

"Anton," Veritas repeated. "Doesn't trigger anything."

"Probably won't. From what Cassius explained to me about the memory wiping, you won't remember much of anything except the most embedded memories. No telling how much, or of what." He smiled. "What do they call you now?"

"Veritas. Ver, for short."

Another smile. "They love their grand gestures, don't they? Veritas. Truth. At least, their version of it. How did you find Cassius?"

Veritas explained about Ben. Milo nodded. "A shame. So much senseless death. Not that it matters in the scheme of things, I suppose. Still, it hurts to hear of it. And I think you would have gotten a lot out of meeting Cassius. He's definitely one of a kind."

"You talk like he's dead."

"He might as well be, as far as you're concerned. They'll try everything to break him, of course, but none of it will work."

"Why do you think they attacked instead of waiting for me to show?"

"Probably because they were afraid you'd tumble to them if they tried to set up an ambush before you got to Cassius's place. And remember they can't be sure which route you might take – roads, or through the woods. So it's safer to wait for you at your destination." Milo sighed. "Come. I can make some coffee on the stove. When did you last eat?"

"I…nothing other than oranges, yesterday morning."

"Then you'll be happy to hear I have plenty of food. And there are fish in the stream and plenty of edible plants and mushrooms, if you know what you're looking for."

"Great."

"Take a load off and I'll get some brewed. Hope you don't mind some energy bars. They're the most efficient to carry, so I have almost a crate of them in my rucksack."

"That would be perfect. But I have a ton of questions."

"I'm sure you do. And I have answers to many of them. Have a seat wherever you like, and once the coffee's going, I'll tell you what I know." He smiled again, and Veritas couldn't help but smile back. Milo sighed again. "Which could take a while."

Chapter 39

Milo sipped from a plastic mug after settling with his back against a tree, and Veritas joined him with his cup of coffee and an expectant expression. Milo set his mug on the ground next to him.

"Why don't you tell me what you've been told first? That will eliminate a lot of repetition," he said.

"The woman said I was part of a military program, sponsored by the Brethren, that had attempted to create super soldiers, but something went wrong and they canceled the program, and only I escaped with my life. Then when we met the Tribe cell leader in Burning Man, he said they wiped my memory to keep me safe, and that the Brethren were planning something really big that would end humanity as we know it. Right after that, they attacked Burning Man and pretty much destroyed it, and we had to go on the run. I chose here because I trusted Ben, and he'd said that I needed to talk to Cassius to learn everything."

Milo nodded. "That's a lot to unpack. And most of it's wrong, or at least more like half-truths. Let's start with the Brethren. What did they tell you about them?"

"That they've been around since the dawn of time and are some kind of messengers of the gods – the Anunnaki, they called them."

Milo took another drink of coffee. "That's true."

"And that the Tribe was a faction of the original group that split off over ideological differences."

"Also true. The Anunnaki were alien visitors who were worshipped by early civilizations as gods. They manipulated evolution so that humans became the dominant species of upright bipeds, but engineered it so they had just enough Neanderthal DNA so they would be useful to them. But they didn't want too much, just a couple of percent, because the Neanderthals perceived the world differently than humans and didn't react to the wetware upgrades, and that wasn't good for the Anunnaki's scheme. They wanted nice, compliant sheep who could be easily controlled. So after sufficient DNA had spread through the human population, they arranged for the Neanderthals to die out, which wasn't that hard to do – they just gave humans enough technology that they had a survival advantage and let nature take its course. The changes they'd made in the human brain with the addition of Neanderthal DNA, as well as from fine-tuning operating system upgrades using viruses, had made *Homo sapiens* more aggressive and prone to violence, so it was natural that the new Neanderthal-Sapiens hybrid would find reasons to destroy their more peaceful neighbors. Very much like today, if you think about it, and as good an explanation as any for why nations act out aggressively for little reason. But the Anunnaki kept upgrading through viruses, and in doing so, we've become ever more aggressive and violent as a species."

"You're saying that aliens created us?"

"Not at all. More like bred us from the available choices."

"Why?"

"Ah, that's the question, isn't it? But back to what you call the Brethren. That makes it sound like one monolithic group, but the first thing you need to know is that it isn't. There's a core group with a cell organization exactly like the Tribe, only with more communication between the cells so they coordinate on how to achieve their ends. And then there's the dark Brethren, which is an inner circle that was set up to keep an eye on the core group. The dark ones are directly in touch with the Anunnaki, whereas the core group operates through their equivalent of priests or prophets, who convey the wishes of the Anunnaki to them."

"They're still communicating today? I thought they disappeared thousands of years ago."

"They departed, but only once they were confident that their messengers – the Brethren – were doing their bidding and could manipulate the earth's population as they wished. They ensured that the core group was always twenty or so years ahead of whatever technology was around at the time, so they could maintain their edge over their fellow man, which is the basis of the legends of ancient knowledge passed along in secret societies. There's truth in that. But the dark Brethren receive the technology more like fifty years ahead, ensuring they always have an advantage even over the core group. It's worked smoothly for thousands of years…at least until recently."

"And the Tribe?"

"Members of the core's inner circle split off when they figured out what the ultimate goal of the Anunnaki was, and they've been fighting to hamstring the Brethren ever since. The super-soldier program's only one example of how they intervened, when we all should have been destroyed. But I'm getting ahead of myself. The program was set up by the core group so that we could be trained to go after the Tribe and eradicate them, all under the pretense of developing the ultimate warrior for the armed forces. But the dark group had other plans and changed the programming on a number of us so we weren't under the control of the core group, but instead under theirs. The problem is that it wasn't the outcome that the Anunnaki wanted – the dark group did it in secret, which they then had to cover up when things didn't turn out as hoped. That's why they ultimately destroyed us."

"But you're here, and so am I."

"Yes. The Tribe was able to help us escape."

"You remember everything? They didn't wipe your memory?"

"No. They wiped yours because they wanted to put you into action if things didn't work out with me."

"I don't understand."

"Let me back up. The Brethren selected orphans when we were two or three years old, or kids like you who were put up for adoption or handed over to the state. The conditioning started young and involved three foundations: spiritual, chemical, and tech. The spiritual was our upbringing at a monastery in Myanmar, where we were taught the ancient techniques of meditation and martial arts that refined our senses. The chemical involved regular doses of agents that expanded our consciousness so we could further perceive reality accurately, rather than as it's presented to us. And the tech was our physical supplementation – our skeletons augmented with polymers so our bones are ten times harder than normal, our musculature juiced with hormones that developed it far beyond anything in nature, and a chip that acted as a booster for our brains, as well as a display system for information that would come in handy in battle. Which makes us faster, stronger, more durable, and more cerebrally developed than just about anything on the planet. All of this created soldiers who could literally slow time when they needed to, who could affect electronic fields within limited ranges, but most importantly, could use the true nature of reality to their advantage in a fight."

"Jordan, the rebel leader, kept saying that too – the part about reality, or perception of it. What did he mean?" Veritas asked.

"How much do you remember about physics?"

Veritas frowned. "Not a ton."

"Then I'll keep this basic. What we see and experience at the material level our normal senses process is called Newtonian physics. Things like gravity, heat, cold, Maxwell's equations, that sort of thing. But at the subatomic level, all the rules of Newtonian physics start to break down. As an example, the quantum computers that are everywhere? They use this difference in subatomic behavior as the basis of their tech. When one quantum particle changes its state, for reasons nobody entirely understands, other particles at a distance react to the change – which is impossible if our understanding of reality is correct, but happens predictably enough to build computers around it."

"What does that have to do with us?"

"Reality isn't anything like what we believe. You've played VR games, right?"

"Of course."

"Then you know that no matter how believable they're designed, what we're seeing isn't real – yet our senses tell us it is when we're hooked in. Over the last generation, it's become impossible to tell what's virtual and what isn't." Milo's expression changed. "What if I told you that tech isn't new? That it's older than civilization? Or at least, that it's been in use on Earth for thousands of years?"

"How? There weren't even computers until, what, maybe a hundred years ago?"

"We didn't get the tech to build them until then, that's true. But like I said before, the core group has been manipulating the entire species' perception of reality for thousands of years with regular updates to our brains, using plagues and viruses."

"Why?"

"Because all of humanity is a kind of distributed computing system in a galaxy-wide organic quantum supercomputer. Every human with the Neanderthal DNA is used as a processing node when they're asleep. A portion of their brain contributes to a master network that partially uses that power to create the reality we experience during our waking hours. But that isn't a true reality, and once you step outside that simulation, you understand it as it actually is – and that turned out to be bad for the super-soldier idea. The irony is that the powers they imbued us with made us completely unsuitable for their purpose. But they didn't figure that out until it was too late. Some of us went insane; our brains couldn't handle the cognitive dissonance, so some became unstoppable mass murderers when deployed, and others became vegetables. But the majority simply refused to follow orders and fight."

"Why not?"

"Everything's connected, and in true reality there's no past, present, or future. The illusion that things are separate is an artifact of the lens we view them through."

"You sound like a dream I had. And old Chinese monk was describing something a lot like that using a river as an example."

"That's one way to explain it. Another is…you know what origami is?"

"Where they fold paper to make animals. Japanese, right?"

Milo nodded. "Correct. Well, the true nature of the universe is like origami. Or like kids with scissors making paper snowflakes by folding a sheet and cutting it."

Veritas's brow furrowed. "You completely lost me."

"Imagine a piece of paper. Like origami, you fold the big piece into ever smaller squares until eventually it's the size of…a stamp. Then you drive a needle all the way through it. Now there's a hole going through dozens of layers of folded paper."

Veritas nodded. "Okay."

"Then you unfold the piece of paper and shine a light through it, and instead of the single hole, you see dozens of holes. So to your eye, based on your perception, you think they're all separate holes. But you're wrong. It's all the same hole, but because your senses can only perceive unfolded reality, it creates an illusion of separateness."

"So reality is a piece of folded paper?"

"That's just an easy way to describe it. It's actually more like a holograph. In a holographic image, which is made by recording wave interference patterns reflected off a target, even the smallest portion of the holographic image, if you were to cut it out and enlarge it with a laser, contains all the information of the larger whole – of the bigger image. If you were to create a holographic image of your face and then cut out a piece of the image the size of the head of a pin, all the wave interference patters are still there – so every part contains all of the whole, even when you make it a separate, smaller piece. Or like a television broadcast, which is just a stream of static, but when you have the right receiver, which is like viewing it through the right lens, it becomes images and sound. The stream is the implicate order of things, whereas the image is the explicate order, which appears to be a separate thing but is just the end result of that stream. Reality is the stream, not the image, but we're programmed to view reality as the image. Make sense?"

"Not really."

"Well, follow that through. If everything is connected and is basically composed of or informed by everything else at some level, and it's all part of that stream, and your lens has been augmented to see it as it truly is versus the normal artificial snapshots, that gives you an amazing edge over someone whose lens is more two-dimensional and doesn't see that all the holes in the paper are actually the same hole, or the image is just a function of the stream."

"How? What kind of edge?"

"In a practical sense, our perception of time is our lens roving over the various holes in the paper. We 'see' the closest one, and then the next one, and the next, and so on. Because of our lens being a continuum that views things in an order of *this,* then *that,* rather than appreciating all simultaneously, we're stuck with a perception of this, then that, then that. But it's all the same hole. The Brethren augmented us so we're able to step outside the continuum and see the entirety. Which enables us to slow our two-dimensional lens, because in reality there's no time between seeing the first hole and the second. We see them simultaneously, so the speed from A to B doesn't affect us – we're freed of that construct. At least in a limited sense. Our lens is still the same one we were born with, but it's got the ability to see more 4D than 2D when we force it to. That comes in handy when a bullet's fired. Instead of it seeming to hit us instantly, we can step outside the continuum and move out of its way with all the time in the world. It makes conventional weapons virtually useless – which makes us unstoppable."

Veritas frowned. "That sort of happened when I broke out of jail." He regarded Milo. "I hear a but…"

"But that same ability to step outside the continuum also enables us to see the pointlessness of the petty squabbles that make humans want to fight, or scheme, or acquire, or do any of the things we've been doing since we climbed out of trees. If everything is an elaborate virtual reality illusion, what's the point of any of it? Why fight anyone if that someone else is just another hole in the paper, like we are – in other words, the same hole viewed from a different perspective? If everything's interconnected and we're all the same energy or consciousness, what's the point of winning or losing a struggle that's entirely artificial? Remember, if there's no time other than that created by our senses, and our position in it on the continuum is just a function of our lenses, then everything's happened already, as has every possibility in what we think of as the future. It's all static, and it's just our awareness that creates the illusion of movement along the continuum."

Milo laughed. "There are theories that are extrapolations of that which drive physicists nuts. Like the many-universe theory, where every atomic event splits reality off into a new tree, leaving a present where something has both happened and hasn't, depending on which universe you're talking. It's kind of like the uncertainty principle, where until a physicist measures the state of a photon, it's both a wave and a particle. It's both things simultaneously, and only becomes one or the other when an observation is made. The cat in the box is both alive and dead until you open the box. Or rather, if it's alive when you open it, it's dead in another parallel universe that branched off when you looked. Or even weirder, there's a universe where you didn't open the box at all, and it's still both alive and dead in that one."

"That sounds…impossible."

"Physics is filled with the impossible. We were taught all this as part of our training, but I keep forgetting you don't remember. But the takeaway is that reality isn't what we think, and everything we do, or someone else does, affects us in some way. The wave interference pattern changes based on their behavior, no matter how seemingly inconsequential. Now multiply that by billions and billions of people, and then billions of billions of billions of nanosecond branches, and we're talking…something most people can't fathom."

"You see all this?"

"It's more like I get brief glimpses of it and can draw conclusions based on what I see. Religions are filled with descriptions of a different reality – that's one of the things they all sort of have in common. Mystical traditions, too. But the vast majority of humanity never does anything but sit at the console playing the VR game, never understanding that they're missing most of the picture – that their lens is tricking them every moment. That's useful to the Anunnaki, but horrible for humanity."

"And they did this so they could use us as computers?"

"More like processor nodes, but you get the picture."

"Why?"

Milo nodded slowly. "That's the best question of them all. And one I can only speculate about. My theory is that, just like governments always need more tax revenue, and VR games need more computing capability, they need more power than we can deliver in our sleep. That's where the current plan comes in. My guess is that the combination of the eradication of everyone who doesn't have the right DNA with installing the Nexus chip in everyone who's left once this virus kills most without it, prepares the survivors to be more powerful, or useful, processors. They can be milked twenty-four seven, just like a computer that's multitasking with something in the background while you update a spreadsheet."

"That's…that would turn everyone into zombies."

"I just got through explaining to you that most people already are – they just don't realize it. So what does it matter if they make it official?"

"You're kidding, right?"

Milo shook his head. "Not at all. In one universe, the Brethren succeed and the world goes on as it has, essentially a slave planet of processing drones being fed a reality that doesn't exist. In another the Brethren fail, and humans are only processing drones when they sleep. Both realities already exist. They always have, and always will. So anything the Tribe thinks it can achieve misses the point entirely, which is that its actions are as much of an illusion as the rest of this mess."

Awareness played across Veritas's face. "Is that why Cassius…"

Milo nodded. "Exactly. He understands it doesn't matter whether they capture him or kill him or not. It's all the same. But he eschews violence, so he won't fight. All he can control is which universe he branches down, or which set of manifest events he chooses to recognize with his lens, and in the universe where he fights, he believes that outcome is worse than the one where he doesn't, even though at a basic level they're all the same."

"But you ran."

"He actually encouraged me to. But you notice I didn't fight. Again, that's a choice I made long ago, which is one of the reasons they brought you out of retirement, so to speak. The Tribe requires a super soldier who can do what it takes to stop the dark Brethren. I refuse to be that soldier. That's what they didn't tell you about wiping your memory: they didn't do it for your own good. They did it in case they couldn't get me to play ball, or maybe even if I had, they might figure two were better than one. So they stole your memories and disabled your abilities until they were forced to update your program so you could be of use to them."

Veritas nodded again. "In saving the world. I can see where they'd think that was worth doing."

"That's where we differ ideologically. Cassius and I believe that nothing is worth sacrificing our integrity for, that no end justifies the means. Why? Because every person's actions affect everyone else at some level, and we can only be responsible for our own – what we put out in the world, or to use the holographic model, the wave interference patterns we create. But obviously not everyone thinks that way. The Tribe, or at least the branch that put you on ice, disagrees." Milo shrugged as though the discussion was over.

Veritas's expression soured. "If I saw things like you, everything would be pointless."

"Quite the opposite. If everything's pointless, then your choices *are* the whole point. Your decisions determine who you are and how you choose to interact with everything else. It's the epitome of free will. It creates meaning in a meaningless situation."

Veritas shook his head. "No, it's deterministic. If you're right, everything is already written, so why do anything at all?"

"We'll have to disagree. If your actions create a different branch, a different universe each time you make a choice, then that's a power that's as close to godlike as any I can imagine."

242

"But that's your conclusion, not fact, right? I mean, it's not carved in stone. The other faction of the Tribe believes differently. What if they're right and you're wrong?"

Milo looked away. "I don't discuss hypotheticals. We all have to be true to ourselves."

Veritas sat in silence, trying to absorb Milo's revelations, but found that his headache had returned. Eventually he rose and took a few steps toward the brook before turning to face Milo.

"How can I get the rest of my capabilities back? I can't make a choice whether to fight or not if I don't have the ability to see firsthand what you're claiming is reality."

Milo grinned. "That I can probably help you with."

"Even though nothing matters and it's all pointless?"

Milo's eyes flashed and he sighed. "I never said nothing matters. I said that my decisions, and how I act on them, are the only things that matter. Everything else is noise."

Chapter 40

Whidbey Island, Washington

Selena struggled against her bindings in frustration as the helicopter set down on the helipad of a mothballed Air Force base. The leader of the commandos was in the copilot seat in the cockpit, leaving her with two members of the team – one, a geeky type she'd heard the leader call Donald, and another who had the stone face of a hardened killer, whom Donald had called Lars as they'd loaded her aboard.

The grounds looked deserted, and when the rotors had stopped turning, Lars slid the cargo door open and waited as the leader made his way to the opening. More helicopters landed farther away on the deserted tarmac, and Selena winced at the roar of their turbines.

She'd decided that whatever they did to her, she'd go to her grave before revealing any of the Tribe's secrets. Fortunately, she knew little about the structure other than her cell, which had been destroyed at Burning Man, and that the cell had been only one of many distributed all over the world. How the group was organized beyond that had been kept a mystery to her, for which she was now grateful – she couldn't reveal what she didn't know.

The leader glared at her with soulless eyes and turned to Donald and Lars.

"Lock her up. We'll interrogate her later," he ordered, and then marched toward one of the gray buildings without looking back.

Lars grabbed her and pulled her roughly toward the door, and

Donald frowned. "Easy. You don't have to break her arm."

"You don't like how I'm doing it, you handle her," Lars snapped, and released her.

Donald helped her out of the helicopter and led her toward the buildings as the other helicopters powered down and black-clad fighters emptied onto the field.

Once at the structures, Donald opened a door and escorted her into the bowels of the building. Every surface was coated with dust; the facility had obviously sat unused for a long time. They reached one of four jailhouse doors with an electric card key reader by its side, and Donald held a magnetic card against it for a moment before it whined and the bolt opened with a clank that echoed along the hallway.

"Inside," Donald said, and Selena complied. Lars stepped into the cell with her and unlocked her cuffs, and then exited and slammed the door behind him. Lars continued down the hall, but Donald lingered. When Lars was gone, he looked Selena over. "I'd cooperate with them. Either way, you won't have a choice. They don't care what happens to you, and they don't answer to anyone."

"What is this place?"

"It used to be an air base near Tacoma. Retired about ten years ago. It was where your boyfriend's program was run before they shut it down."

"I don't have a boyfriend."

"Whatever. The point is, nobody knows you're here, and they're utterly ruthless. Azra, the boss, used to be in the program too. He'd just as soon snap your neck as say hello. Don't mess with them."

"I have no idea why you're doing this."

Donald looked away. "I just follow orders."

"Even if it means murdering helpless civilians, like at Burning Man?"

"I'm just a technician. I never fired a shot."

"You're helping them. That makes you part of it."

Donald grunted and shook his head. "Do whatever he asks. That's your only chance," he said, and walked away, leaving her alone in the cold cell, the sun's morning rays that filtered through a high barred window doing nothing to warm her.

She had no doubt that the interrogation would be brutal. It would probably start with torture and then progress to a cocktail of drugs that would eradicate her will to resist. She'd been warned by Jordan about this sort of questioning and knew there was little she could do other than prepare herself as best she could for what was to come.

Selena walked to the corner of the cell and sat on the floor, massaging her wrists as she recalled Jordan's counsel. She would will herself to a safe place in her mind far away from the cell, where she would be impervious to pain or anything they put her through. She wished she'd been equipped with a false molar that contained a lethal dose of poison if she cracked it open, as Jordan had once offered, but she'd refused, so all she was left with was the techniques she'd learned to minimize the pain. She already knew that there was no hope, and had accepted that as fact – she was badly outnumbered, had no weapon, was up against a ruthless adversary that was prepared to do anything, and nobody was on their way to save her.

Which meant she was dead.

It was a fate she'd been prepared for since becoming an active Tribe operative as a teenager. Even so, a tiny knot of anxiety coiled in her stomach, and she offered a silent prayer that she would die a warrior's death, as had so many of her predecessors, and not dishonor her position as one of humanity's last line of defense.

Azra was pacing in the command office when Donald entered. He fixed the technical director with a hard stare and indicated one of the military-issued metal chairs in front of a desk. Donald sat and waited for the continuation of the argument that had started in Nevada.

"Nothing's happened at the McCleary compound," Azra complained. "We've been holding the old fool there, but nobody's shown up. This feels like a waste of time. This bastard's been ahead of us every step of the way."

"It may take him a while to get there, assuming that's where he's really headed. He could have changed his mind when he figured out that the girl and the pilot knew his destination."

"In which case we'll never catch him." Azra glared at Donald. "I want the upgrade. Now that we know he's out there, we need every advantage, and I'm operating in the dark without full operational capability."

"We've been over this. The risks are too great. The upgrade was always used in conjunction with training to manage the effects. Even so, you know what happened to many of those who received it."

"I don't care. They were weak – I could have told anyone who cared to listen they wouldn't be able to handle it. I'm different. I always was. If we're going to find and neutralize the target, I need to be brought up to full capacity."

Azra had been in the super-soldier program as a last-ditch effort by the DOD to salvage it, but unlike Veritas, he hadn't received the final upgrade or any of the early training and chemical augmentation – he'd been one of the last batch to be processed, where they'd decided to try the chip on unconditioned subjects, but when it had become obvious that the program had gone badly off the rails, the upgrade had been withheld.

"That isn't my decision to make," Donald said. "Take it up with them. You should know I can't do it." In addition to being the technical director of the program, Donald had been in charge of implementing the upgrades.

Azra moved so quickly he was little more than a blur. Donald spilled from the chair and Azra was on top of him, his gloved hand enveloping the top of Donald's head while his other arm choked off his airway.

"Now listen, you little maggot," he hissed in Donald's ear. "You'll do exactly as I say or I'll crush your skull like a walnut. I know you've got the ability to upgrade me, and you're going to do it, or I'll personally take you out in the helicopter and drop you into the Sound from ten thousand feet, understand? Am I clear?"

Azra released Donald and he gasped for breath. When the color had returned to Donald's face, Azra straightened and took his seat again as though nothing had happened. "I know they still have the booths here. I want to be upgraded as soon as possible. Go dust one off, work your magic, but if I'm not being processed within the hour, you're going swimming. And if you breathe a word of this to anyone, including the circle? I'll rip your heart out and make you eat it with your last breath. You read me?"

Donald got off the floor and felt his neck. "You know the risks. If I do this and it goes the way most of the others did, they'll kill me just as surely as you would."

Azra waved the warning away. "Then the question is, do you want to live another hour, or do you want to go for a helo ride right now? If we don't capture this Veritas, I'm just as dead as you are, so I've got nothing to lose. You'd do well to remember that."

"But the girl—"

"She's nothing. Besides, I have an idea. But first you do whatever you need to do to upgrade me — is that clear?"

"I can't be sure the supplies are still here."

"Of course they are." Azra's eyes narrowed. "I know how weasels like you work. You hid some away as insurance. I can see it in your face. So stop wasting time, get it, and prepare a tank." Azra tapped his earbud and growled into it. "Lars, get in here. Now."

Lars came at a run a half minute later, and Azra indicated Donald. "Go with him. If he tries to contact anyone, shoot him. Other than that, I'll monitor his actions via your helmet cam. Stick with him like a second skin."

Lars didn't question the order, but merely nodded.

"It could backfire, Azra. You should reconsider," Donald said.

"I know what I'm doing. You have fifty-eight minutes. Stop stalling," Azra spat, and then turned away to stare out at the helicopters on the tarmac while Lars and Donald left.

An hour later, Donald and Azra were standing in front of a large sensory-deprivation tank freshly filled with warm salt water. Azra stared into it while Donald prepared two syringes, one filled with rust-colored fluid, the other amber. Azra stripped, apparently impervious to the cold air in the chamber, and nodded to Donald.

"I want you to deal with the woman while I'm wasting my time in this thing. Just like we discussed. No surprises. It was a good idea, and it should work."

"Of course. If you're right, by the time you get out, the trap will be laid."

Azra nodded. "You're sure I need a full half-day in the tank?" he asked. "What would happen if I cut it short?"

"That isn't an option," Donald said. "Once I inject the solutions, it'll take twelve hours at the absolute minimum. It's not optional. We actually saw better results with twenty-four-hour isolations, but I'm going by memory."

"I want a suit of armor charged and ready when I come out."

"I'll find one and see to it," Donald said. He set the syringes down and wheeled over an IV pole with a bag of saline hanging from it. "I'll change this out every four hours." Donald held up a tube and pointed to a metal exam table. "Lie down."

After five minutes of preparation, Azra was in the isolation tank, the cannula in place. Donald regarded the naked man without emotion and then stepped away from the cover. "Time will distort," he cautioned. "That's natural. Once you've been injected, there's nothing I can do – you have to remain in the tank until I come for you. These lock from the outside, so if you feel a sense of panic, all you can do is lie still and wait for it to pass."

"I don't panic."

"That's good. See you in twelve hours or so."

Donald pressed a button on the side of the tank and the cover lowered over it and sealed with a soft hiss, leaving Azra in complete darkness, suspended in salt water kept at 98.5 degrees Fahrenheit. Donald moved to the IV tube and injected first the amber fluid and then the russet. When both syringes were empty, he stepped away from the tank and shook his head.

"Goddamned idiot. I hope this shit fries your brain. If it doesn't, it'll be a miracle, but you're the boss," he whispered, and then smiled, recalling that a percentage of the team had been left vegetables by the upgrade, even after weeks of extensive conditioning to prepare their systems for it. He entertained a fleeting fantasy of Azra being unresponsive when he opened the tank to retrieve him, and then frowned. Unfortunately, sociopaths like Azra tended to come through the process better than most, which meant that the likelihood was high the upgrade would do nothing but what it was supposed to.

Although he honestly didn't know how many of the capabilities would be affected by the absence of training. The monks and psychiatrists who'd been part of the program had insisted that the elaborate preparation was critical to managing the new perceptions and heightened awareness, and had pointed out that even with the extensive precautions, too many of the team had either melted down or been left catatonic. Of course, none of them were still alive to ask, so Azra would learn the hard way.

Donald cleared the table of the evidence of his work, humming softly to himself as he methodically repacked the vials. If Azra died or emerged a zucchini, that was the least of his problems. His greater fear, having watched so many in the program lose their minds, was that Azra would be fine.

And what would step from the tank would be the world's worst nightmare – on steroids.

Chapter 41

Milo sat cross-legged across from Veritas, the only sounds the burble of water over rocks in the brook and the cry of morning birds from the trees.

"You understand that if we do this, you could lose all your current memories?" Milo asked.

"Most of which are false – so what do I have to lose?" Veritas drew a long breath. "How does this work, anyway?"

"We were two of the last subjects they upgraded to full capability. One of our features was that we could link to each other in the field if we were damaged and do repairs on the fly. What I'll do is put you into a meditative trance, and then link to you and see if I can restore your default settings. Some of them are active now, which is why you can see the position of the hostiles, as well as my icon. But others have been disabled, including your memories."

"They said they wiped them."

"Right, but I'm not sure what that actually means. The information should still be there; it's just that somehow they've blocked your access to it."

"You think you'll be able to figure it out?"

"We don't have much to lose. Your theory about the EMP causing a reboot isn't a bad one. That shouldn't have damaged you permanently – we're hardened in case something like that happens on the battlefield."

"Did we ever see combat?"

"Oh, sure. Limited engagements. Strafing runs, drops into terrorist zones, that sort of thing. More like experiments than anything else. What we were really developed to do wasn't to fight wars, though. Cassius said that the entire point of the program was to create unbeatable warriors who could be pointed at the Tribe."

"The Tribe…" Veritas echoed.

"Didn't turn out as planned, obviously. They had moles in the program. That's why we're here."

"So you hypnotize me or something, and then…?"

"You'll be under. Don't worry about it."

"What if I need to link to you at some point?"

"Highly unlikely. But the short answer is once we retrieve your memories, you'll remember your training, including how to link and repair."

"How will we know if this works?"

"It'll be pretty obvious. For one thing, if you really focus, you'll be able to project into the future somewhat. Not a lot – maybe five or ten minutes. But your lens will have expanded so you can surf the continuum and see what's coming. It's a feeling like déjà vu."

Veritas nodded. "I've had those. I call them spells, or…the cold. Where everything goes kind of dark and distorts. It's hard to describe, but when I come out of it, I always feel like I'm reliving something that just happened."

"That sounds like glitching. This will be more a clear vision of upcoming events. Which gives you the ability to plan for them, and in most cases, to change them if they aren't in your favor."

"Glitching?"

"Where the fabric of the false reality that's being generated all around us frays at the edges. Think of it as buggy code, where a programmer didn't think through everything, so at the periphery there's just…dislocation. Areas where things don't make sense, and you feel like you've just run out of runway, so to speak. If you aren't conditioned for the experience, it feels really odd – like you described."

"And if you are?"

"You see the bugs in the system for what they are. Artifacts of a virtual reality that isn't 100 percent convincing or consistent."

"You never really said why it is that these…Anunnaki…need more computing power."

"Because I can't be certain. I have my own theories. So did Cassius. But that's all they are."

"I'd be interested in hearing them anyway."

Milo nodded. "There's been a lot of talk about whether humans are living in a simulation. Now, that could be taken literally, as in we're populating a VR game, or metaphorically, as in the reality we're living isn't genuine, for whatever reason. My hunch is that they need more processing power because they've maxed out what can be sustained using our current output. As the population has grown from millions to over ten billion, each of those consciousnesses not only provides processing power, but sucks some."

"Why would they suck power?"

"To sustain the artificial reality when they view it during their waking hours, and to continue to make it believable. Think of it like a VR game – the more players, the more power required to make each one's experience seamless and to make it unique. Imagine how much would be needed to make ten billion people's presents seem real, including full pasts and memories." Milo sighed. "My gut says they've hit a practical limit and need to both reduce the number of eyes and increase the output of those who can serve as processors. That's the only way this makes sense. Cull the herd of those who can't be easily harvested, and increase the productivity of those who can."

"But…why? I mean, what's the point of having the Earth as a slave planet?"

"Now you're into unanswerable questions." Milo smiled. "If you're ready to do this, we can start."

Veritas nodded. "I am."

"Okay. Get comfortable and close your eyes. Just sit without saying or thinking anything, trying to be as in the moment as possible. Eventually I'll say a phrase over and over, and I want you to repeat it in your head as a whisper that grows fainter with each repetition."

"And then what?"

"Just do that. I'll handle the rest."

Veritas adjusted himself so his back was against a tree and closed his eyes. Milo and he sat in silence, listening to the gentle rustle of the trees in the light breeze, and after a long wait, Milo began intoning a two-syllable word nearly under his breath.

Veritas echoed it in his mind and felt himself relaxing and sinking deeper into a calm unlike any he'd experienced. The word eventually seemed to take on a mind of its own, and his focus was able to drift from it as it repeated like a tape loop without any conscious effort. Selena's face appeared at the periphery of his thoughts as a fuzzy rendition, and then was replaced by his mother's face, and then Ben's, each fainter and less clear, as though his mental lens were fogging over and his memories were blurring together into one indistinct morass.

Over time, his awareness narrowed and followed the word to an even deeper, more placid place within himself, and his mind seemed to sever its moorings from his body and drift in an infinite void, absent any sense of space or time or separateness from the greater whole.

Chapter 42

Whidbey Island, Washington

Boots approached Selena's cell from down the corridor and she opened her eyes. Donald appeared at the door, his demeanor obviously anxious. He leaned toward her and whispered, "Come over here. Hurry. We don't have a lot of time."

She rose and took several cautious steps toward the barrier. She could see sweat on the technician's forehead even though it was chilly in the brig. "Yeah?"

"We're supposed to transfer you tonight or tomorrow. I won't be able to do anything once you're no longer here."

"What does that mean?"

He held her stare. "I overheard a discussion a while ago. Azra, the leader of this bunch, talking to his second in command. They plan to kill me once this is over. I know too much. I was one of the original team, but now I'm a liability."

"And?" Selena asked.

He fished in his pocket and extracted a card key. "This opens the door to the comm room. There's a communications console in there from the mission days. It was linked to the soldiers. I ducked in there this morning, and it looks like it still works. You should be able to reach your man on it. He's our only hope of getting out of this alive."

"I don't understand. How can I communicate with him? I don't know where he is."

255

Donald shook his head. "It doesn't matter – the transmitter uses quantum entanglement. It's a cluster of matched particles that can send and receive at any distance. I don't have time to explain everything about how it works, but the simple version is that all of the team members had matter in their implants that was linked to twin matter in the transmitter. Think of it as a real-time radio that doesn't require a receiver on the other end."

Selena frowned. "Why can't you use it to track him?"

Donald thrust the key to her. "Because there's nothing to track. The transmitter is entwined with their implants, but not in a traceable way. All it's good for is to communicate with them, to send a message."

"A message," she repeated.

"Right. If he doesn't rescue us, they're going to kill both of us – once they're finished interrogating you. These people are ruthless. They'll fry your brain with drugs and put you through living hell."

"How am I supposed to get out of this cell and find this transmitter?"

"I'm going to shut down the power to this section of the building for a few seconds once you're ready. That will disarm the doors – there's a backup generator, but I'll disable the circuit for the cells. Once you're out, go the way I came in, and make a left outside the brig door. Follow that hall to the fourth room on the right. Use the key card to get in. When you power on the transmitter, you'll see only one icon. Azra's hasn't been entangled."

"Why not?"

"No point. He wouldn't be able to process the communication without the final upgrade, so there was no reason to."

"What makes you think Veritas would risk his neck to rescue us?"

"He came to the casino instead of just bailing, even with all the helicopters. The only reason was because you were inside. Something tells me that he'll do what he has to do to get you out of here."

"And if you're wrong?"

"The Brethren know your people stole some of the virus and are trying to reverse engineer it. They won't succeed. But I have

256

information that could change that. Information they need. I'm pretty sure they'd do just about anything to save the human race. The problem is that your boy is the only one who'll be able to stand up to Azra once he's upgraded." He hesitated. "I know the prophecy. Either he breaks us out of here so you can save the world, or it's just an old myth."

"Why can't you send the message?" Selena asked.

"He'll be able to hear your voice and see you. I mean, not like a camera or anything – more like in his mind. Tell him you're at the old Whidbey Island Air Force base. But he has to hurry. Once Azra is back online, it'll be too late."

"What do you mean, online?"

"He's being upgraded to full capability. He was one of the last team members, where they tried the implant without the training or chemical augmentation, but he never got the final upgrade – instead, they shut down the program and eliminated the original group. All except for him."

"Why did they spare him?" she asked.

"He's fiercely loyal and was a holy terror on the battlefield before he was modded. I guess they figured that he was more stable because he hadn't undergone the chemical augmentation and because the chip hadn't been fully implemented. But none of that matters. While he's being upgraded, he's in an isolation chamber, so he's incommunicado – and everybody takes their orders from him. So even if they notice you're gone, they'll be rudderless for a while."

Her expression was stony. "And then what?"

"Hopefully Veritas will be able to figure out a way to find us and neutralize Azra. With him out of the way, we'll be able to escape in the chaos."

"Why don't we just try to escape right now? Why wait?"

"We wouldn't get far. Azra would track us down and kill us in no time."

"You want me to risk Veritas's life to save ours," she stated flatly.

"There's no other way." Donald checked his watch. "Azra will be in the tank for at least another three hours. It's not a ton of time, but hopefully it will be enough."

"How do I know I can trust you?"

"I know how to get the information that's necessary to make a vaccine. I'm the only person in the world who isn't in their inner circle who does. They're confident you'll fail. But they didn't factor me into their equation. That's my bargaining chip, assuming we escape – I'm the only person who knows how to access what you need."

"Where is it?"

Donald frowned. "Once we're safe. Until then, it's all in my head."

"I need more than that or no go."

"Do you not understand that they plan to kill us?"

"I've been prepared to die for a long time."

"That's very heroic, but I'm not." He paused. "If you want to stop the virus, you need me alive. Now stop wasting time we don't have. You either do this or we're dead – and billions who could have been saved will also die."

Selena debated telling him that Veritas wasn't functioning at full capacity, but held her tongue. The man's story was too pat, and it didn't make sense to her that he'd place all of his bets on her being able to contact Veritas.

No, he was obviously working his own angle, and he and Azra had decided to use her to lure him onto the island so they could ambush him. Which meant they hadn't found him – he'd gotten away clean.

Donald slid the key card through the food slot. She nodded slowly and pocketed the key card. "How do I turn the transmitter on? How do you even know it works?"

"It's only been a few years. I helped build it. That thing will last a century. There's a red power button on the side and some headphones with a built-in mic and cam. Just tap the only icon on the screen. It'll connect, and then just speak."

"And after I reach him?"

"Hide. This is a big facility, and other than Azra and me, this is the first time any of the commandos have been here, so they'll have a hard time searching it." He stepped away from the door. "I'll shut down the power in five minutes. It'll stay off for twenty seconds. That should be enough to get out of the cellblock."

Selena watched him retrace his steps to the door, her mind racing. She knew he was playing her, but she'd already made peace with the idea she'd taken her last breaths, which made her far more dangerous to them than they'd given her credit for.

With any luck, she could figure out a way to use that to her advantage.

Or die trying.

Chapter 43

Veritas opened his eyes and squinted at Milo, who was still sitting across from him, his expression tranquil. Veritas looked around, and everything seemed brighter, more vivid, and his senses tingled as though he'd come awake from a long, relaxing sleep.

"How long was I out?" he asked.

"Couple of hours. How do you feel?"

"Refreshed. And…like my vision and hearing are turbocharged."

"Good. That's promising. How about your memory? Anything new? Any recollection of our childhood at the monastery?"

Veritas frowned as his mind flooded with images. The ancient monk sitting by the waterfall. Dozens of young boys like himself, shirtless and wearing saffron pants hand-sewn from cloth crafted on village looms, going through the syllabus of martial arts training beneath a harsh sun. Tendrils of morning fog drifting between jagged peaks as he and the rest of the group carried water from a stream to a building perched on a craggy outcropping of gray granite, surrounded by pine trees and impossibly high waterfalls that dropped down the sheer cliff faces to the valley below.

The scene changed, and he was older, in his teens, lying on a straw mattress, sweating from a fever, a young Milo seated by his side holding a bowl of gruel and urging him to eat. Another abrupt shift, and Veritas was pressing an advantage with a staff against another similarly armed youth as at least a hundred boys gathered in a circle watched the bout with impassive stares.

Veritas shook off the vision. Milo nodded and slowly rose, his head cocked to the side. "Get acclimated, and then I'll do my best to walk you through what you're experiencing and try to jog your memory so your training comes back."

"It's…weird. I see us as boys. But also as teenagers, and as…as warriors."

"It'll take some getting used to, but the fact that you can remember that much is promising. I hope the refresher goes the same way. There's no way to compress years of training into a small period, but I shouldn't have to. More like choosing pressure points to trigger your instinctive recollections."

Without warning, Milo whipped a folded pocketknife from his pocket and hurled it at Veritas's head. Time slowed, and a red blinking icon flashed in his mind's eye. Veritas easily sidestepped the knife and scowled. "What the…"

"When I threw that, what went through your mind? How did you react?" Milo asked.

"I…I saw it coming and moved. It displayed in my head as an icon."

"Did you feel like you were barely able to dodge it?"

Veritas thought for a moment. "Not at all. Didn't seem like you threw it very hard. It was easy."

Milo smiled. "Well over a hundred miles per hour. Think of the fastest fastball you ever saw. This was faster."

"Didn't seem like it."

Milo nodded. "That's good. Now toss it back to me and let's try it again. This time I want you to focus on slowing time. Watch the knife approach you, and wait until the last possible instant to move."

Veritas walked to where the knife had landed and did as instructed. Milo hurled it again, and this time Veritas concentrated as it left Milo's hand and sped toward him.

Only instead of speeding, it seemed to take even longer than the prior throw. By the time it was a foot from his head, it seemed like ten seconds had passed, and he leaned a few inches to the side so it winged by his ear without touching him.

Milo grinned. "Very good. I actually threw it harder this time. What you experienced was one of the aspects of your new capabilities. My strength is equivalent to yours, maybe even greater because my chip wasn't wiped, so when I throw, I can do so at close to two hundred miles per hour. You should be able to as well once you've practiced. The point being that you got out of the way with plenty of time to spare."

"That's incredible."

"You can do the same with bullets, cars, pretty much anything, once you get the hang of it. All you're doing is adjusting your lens so it moves along the continuum at a slower rate, although *slower* isn't really accurate since there's no actual speed, just singularity A and B, with you at one end and it at the other. Technically you're viewing the same phenom, only from a different perspective – one that enables you to move at apparent blinding speed to a normal person."

"It seemed to take forever."

Milo nodded. "I know. The other neat trick is you should be able to see forward into the future, although that requires more concentration. Once you get good at it, you can stretch that to ten or fifteen. Master used to call it the elasticity of time."

"Master? The old Chinese guy?"

"That's right. Master Hong. You remember him now?"

"Sort of. It's blurry."

"I wish I could tell you it's going to get clearer, but the truth is I don't know. Judging by your speed in avoiding the knife, my hunch is yes."

It was Veritas's turn to grin. "Why don't you just look into the future ten minutes and tell me?"

"It isn't quite that easy. Besides, it wouldn't change anything."

"What about going backward?"

"You can, but you can only view, not act. That's why books where somebody goes back in time and kills their father or something are pure invention. Remember that everything that can happen already has, both in the future and in the past. There is no real future or past, just our current place in it and the branches we create with our actions."

"So why do we get older, then?"

"At a physical level, there's an arrow of time, and as we move along it, it has an effect on our physiology – the atoms and molecules from which we're made. Basically, the stem cells we're born with slow the rate at which they split, so with each trauma or event, we wind up with fewer of them to heal us. Eventually our tank runs dry, and this physical iteration's done."

"So I'm not going to live forever?"

Milo laughed. "That would be pretty boring after a while, wouldn't it?"

"What about the Anunnaki? The little green men?"

Milo's amusement dissolved. "They inhabit a different dimension than we do. For them, one of our years is the same as about a minute. So while they might seem to live forever, that's not entirely true. Just on our timeline it seems like it."

"Then the same ones that were around in Sumer are here now?"

"Depends on what you mean by here, and now. If you look at it from their perspective, five thousand years would be the equivalent of a week or two to them. They can slow time as well – we're amateurs compared to them."

"I'm still having a hard time accepting this is all real."

"Right. Cognitive dissonance. If it's real, then everything else is false and all of this is theater for our benefit – to keep us from ascending to a higher plane of consciousness, where we wouldn't be as easily manipulated. That's the genius of how they work with the Brethren. They keep them a few decades ahead of the rest of humanity, which is just enough of an edge so they can run things the way they want – but they're still taking their orders from above. They're like the prison bulls who're allowed to run the jails. To an inmate, they might seem like they've got real power, but they're just prisoners with slightly greater freedom. They're still slaves."

Milo showed him a dozen martial arts exercises, and Veritas did his best to mimic them, but with unimpressive results. The movements felt familiar, but his ability to perform them at speed was lacking, and after half an hour Milo stopped and shook his head.

"Not really coming back, is it?" Milo said.

"When will it?"

"I don't know. I was hoping that something would click and your muscle memory would take over, but apparently that's not the case." He frowned. "Maybe after a while longer."

"That's not encouraging."

Milo shrugged. "It is what it is. How do you feel?"

Veritas looked around. "Amazing. Like I'm unstoppable. It's a…a rush. I feel like I can do anything."

Milo nodded. "That's good. Maybe the rest of it will return, then. That feeling of being unstoppable is one of the byproducts of the modifications, which means you're coming up to speed."

When they finished with the exercises, Milo led him to the brook and sat beside it. Veritas joined him, and Milo explained to him how to meditate so that his mind could clear of the distractions of his thoughts, hopefully accelerating the progress of his conditioning returning.

Veritas felt the world drift away. He didn't notice when Milo stood and left, his brow furrowed as he peered at the sky, listening intently, his eyes narrowed to slits.

Chapter 44

Whidbey Island, Washington

Selena was ready when the power went off and the cells darkened. The only light emanated from a row of small windows near the twelve-foot ceilings, but it was just enough to light her way. She opened the door and stepped into the hall, the hair on the back of her arms tingling, and hurried to the end of the corridor, her footsteps silent.

That barrier was also unlocked, and once in the passageway beyond, she rushed to the fourth doorway just as the lights came back on. She held the key card to the reader, and the lock opened with a click, and then she was in the room and feeling for a wall switch.

Harsh white light flooded the chamber, and she spotted the transmitter at the far end. Selena grabbed a chair from beside the door and wedged it below the handle so she wouldn't be interrupted, and made her way to the dust-covered console. She ran her hand over the side of the device, found the power button, and turned it on. The monitor in the center of the console blinked to life, and she took a seat in the swivel chair in front of it and pulled on a headset.

The screen glowed and a pair of blue icons appeared in the center. She glared at it in confusion, and then tapped the first one. The color changed from blue to green, and she cleared her throat and spoke in a low voice, which sounded deafening in her headphones.

"Veritas? Can you hear me? It's Selena. I'm not sure how this works, but I found a transmitter that's supposed to allow me to communicate with you."

A pause stretched for a minute, and she tried again. "Veritas. It's Selena. Answer me if you can."

The headset crackled, and Veritas's voice answered. "Selena? I thought they took you prisoner."

"They did, but I broke out. What about you? How are you doing?"

"So-so. Where are you?"

"Veritas, you need to listen to me carefully. The leader of the men who kidnapped me is named Azra. He's being upgraded with your hardware as we speak. You need to get to San Diego and meet up with my counterparts there. I told you about SexUp. Set up a blind email and leave a message for Gunther in the free boy-on-boy section, and use the words *gargle* and *butter* – doesn't matter what the rest of the message says."

Veritas repeated her instructions. "Where are you, Selena? You say you escaped…"

"They're holding me at a mothballed military base. But that's not important. You need to get to California and do as I say."

"And leave you? Not a chance. Where on the base are you? What's the name of it?"

Her voice broke and she swallowed hard. "Don't try to find me, Veritas. That's what they're hoping you do – this escape was too easy. They want to use me as bait to get you here. I won't do it. You wouldn't stand a chance. There are at least fifty fighters, maybe more."

"Selena…"

"No. It's more important that you reach my people and let them know about Azra, and also that one of the men here claims he's got vital information that will help them with the vaccine. But I don't believe him. I think that's a red herring."

"Selena, tell me where you are."

"Not a chance. You're too important. They're afraid of you.

That's why they're activating Azra. They're going to send him after you."

"I don't care. What matters is you."

"No. That's where you're wrong. It was always you, Veritas. You're our last hope. Please. I don't have much time. You need to do as I say, and don't worry about me. I'll figure something out."

"I'm not going to leave you, Selena."

"I'm sorry, Ver. I really am. But this is goodbye. Remember – Gunther, gargle, and butter. Now I've got to go."

"Selena, don't do this–"

"Goodbye, Veritas. The world's counting on you."

Selena switched off the terminal, removed the headset, and glanced around the room. She spotted a miniature camera mounted in the corner of the ceiling and walked to one of the chairs near a wall cabinet, leapt up in an instant and started pulling at the camera. When it didn't budge, she climbed off the chair, lifted it, and swung it with all her might. One of the legs caught the camera on the second try and shattered the housing, raining glass and plastic on the floor.

She didn't know how much time she had, but she was sure that it wasn't much. She took a deep breath and moved to the door, and then froze at the sound of running boots approaching in the hallway.

Chapter 45

Donald pushed back from the bank of security monitors just as Lars entered the room, his expression dark.

"Well?" Lars snapped, and his eyes moved to the screens. "Did she go for it?"

"I don't know. She was talking too quietly, even with the volume maxed."

"Shit," Lars said. He pointed at the screen, where Selena was standing on a chair, tugging at the camera. "Looks like she figured it out, even completely sleep-deprived."

Selena got off the chair, and then the image changed to a white hiss of static.

Donald leapt to his feet. "Let's go before she has a chance to get out of there."

Three of Lars's men were waiting in the corridor outside the security suite. Donald took off at a trot for the transmitter room, Lars and his thugs on his heels. When they reached it, Donald held his card up to the scanner and Lars stood by his side.

"Remember," Donald cautioned, "Azra wants her alive."

"Get out of the way," Lars growled, pistol in hand.

Donald stepped back, and Lars and his men rushed into the darkened room, weapons at the ready. They were back an instant later.

"She isn't there."

"Damn," Donald said. "She must have bolted right after

destroying the camera. She can't have gotten far." He pointed down the hall. "Put out an alert to your men to be on the lookout for her." He gestured to Lars's men. "You, go that way. We'll head this way. It's either one or the other."

"Does the key card you gave her work on any of the other doors?" Lars interrupted.

"Of course not."

"Then she doesn't have any options," Lars said. "We'll find her." He cursed. "I can't believe she got away that quickly. I told you we should have stationed some men nearby."

Donald shook his head. "We couldn't risk spooking her. She had to believe she was on her own. One sound, and you would have given the whole thing away."

"Right. And this is so much better."

"Come on," Donald said. "We don't have all day."

"Azra's going to lose it if we can't find her. This one's on you. Not how I would have played it," Lars warned.

"You want to stand here and jabber, or track her down?"

Lars indicated the hall they'd come down and motioned to two of the men. "Backtrack, and check all the doors in case one's unlocked and she ducked inside. Remember, she's got street chops, so don't underestimate her," he said, glaring at Donald, his rebuke clear.

Donald ignored him, a ball of acid churning in his stomach.

Selena waited until Donald and the men had departed before daring to move. She'd stood on the chair and pushed one of the acoustic ceiling tiles out of the way, and then kicked the chair to the side and pulled herself up onto the metal frame that supported the drop ceiling. When she was above the drop ceiling, she slid the panel back into place and felt her way along one of the metal beams, the darkness complete except for pinpoints of light that seeped between the tiles along the hallway.

She found a ventilation duct and fumbled along the edge of where the ducting met the vent grid. She paused, listening for any sounds below, and then worked the duct from the grid and climbed inside. It was just large enough to accommodate her.

Selena inched along its length, cringing at every creak her weight caused, moving as quickly as she dared. When she reached a junction, she paused and tried to place the direction she was traveling relative to the hall. If she was right, the junction would take her into a part of the building far from that hallway. By the time they thought to investigate the comm room more closely, she would be long gone, and if her luck held, she'd have lost them.

Donald's treachery had come as no surprise, and she was glad to have called it right.

Now all she had to do was avoid a massive manhunt and somehow figure a way off the island without getting caught.

She sighed and chose the duct on the right. It was arbitrary at that point, but wherever she wound up would be better than locked in the cell again.

An hour later Selena had worked an end of the duct loose and dropped into an equipment room, where pumps were humming and fans whirring. She crept to the door and felt along the jamb, and was relieved to find that there was no card reader, just an old-fashioned lever handle. She tried it, but it didn't budge. Which would work to her advantage, given that anyone looking for her would assume that if they couldn't get in, neither could she.

She had no idea of the layout of the base, but she was sure that eventually they would either tire of the search or conclude she'd somehow evaded them and escaped for good. The third option – that they would find her and recapture her – didn't cross her mind. This time she wouldn't be surprised, as she had been in the casino, and if they located her, she'd force them to shoot her rather than allow them to take her prisoner again.

Whatever happened, she'd done her duty and warned Veritas. She had no regrets over not telling him where she was – Donald's story had been a clever series of lies she'd been too smart to believe, and ensuring Veritas could warn the others rather than allowing herself to be used as bait had been the only call she could have made.

A part of her wished things had turned out differently, but she pushed the thought away. She was first and foremost a warrior in a fight to the death, and couldn't allow herself the distraction of wondering what might have been between herself and Veritas.

She needed some sort of weapon, which spurred her to search for anything in the room that could be used as one. In a corner, she felt the distinctive shape of a metal toolbox. She opened it, and her fingers found the handle of a pipe wrench. Selena removed it and walked to the door, feeling along the pipes, guided by the sliver of light beneath the metal slab. She settled in behind a large collection of pipes and wheeled valves with the wrench in her hand, her only thought to survive as long as she could in the face of impossible odds, or die a death worthy of her ancestry.

Chapter 46

"Milo!" Veritas called, looking around the campsite. The tent was packed and the ground cleared, the area now returned to its bucolic norm.

"Shhh," Milo hissed from the trees. "Over here."

Veritas made for the trees and then hesitated at the sound of a helicopter approaching. Milo was deep in the forest with his backpack on, the tent a bundle in one hand. He gestured to Veritas, who ran to him.

"They'll probably be using infrared," Milo whispered. "Seemed like a good idea to move."

"Where to?"

"There are some caves a half klick north. We should be able to make it without any problem. They're working a grid pattern. This is the second time they've passed south of us." Milo studied Veritas's face. "What is it?"

"Selena just contacted me. On some kind of quantum transmitter."

"I thought that thing had been mothballed for good."

"You know about it?"

"Of course. The problem is that it will show both of us on-screen. And it can be used to intrude into our thoughts, wherever we are."

"So what? Can it track us?"

"No, but they could theoretically distract us by using it, and we'd have no way of stopping it." He glanced at the sky. "Let's run for it. We can talk once we're in the caves. They'll block any thermal detectors."

"Wonder why they didn't wait to ambush me."

"They're probably losing patience – which you can use against them. One of the greatest weapons a fighter has is patience." He took a deep breath. "This way."

Milo took off at dizzying speed, and Veritas was surprised that he could easily keep up this time. He could see the helo behind them on his mental screen, and they put a half mile between themselves and the aircraft in minutes. The terrain rose in a slope as they worked their way north, and when they arrived at a small opening in the foliage, they were considerably higher than before.

Milo led him into the cave and swept a few empty beer bottles to the side before sitting on the stone floor. Veritas entered and sat beside him.

"They're holding her at some base she says we were trained at," he said.

"That would be the Whidbey Island Naval Air Station. They shut it down back around 2024, and we used it as a covert operations base until they terminated the program."

"How far is it from here?"

Milo frowned. "Maybe…a hundred miles." He fixed Veritas with a stare. "What did Selena say, exactly?"

Veritas recounted the discussion. When he finished, Milo grunted. "It was obviously a setup. She was right to be suspicious."

"Maybe. But now that I know where she is, I have to try to get her out of there."

"You'll never make it. They'll have every road blocked. Remember they have infinite resources."

"Maybe, but I made it this far, didn't I?"

"Mostly through luck, from what I can tell. Anyway, you can't do anything for her other than put yourself at risk for no reason. You'd be walking into a trap."

"I have to do something."

Milo shook his head. "You aren't ready. You're still getting used to your own skin. You need more conditioning to be operating at peak."

"She escaped, but she didn't sound like it would last long." Veritas paused, his face grim. "We have to try."

"There's no *we*, Veritas. I chose a different road. This isn't my fight."

"You're helping me now."

"That's not the same as getting involved in your squabble with the Brethren. I won't get dragged into that mess. And you aren't going to be able to do much besides get yourself killed until you've got more skills under your belt."

"I thought you said they'd come back to me."

"I think they will. But that's an opinion, not a guarantee. And there's no telling how long it could take. You can barely execute a decent block or strike. That's a long way from being ready for anything."

Veritas absently ran his fingers through his hair. "What can you tell me about the layout of the base?"

"You really intend to do this?"

"I'm not going to leave her to die."

"You think getting killed is going to help her? Sounds like she was pretty clear about what you should do, wasn't she?"

"Selena doesn't make decisions for me. I'm going to do what I have to do, with or without your help. So tell me as much as you can about the area. What are the approaches? How would you try to get there? There has to be a way they won't expect."

"Veritas, think for a minute. Of course they'll expect it. That was the whole point to having her communicate with you. Which she was smart enough to grasp."

"There's always a way."

"No, that's in movies. In reality, there's almost never one that will work. That's one of the things you learn in the field." He sighed. "If the base has been mothballed, there's a chance that all the team's equipment is still there; it's actually likely, if the transmitter's still working. If that's the case, I'd probably try to get my hands on some of the armor that was developed for us. It's light-years ahead of anything deployed, and our chips are optimized for the suits and the weapons that come with them. If you could do that, you could take on an army and walk away without a scratch – assuming you were working at full capacity, which you aren't."

"And then what?"

"If they capture her again, which they probably will, they'd likely lock her in the brig." Milo described the layout of the base. "Find that, and you find her. Unless they already killed her, and you risked your neck for nothing."

"If they did, they'll pay with their lives."

"See, that's why I don't do this. It's pointless. They kill you; you kill them. And to what end? For vengeance? Justice? These are all theater. They don't matter, and they don't exist except as concepts in your mind. Take some time and use the power I restored. Get a feel for the universe and let go of the hate. You'll see that none of this is anything you want to participate in."

"That's your choice. All I know is that I'm not going to let my friend die if I can do something to save her," Veritas said.

"Your 'friend'? Seems like she's more than that to you if you're willing to take on the best the Brethren can throw at you to rescue her. Which, if I didn't mention it before, is unlikely to happen."

"There's a possibility. You said so yourself. If I get the armor and the weapons, I've got better than even odds of pulling this off."

"I didn't say that. I told you how I'd do it. Which I wouldn't. Because if Azra's been upgraded like you say, you won't just have to worry about a platoon or three of commandos. He'll be the real threat. And if I remember him correctly, he'll be looking to bury you. Nasty customer. I disliked him back in the day, and the upgrade will make him ten times worse. He has none of the preparation and all of the ugliest qualities we spent a lifetime trying to drill out of ourselves."

"If he doesn't have the rest of the conditioning, he'd be beatable even if I'm rusty."

Milo shook his head. "You're not rusty. You can't even remember what you can't remember, so there are whole disciplines that are dormant. The edge you think you have doesn't exist. You're talking about committing suicide to save the life of your…friend. That makes no sense."

"It does to me." Veritas took a breath. "Let's assume you're right about the checkpoints. How would you get to the island?"

They discussed Veritas's limited options while helicopters scoured the area. Eventually the aircraft moved on, and Veritas stood and dusted off his torn jeans. "If you're not going to help me, I'll do this alone. What kind of speed can I make for a sustained run?"

"With our augmentation, we could clock twenty to twenty-five miles per hour all day in training, up to fifty in bursts – roughly four times a normal human. But if you're asking how long it'll take to get to the coast, I'd guess by nighttime you can be there. It's about seventy-five miles as the crow flies, but the terrain gets mountainous, and you're going to have to avoid roads." Milo regarded him doubtfully. "You're making a huge mistake."

"We'll see. According to you it's all theater anyway, so I might as well put on a hell of a show."

Veritas moved to the cave mouth and peered outside. When he was sure the coast was clear, he stepped out into the sunlight and left without a word.

Milo watched him disappear into the woods and pursed his lips in disapproval. "Stupid bastard. You're walking right into their trap. You'll never make it," he whispered, and closed his eyes, the better to follow Veritas's icon on his internal screen before he moved out of range and vanished for good.

Chapter 47

Veritas slowed as dusk darkened the sky, and looked down at the breakwater of a marina in the near distance. Gleaming white rows of boats bobbed gently at the docks, and fog rolled in from the north with the inexorable persistence of a steamroller.

The run from the cave had taken five and a half hours, and even after traversing terrain that would have stopped him flat if he hadn't been augmented, he wasn't fatigued. Despite days without sleep and having pushed himself beyond all reasonable endurance, he felt clearheaded and sharp, his energy level good and his thoughts focused. He didn't know whether his training was returning along with the barrage of memories that flooded his awareness, but he hoped so. He'd done little but think about Selena and how to best infiltrate the base without being discovered, and had developed a plan that had as reasonable a chance of working as any.

Now he needed to liberate a boat and navigate to the island.

Given that he'd never been aboard one, he expected that would present a challenge. Although not as large as it might have been – his inner screen apparently had an intuitive search function he'd been able to call up when he'd needed a map of his route, which he hoped would extend to topics like sailing or hot-wiring marine motors.

He waited as the sun dropped into the sea and then worked his way down to the marina, where a lone security guard in his early twenties was sitting in a booth by the front gate. The parking lot was devoid of cars except for the guard's rusting relic, which augured well for his chances of slipping away with a vessel unnoticed – assuming there were no live-aboards too frugal to spring for wheels. He took up position behind a hedge near the main gate and watched the docks for fifteen minutes. When no lights blinked to life on any of the boats, he turned his attention to the guard, who was riveted to his phone screen, his thumbs working madly as he texted – a retro habit that was in fashion with the young, who eschewed voice-to-text in favor of old-fashioned messaging.

Veritas moved to the edge of the water at lightning speed and ducked under the gangplank. He pulled himself along the underside of the ramp until he was past the locked security gate. He looked over at the guard and, seeing nothing had changed, reached to the edge of the ramp and heaved himself up. He crouched in the darkness and inched to the dock, and then worked his way along the boats until he was at the farthest point from the guard and only a few dozen yards from the breakwater.

A thirty-four-foot Catalina sailboat drew his eye. After another look around, he climbed aboard the boat and inspected the glass-paneled cabin doors. He tried them and, after he confirmed they were locked, stepped away and drove his boot through one with a crash. He reached inside, unlocked it, and was in the cabin in a flash, surveying the breaker panel and comparing it to the image on his mental screen.

Keys strung on a floatation bobber hung by the side of the panel, and he pocketed them and flipped the switches on. The deck below his feet hummed and he returned to the deck, where he removed a silver fabric cover and tried the keys in the diesel engine's ignition. The instrument cluster lit and he tried the starter, and the motor coughed to life after a few sputters and blew smoke across the water.

Veritas didn't wait to see whether the guard would take an interest in him but jumped to the dock to remove the shore power line. He disconnected and untied the lines, and then hopped back onto the boat and eyed the transmission lever, which was a simple forward, neutral, and reverse, with a throttle control beside it.

He backed the boat from the slip and shifted to forward while turning the wheel, and was smiling in self-satisfaction at having managed to clear the dock when a yell sounded from the gate.

"Mr. Jenkins?" the guard called.

Veritas half turned and waved, hoping that the guard would believe he was the boat's owner. A flashlight beam played across the water and settled on the cockpit, and Veritas goosed the throttle while he steered toward the mouth of the breakwater. The guard didn't call out again, which Veritas interpreted as either good, or very bad, news. Because of the distance, the thickening fog, and the limited range of the flashlight, the guard might have assumed that Veritas was Jenkins out for a moonlight cruise.

Now that he was committed, Veritas had no choice but to power on and hope for the best. If the man called the police, it would likely take time for them to arrive, at which point they would probably call the owner to see whether he was at home or on his boat.

The problem being that if the island was on alert, a stolen boat, even twenty-five miles from the base, would give the Brethren ample warning that he was on his way, which would be disastrous. Without the element of surprise, he had no doubt that he would be apprehended as soon as he set foot on shore, and his gambit would cost him and Selena their lives.

Once past the breakwater, the fog thickened to the point where he could hardly see, and he fiddled with the radar until the screen glowed and displayed a twelve-mile range. He issued a silent command, and his internal screen flashed the coordinates of the base, which he entered into the autopilot before setting it. The wheel stiffened in his hand, and soon he was putting along at nine knots, which would put him near the island in two and a half hours. If the radar was correct, he was the only thing on the water, moving at what for him was a fast jog – a sitting duck if a police boat was dispatched to intercept him.

A foghorn lowed in the distance and he shivered involuntarily, the fog around him now a dense blanket. The fuel gauge read half full, so he could easily make it to the island, and the fog would make it impractical to deploy a helicopter, which meant that even if the guard notified the police, they would take their time responding, much less treat a stolen boat that moved at glacial speed as an emergency.

Veritas lowered himself onto a bench seat by the side of the wheel and yawned, resigned to spending the next hours listening for sounds of pursuit, his options nil other than jumping overboard if he'd called the situation wrong.

When nothing happened after an hour, his fatigue caught up with him, and he was nodding off from the gentle rocking of the boat when the sound of another motor reached him from the port side. He was up in a flash and at the controls, eyes glued to the radar. A blip glowed five miles away, and he mentally plotted the other vessel's course as the radar cycled several times. It appeared to be heading away from him, and he exhaled in relief.

Five minutes passed, and he confirmed that the other boat wasn't moving toward him, but was instead pulling away at a faster clip than he was powering north. Still, it was a reminder that he couldn't afford any stupid lapses, and he set about unfurling the mainsail so he could cut the engine when he was closer to the base and approach it in silence. Fortunately for him, the breeze was off his stern, so he didn't have to master sailing beyond the rudiments his screen furnished, and within a short time the boat's speed had increased a few knots as the wind filled the sail and drove it along.

Another hour went by, and Veritas adjusted course to a track that paralleled the shore two and a half miles from the island. Once he was sure of the bearing, he shut down the motor, and the boat slowed to slightly above a crawl. He bit back his impatience and reminded himself that hurrying would result in deadly mistakes, but all he could think of was Selena, who in his mind's eye was staring at him with a panicked expression, surrounded by dark figures in storm trooper outfits, bristling with weapons.

The outline of the island filled the radar screen, and when he calculated that he was two miles from the base, he adjusted the autopilot so it would direct the boat on a course away from the island. He removed his boots, tied them together, and hung them by the laces around his neck; after a moment's hesitation, he slipped into the icy water, the cold so jarring it took his breath away.

When they'd discussed the strategy of swimming to shore, Milo had assured him that his augmentation would enable him to survive in conditions that would kill most long before they reached the base. As the cold seeped through his bones, he offered a silent prayer that Milo was right, because otherwise the freezing water would do the Brethren's work for them.

His jacket dragged as he began swimming for shore, but he doggedly pulled himself along, and after a certain point the frigid current stopped affecting him and he was streaking through the small waves at an astonishing rate. Before he knew it, the island was rising from the water before him and he was crawling up the rocky beach, the few lights on at the base glimmering to his left.

Scores of icons appeared on his mental screen as he shook off water like a wet dog – all of them concentrated inside the buildings. Veritas donned his boots, tied them, and then took off at a run. He closed the distance to the base perimeter in a flash. He was up and over the chain-link fence with ease, and then was a blur in the gloom as he raced toward the building his mental map told him contained the armory – a building with no icons near it.

Eight helicopters sat on the tarmac, their hulking forms black in the dim light. He realized as he drew near the armory that memories of being stationed there were tugging at his awareness, and by the time he was at the door, he had a collage of images of himself training on the field beyond, Milo beside him as they ran an obstacle course at blinding speed.

He forced the impressions away and focused. The door was locked, but he spied a window down the façade and wasted no time shattering it with his elbow.

Once inside he made for the armory, his boots on the concrete floor the only sound in the cavernous space. His heightened vision enabled him to see in the darkness well enough to make out the vault. He tried the door and was surprised to find it open, and then he slipped inside, leaving the door ajar so he could see.

Rows of armored suits hung from wall racks. He moved to the nearest and inspected the power pack on the floor below it. He knelt, felt along its side for the power button, and depressed it, all the while listening intently.

Nothing. Dead.

He tried another, with the same result.

Ten minutes later he'd checked the entire inventory, and none had power, which rendered the suits and Gauss rifles useless.

Which he should have anticipated, but hadn't.

He wondered what else he hadn't foreseen, and frowned. His plan had called for having access to the armor that would give him the critical advantage over the others. Now, he had none besides surprise, and whatever improvements his augmentation had provided him – which were in serious doubt, according to Milo.

Veritas crept from the vault and retraced his steps to the building entry. The brig was two structures away. There were a number of icons inside, but none where his mapping system told him the cells were located. He willed the icons off, their jumble confusing while he was trying to focus, and darted out the door, keeping close to the shadowed wall before crossing an open expanse to the next building. He repeated the maneuver and arrived at the brig, and was moving to the entry door when he spotted a security cam above it.

He vaulted through the air and knocked the camera from its bracket with a blow that sent it flying toward the empty helos. A quick try of the door opened it, and he swung it wide and entered a long hall. He allowed his eyes to adjust to the darkness, and was edging along the corridor when one of the doors on his right opened and he found himself face-to-face with a black-clad gunman.

Veritas rushed the man before he could react. The commando swung his rifle up at Veritas, but he was a fraction of a second too slow, and Veritas punched him in the throat, instantly crushing his larynx. Another brutal strike to the side of his head burst an eardrum, and the man dropped as he fought in vain for air. Veritas wrenched the assault rifle from him as he went down, and watched as he writhed on the floor, his lungs battling for oxygen they'd never receive.

When the man stopped twitching, Veritas quickly searched him and retrieved a pistol and two spare magazines, a combat knife, and four hundred new dollars. He removed the dead man's flak vest and pulled it on. The six extra rifle magazines weighed it down, as did the armored plates in the front and the back.

A radio squealed from the gunman's belt, and Veritas took that as his cue to locate Selena and break her out before the man's absence was noticed. He dragged the corpse back into the room from which he'd emerged, and looked around – it had the appearance of a break room, its tables and counters covered in dust, the door on the far end marked with a unisex bathroom symbol. Seeing nothing he could use as additional weaponry, he returned to the hall and continued toward the cells, the assault rifle at the ready, safety off.

Veritas pushed open the steel door that sealed the cells from the hallway, and stopped to listen.

The cells were empty.

He swore under his breath and considered his next step. If Selena wasn't in a cell, he'd have to search the entire base, and that wasn't going to happen without him getting caught. His face set in grim determination, he moved toward the far door, where his stomach sank at the sight of a card reader. Of course the cellblock would require one to exit, he thought – and then the door burst wide and four commandos piled through it, rifles trained on him, their laser sights' red dots tracing over his chest like crazed fireflies.

Chapter 48

Donald opened the lid to the isolation chamber and stepped away. Azra pulled himself from the tank, and Donald handed him a towel. Azra dried himself and wrapped it around his waist, eyeing Donald suspiciously.

"Has it been twelve hours? Doesn't seem like it."

"Almost eleven."

"Why did you end the treatment prematurely?"

"The target showed up. Our men have him cornered in the brig. I just received the transmission. I figured you'd want to deal with this personally." Donald disconnected the catheter and removed the cannula. "How do you feel?"

Azra stared at him unblinkingly. "Incredible. It's like I was blind, and now I can see."

"Some of the features will take a while to activate. The mental display, your strength and speed...but you should be able to perform better in armor. That will be the most obvious initial effect."

Azra walked to where a suit waited on a rolling rack. "Then hook me up and let's deal with our guest."

Donald helped him into the armor. When he was done, Azra gave him a wicked grin as he slipped the helmet onto his head. The visor covered his eyes, and when Donald powered on the equipment pack on his back, he grunted.

"This is amazing," Azra said.

"I didn't have time to get a Gauss rifle cleaned and ready, but you shouldn't need one for this."

"Doesn't matter. I feel like I could take on a platoon bare-handed. Let's go."

Donald followed him out of the building and to the brig. Halfway there, muffled gunfire shattered the night, and Donald drew his pistol. Azra held out a gloved hand. "Give it to me."

Donald passed him the weapon, and Azra continued toward the building. When they entered the brig, the lights were off and it was silent.

"Where are they?"

"In the cellblock."

They hurried to the wing's security door, and Donald frowned at the sight of a booted foot wedged in the partially open entry. Donald moved to a wall switch and turned on the lights.

Four of the commandos lay in an ocean of blood, their weapons scattered around the area. Azra reached down and collected one of the rifles. "How do I activate the helmet screen?"

"You just have to will it to life. Think *screen on*. That should work."

Azra stood motionless and then nodded. "I see…a lot of yellow icons, and two blue."

"You're one of the blue. He's the other," Donald said.

"He's in the next building."

Donald felt for the radio on his belt. "I'll notify the troops."

"Do so," Azra said, and then took off down the hall, not waiting for Donald.

Veritas had dropped to the floor like his legs had gone out from under him, and he'd taken out the gunmen with four bursts from his M28 assault rifle before they'd been able to return fire, the move instant and unexpected. He'd rolled to one of the walls as he shot, his aim laser precise, while the commandos had been caught by surprise. It was over before it started, and he'd slapped a new magazine in place and taken off at a sprint, knowing the sound of the shots would draw more shooters in no time.

He exited the rear fire door that connected the brig to the adjacent building, his mind racing over his limited options. Any advantage of surprise was now gone, and there were scores of fighters and only one of him. Milo's prophetic warning seemed prescient as he stepped into the warehouse and swept it with the rifle, and he knew there would be no way to escape with his skin, much less find Selena and free her. The stupidity of his impetuous decision struck him with the force of a blow, and he swore under his breath as he blinked his screen to life on the off chance he could find a viable escape route.

He spotted another blue icon racing toward him from the brig and looked around for anything that could serve as cover. That had to be Azra, and judging by the speed, he'd be there in seconds.

Donald caught up to Azra at the warehouse door. "Can I have my pistol back?"

"Negative. I may need it."

Azra twisted the handle and threw the door open, leading with the rifle barrel, his helmet's night vision automatically enabled due to the dearth of light. He stepped over the threshold and eyed the mental image of the location screen. A host of yellow icons were converging on the building, but the other blue icon had merged with his.

The target was in the room. He scanned the surroundings and spied a rifle barrel jutting from a pallet of crates near the wall. His lips curled in a sneer and he raised his weapon, secure that his opponent wouldn't be able to make him out in the gloom without the suit's NV enhancement.

Chapter 49

Veritas released his hold on the rafter and dropped straight onto Azra. His weight knocked the armored man to the ground, and Azra's rifle flew from his hands. Veritas followed up with brutal blows to his exposed neck, which was the only area that wasn't protected by hardened plates.

Azra threw him off and rolled away, and was on his feet before Veritas had regained his balance. The two men faced each other, and Veritas drew the pistol he'd confiscated.

Azra threw himself at Veritas and slammed into him with the force of a freight train. Veritas flew backward with Azra on top of him and fired the gun into Azra's ribs. The shot had no effect, the armor more than a match for the handgun round even at point-blank range, and Azra pressed his advantage and clubbed Veritas's skull with his gloved fists. Veritas tried to block the blows, but Azra was relentless, and one of the strikes knocked the pistol from Veritas's grip and sent it skittering across the floor.

Veritas attempted a rabbit punch to Azra's throat, but the blow went wide, and then Azra was on his feet and kicking Veritas like a soccer ball with his armored boots. The pain from Veritas's ribs was blinding, and a final kick to his skull sent a starburst of agony through his skull and he blacked out.

Azra continued kicking him and then dropped to his knees and grabbed Veritas's head with both hands in preparation to snap his neck.

"Azra! No!" Donald screamed from the doorway. "They want him alive!"

Rage unlike anything Azra had ever felt surged through him, along with elation and an overwhelming urge to feel Veritas's spine break, to crush his skull with his bare hands and watch his brains ooze between his fingers. He tightened his grip, and Donald yelled again.

"You kill him and they'll do the same to us, Azra. Don't do it. You're signing our death warrants. They want to interrogate him, remember?"

Azra looked up at him as though in a trance and then released Veritas just as Lars arrived with nine fighters. Light flooded the warehouse from their lamps, and Azra struggled to his feet and motioned to Veritas.

"Throw him in the brig."

"We found the girl, Azra," Lars said. "She was hiding in the basement. Fought like a hellcat."

"Toss her in with him and alert the men that we're evacuating within the hour," Azra said. "Our job here is done."

Lars regarded Veritas's limp form. "He might need medical care."

Donald shook his head. "No. He's tough. Any damage will heal quickly."

Lars looked at him doubtfully. "He's half dead. You sure?"

"You heard him," Azra snarled. "He'll make it. Lock them up and get the pilots to the helicopters. No point in waiting." He paused. "Drag the dead men to the helos and load them aboard. I don't want any trace we were here when we leave. Hose down the blood and ensure nobody leaves anything that could be tied to us. You have an hour."

Lars grunted his assent. "You got it," he said, and gestured to his men. "You heard him. Carry him to the brig and clean up the mess in there, and then grab your gear and prepare to fall out. I want your quarters spotless when I inspect them. Anyone misses anything, it'll mean a week's pay."

Chapter 50

"Ver, can you hear me?"

Veritas forced his eyes open and found himself staring into Selena's face a foot from his own. "Are you all right?" he managed in a hoarse voice.

"Me? Are you insane? They just about broke every bone in your body."

"Somebody recently told me I'm hardier than I look."

"Seriously. How do you feel?"

"It only hurts when I breathe."

"What happened?"

"I picked a fight with a wrecking ball. I lost."

She shook her head. "I told you not to come. You're supposed to be on your way to my people, not locked up by these monsters. Why didn't you do as I said?"

"I've never been a good listener." He winced and sat up. "I think I felt better after the car hit me."

"Why, Ver? Now you've ruined everything."

"I couldn't leave you hanging, Selena. That's not who I am."

"How did you find this place?"

"I had some help. My memory rebooted."

"How?"

"It's a long story."

"You walked right into their trap. What in God's name were you thinking?"

"Mostly about you."

Her expression softened, and she leaned in and kissed him on the lips. "You're a fool."

"You're not the first to say so." He held her gaze. "I'm sorry, Selena. Believe me. But I had to try. I wouldn't have been able to live with myself if I hadn't."

"The fate of humanity was in your hands, Ver. Now...now the bad guys win."

"If I was humanity's last hope, that says a lot about the shape it's in."

"I'm serious, Ver."

"Kiss me again."

"They're going to kill us."

"I know. So no point in waiting. Kiss me."

She did, and this time her lips lingered on his, her breath sweet against his skin. When she pulled away, he closed his eyes and sighed. "What I wouldn't give for another day of freedom with you."

The sound of helicopters starting on the tarmac reached them, the thrum of the turbines loud enough to rattle the windows. Veritas reached out and touched Selena's face with his fingers as though in wonder, and wiped away a single tear that trickled down her cheek. "You've ruined everything, Ver," she said. "I...I was ready for whatever happened. But now..."

"I couldn't leave you, Selena. You have to know that. If this is how it ends, then that's how it was meant to be."

She frowned. "Did you ever speak to Cassius? I gather you were nearby, given how fast you reached the base."

"No. He was taken by the Brethren. Maybe executed. I don't know which."

"So it was a waste of time? That almost makes this worse."

"Not completely," he said.

Selena was about to respond when the door at the end of the hall rattled and then opened. A figure approached down the darkened corridor, and Selena gasped when she saw who it was.

"You!"

"I'm here to get you out," Donald whispered. "We don't have much time. They're going to come for you any minute and load him into the helicopter." He eyed Selena. "You, they plan to let the men use until they're tired of it, and then interrogate you and put a bullet in your head."

She glared at him. "I heard you in the hallway outside the comm room. You're a lying sack of shit."

"I had to pretend to be playing along." He adjusted the assault rifle strap on his shoulder and swiped his key card. The jail door swung open. "Can he run?"

Veritas rose unsteadily. "Who's this?"

"Don't you recognize me?" Donald asked. "I taught you how to put on your armor, not to mention tuned your chip and repaired anything technical that went wrong."

"I've had a lot on my mind."

"Well? Can you run?" Donald repeated.

"I'll manage."

"Don't trust him," Selena warned.

Veritas looked Donald up and down. "Give me the rifle and I'll believe you're legit."

Donald's eyes narrowed, but he slid the sling from his shoulder and handed Veritas the weapon. "Careful. There's one in the chamber. Safety's on."

Veritas glanced at Selena. "Well? You want the gun?"

She nodded, and he handed it to her. She ejected the magazine and verified it had bullets in it, and then slapped it back into place and tossed it to Veritas. "You remember how to use it?"

"Like riding a bike." He looked to Donald. "Let's go."

Donald led them out of the cellblock to a rear exit, which was unguarded. He swiped his card, and then they were in the night air, the fog from the strait thicker than when Veritas had arrived. Donald took off at a run toward the water, out of sight of the helicopters on the other side of the building, and Selena and Veritas trailed him, Veritas grimacing with every step but driving himself forward despite the pain.

They arrived at the water's edge, and Donald pointed to an inflatable boat pulled onto the shore. "It's a good thing it's fogged in. They won't be able to track us with the helos in this soup."

"Where are we going?" Selena asked, her tone still distrustful.

"As far from this island as we can get," Donald answered. "We'll figure the rest out on the way. All I know is they're going to kill me once this is over, and I'm not waiting around. I wasn't kidding that I have info that will make me the most important person on the planet to your people. I'll make getting us to safety their problem."

He approached the boat and was pushing it off the shore when a voice rang out.

"That's far enough."

Chapter 51

Azra and Lars materialized out of the fog, rifles leveled at them. Veritas saw Azra's weapon, and his shoulders slumped.

Donald reached for his pistol, and Azra fired a burst that whizzed by his head. "Don't move, you treacherous scum," he growled. "The next shots take off your head."

Donald froze. Azra continued toward him. "Not that I have any reason to keep you alive any longer."

"I pulled you out of the tank too soon," Donald said. "You're going to need me when the symptoms of early withdrawal kick in. There's nobody else who knows the tech well enough to help you. If you kill me, you're damning yourself to a short life of pure hell."

Azra reached the water's edge and pointed his weapon at Donald's head. "You're bluffing."

"The chances of it going sideways on you are greater than eighty percent. There's a reason I told you that twelve hours was the minimum. But if you think you know better, you'll get your reward for being wrong."

Azra shifted his aim to Donald's legs. "Then I'll just blow your kneecaps off. You won't need your legs."

Lars motioned at Veritas with his rifle barrel. "Drop the gun," he ordered.

Veritas's gaze flitted to Selena, and she nodded slightly. He tossed the rifle on the gravel in front of him and slowly raised his hands over his head, as did Selena.

Lars laughed. "This is the superman who was so tough–"

A form flew from the water and tackled him before he could react, dropping him against the shale and sending his rifle flying. The weapon clattered against the bank, and Veritas dove for his assault rifle when Azra swiveled toward Lars and his attacker with his gun raised.

Veritas snagged his rifle and thumbed the safety to full auto and blasted a ten-round burst into Azra's chest an instant before he could fire. The rounds didn't penetrate the armor, but their force knocked him into the water. He lost his footing and fell backward with a splash, and then Lars was on his feet and drawing his pistol from its holster.

Veritas fired a dozen rounds at him. Several of the first shattered the ceramic plate in his vest, and the last six drilled through the shards and tore his lungs and heart into hamburger as they tumbled and deformed inside him.

Lars jerked like a marionette, and then Donald's pistol was free and he fired three times. The rounds struck Lars in the neck and faceplate, and his chin disintegrated in a spray of bone and blood.

Azra broke from the surface with his weapon in hand, and Veritas emptied his rifle at him, aiming for the vulnerable area above the chest plate and below the helmet. Azra cried out and dropped the gun, and his hands flew to his neck as Veritas's magazine ran dry.

Donald swiveled toward Azra and squeezed off seven shots. Azra tumbled backward into the black water, still clutching his neck, and disappeared beneath the surface.

Everyone stood frozen, waiting to see what happened next. When Azra didn't reappear, Veritas rushed to Lars's corpse and retrieved his spare magazines. He slammed one into his gun, freed Lars's pistol, and slipped it into his belt.

The figure who'd tackled Lars pushed himself to his feet.

Veritas smiled. "I thought you said this wasn't your fight?"

Milo nodded. "That's right. But it looked like you could use a little help."

Veritas motioned to Milo and looked to Selena and Donald. "This is—"

"Milo," Donald said. "I remember you, of course."

"Donald, right?" Milo asked.

Donald nodded. "How did you manage to escape the purge?"

"It's a long story." Milo held out a hand to Selena. "You must be Selena."

Her face radiated confusion. "Who…"

"He's another one of us. The only other surviving super soldier," Veritas explained.

"Ah."

Milo nodded to Selena. "Your people know all about me," he said. "I'm surprised you don't."

"They don't tell me everything."

"So you're going to help after all?" Veritas asked Milo.

Milo shook his head. "No. I'm here for the transmitter. I don't like anyone to have the ability to get inside my head." He turned to Donald. "How many transmitters are there?"

"This is the only one."

"Where is it?"

Donald gave him a quick rundown of its location.

Milo nodded and listened for an instant. "Sounds like the bad guys are on their way here. That should keep them busy while I'm destroying the damn thing." He smiled again at Veritas. "Good luck, my brother."

"We can't wait for you," Selena warned.

He nodded. "I'm not asking you to. In fact, if I were you, I'd get the hell out of here. I'll be fine."

Milo bolted away from them, and within seconds he'd melted into the fog. Donald called to Selena and Veritas. "Help me get the boat into the water. They'll be here any second."

They did as asked, and Donald was pulling on the oars with all his might when they heard shouts through the haze. A few shots rang out from the shore, but they were scattered and aimless, fired out of frustration at ghosts in the mist.

"Let me row. I can make better time," Veritas whispered to him.

Donald shrugged and shifted back toward the small outboard motor, allowing Veritas to take the oars. Veritas's augmented strength soon had them cutting across the waves at a fair clip, and Donald smiled in relief at Selena.

Veritas eyed him. "Who designed the armor?"

"Why?"

"I thought it was odd that it left his neck exposed."

Donald chuckled. "There's a section that bolts onto the chest plate that I left off when I suited him up. I told him I couldn't find it."

"Why?"

"I figured that if I needed to shoot him, I'd leave a vulnerable spot so I could do some damage. Turns out that was a good call."

"Where to now?" Selena asked.

"That's up to you," Donald answered. "I've done everything I can."

"You said you know how to find/steal/locate the information we'll need to create a vaccine. That should be the priority."

He shook his head. "Not a chance. Once I do that, your group has no reason to protect me."

"Of course we do. You're a treasure trove of information about the super-soldier program, as well as the dark Brotherhood."

"But push comes to shove, that isn't as powerful a motivator as the vaccine, and we both know it."

"If they've got the roads and airports covered, we're not going to be able to do much. But if you have the cure in your hand, they'd move heaven and earth to keep it safe, wouldn't they?" she countered. "Besides, you're assuming I can pick up a phone and reach a decision maker. That's not how we work. It could take days or weeks to find another cell and for our situation to work its way up the ladder. Time we don't have – that the world doesn't have. But if I say we have the info and they need to get us out now, as you said, they would do just about anything to get it."

"Are the Brethren aware you might know about this?" Veritas asked. "If so, once you're reported missing, they'll probably shut down every avenue to get to the information, at which point your value drops to zero, doesn't it?"

That gave Donald pause. His expression confirmed Veritas's conclusion.

"He's right," Selena said. "They'll lock down everything." She paused. "How far away is it? We may already be too late."

Donald sighed and sat back against the transom. "Not that far. Seattle. There's a professor who works at Costco University who's one of their creatures. If we can get his password, we can get into his system. It'll be encrypted, but he's got all of the information on his system or somewhere in their servers."

"How do you know this?" Selena asked.

"I've been working on it for months. It was my insurance policy. I saw this day coming from a mile away, so I hacked and bugged until I'd cracked their communications using Azra's access. Some of it was deduction, but I'm right. In addition to his professorship, he's a consultant for a big bioengineering military contractor. It's got to be him – he's got a ton of money from questionable sources, he's got the technical expertise and access to the resources required to engineer it, and he works with a company capable of executing. That's a pretty narrow set of parameters to be coincidence."

"How far are we from Seattle?" Veritas asked.

"About fifty miles," Donald replied. "You should be able to pull up a map on your mental display."

Veritas grunted. "I keep forgetting about that."

"Don't. You're going to need every edge you can get if we're going to be alive this time tomorrow."

"How fast will the outboard go?"

"Probably fifteen, twenty miles per hour." Donald studied his watch. "We could be there by…three or four. But I don't want to risk it until we're well away from the island."

"How can we get the password?" Veritas asked.

"The only way is from the professor, obviously, because he changes it regularly," Donald said.

"How do you know?"

"Don't you think it already occurred to me to try? It's set up so you can't hack it. I spent three months trying, and nothing. He changes it every month."

"How about a key logger?" Selena asked.

Donald shook his head. "Too easy to spot. He's sophisticated. Might as well sound an alarm."

"Then how do we get in?" Veritas asked.

Donald smiled in the fog. "We obviously need his help."

"And how do we do that?" Selena asked.

Veritas's expression hardened. "We do whatever we need to in order to convince him."

Chapter 52

Wolf Bay, Washington

Veritas rowed the Zodiac the final hundred yards to an open stretch of shore, the darkness around them thick as oil.

"The professor lives in a big place on the water. And he has a seventy-two-foot yacht moored out back," Donald said. "I've studied the property. The dock and estate are protected by an alarm system with the works: motion detectors, pressure pads, and infrared sensors. A straight shot from the water's out of the question."

"How can you be sure he doesn't have any bodyguards?" Selena whispered.

"He's not one of the inner circle – more a highly paid employee who doesn't mind selling out the human race if he winds up one of the richest survivors. He leads a relatively low-key lifestyle, though. The house, boat, and car are his only real extravagances. To look at him, he's just a simple academic who's managed to make some play money from his biotech gig. I've been watching the house for a while from a satellite I hacked. Never seen anyone patrolling the grounds."

"There could be guards inside," she countered.

"Anything's possible, but it's doubtful. He's not one of them. He just works for them, so who's he protecting himself from?"

"Dogs?"

Donald shook his head. "Don't think so."

"I'm liking this less and less."

Veritas interrupted. "If there are guards or dogs, we'll deal with it. The big question is whether we can get past the security system."

"That should be pretty straightforward. I know what kind it is, and there are ways around it if you've done your homework."

"Which it sounds like you have."

"We'll find out soon enough."

The boat's rubber bow bumped the shore, and Selena hopped onto the rocky beach and pulled it aground. Veritas jumped out to help her, and Donald followed once the boat was out of the water.

"Which one is it?" Veritas asked.

"This way."

The professor's house was near the end of a long row of waterfront homes in a privileged enclave that still managed to be upper middle class rather than filthy rich, at least at four in the morning. The houses were expansive, on huge lots, but modest compared to the truly affluent areas owned by high-tech royalty.

They made their way along the sidewalk to a grove of trees thirty yards from the house, and eyed the hulking structure in the fog. A pair of porch lights glimmered, but there were none on in the house, and there was no evidence of guards.

"You're sure he lives alone?" Selena whispered.

Donald nodded. "He's a lifelong bachelor."

"The place is the size of a small hotel," Veritas said. "Seems odd that it's just him."

"This is practically a shack by the scale of some of the big-money places up in Bellingham and on the western shore." He glanced across the street and then back at the house. "I'll disable the alarm and give you the word when everything's shut down."

Selena hefted one of the M16s they'd taken from the gunfight and stared hard at Donald. "I'm going with you."

"That's not necessary…"

"I'd hate for you to get lost and we never see you again."

Donald shrugged, and the two of them moved toward the house in a crouch, sticking to the tall hedges that ran along the property line.

Veritas hoped Donald knew what he was doing. He seemed competent, but nothing so far had gone well for them, and he was distrustful of the scenario. Veritas understood Selena's hesitation about him. He knew from watching her she could take care of herself, but he was still anxious until they returned, their expressions tense.

"Well?" he asked.

"It's disabled," Donald answered.

Veritas nodded. "Then let's do this."

The three of them made their way to an enormous wrought-iron gate and swung it open. Selena winced at the creak of hinges, and then they were through and crossing a lawn the size of a soccer field. Donald led them around the side and stopped at the rear porch.

Selena frowned. "How are we going to get in?"

After trying the door, Veritas slammed the butt of his rifle against one of the glass panes in its center.

The gun bounced off like it was made of rubber.

Donald shook his head. "I could have told you that the security measures were impressive. No way you're going to be able to break that. It'll withstand a shotgun blast."

"How about the second-floor windows?" Selena asked.

"That's what I was going to suggest," Donald said.

Selena regarded Veritas. "You up for it?"

"Try to stop me."

Veritas slid the weapon's sling over his shoulder and scanned the house. The wood shingled exterior didn't offer much in the way of handholds, but a drainpipe ran to the roof at the corner. He approached it, tested it to verify it would hold his weight, and then climbed hand over hand, his boots gripping either side for support.

He was almost to the second story when the pipe groaned. He froze as it pulled free of the roof and began to lean away from the house.

"Veritas!" Selena cried from below.

He pushed with his legs and threw himself toward the window on his right side. His fingers locked onto the sill as the pipe continued its slow fall to the ground. It stopped halfway and hung in space in an uneasy equilibrium once Veritas's weight was removed, trembling like a branch in the fog.

Veritas heaved himself upward until he was perched on the sill and tried the window, which was locked. He cursed and removed his pistol from his belt while clinging to the frame with his other hand, and shattered the upper pane with a sharp blow. He almost fell as his balance momentarily wavered, and then he caught himself and reached up to unlatch the lock.

The window slid up with a rattle, and he swung his legs into the house and dropped to the floor, the pistol gripped in front of him. He found himself in a long hallway without any illumination other than the otherworldly glow from the open window, and another at the front of the house. Donald had told him the master was in the front on the second story, and he debated barging in on the sleeping man without Selena and Donald, and then discarded the idea.

He crept to the stairs, descended to the main floor, and made his way to the back door through the kitchen. Donald and Selena were waiting on the porch. He held a finger to his lips when he opened the door, and they nodded before following him up the stairs to the master.

Veritas turned the doorknob and winced at the scraping of the antique hardware. He listened with his ear to the mahogany panel and, when he heard nothing, eased the slab open and stepped into the room.

"Stop right there or I'll shoot," a tremulous voice warned from the gloom.

Chapter 53

Veritas flew across the room to where a youth in his late teens stood naked by a four-poster bed, a chromed revolver in his hand. He moved so fast the youth barely had time to adjust his aim before Veritas slammed him against the wall and knocked the gun from his grasp. The young man cried out in pain, and Veritas delivered a strike to the side of his neck, and he crumpled to the floor with a moan.

An old man sat up in bed, watching in horror as Veritas turned toward him. Selena stepped into the room and flipped on the lights, and the man gasped before his face hardened and he gave them an arctic glare.

"How the hell did you get—" he sputtered.

Veritas cut him off with a curt gesture and spoke to Selena.

"Tie the boy up. Gag him. I'm sure the professor has ties or something in the closet."

The professor shook his head. "You'll never get away with this. The police are already on their way here. You've triggered a silent alarm. Your only hope is to leave now before they arrive."

"We're not after money," Selena said.

"I...I don't understand."

Donald approached the bed. "We know about the virus, Professor. I traced the file to your university server, but couldn't get any further without the password. We want the password."

The blood drained from the professor's face, and he swallowed hard. "You..."

"Yes. We're well aware of your standing with the Brethren," Selena said, returning with a handful of silk neckties. "Which should tell you that we'll do whatever's necessary to get the password. And we're in a hurry."

"I...I don't know what you're talking about."

"Yes, you do. You developed a virus for some very bad people, and you've got all the data required to make a vaccine. No point in lying. We know it all," Donald said.

"I'll take great pleasure in skinning you alive to get the password," Selena said, her tone conversational. "You'll look like a science experiment by the time I'm done."

"You're mad."

Veritas smiled. "This can work two ways. You can give us what we need, or you can experience the tortures of the damned and be begging to tell us. I don't much care which," he said. "But my friend here was telling me that she really hoped you'd refuse. Apparently she's taking your mass murdering most of the world personally."

Selena began tying the youth on the floor up and looked to Donald. "See if you can find some bleach and a nice sharp carving knife. Oh, and some garbage bags. No point in leaving a bloody mess in this beautiful house." She regarded the young man. "Maybe I'll start with him so the professor can see how household solvents feel on nerve endings and freshly exposed epidermis. If that doesn't work, there's always a torch. A pity we don't have more time – I can make it last for days with a torch."

"The police will be here in minutes," the professor blurted.

Donald glanced back over his shoulder as he left to find the items she'd requested. "I disabled your alarm. Nobody's coming. She's dead serious."

"Impossible."

"Tell me that in five more minutes when the cavalry hasn't come over the hill," Donald said, and left.

"So do you drink baby blood as part of your deal?" Veritas asked the professor as Selena finished binding the youth. "I hear that's big with death cults. Keep you sprightly?"

"Who is this imbecile?" the professor demanded.

"How much did they pay you to commit genocide on a global scale?" Veritas continued. "Are we talking millions or billions?"

"I told you I have no idea what you're talking about."

"Maybe I'm not getting through to you," Selena said. "I'm going to blind you with bleach. Then I'll puncture both eyes and make you eat them. But that's just the warm-up. I wasn't kidding about skinning you. I've found it's the absolutely best way to ensure I'm being told the truth. Once I cut out your tongue and slice off your fingers, I might leave you alive just so you spend the rest of your miserable existence in unbearable agony. Actually, that sounds like a perfect way to cap it off. Leave you looking like a hairless mole – deaf, mute, and blind. Maybe cut off your toes, too, so they can't graft them on and use them for fingers. That sound like a deal? Because when he gets back up those stairs with the stuff, I'm not asking again. Make your choice, because once I start, there's no going back."

"I...I work for the government. This is...this is insane."

"Is that who they told you that you were working for?" Selena asked. "I mean, maybe you are. But that's not the final customer for your little bug."

"What do you mean? It's for the DOD's bioweapon program."

Selena rolled her eyes.

"You poor shmuck," Veritas said. "You actually believed that?"

"They're going to release the second rev once the first has eliminated everyone that doesn't fit their profile," Selena snapped. "Which will be billions. You think that's something the government would do?"

"I...that's impossible. They'd never..."

"It's happening right now," Veritas said. "The flu that's sweeping the world? That's your creation."

Footsteps approached from down the hall, and Donald appeared in the doorway, a jug of bleach in one hand and a wicked-looking bread knife and a roll of garbage bags in the other. Selena glared at the professor and raised an eyebrow. "Billions will die if we don't create a vaccine. If you think I won't turn you into a boneless ham to save them, you're sorely mistaken."

The professor swallowed, and a bead of sweat ran down his face in spite of the room's chill. "All right. I believe you. But there's no password to give you – it's all biometric now. There's a retinal scanner on both my university and my work systems, and we switched over to key cards rather than passwords a few months ago. You need me to get into either of them. The company's more protected than Fort Knox, so you can forget that. And there's no way you'll be able to access my offices at the university unless I'm with you – you simply wouldn't make it onto the grounds without passes, and as to the building…ever since the riots, it's locked down like a bunker."

Selena nodded slowly. "You understand that if you try to alert anyone, you're signing your death warrant?"

"You've made that perfectly clear. But once you have the information – what then?"

"We'll see," she said. "If you really didn't know what your work was going to be used for, then I have no gripe with you."

"I swear I didn't. I mean, what you're describing is…it's monstrous. Beyond monstrous."

"Put on some clothes. We're going to the university," Veritas growled.

"What? Now?"

"That's right. We need to be in and out before the campus is crawling with students."

"It's the middle of the night."

"No, it'll be dawn in an hour or two. Now get dressed and stop stalling. The cops aren't coming," Selena said, and walked over to where Donald was waiting. The naked professor climbed out of bed and made his way to the closet under Veritas's watchful eye.

"You know he's lying, right?" Donald murmured so softly she could barely make out his words.

"Doesn't matter. Bring the knife and the bleach so he stays motivated."

"Were you really going to…?"

She took his arm and moved him into the hallway. "I'll do whatever's necessary. Whatever. There are no limits. We're in end game."

The professor was dressed in minutes. Selena gathered the young man's revolver and hefted its weight as she waited for the professor to tie his shoes with shaking hands. She pocketed the gun, and they escorted the professor downstairs and to the three-car garage, where Veritas stowed the rifles in the trunk of a new Mercedes hybrid sedan that seemed as big as a cable car.

"You drive," Selena instructed the professor. "Ver, sit behind him. If he tries to pull anything, put a bullet in his spine."

"You're going to kill me, aren't you?" he stammered.

"If you don't start the car and get going, I just might," she replied.

The streets were deserted in the predawn, the fog thick on the ground as they made their way to Boeing University – at one time the University of Washington. The professor appeared lost in thought as the auto-drive navigated the ghostly streets. He was still sweating in spite of the air conditioning, and occasionally snuck a look at Veritas in the rearview mirror, his eyes panicked at the gun-wielding apparition in the rear seat.

A police cruiser, one of the new hovercraft models, seemed to float out of the fog from an alley on their left and cruised past them with lights blazing but siren off. Selena could feel the professor tense at the sight of the vehicle, and shifted the revolver in her lap so it was pointed at him.

"Easy. Nice and easy," she said, her tone calm and soothing.

Donald drilled the professor on where exactly on his system the relevant information could be found, and Veritas listened intently, noting the discussion of directories and files that would get them into the classified server.

"It's a big file," the professor said.

"We'll manage," Donald fired back.

The university gates loomed in front of them. "Switch off the auto-drive," Selena ordered.

They approached the guard station at the entrance, and two men in riot gear stepped from the building, shotguns slung over their shoulders. The professor dropped the window a half foot, and one of the men peered in at him. "What brings you out with the chickens?" he asked.

"I have guests in from Europe, and I want to give them a tour of the labs before anyone arrives."

The guard eyeballed Selena and then peered into the back before asking for the professor's ID. "Strictly protocol," he explained apologetically. "And your guests? Names?"

"Vanessa Blair, Eddie Lerner, and Lazlo Radijec," Selena said.

The man frowned. "Can you spell the last one?"

Selena did, hoping the guard didn't ask why the professor's forehead had sprouted tiny beads of sweat. If he noticed, he didn't say anything, and handed the professor's ID back to him with a small salute. "Have a good one," he said, and then strode back to the guard shack without further comment.

"There's another checkpoint farther inside the campus," the professor said. "But they know my car, so they won't stop us."

Selena noticed his knuckles were white on the polished wood steering wheel, and put the revolver back in her pocket so she wouldn't further spook him. They wended their way along the campus main artery, and she was starting to relax when the professor stomped on the accelerator.

G-forces pushed her back in the seat as the car rocketed forward with near impossible force, and then it smashed into the base of a stone pedestrian overpass at over a hundred miles per hour in an explosion of metal and glass.

Chapter 54

"Jesus," Selena exclaimed, stunned by the high-speed collision. She pushed the air bags out of the way and unbuckled her seatbelt. "Everybody okay?"

"I'm fine," Veritas said. He paused. "How about you?"

"Hurts like hell where the seatbelt got me, but it's just bruised."

Veritas looked over at Donald. "Donald's hurt. He wasn't strapped in. He got thrown around pretty hard."

Blood was coursing down Donald's face where his head had plowed into the media screen on the back of Selena's seat, and the jagged edge of his shin bone protruded through the left leg of his cargo pants from where his door panel had crumpled upon impact, snapping his tibia. The side airbags had instantly deflated after the collision but had done little to protect him in the crash. He groaned and Veritas leaned down to him.

"How bad are you hurt?" Veritas asked.

Donald blinked away blood. "Bad. I...my ribs feel like they're broken, and it's..." He coughed. Pink foam frothed from his mouth and nose.

"Shit," Veritas muttered. It was obvious he was badly injured.

"Ver? He wasn't strapped in. There's no pulse. He...he's dead." Selena had her fingers on the professor's carotid artery. His head lolled to the side at an unnatural angle and his unblinking eyes were wide. "We need to get out of here before the cops arrive."

"The cops will be the least of our problems. Once they hear it was the professor, they'll be swarming the area," Veritas said.

Donald coughed blood again and wheezed at Veritas. "In my...pocket. A...thumb drive...for the...data."

"We aren't leaving you here," Veritas said.

"Get...it..."

Veritas felt in Donald's pants and extracted a wad of new dollars as well as a pocketknife and a USB drive. He removed Donald's gun and slipped it into his waistband beside Lars's, and then tried to open his door so he could pull Donald from the car.

The door wouldn't budge. Veritas reached for Donald's, but it was jammed as well.

Flame flickered from around the hood, and Selena smashed her window with the revolver, shattering it. She kicked out the glass and looked back at Veritas. "Do the same on your side. The cage is mangled. You'll never get the doors open."

Donald croaked a few words. "The key...card..." He fought for breath and was rewarded with a sickly gurgle. "Veritas...your chip...can...copy...his retina...but...not...hundred percent."

Veritas frowned, not understanding what Donald was saying, and then broke his window and kicked out the glass. "This is going to hurt, Donald. I need to drag you through the opening."

"Gah."

"Hurry," Selena urged. "I smell gas."

Veritas grabbed Donald beneath his arms, slid him onto his side of the car, and crawled through the window. When he was out, he reached in and dragged Donald through the gap and to the trees that lined the jogging path. Donald coughed again as Veritas laid him on the grass, but this time instead of pink foam, a crimson river coursed from his nose and mouth.

"He's not going to make it," Veritas said.

Selena nodded. "What was he saying about copying the professor's retina?"

Orange flame licked from under the ruined hood, and they stepped farther away. Donald coughed a final time and spasmed before shuddering and lying still. Selena exhaled and looked to Veritas. "We need the data, Ver. Get the card and try to copy his retina."

"I don't know how, Selena. I'm still learning. Nobody gave me a manual."

"Shit."

Veritas pushed her away. "Get back. This thing's going to blow any second."

Selena started to protest, but Veritas was already heading back to the car. He broke the window with Donald's gun and knocked out the sheet of fractured safety glass, and then rummaged through the professor's pockets until he found his wallet. He checked it for the key card and, when he found it, pocketed it and studied the professor's bloody face.

Veritas leaned over him and stared him in the eyes, but nothing activated on his mental screen. He willed it to do something, but a loud crack from beneath what remained of the hood startled him. More flames rose into the darkness, accompanied by black smoke, and the odor of gasoline intensified.

"Veritas!" Selena cried as more smoke belched from the engine compartment.

"Get back!" he warned, and then leaned toward the professor again, knife in hand.

He ran to Selena and knocked her to the ground just as the car erupted in a fireball as the fuel caught, engulfing the vehicle in flames. Heat blasted over them, and then he was on his feet and pulling Selena to hers.

"This way," he said, and made for the pedestrian path. "They'll be here any second."

"What about Donald?"

"There's nothing we can do for him now."

Sirens wailed in the distance and the sound of running men reached them. Flashlight beams illuminated the fog, bouncing as security guards neared the crash site.

He grabbed her hand. "Can you run?"

"Yes. I'm just sort of in shock, I think."

"Come on."

Veritas guided her through the gloom and paused at a bench a hundred yards down the path.

"Can you see anything?" she asked.

"No. Too much fog. But we have to assume the Brethren will throw everything they have at us once the professor's identified."

"Damn. We were so close."

"I'm still going to go for it. But you should get out of here."

She shook her head. "Not a chance. I'll help."

"It'll be way harder trying to get two of us into his office."

"Then I'll park myself outside and keep watch." She frowned. "Stay here."

"Where are you going?"

"All the guards will be at the wreck. I'll snag one of their radios so I can listen in on what they're doing."

Selena sprinted down the path and barely heard Veritas warn her to be careful.

She found the guard post as the sirens drew nearer, and spotted a half-empty rack with three small handheld radios in it. She looked around to confirm she wasn't being observed, and then snatched them and took off at a run.

When she rejoined Veritas, she handed him one. "This way we can communicate."

"You can't say anything on it or they'll know we're still here."

Selena shook her head and switched one to a different channel, and then did the same on a second and handed it to him. "I'll monitor their channel, and if anything happens that will affect you, I'll let you know."

"Smart."

"They teach smart in cop school."

Veritas clipped the radio to his jeans and then thought better of it and put it in his jacket pocket. He removed the professor's wallet and rummaged through the cards until he found the key card, and then slid the high-denomination new dollars from it and handed Selena the wallet and money.

"That might come in handy if we make it out of this." Voices reached them from the wreckage. He leaned toward her. "We're not that far from the professor's building. I pulled up a map on my display."

"You think you can get in?"

"I'll figure it out."

She nodded. "Did the retinal copy work?"

Veritas's expression hardened. "Sort of."

"What does that mean? How are you going to access his system?"

Veritas inhaled deeply and looked into the fog. "You don't want to know."

Chapter 55

The professor's office in the Microsoft Department of Bioengineering building was pitch black. The only light came from the lobby, where a lone guard was sitting behind a counter watching something on a handheld. Veritas studied the building exterior, which had obviously been built in the last five years, and whispered to Selena, "Donald said his office is on the third floor. But it's going to be impossible to get in through the lobby without taking out the guard. You think we can risk it?"

"If you're only going to be in there for a few minutes, sure. But he said it was a big file, so it could take a while."

"I was afraid you'd say that. How much longer until sunup?" Veritas asked.

"Maybe forty minutes. The car clock said it was five twenty. But I can't be sure. I'd say assume six, and if it comes up later, super."

"That doesn't leave us a lot of time."

"Tell me about it." She paused. "How are you thinking of getting in?"

Veritas closed his eyes and a vivid image leapt into the forefront of his consciousness. Whether this was a vision of the future or just an inspired idea, he had no idea, but he immediately saw the way forward. He pointed at the building. "See those vertical steel beams between the glass? Looks like they're mounted to them, with maybe a foot between the panes?"

"You're going to somehow dematerialize and slip through?"

314

He laughed in spite of the tension he felt. "No. I'll go in through the roof. I can climb up the girders."

She counted the floors. "Nine stories?"

"I didn't say it would be fun. But I don't see any other way, do you? No way is that guard going to let me by, and if I incapacitate him, with everything else happening, they'll be on it immediately."

Selena adjusted the volume of her other radio. They'd been listening to the frantic back-and-forth as the ambulances and police had arrived, but so far nothing had happened that posed an immediate threat. "Be careful, Ver. Too many close calls for one night."

He grinned with confidence he didn't feel. "It'll be easy."

She stood on her tiptoes and kissed him. "Come back to me in one piece, okay? Now go."

Veritas bolted toward the building and crossed the lawn in a blur, and then was hoisting himself up the beam hand over hand, his arms surprisingly strong given the beating he'd taken only hours earlier.

The steel was slick from condensation, but his grip was solid, and three minutes later he was hauling himself over the lip. He stopped once on the roof and caught his breath, and then ran for the door beside the top of the elevator shaft.

Which was locked.

"Damn," he said. He'd hoped that they wouldn't lock a door with no access to anyone but seagulls, but some conscientious maintenance man had. He studied the shaft and then removed the pocketknife from his pocket and set to work on the screws that held a vent grid in place. They proved more resistant than he'd thought, and he burned five minutes removing them before he could lift the cover and climb through it.

A concrete stairway ran beside the elevator shaft, and he descended to the third floor. When he cracked the door on the landing, the halls were barely visible, the only light seeping in through a floor-to-ceiling glass panel at the other end.

Veritas checked the ceiling for security cams and spotted a telltale globe by the elevator. He considered smashing it with his pistol, but reconsidered before doing so – the damage would already be done when he approached it, and since he was already public enemy number one, there was no point.

The professor's door was easy to find, given the ornate plaque mounted above the card reader. He slid the card into the slot. The light strip blinked green three times, and he opened it and stepped in.

He passed a reception area with a single desk and continued to the professor's private office, which was surprisingly small. An antique desk sat in front of a matching credenza, and a tall, dark wood bookcase overflowing with reference books occupied an entire wall.

Veritas crossed the room in a few strides and shut the blinds, and then sat at the desk and powered up the computer. The screen blinked to life, and he inserted the card into the reader when prompted. The system demanded biometric confirmation of his identity, and he removed the bandana in which the professor's eye was wrapped, which he'd cut out using Donald's knife. He wiped the last of the blood from the cornea and held it up to the screen-mounted reader, and the system flickered and then welcomed him with a mauve screen with a smiley face.

Veritas closed his eyes and the discussion with the professor in the car replayed word for word – one of the benefits of his chip, he realized. He opened them and tapped the keys, and soon he was in the biotech company's network using the stored passwords in one of the obscurely named files the professor had created so he wouldn't forget them.

The directory tree to the one he needed was simple to navigate, and when he found the relevant file, he downloaded it to the professor's computer. He waited as it streamed from six miles away, and almost jumped out of his seat when the radio in his pocket screeched like an angry bird.

"Helicopters on their way in," Selena warned. "Probably your friends from the base, or maybe DSS."

"I'm waiting for it to download."

"You're out of time."

"It says another two minutes."

"They're landing." There was a long pause. "Shit. There must be fifty troops. Half are headed our way."

"Get out of there."

"Not without you."

"Don't argue. Get off the grounds while you can. I'll meet you when I'm done."

"Ver—"

"I need to focus. Please, Selena. Just do it. Hang on to your radio. I'll contact you when I'm clear."

"I hate this."

"That makes two of us."

He turned down the volume and regarded the screen. When it signaled the file had been downloaded, he disconnected from the company network and inserted the thumb drive so he could copy it.

The power died.

Veritas instantly knew what had happened, and felt for the server, which was a compact box the size of a paperback book. He disconnected it, stood, transferred Lars's pistol to his jacket and Donald's to the front of his jeans, and then slid the server down the back of his pants so his hands remained free.

There was no question that they would be at the office in no time, so he rushed to the door and ran down the hall to the stairwell. His mental screen lit up with yellow icons, but he didn't need it to hear at least ten men ascending the steps.

He leaned over the rail and Lars's pistol barked a half dozen times, the gun deafening in the confined space. Three of the icons turned red and answering fire exploded from below, masking the sound of his boots as he took the stairs three at a time. Rounds ricocheted off the walls, and he remembered Milo's coaching and focused on slowing reality.

Veritas continued climbing higher, but the bullets seemed to be drilling through gelatin, slowed to the point where he could see them and easily dodge the few that might have posed a danger. He didn't let up on his pace up the steps, but everything else seemed to be moving in slow motion, and he felt as though he could reach out and slap the offending rounds out of the air if he wanted to.

He reached the roof about the time his screen told him his pursuers had reached the third floor, and he burst through the door and ran to the edge. Below, a throng of black-clad shooters had cordoned off the building entrance, and more were streaming inside, moving like slow-motion ants in the artificially decelerated reality. He hurried to the other side of the building and saw a smaller group gathered by the rear fire entrance.

He darted to the left side and saw nobody below, and didn't hesitate to lower his body over the side while clinging to the roof with his hands. When he was hanging off the side, he clutched the steel beam in front of him and lowered himself as fast as he dared, which seemed glacial to him, but in real time was probably four times normal.

Once on the ground he whipped both pistols free and ran for the trees. The stutter of an assault rifle from behind him broke the quiet of the predawn, and he dropped and rolled as rounds spiraled above him at the speed of lazily thrown softballs. He spun and drew a bead on the shooter by the building, and fired three times. Two of his shots hit the man in the chest, knocking him backward. Veritas knew that the composite plate in his tactical vest would stop the pistol rounds, but he'd likely have a hell of a bruise where they'd struck.

He jumped to his feet and continued toward the trees as a raft of shooting from the roof drove him forward. Again the bullets rained around him at the speed of badminton birdies, and he found them so easy to dodge it was laughable. His mental display calculated their trajectories in real time, and all he had to do was avoid their impact points to be in the clear.

Once in the trees, time sped back to normal, and a sensation like emerging from a swimming pool washed over him. He ran for all he was worth, well aware that his pursuers would pull out all the stops to catch him, and that the advantage that the fog and darkness had lent him would soon disappear like morning dew.

Veritas reached a stone wall topped by ornate wrought-iron fencing, and barely slowed to replace his pistols before vaulting effortlessly up the side and throwing himself over it. He landed on his feet and took off like a scared rabbit, sirens and squawking radios from the campus following him as he ran. More shooting echoed through the trees but to no avail, and within moments of beginning his final dash, Veritas vanished into the gloom.

Chapter 56

Veritas sat on the floor of a squalid room, watching Selena finish uploading the file from the professor's server to a blind account in New Russia, which would immediately bounce to another private server in Maui, before finally being auto-transmitted to the Tribe lab somewhere on the U.S. mainland.

Her posting on SexUp had generated a nearly immediate response, and she'd communicated with the Southern California Tribe cell, who'd relayed her news up the chain. That had been four hours ago, after making their way to the South Park area of Seattle on foot – a district that, like Oakland, had been abandoned by the city government when it had become uncontrollable after riots and was now a cesspool of warring gangs and rampant criminality.

The professor's wad of cash had come in handy, and she'd been able to buy more ammo for Veritas's weapons and a stolen monitor and keyboard from a corner dope dealer. They'd found a flophouse with fiber-optic internet and barely running water located in a converted mini-mall fortified with barbed wire and sandbagged machine-gun nests manned by hard-looking veterans who appeared eager to put their combat skills to use.

She sighed and looked at Veritas, who offered a tired smile.

"Well?" he asked.

"Mission accomplished."

"That was what they were looking for?"

Selena nodded and set the keyboard on the floor. "Apparently so."

"What's to stop them from tweaking it and releasing a new variant that your vaccine won't work on?"

"In reality? Nothing. But it'll take time, and that gives us more chances to put an end to them once and for all. Which is where you come in."

"I told you, I'm not sure I want to play."

"It's the future of humanity, Ver."

"I get that. But nobody seems to care much what I want. Just how useful I could be."

She nodded again. "I completely understand. But some things are bigger than us as individuals. And this isn't over. They're never going to let up. Now that they know you exist, they have to kill you, or the prophecy says you'll bring them down."

"I keep hearing about this prophecy, but it doesn't mean anything to me. Look, Selena, I did all of this because of you. I wasn't about to leave you to die. But now that we're safe…"

"That's what I'm trying to tell you, Ver. We'll never be safe as long as they're out there. Nobody will. They aren't going to give up. This was just a temporary setback for them. We're the only thing standing between them and Armageddon."

"Selena, you signed up for this. I didn't. I need time to think through what I want."

She moved to him and sat cross-legged across from him, and leaned forward to kiss him on the mouth. "What do you want, Veritas?"

He kissed her back. "A shower sounds pretty good."

Selena nodded. "And maybe we can find clothes? These are getting a little ripe."

"And some food and sleep. I'm beat. You must be about to faint."

"I've had better days." She smiled. "What happened to Moxie?"

"I left him with Mabel. She said she'd watch him until I could come for him."

"You planning to?"

He returned her smile. "He's about all I have in the world, besides you."

"That's our next stop?"

"Maybe not our next, but it's going to be a stop, one way or the other."

The server beeped. She rose and eyed the screen. "They said they'd do their best to make arrangements to get us to a secure location within twenty-four hours."

"What does that mean, their best?"

"It means it'll happen. And there's something else. They said the guy you came to Washington to see? He was taken prisoner and is in custody. So he's still alive – at least for now."

"I wonder why the Brethren didn't off him."

"Good question." She strolled over to the queen-size mattress on the floor by an open window, where the faint sound of music drifted through the bars.

Oooh, stick it in, stick it, stick it, stick it in…

"You can't escape that shit, can you?" he grumbled. "If we were on a desert island, they'd manage to pipe it in by satellite."

It was her turn to smile. "Let's see if we can buy some food and clothes, and then we can shower and grab a little sleep." She held out her hand to him. "Although you have to admit it's got a catchy beat."

"We're doomed."

Selena laughed. "Probably. But in the meantime, we might as well make the most of it, right?"

He took her hand and pulled her close, and kissed her again. "I'm not letting you out of my sight, Selena."

Another smile, and she put her arms around his neck. "That sounds like a negotiation."

"I'm serious."

"So am I."

About the Author

Featured in *The Wall Street Journal*, *The Times*, and *The Chicago Tribune*, Russell Blake is *The NY Times* and *USA Today* bestselling author of over forty novels, including *Fatal Exchange*, *Fatal Deception*, *The Geronimo Breach*, *Zero Sum*, *King of Swords*, *Night of the Assassin*, *Revenge of the Assassin*, *Return of the Assassin*, *Blood of the Assassin*, *Requiem for the Assassin*, *Rage of the Assassin* The *Delphi Chronicle* trilogy, *The Voynich Cypher*, *Silver Justice*, *JET*, *JET – Ops Files*, *JET – Ops Files: Terror Alert*, *JET II – Betrayal*, *JET III – Vengeance*, *JET IV – Reckoning*, *JET V – Legacy*, *JET VI – Justice*, *JET VII – Sanctuary*, *JET VIII – Survival*, *JET IX – Escape*, *JET X – Incarceration*, *JET XI – Forsaken*, *Upon a Pale Horse*, *BLACK*, *BLACK is Back*, *BLACK is The New Black*, *BLACK to Reality*, *BLACK in the Box*, *Deadly Calm*, *Ramsey's Gold*, *Emerald Buddha*, *The Goddess Legacy*, *The Day After Never – Blood Honor*, *The Day After Never – Purgatory Road*, *The Day After Never – Covenant*, *The Day After Never – Retribution*, *The Goddess Legacy*, *A Girl Apart*, and *Quantum Synapse*.

Non-fiction includes the international bestseller *An Angel With Fur* (animal biography) and *How To Sell A Gazillion eBooks In No Time*, a parody of all things writing-related.

Blake is co-author of *The Eye of Heaven* and *The Solomon Curse*, with legendary author Clive Cussler. Blake's novel *King of Swords* has been translated into German by Amazon Crossing, *The Voynich Cypher* into Bulgarian, and his JET novels into Spanish, German, and Czech.

Blake writes under the moniker R.E. Blake in the NA/YA/Contemporary Romance genres. Novels include *Less Than Nothing*, *More Than Anything*, and *Best Of Everything*.

Having resided in Mexico for a dozen years, Blake enjoys his dogs, fishing, boating, tequila and writing, while battling world domination by clowns. His thoughts, such as they are, can be found at his blog: RussellBlake.com

Books by Russell Blake

Co-authored with Clive Cussler

THE EYE OF HEAVEN
THE SOLOMON CURSE

Thrillers

FATAL EXCHANGE
FATAL DECEPTION
THE GERONIMO BREACH
ZERO SUM
THE DELPHI CHRONICLE TRILOGY
THE VOYNICH CYPHER
SILVER JUSTICE
UPON A PALE HORSE
DEADLY CALM
RAMSEY'S GOLD
EMERALD BUDDHA
THE GODDESS LEGACY
A GIRL APART
QUANTUM SYNAPSE

The Assassin Series

KING OF SWORDS
NIGHT OF THE ASSASSIN
RETURN OF THE ASSASSIN
REVENGE OF THE ASSASSIN
BLOOD OF THE ASSASSIN
REQUIEM FOR THE ASSASSIN
RAGE OF THE ASSASSIN

Made in the
USA
Middletown, DE